Sal stared at the canvas. What was it she was trying to say? If John could make some sort of sense out of the chaos surrounding his life, surely she could do the same. When he had come home the night before, exhausted and shaken by his experience on the streets, her own complaints had seemed petty by comparison.

And now, here they were, living with killing all around them, in spite of John's role in the affair.

She picked up her palate knife and started to turn toward the canvas when she heard a scraping noise behind her. She jerked her head around to see two men standing in the open barn door. They were wearing ski masks.

"What do you want?" she whispered hoarsely, terror rising in her throat.

The bigger of the two men stepped forward. "Take that shirt off and show us what you got."

There was nowhere to run. She was trapped....

## ABOUT THE AUTHOR

George Mettler was born in Tampa, Florida, educated at Jesuit High School, Loyola University of the South, New Orleans, Louisiana, Mercer Law School, Macon, Georgia and Stetson College of Law, St. Petersburg, Florida. He holds a BA in journalism and a J.D. in law. Mettler has been an Army officer, an FBI agent, a newspaper reporter/editor, a college professor and a practicing attorney. He has published several works of fiction and a text on criminology. He is married and the father of two sons. He has lived in many parts of the world and presently practices law in Tampa.

# DOWN HOME

*a novel by*

**George Mettler**

FAWCETT GOLD MEDAL • NEW YORK

DOWN HOME

Copyright © 1981 George Mettler

All rights reserved

Published by Fawcett Gold Medal Books, a unit of CBS Publications, the Consumer Publishing Division of CBS Inc.

All the characters in this book are fictitious, and any resemblance to actual persons living or dead is purely coincidental.

ISBN: 0-449-14403-8

Printed in the United States of America

First Fawcett Gold Medal printing: May 1981

10 9 8 7 6 5 4 3 2 1

This book is for the *fambly*:
Darlene, Jaime and Sean,
with love.

*The land is full of bloody crimes,
and the city is full of violence.*

Ezekiel

# PROLOGUE

**He began firing without sound or warning. Just stepped** out from behind the cover of the giant magnolia tree at the back side of the house and started shooting. His right arm was extended, his elbow and wrist locked tightly, his knees bent and his weight carefully balanced on his widespread feet. His stance was perfect and so was his aim.

The first bullet struck the girl about an inch above her right eye. Blood and brain matter splattered the board wall behind the gyrating porch swing.

The recoil raised his arm, but without unlocking his wrist or elbow he zeroed in on the funny-looking man with the wilted little penis still protruding from his unzipped fly. As the man bolted in a lumbering panic toward the end of the shadowed porch the second shot opened his head just below the left ear, spattering the hydrangea bushes with thick gouts of bloody material.

Then, almost as reflex action, he swung his aim back toward the kitchen door and fired again as a pimply-faced boy in a pair of jockey shorts burst onto the porch with a fire poker clutched in his hand. An expression of bewildered rage split the boy's face even as the slug tore open his sweaty chest like the point of a knife splitting a ripe melon.

The intruder walked up on the porch as calmly as a postman making a special delivery. He exhibited no surprise when he was met inside the door by a woman with a meat cleaver in her upraised hand. He dropped to one knee and squeezed off a fourth round from the U. S. Army .45 that obliterated the woman's crotch.

An old man whose face appeared in the doorway across the kitchen was the next to go, along with the intruder's shoulder socket. The automatic and the old man's shotgun delivered their deafening loads in unison.

The intruder crawled across the cold linoleum floor, passed the old man's mutilated corpse and paused to rest in the living room. When he heard a sudden metallic sound in the adjoining hallway he rolled onto his side and fired.

The hard cold slug struck the naked child squarely in the chest.

He stared at the twisted little body in the dimly lighted hallway, then raised the gun and inserted the smoking muzzle into his mouth.

# PART ONE

# Chapter One

**The day began like any other day in the sultry summer** ritualism of Taliawiga County.

Shortly before six the whippoorwill, perched in a tree down by the branch, sang its morning song. John Winter had been awake for some ten or fifteen minutes. He checked the clock beside the bed, pushing down the seldom-used alarm plunger, yawned and stretched his naked limbs. But then he lay quietly for some moments longer, watching the brilliant sunlight as it made its ascent through the trees outside the window.

Morning was the time of day John liked best in all seasons and, as was his custom, he was wide awake. A morning man, he always woke instantly full of vim and vigor. Much to Sal's sleepy-headed chagrin. It was indecent, she complained, for any civilized person to act that way before nine o'clock. That particular contrast in character traits had required a certain nice accommodation throughout the years of their relationship.

John was smiling in the half-light, at peace with himself and the world. At long last, he thought. He felt as if he had somehow assimilated the morning silence of the old farmhouse, broken only by the pulsating record-keeping of the antiquated grandfather clock. The clock—*his* grandfather's clock—stood halfway down the hard oak corridor that ran through the massive frame house like a superhighway. He breathed deeply in rhythm with the pulsing time but carefully, so as not to disturb Sal, waiting for the old clock to strike the hour with its heavy resonant tones. He loved the clock almost as much as he had loved the crusty old man.

Gone now, unbelievably, these last twenty years. Victim to the invincibility of time.

John stretched his muscular arms up over his head and pressed his feet hard against the footboard. Another inch, Sal said, and he would hang off the bed. John breathed deeply of the fresh country air as it billowed the curtains into the stillness of the room. He could smell the rich woman-scent of his wife too, as she turned heavily on her side with a sigh of annoyance and pulled an extra pillow over her head in an attempt to block out the shrieking birdcall. His smile widened as he recalled the use to which the extra pillow had been put the night before.

When the clock began to toll the hour John sighed, threw back the sheet and sat up on the side of the bed. He looked down at Sal's golden backside, at her buttocks and legs, and felt an involuntary tingle in his groin. Asleep, she was more appealing than most other women he knew at their wide-awake best. Other men reacted to her warm earthy sensuousness too. He had seen friends and strangers in the street go weak in the knees merely at the sight of her, and figured it had something to do with the whisper of Indian blood in her veins. Even Homer Stokes, the urbane Galahad of Taliawiga County, had remarked at a recent party that Sal was just the sort of healthy young woman that caused Presidents to lust in their Christian hearts. Laughing, John reached out and rubbed the tips of his fingers lightly over the rash of goose pimples that had begun to march across her exposed buttocks.

That, too, was part of his morning ritual of late. He always paused to reassure himself of his good fortune. On the rare instances when he woke and found her already out of bed—in the bathroom, perhaps, or attending one of the children—anxiety would flash uncontrollably through his veins like a virus. Ever since they had come home from Europe he had harbored a silent dread that their return might somehow have been a mistake. Rubbing his hand over her smooth warm buttocks of a morning was curiously reassuring, like having his own private talisman, his soft furry rabbit's foot. His grin broadened. My good luck piece, he thought, and Sal began to stir like a cat disturbed in her sleep. He removed his hand and spread the sheet back over her body. He would let her sleep a bit longer. She needed every minute's rest she could get. The kids would be clamoring for her attention soon enough.

The bird was still raising the hue and cry and the room

had begun to lighten as the sun worked its way up toward the top of the window frame. He rummaged quietly about for his jeans and a shirt, then moved softly toward the bathroom in his bare feet. But he lingered momentarily in the connecting doorway, for some reason unwilling to break the spell of the moment.

He loved Sal so damned much—sometimes it was a little embarrassing—and he wanted things to be just right for all of them. But he was never quite certain. He *thought* she was well and happy now. But she had the capacity for such self-control and internalization. The Choctaw brush, again. She was deep water and no matter how gently stirred would not come clear until she was ready.

He could usually guess fairly accurately at the character of her mood by the direction of her painting in progress. Thank God she had more or less finished with the pre-European dark period, the serpentine forms and the heavy twisted jungle foliage. He knew what all *that* had been about and dreaded the thought of anything happening that might plunge her back into the depressive sloughs of her tragic past. But her work had been so light and sunny and bright during the European sojourn that he had almost lost the nagging edge of concern that always lay just below the surface of his consciousness. She *seemed* all right. So rosy and joyful in these first months since the birth of their daughter, stronger even than after Davey's birth. Sal had begun to paint again, too. But it was too soon to tell in which direction her mood would take her art. Or was it the other way around?

He buttoned his cotton work shirt and thought again of how happy she had been during those three sun-filled years in Italy. Maybe he shouldn't have brought her back here. She didn't really belong in Adelphi. He knew it, Sal knew it, and his mother knew it.

He was suddenly annoyed, as he most always was at the thought of his mother's unbending ways. Could the old duck really suppose he didn't know how she carried on? Hell, it was impossible to keep such things quiet in a place like Taliawiga County. But then maybe she just doesn't give a damn, he thought. Maybe she *wanted* them to know how she felt about their marriage without having to face the issue head on.

John grunted deep in his chest. That would be characteristic of his mother's style all right. A true daughter of her Confederate heritage, circumlocution had always been her way. But by god it wouldn't work this time, not by a long shot, he thought adamantly. Sal had suffered enough because of her own lineage and he'd be damned if he would let the hypocrisies of the Winter clan cause her any further injury.

He felt the little poisonous jets of gas spraying against his stomach lining as the old resentment rose up in him again. What the hell right had his mother to be so uppity and all-fired high and mighty anyway, he thought angrily.

He closed the door more loudly than he had intended, and headed toward the bathroom.

# Chapter Two

**On that same morning, Sonny-Boy Cubbage was having** no luck getting into his bathroom. He found himself locked out for the third time since he got up. First, his granddaddy had been getting himself "squared away" for the day's television viewing. The old soldier's reveilles came at a somewhat later hour nowadays but with much the same precision of motion if not a similar quality of purpose.

Next Sonny-Boy had had to wait for his mother to prepare herself for duty at the reception desk of the nearby Adelphi Motel, and now Sissie was up a good hour earlier than usual and bolted obstinately behind the bathroom door.

If only they had a second bathroom, or even a serviceable outhouse. It was too large a family for one bathroom, especially since Sissie had come back home. But just you try to get the old tightwad to part with a nickel for something he didn't get the primary benefit from and that would sure enough be a red-letter day in hell. Why should *he* worry? Out on the road all the time; real nice hotels to stay in; private showers, room service, movies and whatever in bed. What the heck did he care about *us* jumping around with tears in our eyes to keep from pissing on the walls?

"Shoot. He don't care," Sonny-Boy groaned aloud. His stomach began to knot up, as it always did at the thought of his domineering little father. He began hopping from one foot to the other in his discomfort. If Sissie didn't come out soon he would have to take a leak into the hydrangea bushes off the end of the back porch again.

A sudden prickly heat began to flush through his veins. He knew that Naomi Hicks had seen him the last time he had peed in the bushes. And he knew that she knew that he watched her undressing in her room at night when Andy Joe was out of town. The hair on the back of his neck began to crawl. Their rooms were right across from each other, so close they could almost reach out and touch. In the summer months, with the windows open, he could sometimes hear them making love late in the night. In the summer months the eighteen-year-old Sonny-Boy still jerked off regularly three or four nights a week.

He was beginning to erect as Sissie suddenly emerged from the bathroom, brushing past her brother as she might a stranger in a hotel corridor.

"Boy, you ever let Daddy see you walkin' around like that," he said, watching in amazement as she padded down the hallway in her bare feet and a pair of white lace panties.

At the door to the bedroom that she reluctantly shared with her baby sister Layde she turned and looked at him, a sour grin on her feral face. Her little white teeth were sharp and predatory, her mouth almost too full for the narrow shape of her chin. But it was the eyes—along with the acidic tongue—that always riveted Sonny-Boy to the spot. Slate gray and almost expressionless, the eyes seemed to say that the only thing she had ever felt in her life was a total absence of feeling.

"But Daddy ain't here," she said coldly, "—an' what he don't know won't hurt him, now will it, Sonny-Boy?"

She hooked her thumb in her panties and began to twist the elastic band. Her girlish chest was not much fuller than his own, but her legs and buttocks were as good as any Playmate's he had ever seen. He hated the way she always flaunted herself in front of him like that but was unable to resist looking at her all the same.

She lowered the top of her pants until the pubic hairs

began to show, then laughed at the choked expression on his face and closed the bedroom door.

Sonny-Boy had scarcely got on the toilet with his erection in hand when she knocked insistently on the door.

"No. Not—now."

"Open the door."

"Go away, Sissie."

"You open this door, Sonny-Boy, or I'll make you pay through the nose for this!"

Instead, he opened her purse. It was on the clothes hamper across from the toilet. A hit of marijuana was thrown casually in with the rest of the junk she carried around with her, and he thought of what old Chester Biggs would do to a girl like Sissie if the sheriff was ever to catch her with that stuff in her possession.

"Sonny-Boy!"

He slid back the bolt, carefully concealing his swollen condition behind the cracked door, and handed her the purse.

She snatched it from him and, as usual, hammered in the last word. "What the hell you doin' in there so long ennyway—beatin' off again?"

# Chapter Three

On the other side of Adelphi, almost beyond the city limits, in a narrow rectangular warren of tin-roofed tar-paper shacks, Josie Fletcher knocked lightly on her daughter's bedroom door. "Ellie, honey? Hit's time to be gittin' up an' ready fo' school."

"Mornin', Momma," the girl said from inside the room. "I been ready an' reading for an hour now."

"Land sakes," said Josie, and Ellie, propped up on her pillows with a copy of Ralph Ellison's *Invisible Man* in her lap, could hear her mother's deep-throated chuckle as she padded down the linoleum-covered hallway toward the little kitchen at the back of the house.

Marking her place in the book with the library card, Ellie swung her smooth brown legs over the side of the bed. She was already dressed, except for her shoes, so she slipped into a pair of sandals and went to the kitchen to help her mother with breakfast.

Their morning routine was a simple affair. Her brother, Otha, had been gone from home a little more than three years. The last they had heard, he had settled up in Atlanta. Not that they had heard it from Otha, thought Ellie. Otha had never written, not so much as a postcard, since he had gone off to join one of those black militant groups always talking about how they was gonna do this and that and how Whitey sooner or later—more likely sooner—was gonna eat more crow than his ol' hookworm constitution would be able to digest. They had read about Otha in the Atlanta paper, even saw his picture once, although he was only one of a group standing up there as big as you pleased on the steps of the golden-domed capitol building. But Ellie missed him. As much trouble as he had always been, she missed her brother and wished he would just come on back home and mind his own business. But she knew better than that. He wouldn't come back to Adelphi, not for love nor money. And even if he wanted to, ol' Sheriff Biggs probably wouldn't let him set foot across the county line.

On weekday mornings, mother and daughter would eat breakfast together and then leave the house together, Josie on the way to her backbreaking labors in the steaming kitchen of the Adelphi Motel and Ellie to her senior classroom at the local high school. Grannie Eagle and Mandy would eat when they got up an hour or so later.

On this hot humid morning too, mother and daughter left the house together shortly before eight o'clock. Already the neighborhood was aswarm with sound and motion. The roads were unpaved and there were no sidewalks or streetlights and no way for the rainwater to run off, save for the twisting ruts and gashes that mutilated the clay surface of the earth. Gray-planked tar-paper shacks seemed to lean toward one another for support, looking as if a high wind might tumble them all like a cluster of dominoes.

Ellie and her mother held hands as they walked down toward the bus stop. Josie was prim and starched in her fresh blue uniform, and Ellie looked much younger than sixteen in a dark skirt and a clean white lace blouse. Nearly every house they passed boasted a big iron pot in the back yard bubbling a similar stew of boiling laundry. Radios and TV sets blared news or gospel music out of the front doors of most houses. Dogs were yapping all over the neighborhood, chickens prancing and clucking about, and a few bare-bottomed babies were scampering around in the junk-littered yards. The odor of frying foods and outdoor privies scented the morning breeze. Officially the neighborhood was listed on the township maps as Shad Row. No less original, nearly everyone in Taliawiga County called it simply Niggertown.

When the school bus arrived at the stop Ellie and Josie hugged and kissed affectionately, then Josie held her daughter's heavy armload of books while the girl climbed up on the steps. Josie thought Ellie walked just fine; it was only when she tried to jump or climb that it became noticeable that her right leg was just a tad shorter than her left.

Josie waved, stepped back away from the exhaust of the bus and waited patiently for the dust to settle before crossing the road.

She looked at her watch. There was just enough time to go by the post office to pick up the monthly check that would be waiting in the numbered box. It had always been there, every month for the last sixteen years. She crossed the road and started off on the two-mile trek to the post office on the square in Adelphi.

Josie had expected the checks to stop when the old colonel died. But they just kept on coming. She had stopped asking *why* they came many years before.

# Chapter Four

John Winter was in the kitchen. He had shaved and trimmed his moustache and dressed in the faded jeans and an old cotton work shirt. Standing barefoot on the cold linoleum floor, as he drank a glass of orange juice and started a fresh pot of coffee. While the coffee was perking he cracked an egg into a dish, scooped out the yolk with a tablespoon and dropped the white and the shells into the pot to supply the glossy sheen his grandfather had taught him to appreciate. The window above the sink was open and the aroma of the coffee was joined by other fresh scents of the early morning.

He leaned into the window and drew a deep draught of fresh air into his lungs. His brow wrinkled involuntarily as he thought suddenly of the unexpected phone call from Thurlow Wheems earlier in the week. What in the world had made his old boss in the U. S. Attorney's office suppose that John might want to go back to work for him in Atlanta at *any* increase in salary? And all that crapola about being just about the best young trial attorney in Georgia! Talent to burn just going to waste in the dull sterility of a second-rate college classroom. Couldn't teach them niggers and tobacco road honkies to spell C-A-T in a million years and that was the good Lord's truth.

Old Thurlow sure as hell hadn't changed much, John thought sourly, except maybe to grow a little dumber if he thought John could be enticed back into the rat race of the U. S. Attorney's office. What the devil was wrong with the man? How could he ever imagine that John might work for him again in view of the special circumstances of their parting five, no, closer to six years ago? Doesn't he know that Sal is still with me? Doesn't he *care* anymore? Or is that just another day and time long gone and forgotten, if not exactly forgiven? Well, *I* haven't forgotten, thought John. I haven't forgotten the way they savaged and abused her all in the name of God, Justice and Patriotism. And I damned sure haven't forgiven the likes of Thurlow Wheems!

The mere thought of the man and his insidious ways caused a spurt of tension to leap in his veins. At such moments he wished he were a smoking man; merely the *act* of lighting up seemed to afford people at least the illusion of relief. And he damned sure couldn't crack open a bottle of bourbon at seven o'clock in the morning.

But then his thoughts were interrupted by the sound of chopping in the garden. He set out two bowls of dry dog food on the back steps, looked around for his two feisty dogs and then went on down to chat with his handyman.

"Moses? Gettin' an early start, as usual?"

"Mawnin', Mistuh Jawn. Yo' knows how I likes to git at it real soon fo' dat ol' sun mek me crazy in de haid."

"Been stoking up these last few days all right. Have us all prayin' for winter we have another week or so like this one."

"Somethin' to do with all them there bombs an' all, you ast me. Course de President he don' nevah want to hear no opinions of *mine*."

"Jimmy don't listen to ennybody but Bert 'n' Billy."

"Don' listen t' Billy an' he goin' up dere an' pee on the po' man's laig."

Both their faces seemed to split into sections. Like two peas in a pod, Sal would say. One white, the other black as ink. If she could hear them now she would be bobbing away, saying to herself, There he goes again, talking like a field hand, her man of all seasons and many languages. He was a chameleon, she said, capable of blending in with any environment in which he found himself. And according to Thurlow Wheems, it was one of the reasons he had been such a damned fine lawyer.

"You seen Clyde and J. Edgar around this morning, Moses?"

The old man grunted as he chopped into the dry red earth. "Shoot, dem ol' dawgs was over yonder the other side of the ol' Sutton place come milkin' time."

John laughed and waved a gnat away from his eyes. "Old man Sutton was sore as a carbuncle one day last week," he said. "Called me on the phone and raised holy hell about my collies marauding in one of his hen houses."

He knew Moses was in the throes of a laughing jag by the tightening of the skin on top of his bald head. Moses had been with the family for a lot longer than John could remember. John couldn't begin to guess his age. He was old the day John was born nearly forty years ago.

John walked along the arrow-straight rows of vegetables, leaving the old man to his work. The garden was shaping up real fine this year, John reflected. If there was not too much rain the tomatoes and sweet corn would be wonderful. During the summer break at the university he would help Sal with the canning and they would be in good shape for the coming winter. They wouldn't want for meat, either. Moses was fattening up a calf and a couple of hogs and the woods were infested again with wild animals. Come fall the freezer would be groaning with its weight of venison, rabbit, squirrel, dove and quail. But no animal was ever killed merely for sport in his woods, not even a game bird. Even if he had still been interested in hunting for its own sake, John knew that Sal would never have countenanced such wanton destruction.

He stopped and looked up at the massive old house and wondered if Sal was still asleep. The whippoorwill was still at it in a perch somewhere down by the branch that meandered in front of the house. It was a true test of Sal's pacific principles that she hadn't turned him loose to shotgun that detested bird. Of course John was by now rather attached to the much maligned fellow and would hate to see anything happen to him.

God, I love all this, he thought, and glanced suddenly around as if someone had unexpectedly spoken out loud. And perhaps he had; he really wasn't sure. He drew a deep breath and just stood there, immobile in the middle of the garden. He could hear and see and feel the earth beneath his bare feet; he could sense the myriad growing things surrounding him. Instead of jogging, he would get out and work in the soil after breakfast, he decided with elation. There would still be just enough time to shower and change clothes and make it over to the university in time for his ten o'clock lecture.

He started back to the house for his coffee. As he passed Moses the old Negro paused in his work and a scowl as dark as thunder settled over his face. "I dunno *how* minny times

I done *tol'* you, Mistuh Jawn. Yo' bettuh stop walkin' aroun' like that wifout no shoes on. Yo' gonna step on a big ol' moccasin one of these days an' he gonna eat yo' foot right off."

John laughed and could hear the old man muttering to himself as he returned to his hoeing. "Nevah would lissen, even as a chile. Hardheaded jes like his ol' gran'daddy Flood."

In the kitchen John poured a large pewter mug of coffee and took it out onto the front porch. The veranda, his grand-momma used to call it. He settled into his favorite rocker and propped his feet up on the wood railing.

Leave all this for that madhouse up in Atlanta? In a pig's eye, he thought, carefully sipping at the hot steaming coffee. Porch sitting of a morning was yet another extension of his daily ritual, at least when the weather was fine. In winter he had his morning coffee in the den before a roaring split-oak fire. His granddaddy had built the big open fireplace in the den—and the one in the living room too—with huge irregular-sized slabs of rock and fieldstone that he and Moses had hauled up out of the creekbed so many decades ago. The rest of the fine old house had just sort of grown up around the two massive rock fireplaces and their matching chimneys. John never thought of his house or returned to it, no matter how brief his absence, without experiencing a rush of excitement that he had never known for anything or anyone else until he had met Sal.

It's ironic, he thought. After all these years and here I am right back where I started from. And happy about it. Old Tom Wolfe was a good enough writer all right, but that didn't mean he always had to know what he was talking about. Some people *could* damn well go home again.

Not that John Winter hadn't tried his all-fired best to find another road. It was just that all roads, if traveled long enough, seemed to lead back home. At least that was the way it had been for him. College in Athens, and—despite his spoiled and precocious sweetheart Rachel Pettigrew—law school at Georgetown, almost two years in Korea via the courtesy of the U. S. Army, a year and a half in Washington with the Justice Department, three years in Atlanta as an Assistant U. S. Attorney, and the three expatriate years in Europe with Sal before coming back home. He still found it difficult to believe that he could have adjusted so readily to the life that he now led. For John Winter was a lawyer who no longer practiced law, a gentleman farmer, a university professor with a large student following and an author of no little promise as a social critic and observer. He was, in short, a man who at long last was on the verge of coming to terms with himself and his environment.

But what about Sal? Was it the right thing to have done for *her?* The subtle tightening of his jaw muscles betrayed the chill that swept over him at this disturbing thought. And the children—was it good for *them* to be raised in such a provincial environment? And to make matters worse, there was so much family history to live down. His and Sal's alike. But then, did it really matter *where* one attempted to manage the ragged ends of the past?

He stood up abruptly and walked to the far end of the porch. A tall, slender man, he didn't look his thirty-seven years. He looked like a man who had not gained five pounds in the last twenty years, nor added more than an inch to his waist or more than a decade to his age. He leaned against one of the rough cedar posts and tried to manage the direction of his thoughts.

Through the trees and up the oak-fringed mountain that rose steeply beyond the branch, he could glimpse the remains among the foliage of the old stone-faced dugout that his granddaddy had fashioned into the wall of rock so long ago. The old man had lived there with his wife and younger brother and John's mother while the original homestead was being built. Only the stone window boxes and chimney were still intact now. One of these days John would have to rebuild the cabin for Davey to play in, as he had done as a boy, and to retreat to in the inevitable moments of youthful shame and crises. And he would have to see to it soon, he thought, looking attentively at a small oak in the front yard. He had planted the tree on his son's first birthday, shortly after their return from Europe. It was a fine strong sapling. In its time it would make a massive oak.

And maybe that was the answer. Perhaps it had been a mistake for him to come back, and for Sal. Perhaps it was too late for them, but not for young Davey. Maybe the dream could yet be realized in his son. Maybe *that* was the answer to it all.

He could smell the bacon and eggs frying and knew that his family was astir. Baby Cathy was probably still asleep but he thought he could hear Davey's strident voice from somewhere in the back of the house. I have no *right* to be so damned pessimistic, he thought. Not anymore. With a woman and children that you love, all that changes completely and forever. I have a good life now. I'm building something here that will last. Hard work and disciplined thinking is the indicated prescription for a random case of the shakes. That and a massive dose of love.

"John—? Oh, John! Come to breakfast."

He turned around and answered his wife through the window screen. "Coming, hon."

"Hey, Papa-Daddy! Guess what we's havin' for breskiss?"

John was smiling as he headed for the door. No one and nothing was going to interfere with his life again, he thought fiercely.

# Chapter Five

**"You gonna eat the rest of that there glop?"**

"Just the coffee," said Eddie James, and he lit a cigarette as the bosomy waitress cleared away the remains of his breakfast.

His lower back ached, and he had picked up a rash of troublesome mosquito bites in the roadside park. He had been reluctant to stop and lose the time sleeping, but knew he couldn't make it in one straight shot no matter how much of a hurry he was in. Besides, he was having one of those attacks again. The dizziness, the whirring sound in his ears and the throbbing pain right between his eyes. It began as he was driving just north of Cairo, Illinois, on Route 66. He knew he had to stop and rest or he would wind up in a muddy ditch with a broken neck and nothing at all accomplished for his pains. And he just couldn't risk anything like that. Too much was at stake. He had planned it too well to abort his mission because of impatience.

He didn't really have to hurry anyway, he thought, as he drew the folded envelope out of his shirt pocket. He knew where they were. He took a sip of the lukewarm coffee and stared at the envelope for a long moment. The black eyes were hard as granite. The jaw muscles in his smooth dark face pulsated as he began to grind his teeth.

He stared at the envelope, at the return address and the faded Georgia postmark. He didn't have to read the letter again. He knew exactly what it said, word for word.

"Will there be anything else?"

"What?"

"I said is there anything else we can get for you?"

The provocation implicit in her tone jarred Eddie out of his reverie. He smiled as he looked from the waitress's freckled cowlike face to a young girl in a back booth wearing a soiled shift, braless, sipping a Coke and reading a dog-eared movie magazine. She too looked up at the sound of the waitress's voice. Nor was it unusual for Eddie to be approached in such a way. He was an exceptionally handsome young man, in a dark but delicate, almost pretty way. His copper-colored skin was as smooth as a baby's, his flashing smile as striking as a movie star's. He usually got a kick out of the reaction of women to his looks. He got a lot of kicks. Recently a woman lawyer in Chicago had offered to pimp for him and promised to make him a wealthy man in ten years' time. But Eddie didn't have ten years to spare.

"Well?"

"Naw, I'm in a hurry," he told the waitress, "and I got a long way to go." He folded the envelope and returned it to his shirt pocket. Then he dug into his jeans and pulled out a wad of bills.

The cafe was not overburdened with business at the moment. There had only been a couple of customers since Eddie's arrival, and now the place was empty. The woman was obviously sorry not to make the extra money. As he paid, he saw her notice the scar on his arm. "Wow," she said. "Where in the world didja get *that* monster?"

She handed him his change and she stared in rapt fascination at the grotesque scar that extended from his left elbow to a spot just above his wristbone.

"A house party in Southeast Asia," he shrugged, with no discernible bitterness in his pleasant voice.

"Oh cheez, I lost my little brother in Nam," the waitress said, fumbling with his change.

"A lotta brothers got lost in that place all right."

"Barry Crimmons," she said thickly. "I don't suppose—"

"I don't remember names, lady. Only faces."

He left a good tip beside his cup and started for the door.

"Hey. You come on back sometime when you ain't in such a hurry, hear. And it won't cost you a thing."

Though his head was spinning again, Eddie smiled at the waitress and at the girl in the booth, and then flashed them a peace sign before he left.

# Chapter Six

By the time Lucy Pittman worked up the nerve to go into her bedroom to wake her son it was almost 10 A.M. The task was one she looked forward to about as much as she would to the privilege of dancing the hoochie-coochie in a den of constipated rattlesnakes. Her son was *that* mean and unpredictable.

He was lying on his side with the sheet twisted between his bulbous knees. He was naked and his little erect penis was pointing at her like a stabbing accusation.

She almost backed out of the room. It was too risky. If he woke in one of his impossible moods... She stood there staring at him with a mixture of fear and wonder and loathing bubbling her blood.

He was twenty years old, with long blond unkempt hair, blue dope-washed eyes and a big lumpy body that made him look like an albino gorilla. As a boy he had been nicknamed Monk. It was derogatory of course, but the fool had preferred it to his given name of Elton. He claimed it was, of all things, more masculine. His hands were big and spatulate, his feet enormous and medically flat (they had kept him out of Vietnam, though he often affected the pose of having been a draft resister), and his shoulders were broad and stooped. The only things small about him, she reflected, were his brain and that silly-looking stunted penis.

Lucy wondered how long Elton would hang around this time. How many more nights would she have to sleep on the sofa? She found it impossible to manage her affairs with him hanging around day and night. People were scared of him. They wouldn't come near the place if they knew he was there, and the word was already getting around. Even Billy Mack Trumbo had canceled out on her yesterday, and poor old Billy Mack couldn't go more than a week or so without his special treatment.

Lucy fingered the money in the pocket of her soiled bathrobe and wondered how much it would cost her. Was he already in trouble, or just cruising? Whatever it cost, she had to get him out.

She took a deep breath to settle her nerves, and then moved quietly over to the bed. Carefully she pulled the sheet from between his legs and tried to get it down over his sticklike erection. It was not a bit bigger now than when he was nine or ten. She remembered the time, a year or so ago, when he had drunkenly beat her up and raped her in the ass and she hadn't even felt it.

"Gotcha!" he said suddenly, catching hold of her wrist and twisting her down on the bed.

"Elton, don't!"

"Lick it."

He twisted her wrist so far over she expected to hear the bone snap. The pain was unbearable. She stuck her tongue out and touched the end of his penis as if it were the head of a snake.

"Oh, Elton, please, *please*," she said and began to sob.

"Now that's better, Momma. Please is a whole lot better."

He pushed her viciously off the bed. She cracked her spine against a knob on the mahogany chiffonier and feared for a moment that she might pass out. But unconsciousness was unthinkable with Elton in the same room. She began to struggle to her feet, carefully closing the bathrobe over her pendulous breasts.

"Okay, old girl. So what the hell you want sniffin' around my room like a old fox in a henhouse?"

"I want you to get up and get out of here," she said bravely through her tears. "I want you to get *out*."

"Business?" he asked contemptuously, scratching at his testicles with his meaty fingers. "So early in the mornin'? You must be out to corner the fucking market, Momma."

"It's *not* early," she said defiantly. "It's almost ten o'clock."

"So? What are you, the town alarm clock too?"

Her resistance seemed to crumble. She dug into her pocket and, pulling out a cigarette, lit it with an unsteady hand. She inhaled ravenously, as if the smoke possessed a tangible quality that she could chew on.

"Those things are gonna kill you someday, Momma. If you don't die first from all that there high-priced semen in your lungs. You ever try to imagine what your pore ol' lungs must look like with all that squiggly goo workin' around down in there? Cancer or come, Momma. One of the two is sure Lord gonna do you in one of these fine days."

Lucy Pittman went into another pocket and extracted a wad of bills. "Here's a few bucks, Elton. You know, to see you through till you can make your plans."

"Well now, I appreciate that, Momma. I surely do. I know how hard you work and all." He got up abruptly and snatched the money out of her hand and began to count aloud.

"Sixty, eighty, a hundred...Say now, business must be purty good, hey old girl? Must be the season or somethin'. I'm real proud of you though, you know what I mean? My fuckin' old lady out there ever' day 'n' night workin' her ass off to put the bread on the table for the liddle fambly."

He reached out and slapped her so hard that she spun a full circle right where she stood. She screamed as she came around and he slapped her again. This time she landed on the floor in the corner of the room.

"Elton, *no!*" she screeched as he pulled her to her feet by the hair of her head.

"Where's the rest of it, bitch? And don't you give me no shit, you hear me now."

"There ain't no more, Elton. I *swear*. I didn't know you was coming home. I ain't got no more cash laid by."

"Then you damn well better *make* some more, you hear? An' *fast*."

He shoved his mother back against the wall and picked the cigarette up off the floor. When he grinned at her she felt the blood in her veins turn to ice water.

"Oh God, no."

He moved toward her, smiling still, rolling the burning cigarette between his fingers.

"Please don't," she whispered.

He towered over her as he said, "I want bread, old girl. I want a lot of bread and I want it quick. I ain't got no plans of stayin' around this fuckin' place no longer'n I have to. So you just better do your part in buildin' up the old travel fund. Click?"

"Yes, Elton. Yes. Only please go now. Please."

He grinned again and moved against her so that she felt the swelling of his diminutive erection against her hipbone. He pulled open her robe and caught her big left tit in his enormous paw.

"Oh God," she gasped and there were tears filling her eyes as he began to squeeze. Her face grew dark and mottled and was soon contorted with pain. Elton merely giggled and licked at the dried spittle caking the corners of his mouth.

At last, when the agony became too exquisite to bear, Lucy whispered through tightly clenched teeth: "It's after ten, Elton. He...he said he'd be here by half past."

Grinning wolfishly, her son began to move the burning ash of the cigarette toward her viscid nipple. When it was close enough to singe the flesh, he asked indifferently, "An' who the hell is 'he'?"

"Sheriff Biggs," she said.

His penis wilted and he let go of her breast as if it were a coiled rattlesnake.

Snarling, he slapped her viciously on the side of the head, knocking her down, and then stepped on her crumpled body in his haste to get over to his clothing.

# Chapter Seven

Sal could no longer deny it, even to herself: she was worried about John. Mostly because he was so concerned about her. Even though he tried to conceal it, it was always there, lurking beneath the surface. She tried to reassure him, to convince him that she was all right now. But it hadn't worked. Ever since they had left Europe, the old fearful uncertainty had begun to plague them again.

And it was all so unnecessary, she thought. She *was* all right now. She had never been happier and more content in her life; at least in her adult life. Why couldn't John see it? Why wouldn't he *believe* her?

Sal had deposited the kids with John's mother earlier—much as she disliked having to do it—and then drove into Adelphi to do the errands that had accumulated during the week. After the post office, she went to Adams-Brisco to pick up six hydrangea plants that Elmoose Brantley had been holding for her, and then to the hardware store with a list of items that John needed for his handyman chores over the weekend.

She smiled to herself at the thought of how handy he had been the night before. She knew what most of the good women of Adelphi would think of her if they had any idea about the intensity of her feelings for John, physical as well as emotional. Even the university crowd was more straightlaced than she had ever imagined such people would be. Of course Adelphi University was not exactly Berkeley.

She couldn't help it anyway; she loved him and that was all there was to it. She loved him more than life itself. Suddenly, she got that faraway look that so often came over her without any warning. There was every reason to suppose that had it not been for John she would have had no life at all.

I'm getting moody, she thought. I mustn't get moody. It's the heat. This afternoon I'll take the kids to the motel for a swim.

"Mawnin' there, Pocahontas. Everybody all right out to your place?"

"Good morning, Aaron. We're all just fine. And you and Sophie?"

"God's in His heaven an' all's right with the tribe of Goetz."

"It's a beautiful day, that's for sure."

"Gettin' purtier by the moment an' tha's a fact," the man said, grinning all over himself and making not even the slightest effort to conceal his appreciative examination of Sal's healthy bosom.

She was a delight to see, and although she was not unaware of her striking good looks she was as unaffected as only the truly handsome can be. And Aaron was right, she did look like a TV version of an Indian princess. Long straight raven-black hair, dark luminous eyes that were oval in shape and heavily lashed. Her healthy complexion sustained a year-round tan that deepened in summer to a dark honey color. Tall, supple and graceful of movement, she always dressed simply and with uncalculated sensuousness. Of course she was all the more sensuous precisely because it was unpremeditated. Today she was dressed in Levi's, sandals and a white cotton tank top.

Sal smiled and with a toss of her long hair unprised Aaron's optic clasp on her breasts and handed him the list of items she needed. Men, she thought with good-natured forbearance, as Aaron bustled off to fill her order.

She thought quickly back over what John had told her about the Goetz family. They were Adelphi's token Jews. Where they had come from and why, no one exactly knew. No stranger could have guessed Aaron's origins, either from his appearance or his dialect. With his flowing white mane of wavy hair and his outrageously cultivated Southern accent and manner of dress, he could out-Claghorn Senator Talmadge any day of the week. John said he spoke better redneck than any bona fide native son of Taliawiga County. Homer Stokes contended in his cultured tones that Aaron was a Zionist spy assigned to pierce the heart of the enemy camp.

If Aaron had any enemies, Sal didn't want them for friends.

Then she remembered the light bulb.

It was not on the list. One of the high-voltage bulbs for the backyard had burned out the night before. Although they loved the splendid isolation of their home—as John's grandfather had described it—it did necessitate certain special considerations. Though John was seldom away from home overnight, he was away occasionally after dark. Sal had not looked at their surroundings in quite the same way after a young mother and her child had been brutally murdered on a county farm the previous year in a case that was still unsolved. The police and most everyone else were apparently satisfied that the crime had not been committed by a resident of Taliawiga County. As Sheriff Biggs put it: "It was most likely one of them there dope fiends roamin' along the Innerstate on his way down to Floridy."

The mere thought of physical violence still made her ill. She tried not to think of such things anymore. It had been years...nothing could undo what had already happened.

"Hey, Sal. You feelin' all right there, honey?"

"Oh." She put her hand over her mouth and leaned against the counter. "I'm fine, Aaron." Her skin was hot and clammy, her hands and feet cold as ice. "I'm okay, really."

"You don't look so good to me. Mebbe I better take these things out to the car for you."

"No, thanks. I can manage." She took the packages and said, "I'm perfectly all right."

"You don't look all right to me," he insisted, scowling as she started for the door. "Now you just go on home an' get off your feet, you hear me now?"

On the sidewalk she leaned against a parking meter and began taking great drafts of fresh air into her lungs until her head started to clear. It has been so long, she thought. I was sure I was over all that. No wonder John is worried.

But it was passing now. She would be all right. I *am* all right, she insisted and pushed herself away from the parking meter.

"Sal. Oh, Sal!"

As the clock in the courthouse tower began to chime the hour, she heard someone calling her name. She pushed the hair out of her eyes, shaded her gaze from the glaring sun and looked around the courthouse square. The benches were groaning under the weight of dying old men in white straw hats, coveralls or cotton summer suits, while blacks streamed in and out of the courthouse in sufficient numbers to cause the registrar of voters to have nightmares. Finally, Sal located Homer Stokes waving to her from the steps.

She took a deep breath and waved back. She was all right now. Until the next time.

Homer carried his hand to his mouth and tilted his head back sharply. Sal pointed up to the clock and shook her head, *No time.* She just wasn't in the mood for coffee and chitchat, not even with Homer.

Homer was their best friend in Adelphi, what the books called "a real Southern gentleman." A small-town Southerner named Homer Ray Stokes ought by rights to have been short, fat, red-haired and red-necked, and not right bright in the bargain. Homer was tall, dark and lanky-Lincolnesque. He habitually dressed in winter tweeds and summer linens, ubiquitously smoked a blackened meerschaum pipe and spoke with a clipped quasi-British accent acquired as a Rhodes scholar at Oxford. He was a graduate of the St. Louis school of journalism and he o⸺ ⸺ ⸺ the local newspaper. He was a graduate of Harv⸺ ⸺ness school and he owned the town's bank. He also ⸺ned a thousand acres more or less of pasture and woodland, two or three hundred head of cattle and a thriving commercial catfish pond. He was the richest man in middle Georgia, by inheritance, and had never hit a consistent lick at a snake in his life. Sipping champagne, he wrote romantic poetry far into the night which he routinely destroyed when reread by the light of day. A confirmed bachelor John's age, he lived in an antebellum mansion on a hill overlooking Adelphi with his widowed mother, who hadn't spoken to him in nearly twenty years.

Sal pantomimed the shoveling of food into her mouth and Homer nodded his assent, waved again and went inside the courthouse. Sal started slowly down the sidewalk to her car, and decided to have roast chicken and potatoes for Sunday supper. It was one of Homer's favorite dishes and they still had a couple of bottles of Montrachet that he had brought the last time he came to eat.

After she put her packages in the trunk, Sal turned to find Sheriff Biggs examining her denimed rear end while waiting in his county car for a red light to change. She felt her pulse leap and she moved quickly into the car. The mere sight of the man disturbed her. It was his little pig's eyes that shook her more than anything. More than the fat ham of a face, the gargantuan belly cinched by the thick black holster, the jackboots. God, how she hated those symbols of official macho chauvinism. How often had she faced that image across the barricades in the turbulent days of the late sixties. But she wasn't going to think of that. The likes of Chester Biggs wasn't going to force her to think of all that.

Nor would she let him know she was afraid of him. She sat there stiffly behind the wheel and stared him down. Finally he took the cigar out of his mouth and nodded a grudging hello, which she coldly ignored.

His face reddened like an angry boil. He jammed the cigar between his teeth and blasted the cruiser through a caution light, barely missing a cement truck that was already into the intersection.

She sat there for a moment before starting the engine. Had anyone suggested a few years before that Sally Massingale would one day be living in a place like Adelphi, Georgia, she would have thought him mad. In those days she thought of Georgia as a place some Civil War general had tried to burn off the map, and where the lunatic Scarlett O'Hara had spurned the sort of man that every schoolgirl in her right mind dreamed of enslaving.

No rhyme or reason had brought her to Georgia in the first instance. She had known no one in this state and had no family here. She had no family anywhere. Perhaps that was why she had come.

Her heart suddenly skipped a beat. After the death of her parents she had wandered with unreasoning vagueness from one city and state to another. Too weary to continue, she had simply stopped one day and unpacked her only suitcase. It was a week or so before she had consciously realized she was in Atlanta.

Eight years ago, she thought. And time receded before her eyes with uncompromising dedication to reality. The mission compound, the plaster and plywood chapel, the toneless organ, the encroaching lushness of the South American rain forests...the clattering rifle bolts, the strident command of the rebel chieftain and the obedient clap of responding gunfire. Orphaned at sixteen, she had had no friends or relatives to turn to in all the world.

Without realizing it, Sal started to cry. She gripped the steering wheel so tightly that her knuckles turned white. It was the old feeling again beginning to well up inside her, a feeling compounded of ache and sorrow and bitter recriminations. They had had no *right* to live that way! They had children and earthly responsibilities; a daughter who was not a lily of the field and a young son who was anything but a sparrow. It was not fair. It was wrong. It was the unforgivable sin.

No. Hers was the sin not to be forgiven, she thought sadly. She had survived.

Her parents had been Protestant missionaries. Because of her mother's Indian blood, her father's career was forever impeded, and they had spent most of their impractical lives in one South American country after another, taking the word of God to the heathen horde. When the trouble started Sal had been confined to a hospital room in the capital recuperating from an operation for appendicitis. After the atrocity at the mission, the U. S. Embassy immediately shipped her to safety in Miami and to two years of misery in a church-sponsored orphanage.

A blaring car horn and a screech of tires in the nearby intersection ⸻red Sal out of her traumatic reverie. She blinked aw⸻ her tears as she noticed Bobcat Tribble, the e⸻ ⸻ ⸻inal lawyer, watching her. His thinning hair and ⸻ ⸻ce were as rumpled as his white linen suit. Tribble possesse⸻ ⸻e of the saddest faces she had ever seen. He looked like an old whipped dog spoiling for one more fight. But why is the old lecher staring so intently at me? she wondered. I hardly know him.

And what am I doing here? she thought, genuinely perplexed by the question. After all that, and after all that happened to me at the orphanage, how in the world did I wind up in a place like *this?*

She wiped her cheeks with the back of her hand and started the engine.

Adelphi was not and never could be her home. On the other hand, where was home? She had never known any sense of permanence, not with a family like hers. The only stability she had ever known, before John had rescued her from all that activist mania up in Atlanta, was in her art. But now there was John, and Davey, and little Cathy. They were her life and her stability, her sanity and her hope.

She backed out of the parking slot and shifted gears. She didn't really care where she lived, she thought. Just so long as I have my family and my work. Life is never hopeless as long as you have someone or something outside yourself to cling to.

Her eyes were dry again as she turned the corner on Main Street and drove past the stately old courthouse on her way home.

# Chapter Eight

**Eddie James was hard on the approach to Chattanooga** in his determined Sherman-like push toward Georgia. If the weather held he would make Atlanta by midafternoon.

But for the last hour he had been anxiously watching the black clouds as they boiled up on the Chattanooga horizon. Rain might cool things off but would slow him down too.

His back ached and his temples were beginning to throb again. The pain came more regularly lately, and more severely too. He checked his watch and the skyline ahead, and increased the pressure of his foot on the accelerator.

# Chapter Nine

"...and so the issue of violence is of central importance to the student of criminology. It is of crucial concern to the average citizen too. We live in a time when violence is apparently endemic to our daily lives. But is there anything new or unusual about this phenomenon? Is it a social condition original to our own day and time, or has violence always been a central condition of man's social experience? American man, in particular?"

John removed his horn-rims and looked out across the upturned faces in the crowded classroom. Not all of his students were favoring him with their undivided attention. A few were so near the edge of sleep he expected them to topple headfirst onto the floor at any moment. A black dude in a chartreuse leisure suit was studiously paring his manicured nails with a switchblade the size of a Moroccan scimitar, and toward the back of the room a little white girl about the size of a bird was frantically working on her homework for the next class. But most of the others were bright-eyed and alert. Sonny-Boy Cubbage, as usual, was front row center and hadn't missed a word. Next to Sonny-Boy sat Lynelda Anderson, crossing and uncrossing her legs in a distractingly non-academic fashion.

"...of course it is historically indisputable that man's earliest response to offenses, fancied and real, was one of personal retaliation and vengeance."

Many of the students were off-duty police officers, probation and parole counselors, and correctional personnel, all from a variety of agencies within the community. Much to

John's displeasure most of the policemen came to class armed whether in uniform or not. And although a number of complaints had been lodged with the university administration nothing as yet had been done about the situation. John had complained to the president himself on the grounds that the confrontation was much too one-sided, that even if he was allowed to arm himself in self-defense he would still be severely outgunned. But apparently President Reed was not impressed by the droll wit of his resident criminologist and nothing had been accomplished by way of an arms embargo.

"It is interesting to note," said John—and precisely at that moment Mrs. Anderson made it historically indisputable that she was not wearing underpants—"that some modern scientists are now contending that man's primary characteristic is not an instinct toward violence and destruction after all, but rather one of cooperation and self-preservation." Though he stumbled slightly over his words in the face of such distracting competition from Lynelda, John managed not to lose his train of thought entirely.

"And without this willingness to cooperate," he concluded, "man could not have survived at all."

"Oh they's cooperatin' all right," growled a burly hulk in uniform on the back row. "To see just how fast they can rob an' kill the rest of us."

It was John's custom to end on a note of laughter or whenever a spirited argument was reaching its peak. For the first time since his lecture had begun he seemed to have the attention of the entire class. So he promptly dismissed the class ten minutes early and gathered up his books.

John Winter's popularity with students was a subtle compound of a variety of ingredients. He was a thorough professional in his field. He understood the law and how it operated as well as any man could. He was a minor celebrity due to the recent success of his book on crime in American society, not to mention his reputation as one of Georgia's former outstanding football players. His Socratic method of teaching, though initially unsettling, was ultimately effective and rewarding to student and teacher alike. Most students liked him primarily because they sensed that he liked them. And he cared about them. It was more than they felt they could say about two-thirds of the rest of the faculty. Some of the females liked him for a variety of other reasons.

"I've just gotta do *something* about that last test grade,"

Lynelda Anderson was saying in her soft throaty voice, as they strolled along the corridor toward his office.

John stopped and drew her over to the wall. "Just what do you have in mind?" he asked in a low confidential tone.

Her green heavily painted eyelids widened as she detected the first opening he had ever allowed. "Anything," she said meaningfully. "Dr. Winter, I would just do *anything* for you."

"Good," he smiled, looked conspiratorially up and down the corridor and leaned down toward her. "Go home, tell your hubby to lock himself in the bathroom all weekend, and then you study your pretty little tail off for a change."

"Oh!" she said, stamping her foot. *"You."*

John had barely settled at his desk, still chuckling to himself, when Sonny-Boy appeared in the open doorway.

"Hi ya, Doc. Gotta minute?"

"Sure, Sonny-Boy. Come on in. You want a cup of coffee?"

"No, thanks. I got another class in a minute. I just wanted to...uh...well, talk to you for a minute or two."

"What's up?"

"Well, I only got a couple minutes. I won't take up much of your time. Course I could come back some other time iffen you ain't got time to talk now."

"Sonny-Boy, if you don't get on with it the bell's gonna ring before you even get started."

"Yeah." He grinned sheepishly and bobbed his head from side to side.

"You got a girl in trouble?"

"Aw, Doc."

"Sit down," he smiled. "Any news about your application?"

"Naw. Those people won't tell me nothin'. But I hear I can get on over to the sheriff's office ennytime I wants."

"That's probably true," said John.

"But I druther wait an' see what happens over to the P.D."

"I don't blame you."

"Doc, I know I got a long way to go, me wantin' to be an FBI agent an' all. College an' then law school. But iffen I could get me some real good experience out on the street, you know, in uniform an' all, why, that wouldn't hurt me none either, would it?"

"No, it wouldn't hurt, Sonny-Boy."

"You reckon the FBI might give me credit for that kind of experience? Experience right out there on the street?"

"Sonny-Boy, I'm sure the FBI will consider your entire

record, all of your experience and qualifications." What the hell, thought John. What else *can* I say?

Sonny-Boy brightened. "I think experience with the P.D. will be a lot better than with the sheriff," he allowed solemnly.

"It pays better too."

"Yeah, but if I don't hear something soon..."

"You go with the sheriff and you'll have to quit school, remember. We don't have a friend over there like we do in Captain Tate."

"Wudden you think they'd wanta cooperate—"

"Biggs didn't even graduate from high school, Sonny-Boy."

"An' the dumb fucker seems proud of it."

John laughed and poured himself a cup of coffee from an illegal hot plate on a table beneath the window overlooking the spacious pine-studded campus. Sonny-Boy watched him with unconcealed admiration. He liked Dr. Winter better than any of his professors. In fact, he liked him better than any adult he knew, including the members of his own family. *Especially* including the members of his own family. There was no one else he could turn to.

"Okay, Sonny-Boy. Out with it. What's bothering you?"

The boy looked sideways at him and shrugged his bony shoulders. "Aw, Doc. It's Sissie again, man. I just don't know what to do about her."

"I thought she was pretty well settled down by now."

He made a face and shook his head. "No way, man. No way."

"She still enrolled in the nursing department?"

"She takes a couple courses, just to keep the old man off her back. But she ain't serious about nursin', man. She ain't serious about nothin' 'cept raisin' hell."

John took a sip of coffee and glanced at his desk calendar. He had an appointment with Dean Witcomb at twelve-thirty and would barely have time to grab a sandwich. He wondered what Cecil Witcomb had on his mind.

"Well now, look, Sonny-Boy," he began, turning his attention back to his visitor. "Maybe Sissie's just not certain what she wants to do with her life yet. You're lucky in that respect."

Sonny-Boy's head was shaking like one of those toy dogs in the back window of a car. "She's always been wild, Doc. And too damn smart for her britches, if you know what I mean. Wild and smart-alecky. But ever since she went up

North..." He paused and licked at his lips anxiously. "I dunno...she's diffrunt now. Before it was kid stuff. Now..."

"She's no longer a kid," said John, thinking of the predatory look in the girl's eye, the provocative manner of dress and her sultry suggestive ways.

"Ever since she come back there's been something strange goin' on. She was always wild an' sassy, but since she went up North she really changed. I don't know exactly what happened up there, I don't even know where she was for sure. Or how my old man found out where she was stayin'. But he went up an' got her though an' brung her back home, an' neither one of 'em's ever said doodley-squat about it since."

John took a deep breath and a thoughtful sip of coffee and tried to figure just what Dean Witcomb might be up to. Probably wants to con me into speaking to another one of those stodgy civic club dinners that he so loves to attend. I'm on the verge of turning into a one-man speaking bureau.

"Of course I don't know anything about it, Sonny-Boy. But maybe things will just sort themselves out in time. They most always do, you know." There. Now how was that for puerile academic drivel of the worst sort? Come to Doc Winter, the snake oil salesman of Taliawiga County, and he'll lift your burdens with a handy aphorism or two.

"You think maybe Sissie's home to stay this time?" John asked into the awkward silence.

"I dunno, Doc. And tha's just it, man. I hope she don't." He was visibly agitated now and could scarcely keep his seat. "I mean, she's headin' for trouble, see. An' I'm scared it's gonna rub off on *me*."

"What kind of trouble, Sonny-Boy? Be more specific."

"She's messin' around with some purty bad actors, believe you me. Like those black dudes down at the Ace of Spades. An' she's got somethin' goin' with some ol' big-shot lawyer over in Macon an' I don't know what all else. Ever since she come back from up North, man. I don't know what happened. Now ennytime Daddy ain't around she just goes hog-wild. Like when that Elton Pittman creep showed up in town a week or so ago. You know Sissie ain't even got no better sense than to be messin' around with *him*."

"Lucy Pittman's boy?"

"Tha's the one."

"I thought he was supposed to be in jail or prison upcountry somewhere for armed robbery or something."

"He's home now."

40

"Or was it a dope bust? I can't remember—"

"Dope," said Sonny-Boy. "He pistol-whipped a female dealer who tried to overcharge him, according to *his* story. Ennyway, he's out again now an' he's been sniffin' around our Sissie ever' time Daddy turns his back."

"From what I've heard about your father—"

"He'll kill the gorilla."

The bell rang and Sonny-Boy jumped as though he had been shot.

"Well, I got another class," he said, "so I better shove along. But I sure would like to talk to you again sometime, y'know. I mean, not as a teacher. I mean, you're a lawyer an' all, even if you don't practice no more. Mebbe I could even pay you a liddle something, you know, for all your time an' advice."

John put his cup down and stood up. "Don't be silly, Sonny-Boy. I don't want your money." He walked him to the door, adding, "You come see me anytime, understand? I don't know what I can do to help, but I'll be glad to talk with you."

The boy's pimply face brightened as if John had flipped a light switch. "Gee, thanks, Doc. I really mean it. Like, I mean, I didden know where else to go—"

"You better go on to class," said John, looking up at the clock above the door in the reception room.

Sonny-Boy grinned and started up like a bag of disassembled bones. God help us all, thought John, if this kid ever does succeed in getting a license to wear a badge and carry a gun. "FBI, my foot," he said aloud, meeting his secretary's eye across the room, and they laughed like co-conspirators.

"Still, you remember what he was like *last* year, Marilou?"

He decided to wander on over to the cafeteria for a sandwich and some iced tea before stopping in to see what Dean Witcomb wanted.

# Chapter Ten

**Sissie had been waiting for almost an hour in the lavish** reception room of Joyner and Joyner, father and son attorneys-at-law. But she didn't mind; she could be as patient as the next person when there was something in it for her. And boy, was there ever gonna be something in it for her, she smiled. Come the day of judgment.

She looked at her watch. She had nothing else to do until three when she had agreed to meet that big black guy from Atlanta down at the Ace of Spades. If his connections were anything like what people said... And speaking of connections. She looked out the picture window that opened onto the street below, just as Bobcat Tribble parked his ancient Caddy in front of his law office and shuffled inside.

Maybe I oughta pay him a visit too, she thought, wiggling her toes over the edges of her sandals in the lush shag carpet. After she finished with Gordon here, maybe she ought to just sashay on over yonder and have herself a go at Mr. Bobcat Tribble. Sissie's smile was never more attractive than when it was lit by considerations of hard cold business calculation.

But she knew it wasn't really a very good idea. She scarcely knew Tribble. In fact, he might not even remember her at all. Their single encounter had been over a year ago, before she had gone north to Chicago. And he had been pretty drunk as it was, and probably had little or no recognition of what he had done, or even *who* he had done, she thought, smirking over the memory.

She had been at a roadside tavern out near Lake Taliawiga when it happened. Tribble walked blindly into the ladies'

42

room and there she sat, skirt hiked up around her waist, sticking in a fresh Tampax. It was just like in a porno movie. He charged into that stall like a rampaging bull and socked it to her without even giving her time to get the damned Tampax out of the way. Old Doc Whipple hadn't said anything when he had to fish it out for her the next day, but he had sure as hell given her a look that said he was fit to be tied.

Sissie had been thinking about Tribble off and on ever since, wondering if he were a likely mark. He certainly wouldn't be as easy to handle as Gordon Joyner of Joyner and Joyner. Gordon was a nincompoop. Tribble *acted* the senile fool at times but she knew better than to underestimate him. Still, he might be manageable if the randy old fool were played just right. For all his perverse eccentricities, he was still the best criminal lawyer in middle Georgia.

"Miss Cubbage? Mr. Joyner will see you now."

If Sissie felt the least bit self-conscious about her worn jeans and washed-out halter in such splendid surroundings, it certainly didn't show. She got up and walked serenely across the Grecian blue sea of carpeting like a blond Jacqueline Kennedy Onassis, entering the lawyer's private office without bothering to knock.

"I've told you not to come here dressed like that," said Gordon Joyner, turning from his antique rolltop desk and coming to meet her.

"It's all I got, Jedge. Now if you wanta kick in a liddle on the ol' clothing allowance..."

She moved as if she were going to kiss him on the mouth, but he quickly avoided the gesture—as she knew he would—by hugging her roughly and patting her self-consciously on the ass. In all the time they had known each other he had never once kissed her on the mouth. But she merely laughed and sat down on the sofa, causing him to wince as she crossed her legs Indian-fashion on the silken seat cover.

"You want something to drink?"

"Just a Coca-Cola."

He poured her Coke at a teak-paneled bar in the corner and mixed a bourbon and water for himself. Then he sat across from her in a genuine early American wing chair that looked as if it must have cost as much as the secondhand VW beetle that Sissie drove, courtesy of her loving daddy.

Joyner was a fastidious man, and he crossed his legs carefully so as not to spoil the crease in his expensive gray slacks.

He was wearing an expensive blue blazer and a very expensive paisley tie. A short dark well-built man of about thirty-five, he looked exactly like a weaker version of the dark powerful old man in the big painting on the wall across the room. His congressman daddy was seldom in Adelphi and Sissie had never had the opportunity to see him in the flesh. She knew one thing though, instinctively; if the old fucker ever got her between the sheets, unlike his son, he would make her do a good night's work for her pay.

"You got it with you?"

"Watcha got in mind?" Sissie said coyly, examining the gold-leafed family portrait on a shelf behind Gordon's head. The four boys looked exactly like Gordon, even down to the weak receding chin. The wife looked like a dried-out piece of seaweed.

"Have you got it, Sissie?"

"Course I got it, man." She wet the tip of her little pink tongue in the carbonated fizz that was still bubbling around the rim of her glass.

"How much?"

"Two hits."

"And the cost?"

"A couple hundred."

"Your ass!"

"Uh uh. That costs more," she smiled, licking her lips with the tip of her tongue.

"Don't you try to jack me around, Sissie. You know I can't be jacked around."

"Sure," she smiled. "I know you can't be jacked around, Gordie."

"I'm not the type."

"You ain't the type to be jacked around, are you?"

"Lord, girl," he croaked. "Keep that tongue inside your mouth."

She laughed huskily. "It's quality shit, Gordon. Worth two hundred."

"I don't know..."

"You ever known me to give you bad stuff?"

He made a choking sound down in his throat. "You *gotta* kick in somethin' more for that kind of bread."

Sissie smiled and took a sip of her drink. Then she stuck her tongue out and touched the tip to the end of her nose. She giggled as she saw the electric shock hit him between the eyes and his legs at the same instant.

She got up and started to unbutton her jeans, but he stopped her.

"I have to be in court in twenty minutes."

He looked more as if he would soon be in the intensive care unit with a massive cardiac arrest. Sissie knelt in front of his chair and unzipped his fly.

"Don't you mess my slacks, you hear me now?"

She grinned and began to massage his member. "You ever known me to spill, Jedge?"

# Chapter Eleven

**Dean Witcomb was about as nervous as one of Tennes**see Williams's cats tiptoeing over a hot tin roof. He was a simple, transparent man who labored under the burden of a basically honest nature. He completely lacked any facility for dissembling. A shaving patch over a cut chin smacked of deceitfulness to Cecil Witcomb. It was all but a fatal flaw to administrative advancement in the field of higher education.

Though John knew perfectly well that something more than polite chitchat was on the dean's mind, he was resolved simply to wait the man out.

"And you've been with us now—let me see—almost three years, isn't it?" the dean was saying.

As if he didn't know precisely to the day how long John Winter had been with the university.

"Three years the end of this quarter. I hope you aren't about to tell me it's my last."

"What?" The dean sat up even more rigidly in his chair, the skin tightening visibly around his thin-lipped mouth.

Then he caught on. "Oh, I see. Good heavens, John. You gave me quite a start for a moment, even suggesting the possibility of your leaving the university."

John smiled. Cecil Witcomb always intoned the words "the university" with the same awed reverence that other men reserved for use when referring to the church or the party.

"You *are* happy here, aren't you, John?" he suddenly asked.

What the hell, thought John. "Well yes, Cecil," he said cautiously. "I'm a happy man."

"That's wonderful, John. Simply wonderful. And needless to say, we are very pleased indeed with the way matters have worked out from our standpoint. The criminal justice courses have never been so well attended. For your information, enrollment in your own classes has risen some five hundred per cent in the three years you've been here."

John nodded and reached for a cup of coffee that sat on a small table beside his upholstered chair.

"I'm sure I don't have to tell you," the dean continued, "that when you first came to us we...well...were not at all certain as to how the arrangement would work out." He hesitated and cleared his throat uncomfortably. "In the first instance, your beginning salary was no more than a third of what you might have made as a lawyer."

"It still is," John said matter-of-factly.

"Yes, well...the university system, you know..."

"Yes, I know."

"In any case, we were aware of the book you'd published while in Europe, of course, though we had no idea that it would, ah, prove so financially successful for you."

"Now I get it. You're trying to tell me it's necessary to cut my salary—such as it is—and you're glad I have a little something to live on."

"No, no. It's nothing like that, I assure you," said the dean with a small forced chuckle.

"Besides, it really isn't all *that* much money, Cecil. I haven't exactly knocked Galbraith out of the best-seller's box as yet."

"But it *has* done very well, John. And we are extremely proud of you."

"I think maybe a monkey could write on the subject of crime today and get it published somewhere."

"But not critically praised the way your book has been.

How many colleges and universities have adopted it now? Quite a number, I'm told."

"Quite a number," John said. "But I really don't keep close tabs on the actual figures."

"And the new book? It's progressing well, I trust?"

"About half done, I reckon. At my current pace I should finish by Christmas, well ahead of the contract date."

"Oh that's splendid," said Witcomb, leaning forward to stir his coffee. "Absolutely."

The nice thing about it as far as John was concerned was that Cecil really meant it. Unlike some of his other colleagues, the dean was truly pleased at someone else's success. But John still wished to hell he would get on with whatever was really on his mind. He looked at his watch. It was getting late. He wanted to get home in time to take Davey down to the pond for a little fishing before supper.

Still, he wasn't going to help or prod the dean along. He had learned a long time ago to hold his own counsel and wait the other man out. His colleagues in the D.A.'s office had often marveled at his ability to use his own silence in plea bargaining sessions as a positive tactic of negotiation.

"And Sal? Is she well and happy with her life here in middle Georgia?"

The question was a bit of a surprise and caused John to hesitate slightly, but the dean didn't seem to notice it. "Oh sure. Sal's fine," he said. "She's got the baby pretty much on a routine now. I think she'll be coming out to some of the campus functions again pretty soon now."

"That's wonderful, John. Lavonne asks about her quite often. We'll all be so happy to see her."

John said, "She's even beginning to paint again," and reached for his coffee.

"Oh that *is* good news."

"No major projects, mind you. Not yet. But she does get in an hour, perhaps two, each day out in the studio-barn."

"The marvelous picture she donated to the library is still the focal point of our institutional collection."

John smiled thinly. "There are those who might disagree."

"Oh yes, well." The dean was acutely uncomfortable now. "Not everyone appreciates—or even *understands*—modern art, John."

"Especially those—"

"Now, John."

John grinned sourly, and nodded. "How is he, Cecil?"

The dean shook his head. "Not terribly well. It's mostly age, of course. But then he does have—ah—other problems."

"He does indeed."

The dean actually seemed to shrink in stature merely at the mention of the university's aging president. John had often wondered how this taciturn, scholarly, introverted Midwesterner had co-habited so well for nearly ten years now with Adelphi's glib, superficial, charming and oh-so-very-Southern chief honcho. Oliver Wendell Reed, crusty and bordering upon senility now in his eighth decade, had been Adelphi University's president for more than twenty years. He was still a powerful force to be reckoned with in civic and governmental circles as well as educational. But he was running down, there was no longer any doubt about it. He still started each day with a six o'clock canter on his favorite mare, then breakfasted on an undeviating routine of homemade hot buttered biscuits, grits and redeye gravy, lacing his coffee with 90 proof bourbon. But by early afternoon he had begun to eschew the coffee in favor of the "sweet'ner." Come nightfall he was regularly in his cups.

It was well known that Reed had relinquished most of the academic concerns of the institution to Dean Witcomb some five years before. But he clung tenaciously to the school's financial reins. The university was growing with the times while time was killing Oliver Wendell Reed in ruthlessly regular increments. Even so, he retained the power and the willingness to use it to crush anyone in the institution who attempted to oppose him.

The telephone rang and Dean Witcomb jumped as if he had been goosed by an electric prod.

"Please, Mrs. Starbell, no interruptions. Yes. Yes, I know. I'll be there. I may be one or two minutes late, but I'll be there."

The interruption gave John a moment longer to reflect upon the dean's relationship with the Old Man. Perhaps that is how Cecil has survived so long, he thought. By never opposing the old boy. He couldn't think of a single instance in which Witcomb had gone against the known wishes of the president. On the other hand, there had been considerable academic advancement since Witcomb had become dean. Coincidental? Or was there another side to the self-effacing fellow that didn't readily meet the eye?

"I'm sorry about that interruption," Witcomb said when he hung up the phone. "I have a meeting with the president"—Cecil *never* referred to Reed as the Old Man; not even in the privacy of his own thoughts, John was sure—"at three, one of those interminable budgetary sessions that I can seldom make hide nor hair of."

"Well, don't let me keep you, Cecil."

John was halfway out of his chair with his and Davey's hooks baited and in the water before the dean was able to get control of the situation again.

"No, no. Don't leave just yet, John. There's something very important that I should like to discuss with you."

John dropped back into his chair and the dean got abruptly to his feet and came around the desk. Tall, spare, Lyndon Johnson hair and glasses, no more than fifty going on sixty-five. The dean sat on the sofa across from John now and began to dry-wash his hands like an undertaker about to launch his ten-thousand-dollar pitch.

"Look here, John. Are you planning to stay on with us?"

Now that's another surprise, thought John. What the hell is going on? "Of course I'm planning to stay, Cecil. If you still want me."

"Oh we want you all right, most certainly. But there is still the notion in the minds of at least some of the trustees that you may, well, 'pack it in,' as old Hiram Whiddow put it the other night, and return to the practice of law."

"I have no such plans, Cecil."

The dean cleared his throat and said, "And there's been some mention of, well, a possible political move in the near future."

Cecil Witcomb had the capacity to shock after all. John could not conceal his incredulity. "Politics? *Me?*"

"There has been talk, John. A number of offices will be opening up in the fall—my goodness, even Senator Talmadge can expect stiff opposition in view of his latest, ah, difficulties."

John Winter's mouth was beginning to hang open.

"In any case," the dean said, "at least a few of the trustees are under the impression that you are a likely candidate for elective office in the near future."

John leaned back in his chair, barely able to restrain a scatological expression. "Well now, I'll just tell you what you can do for me, Cecil. Though I have no idea why this whole thing has come up, or why it should really matter to anyone one way or the other, you just tell those old boys for me that when it comes to an aversion to holding political office General Sherman was a mealymouthed, pussyfooting marshmallow of indecision compared to John Winter."

Witcomb stared at him for a moment and then burst out laughing. He put back his head and laughed so hard that both his feet raised up off the floor. John could see the relief washing over the man's face, though he had no idea why his response should be of such importance. But he had the feeling that he was going to find out real soon.

"John, cards on the table now." The dean leaned forward and looked at him earnestly. "I...we...all of us want you to become chairman of the Division of Social Sciences in the fall."

# Chapter Twelve

**Ellie Fletcher waited on a corner across from the school** with her books clutched tightly against her schoolgirl's breasts. The afternoon school bus had been gone for some ten or fifteen minutes and she was beginning to worry. Marvin had promised to pick her up at three o'clock sharp and take her home. Although Josie would not be home yet from her labors in the kitchen of the Adelphi Hotel, Ellie would not conceal from her mother the fact that she had been late getting home from school. It wasn't that kind of relationship.

And Josie would surely be upset. She didn't like for Ellie to stay in town after school was over. There were far too many dangers for young people to be left so much on their own these days, especially with all the drugs being peddled around the school yards and the other bad things so many of the kids seemed to be getting into lately. It was bad enough for anybody's children—it was unthinkable for her Ellie. *Her* girl was going to amount to something, praise the Lord, Josie knew. Sixteen, sweet, innocent and clean as fresh-boiled sheets, she was going to *be* somebody. Straight A's, an academic scholarship to college and money in the bank drawing interest all these many years. Elmarie Fletcher would be a credit to her race and to the family name. Josie felt sure Ellie was going to help make the world a better place in which to live instead of trying to tear it all down like her brother Otha.

Ellie resettled the books in her arms and shifted her weight onto her good leg. Except for the half-moon stains under her arms, she looked just as clean and fresh as she had when she stepped out of the house that morning.

She heard a car, and recognized the sound of the engine as it came up the side street behind her now. She had noticed the white man looking at her when the car had passed in front of her on Main Street.

She moved quickly away from the curb and up on the sidewalk as far as she could without stepping on the lawn in front of Miss Maddie Yates's white frame house. She knew that if she so much as bruised a leaf in the old lady's yard she would be reported to the principal and possibly even to Sheriff Biggs. Even now she could see the old lady hovering alertly behind the curtain at the front window. Any other time Ellie would have smiled and waved hello. But now she tensed as the car slowed to a stop near the intersection.

She kept her back turned, listening to the ragged idle of the engine. She didn't have to look at the man to know what he was up to. She had seen the look he gave her as he went past the first time. She had been seeing that look from white men ever since she was a little girl. No one had ever told her what it meant; no one had to.

"Hey there, sugar-chile. You know what time it is?"

She froze.

"You tell me what time it is I'll give you somethin' real nice."

She clamped down on her teeth so hard her jaws began to ache. *Please don't.*

"You like candy? I got a piece of candy here goes just right with a liddle dish of chocklate like you."

Ellie clenched her eyes in an effort to hold back the tears. She wasn't really afraid the man would actually harm her. His kind seldom made a move unless encouraged. But what made it so bad for her and most of her friends was the fact that a few girls would actually go along with what the man wanted. Annie Lee Simms, for example, was always bragging that she had been with more white men than you could shake a stick at—for the right price, of course.

The man pressed down lightly on the accelerator, but not enough to move the car.

"C'mon, honey-chile. It won't hurt you none, I promise. A tallywacker's all the same no matter what color it is."

It wasn't fear that moved her to tears now, it was the shame and humiliation, and the awful sense of hopelessness, of being treated like an animal. A nigger. And a cripple in the bargain. Nothing on earth would ever change all of that. Not money, not education, not even religion.

Tears began to fall out of the corners of her eyes and she had to bite her lip to hold back the sobs.

"Lissun here, you liddle black shitass. How much you think that ol' smelly nigger cunt of yores is worth ennyhow? I got me a good mind to come on over there—"

Ellie's heart almost leaped into her throat when she heard the familiar sound of Marvin's battered old pickup truck as it swung over to the curb on Main Street.

The white man's car shot out across the intersection and Ellie jumped into Marvin's truck as quickly as she could manage. She dropped her books and promptly burst into a flood of scalding tears.

# Chapter Thirteen

"A little help from the fellas, if you please."

John began to stack the dinner plates while Davey proceeded to decorate the carpet with loops and swirls of soggy spaghetti.

"John, see what he's doing!"

"Hey, Davey, boy. Easy, man. Easy."

"Here ya go, Mom," the boy said dutifully, handing his mother a salad plate upside down.

Sal gave John a dark look and tossed her long black hair over her shoulder. "It isn't funny, John."

"Then why are you laughing?" he demanded.

"Don't laugh, Momma," Davey scolded her, reaching for a basket of garlic bread and overturning the glass in which she was saving her last swallow of wine.

John vacuumed under the table and while Sal loaded the dishwasher, he got Davey settled in the bathtub with his plastic armada and a bosun's whistle.

Davey was still going strong while John was beginning to wear down. After his talk with Cecil Witcomb, John had played two sets of tennis on the campus courts with one of his fellow professors, and then had gone down to the pond with Davey for an hour's fishing before supper.

It had been a fine evening for fishing. Davey caught two good-sized perch for the skillet and chortled to beat the band. John watched the barefooted boy prancing about with his catch, the sultry wind lifting his powder-soft hair, and in that moment realized in a flash why he was such a happy man.

John walked out to the kitchen to finish his own glass of wine.

"Hey."

Sal gave him a sheepish look and licked her lips as he picked up his empty glass. He leaned over and kissed her on the mouth.

"It's better this way anyhow," he said, and licked his lips, too.

She put the glass in the dishwasher, then turned and put her arms around his neck. She kissed him deeply and said, "Nothing's too good for Mein Leader. Today the chairmanship, tomorrow the vorld."

"I'm telling you, Sal, you could have knocked me over with the proverbial feather."

"I'm so proud of you."

"Well, I haven't accepted yet."

"Even so, you must be very pleased that you're wanted."

"I don't know. There's something peculiar about the whole thing. Cecil didn't tell me everything."

"What do you mean, peculiar?" She punched the appropriate buttons and the dishwasher took off.

"I don't know, honey. I just don't know."

"I know one thing—Homer will be pleased."

John smiled. "If I accept, he'll interpret it as evidence of some tiny vestige of ambition that has refused to die in spite of all my conscious efforts."

"He's coming to dinner tomorrow, remember."

John began cutting the orange slices while Sal heated the brandy for the *café brûlot*.

"Oh Lord. I hope he's not gonna start in again on all that political crap."

"Do you think he's been saying anything? I mean, is that maybe how the trustees got hold of those rumors?"

"I don't know," John sighed. "I just wish the rascal would find something to do with all his time and money."

"Why won't he go to work in one of his mills? Or the bank? Or take over the *Oracle*, he loves literature so much."

"Honey, I wouldn't exactly call the Adelphi *Oracle* literature."

Sal laughed too. "A man with all his money and independence, and so much intelligence and talent. Why won't he just take hold of his life? He ought to do something, *anything,* just to get out of that mausoleum and away from that horrendous old woman. I saw him in town this morning, by the way. Why won't he just take hold, John?"

"Who knows," he shrugged.

"If you don't, nobody does. You're his best friend."

"Yeah, I know. But there's still that line, Sal. He holds back a lot. Something fundamental, I'm sure. Nobody has ever got really next to Homer. Even as a kid, there was always that line."

"Do they really live in that old mansion up there together without speaking?"

"Almost twenty years now," he nodded.

"Do you know her? I mean, to talk to?"

"I used to, when we were kids. But she cut me off too when the big break came."

"And all because he won't write poetry?"

"He *does* write poetry. It's just not good enough to publish. What she *really* wants—wanted—it's too late now—was for Homer to write a small quantity of deathless classical poetry, die young of some 'poetic' incurable disease and leave her a lifetime to perpetuate his work and his memory."

Sal actually appeared to shudder. "Lord. The Southern mother—"

"Now don't you start in on pore ol' Ida Belle."

"No. Let's don't get started on *her*." She began to laugh, dryly, but good-naturedly. There really wasn't a malicious bone in Sal's body. "You have no idea what she was doing when I dropped the kids by the house this morning."

"I thought we weren't going to start on the Dowager."

"Yeah, you're right," she agreed. "Trying to figure Homer Stokes out is task enough for one night."

"Don't *try* to figure him out," said John. "Nor his mother and Ida Belle, nor any of the others. Nobody and nothing about this manic land of corn pone, grits and redeye gravy makes the least *bit* of sense. Never has and never will. So just don't mess with it."

She stared at him for a moment and finally said, "Then what in the world are *we* doing here?"

He stared back at her, then shrugged his bony shoulders. "It's home, Sal."

There was nothing else to say to that, so they finished getting the after-dinner coffee ready in silence. When John turned around to look at her, she was standing with a spoon in her hand, her body resting against the sink, thoughtfully examining the middle distance between them.

"Maybe...maybe Homer just needs a good woman," she suggested, almost as if she were thinking aloud.

"And maybe that's the trouble—there just aren't enough of those to go around."

She threw a wet dishrag at him and it wrapped soggily over the end of his chin. "Hey!" he yelped, and started at her with the wet cloth.

"Don't you *dare*."

"Hey, Dad! What's goin' on out there?"

"Hush up," he laughed, as he tried to push the wet cloth over the top of Sal's halter. "You'll wake the baby."

"Now you've done it," said Sal, pushing at his hands. "Next thing you know Davey'll be in here looking for a romp."

"Hey, Momma!"

"Hold it *down*, Davey," John said as he kissed the boy's mother again.

It was seven o'clock. John went to the living room and turned on the national news. Sal came to the door while the credits were in progress.

"Why do you suppose Homer never married, John?"

He looked up, surprised, and said, "I thought you knew. I got you first."

She stared at him for a moment, then smiled. "Silly."

"Nothing like it," he said, and settled down to watch the news.

"Hey, Papa! Is that my ol' friend Walder Concrite?"

"Stop that yelling, Davey," John yelled above the nightly commentator's mellifluous voice.

Toward the end of the last segment Davey came into the room dripping wet with a towel slung over his shoulder. "Is that guy with the gun a good guy or a bad guy, Dad?"

"Davey—for Pete's sake—get over here."

John crossed the room to meet his son, stooped down and began to dry him off while the boy absorbed more than a few details concerning the latest atrocities in the Middle East.

"Why's that man got a gun, Papa?"

"He's a soldier, Davey. Remember, soldiers and policemen have to carry guns. Now hold still so I can dry your hair."

"Why, Papa?"

"Because you go to bed with a wet head it'll make your brains soggy."

"Aw, Papa. I mean why do sojurs and policemen gotta carry guns?"

John leaned back on his heels and looked at his son. He

noticed how quiet it had become out in the kitchen. They were both awaiting his answer.

"They have to carry guns," he said cautiously, "so they can protect good people from bad people. It would be better if they didn't have to but—"

"Is Uncle Homer a bad man?"

"Of course not."

"He has a gun an' he ain't a sojur or a policeman."

John hesitated, sat cross-legged on the floor and took a deep breath. "Son, Uncle Homer is a very rich man. He...well...he just feels a little safer, that's all, if he has his own gun for protection."

"Are we rich too, Papa? Like Uncle Homer?"

"No, son. I'm afraid not. There aren't many people as rich as Uncle Homer."

"If he didn't have so much money he wouldn't have to be afraid. Then he wouldn't need a gun."

Out of the mouths of babes, thought John. "He's coming to supper tomorrow night. Maybe you better talk to him about it."

"Yeah, okay. But I still don't see why he needs a gun."

"Davey, he just feels *safer* with his own gun."

The boy thought about it for a moment and then said, "I think mebbe we oughta have a gun too."

"No."

"We'd be a lot safer if we had a gun."

"We're safe enough," John said. "Now hold still and let me finish your hair."

With his head inside the towel, the boy said, "Dad? Why does Uncle Homer kill all those birds an' rabbits?"

Oh Lord, thought John. What do I say? I can't keep stalling him on this. What do I do, give him the Hemingway answer? That Homer kills animals to keep from killing himself? No, he couldn't say anything like that.

"Well, Davey, that's called hunting."

"You have your gran'pa's old shotgun but you don't shoot things like Uncle Homer does."

"That's true. But I shoot things occasionally when we need something to eat."

"Didja shoot us the busgetti for tonight?"

"No," he laughed. "I didn't have to shoot the spaghetti."

Walter Cronkite coughed, cleared his throat and said, "And that's the way it is...Good night for CBS News."

John got to his feet as Davey yelled, "G'night, Walder!"

and then raced his father down the hall to his bedroom. "I won! I won!" he shouted, hopping up on the bed and bouncing up and down as if he were on a trampoline. "Where's Momma?"

"She'll be here in a minute. Now you calm it down, Davey."

He leaned over and kissed the boy on the forehead. Davey purred, threw his arms around his dad's neck and kissed him wetly on the mouth.

"Night, son. Papa loves you."

"I love you too. Papa?"

Sal met John in the doorway and they touched hands.

"What is it, son?"

"I really think we oughta have a gun."

John could feel the tension in Sal's hand. "We have a shotgun, Davey. That's enough."

"Can you protect us with a shotgun?"

"I'll protect you, don't you worry about such things. Now you just get some sleep."

"Okay. But when I get big...I think I wanta have a *real* gun."

John and Sal looked at each other. It was not a happy exchange.

"When you get big," John said, "you'll have to make that decision for yourself. We hope you'll do the right thing."

"Can I have a story now, Momma?"

"Yes, honey. You can have a story now." Sal leaned up and kissed John softly on the neck. "I love you," she whispered. Then she sat down on the bed and said, "What do you want to hear tonight?"

John was halfway down the hall when Cathy woke up. He went to her room and found her tangled in the covers, squalling at the top of her lungs in a most unladylike fashion. He got her up and on his shoulder and began to sing her back to sleep.

She was still whimpering a few minutes later when Sal slipped into the room. "Want me to take over?"

He handed her the child and whispered, "The *enfant terrible?*"

"Subdued," she smiled and settled down in the rocker with the baby on her pillowy bosom.

John went on to the living room and selected a series of Beethoven piano concertos from their extensive record collection. He stacked them on the spindle, lowered the volume and went back to check on Davey.

"Cover me up, Papa."

"Jesus."

"O-woo-woo. Papa said a cuss word."

"I was *not* cussing. I was praying." He pulled the sheet up to Davey's and the stuffed tiger's eyes. "Now will you *please* go to sleep without any more trouble."

"I wanna kiss."

They hugged and kissed goodnight again. As usual, when John held his son in his arms he had the fleeting impression he was hugging himself. John had never known the experience of a father's embrace and it had haunted him all his life.

"Night, Papa-Daddy."

"Night, son."

He got as far as the door.

"Papa!"

"What?" John closed the door and waited, and began to grind his teeth.

"I love you."

# Chapter Fourteen

The old car rattled along the unlighted, unpaved road and slid to a halt at the next intersection. Eddie James leaned over the steering wheel and tried to read the road marker in the arc of his own headlights.

Then he suddenly caught his breath. Turning slowly into the intersection was a police cruiser.

He watched tensely as the one-man patrol edged along on the narrow road beside him. His hand began to inch carefully along the seat. He gripped the handle of the U. S. Army .45 and held his breath until his chest began to ache. If the cop stopped, he knew what he had to do. He wasn't about to have it all blow up in his face now. He pulled the gun into his lap, his mouth so dry he could scarcely swallow.

The cop looked at him in passing but didn't seem particularly interested. He watched the taillights flickering in his rearview mirror and then breathed a sigh of relief when the cruiser turned out of sight.

He was not familiar with Adelphi or Taliawiga County by experience, but he knew the area as well as the back of his own hand. He had studied the maps for weeks, imprinting on his mind every twist and turn that would take him to their doorstep.

It was a little more difficult at night, that was all. He would have to take his time, be careful, be patient just a little while longer. He could taste the excitement rising in his mouth.

He had known that taste before. He could remember it all as if it were only yesterday. Thinking about it, his vision started to spin and a terrible pain began to throb at his temple.

# Chapter Fifteen

"I *told* you never to call me at home, jackoff. I'll call you."

"I gotta talk to you, Sissie."

"So now that you're on the phone, talk."

"No, girl. I gotta see you. I gotta see ya an' we gotta talk."

"You needin' a fix, Elton? You all strung out again, man?"

"That ain't it," he groaned.

She laughed and said, "You wouldn't be needin' another batch of them there pictures, would you?"

"I wanta see *you*, Sissie. Right now. T'night, goddammit!"

"Hey now, you lissen here, asshole. Who you think you're ordering around?"

"Please, Sissie. *Please*. I need to see you."

"You don't order me around. Nobody orders me around. Specially no asshole like you gonna order me around." She paused, hitched up her skirt so that Sonny-Boy could get a good shot from his room across the hall and said curtly, "Besides, I ain't in the mood for none of that crap t'night."

"I gotta *see* ya, Sissie. I just gotta," Elton whimpered.

She was tempted to tell him to shove it, but the big clod sounded as if he was about to cry or something. She didn't want to see him, but she didn't want to provoke him either. You never could tell what the crazy bastard might do if he got a wild hair up his ass. Besides, she didn't want to screw up a good deal. Elton was an idiot but he had his uses. Anyway, he wouldn't be around long. Even though he was a pest, he never stayed around long. He was always getting into trouble of one kind or another and had to hit the road to keep out of the way of the cops.

"Sissie?" His voice was a whine now and she could hear him sniffing in her ear. "I *gotta* see you, Sissie. I mean it, girl. This time I've really done it. Boy oh boy oh boy."

She paused, lowered her voice and then said, "Okay. You might as well come on over."

"Oh no. Yore daddy said if he ever caught me—"

"Daddy ain't home, man. You wanta see me you c'mon over."

She hung up and turned around. Her mother was standing in the doorway with anxious, cowlike eyes.

"One of these days yore gonna hear somethin'," Sissie said, her voice dripping with sarcasm.

"Who was that?"

Sissie shrugged and began to scratch her crotch.

"It was that Pittman boy, wadden it? I know it was, Sissie. Now you just tell me if it wadden that Pittman boy again."

"An' what the hell if it was?" Sissie flared.

"You know yore father—"

"Daddy ain't home now, is he, Ma? An' what he don't know won't hurt him. Or me. Or you."

"He'll find out," her mother said, twisting a dish towel in

front of her aproned bosom. "You know he will. Yore daddy don't want the likes of Elton Pittman hanging around here, girl. An' you know he's a-gonna find out."

"You keep yore big ol' mouth shut he won't find out nothin'. An' you *better* keep shut, you hear me now?"

For a moment they just stared at each other. Then Sissie grinned crookedly and began to scratch at her crotch with an exaggerated motion of mock sensuality.

"You know what I mean, Ma?"

Her mother began to tremble in all her limbs, and she looked as if she might collapse. Sissie began to laugh, an ugly sound that seemed to wrap around her mother's heart like a bullwhip. She began to gasp as Sissie brushed past her and sashayed down the hall to her room.

Sissie wasn't wearing a bra and she took off her pants just in case. She really didn't feel like messing around, since earlier she had copped Gordon's joint and screwed with that black in the back room at the Ace of Spades. It had already been a busy day.

Sitting at her desk, she unlocked the center drawer, removed a green leather-bound diary and opened it to the current date. Then she picked up a ballpoint pen and reflected upon the day's events before beginning to write. She started laughing as she recalled Gordon's hysterical antics when she had purposely spit a few drops of semen on the fly of his pants.

But she had to hurry now. The way Elton was so worked up, it wouldn't take him long to get to her house. What the hell, she thought, all I have to do is pull that silly little peter of his and I can get anything I want out of him.

All she had to do was decide what she wanted this time.

# Chapter Sixteen

"I don't know what he has in mind, Sal. But it's something more than my taking Arthur Waley's place. I'm sure of that."

They were rocking in their chairs on the front porch, sipping the *café brûlot,* listening to the night music from the woods and trying to puzzle out Dean Witcomb's behavior that afternoon.

"I still don't see why you find it so perplexing, John. Why *shouldn't* they prefer you as chairman to old Priss-and-Boots Arthur Waley?"

They rocked in silence for a few moments, both given over to their own thoughts. John went back over his conversation with Dean Witcomb in an effort to read between the lines.

Arthur Waley couldn't handle the job any longer, the dean had explained. The job had grown too large for him. He couldn't function under administrative pressure and had no facility for delegating authority. Moreover, he no longer commanded the respect of the faculty members in his division. John had protested that the poor man was undermined by diverting personal pressures; everyone knew he was having money problems with a former wife while his girl friend was pressuring him to formalize their living arrangement.

But the dean was ready for that suggestion. "Arthur Waley *wants* to step down, despite the reduction in pay, and return full-time to the classroom."

But John didn't *want* to be an administrator, even if there was an increase in salary; he *liked* being in the classroom and wanted to stay there. And a twelve-month contract would curtail his summer travels. He didn't like working eight to five, and he hated to wear a tie every day. But Dean Witcomb parried all such objections with the dexterity of a fencing master.

Then John tried to raise his lack of credentials and status as an obstacle. But Witcomb said his J.D. was the equivalent of a Ph.D., and the board of trustees had already given the proposal its blessing. In September John was to be promoted to associate professor. He could still teach one class each semester and brief periods of administrative furlough would be extended to enable him to complete his book.

And then Cecil had said the oddest thing of all: "You mustn't spoil things, John. This isn't just something I've cooked up overnight, you know. President Reed won't be around forever. We must make plans, with vision, foresight, imagination. We must think of the future welfare of the university."

"So, what have you decided?" Sal asked, pouring them each another cup of coffee.

"I haven't decided anything," said John. "Not really. I promised Cecil that I'd at least think about it though. I said I'd talk it over with you and let him know in a couple of weeks."

"With me? What have I got to do with it?"

"You're my wife. Whatever I decide affects you too."

She smiled in the shadows. "It's your career that matters, darling. I can and will paint anywhere."

He laughed. "Whither thou goest, etc., etc., huh?"

"Something like that," she nodded.

He reached across the coffee table and stroked her arm gently. It was about what he had expected her to say. She had never yet attempted to dictate the direction their lives ought to follow. It wasn't her style. She influenced him in more subtle ways.

John thought suddenly of their first meeting. Atlanta. The U. S. Attorney's office. Thurlow Wheems. At least he hadn't heard from that old bastard anymore lately. John hadn't told Sal about the phone calls from Wheem's. He didn't like keeping things from her, but in this instance he thought it was justified. He smiled tightly in the darkness as he thought of his final assignment in the federal prosecutor's office.

He had always considered his job in the nature of a postgraduate course in the criminal law. And Sal had been the occasion for his best grade. By the time he met her she had established herself as a fine artist and a militant feminist and civil rights activist as well. She was on the barricades in support of the antiwar movement and just for good measure was a vocal opponent of the death penalty. Which did not bode well for a happy residence in Atlanta. Thurlow Wheems just happened to favor the complete extermination of the yellow race and was a devout adherent of the efficacy of the death penalty in the sovereign state of Georgia.

"I don't care how you do it," Wheems had told John one sultry summer morning, "but I want you to get an indictment against that Massingale broad, you hear me now. I want you to nail her sloppy ass to the wall, Johnny-boy, to the wall! Along with all the rest of them long-haired commie goons an' nigger lovers she hangs around with."

Well, John had nailed her all right, but it wasn't exactly what old Thurlow had in mind. Wheems almost threw a catfit when his favorite young assistant resigned his office a month later, severed all connections with the prosecutor's office and moved into Sal's studio-apartment on the wrong side of Peachtree Road.

"What in the world are you laughing at?"

"What—? Oh. I was just thinking."

"That's liable to get us in trouble."

"I hadn't thought of that."

She smiled. "You just haven't got around to it yet."

# Chapter Seventeen

He began firing without sound or warning. Just stepped out from behind the cover of the giant magnolia tree at the back side of the house and started shooting. His right arm was extended, his elbow and wrist tightly locked, his knees bent and his weight carefully balanced on his widespread feet. His stance was perfect and so was his aim.

The first bullet struck Sissie about an inch below her right eye. Blood and brain matter splattered the board wall behind the gyrating porch swing.

The recoil raised his arm, but he never unlocked his wrist or elbow as he zeroed in on the funny-looking man with the wilted little penis still protruding from his unzipped fly. As Elton bolted in a panic toward the end of the shadowed porch the second shot opened his head just below the left ear, spattering the hydrangea bushes with thick gouts of bloody material.

Then, almost as reflex action, Eddie James swung his aim back toward the kitchen door and fired again as Sonny-Boy burst onto the back porch in a pair of jockey shorts with a fire poker clutched in his hand. An expression of bewildered outrage split Sonny-Boy's face even as the slug tore open his smooth sweaty chest like the point of a knife splitting a ripe melon.

The acrid smell of gunpowder was like a burning joss stick on the summer breeze. Eddie James walked up on the porch now as calmly as a postman making a special delivery. He exhibited no surprise when he opened the screen door and was immediately attacked by a shrieking woman with a meat cleaver in her upraised hand.

He dropped quickly to one knee as the cleaver opened a bloody gash in his shoulder that he didn't even feel, then squeezed off a fourth round from the U. S. Army .45 that obliterated the woman's crotch. The sudden stillness alerted Eddie James to the danger. He looked up over Gladys Cubbage's body—sprawled on the kitchen table like an underdone pot roast—as an old man in a rumpled pair of khakis with faded chevrons on the sleeves swung into slow-motion action with a double-barreled shotgun.

The roar of the two guns was as one.

Beside him, the doorjamb shattered with Eddie's own flesh even as the old warrior's face disintegrated beyond recognition.

Eddie crawled across the cold linoleum floor and came to rest on the doorsill leading to the living room. On a color TV set in the corner of the room a bald-headed police detective was passing out suckers and making wry comments about the nature of his work.

Instinctively, Eddie rolled over and fired when he heard the sudden metallic sound in the adjoining hallway. The hard cold slug struck the naked child squarely in the chest. Her wet soapy body was propelled backward along the floor, coming to rest beside the open door to the bathroom. In the no-man's-land between Eddie James and the child a small plastic duck rocked back and forth, making a metallic clicking sound on the cold linoleum.

Eddie stared at the child in the dimly lighted hallway. The hairless gash between her smooth twisted legs matched the huge swollen wound in her tiny chest. His eyes began to fill, and he began to choke on his rising gorge.

He raised the gun once again and inserted the smoking muzzle into his mouth.

# PART TWO

# Chapter Eighteen

The insistent clamor of the phone savaged the heavy stillness of the dark sultry room. At first there was no corresponding movement in the bed, but as the phone continued to shriek its alarm the larger of the two covered mounds began to stir.

Oh shit, Charlie Tate thought, turning onto his side. Wouldn't you just know it would hit the fan on the weekend.

Oh please, she thought. Don't let it be *him* again. Not now. Not with Charles here.

"Hello, goddammit!"

"Cap'n Tate?"

"Naw, he's outa town again an' this here is Cassonova. Now who the hell is *this?*"

"Hemphill, sir. Lieutenant Burke, he said to call you? Said you'd prolly wanta handle this'un yourself."

Charlie Tate slid from under the sheet, groped for a cigarette on the nightstand and sat up with his bare feet on the carpet one on top of the other. His white pajamas gleamed, iridescent in the darkness. "Okay, Hemphill," he said. "So what have you got?"

"Homicide, Cap'n."

"Where's the body?" he asked matter-of-factly, as another businessman might inquire of an employee concerning a misplaced piece of furniture, a truck farmer a sack of baking potatoes.

"Bodies, sir. Six of 'em."

"What?"

"Nine, actually. Six dead on the spot. One died on the way

to the hospital, and they's two more possibles on the operating table right now."

"What the hell is going on, Hempstead!"

"Hemphill, sir."

"Fuckhead for all I care!" Tate bellowed, abandoning the search for his slippers and throwing the unlighted cigarette across the room.

"Well sir, it's, uh, like I'm trying to tell you, sir. These people were killed out near the county line—"

"That goddamn Biggs ain't in on this thing, is he?" demanded Tate, standing beside the bed.

"Nossir, the sheriff ain't got no jurisdiction on this one."

"Well, get on with it."

"This fambly got itself plumb wiped out an' two of our own boys got shot trying to take the sonofabitch what done it into custody."

Tate felt his heart sink. He sat down again on the side of the bed. "Are they—"

"Billy T. Musgrove's dead, Cap'n. Bubba Grooms is on the chopping block right now."

"What about the cocksucker that done it?"

"We got him, Cap'n. He's in the hospital too."

Tate stood up abruptly. "Well now, you hold onto him real good'n tight," he said and banged the phone down in its cradle.


When Holly Tate heard the car engine turn over she breathed a sigh of relief. She always felt relief when Charlie left the house. She heard the tires on the gravel driveway, a sound like crunching bone. Hers.

If only he would call now, she thought.

She turned onto her back and her heart began to pound. She raised her knees under the coolness of the sheet and pressed her hands down hard against the knotting pain in her abdomen. He *might* call. She looked at the illuminated face of the clock. It was only a little past midnight. She wondered if it was perhaps someone in the neighborhood. Or one of the men down at the Police Department.

*Charles would kill us.*

She raised her gown above her waist and caressed the insides of her thighs. If only she knew who he was, his name, anything about him. She looked at the telephone in the darkness, willing it to ring, and her fingers began to move.

*He'll kill us if he finds out.*

She closed her eyes and, moaning softly down in her throat, began to stroke the liquid folds of her sex.

# Chapter Nineteen

"Jesus H. Christ!"

"It's a real mess, Charlie."

"I can see that all right." Tate stood on the front porch, drawing a few last-minute drafts of fresh air into his lungs, scanning the activity inside the house through the front screened door. His chief-ranking assistant by virtue of years in service, Lieutenant Fred Burke, was all puffed up beside him like a pregnant blowfish.

"But you ain't seen the kid yet—" Burke gasped.

"There ain't no hurry. I bet you dollars to doughnuts she ain't goin' nowhere."

More people, official and otherwise, were arriving by the moment. So far, the patrolmen on security duty were doing a pretty good job, but Captain Tate decided he would need to get a couple more boys on the line in the next few minutes.

"Looks like a goddam Hollywood pre-meer out there," he grumbled, looking out across the yard.

By the time he had arrived the scene had come alive. A fleet of squad cars, their red dome bubbles flashing like strobe lights in a roadside honky-tonk, were nosed in out front at the curb like piglets fighting to get at their momma's titties. Four white sharklike ambulances were dancing in attendance, awaiting their remaining litter of one-way passengers. It seemed that every light in the neighborhood was blazing; Georgia Power would be thankful for murder and mayhem in the suburbs. Of course the newshounds had already scented blood. The cameras of at least two local TV stations were setting up as close as the police barriers would allow. When he arrived, Captain Tate brushed off a volley of questions—barely resisting an urge to shove the microphone that a reporter pushed into his face up the guy's inquiring asshole—and hurried on up to the house.

"Who you got working the crowd, Fred?"

"Huh? I mean, well, shoot—we already got the guy what done it, Charlie."

"You jackoff. What makes you think the guy you got was working solo?" Tate knew from long experience that more than one criminal since that Raskolnikov fellow Doc Winters told about in his class had returned to the scene of the crime to get an additional set of kicks. "Now you get somebody out there, Fred, an' you do it fast," he said.

Though he covered it well, the captain was in no real hurry to go inside. He could still remember the bodies of the two spinster sisters they had found in the rooming house over on Lee Street a month or so earlier. Nobody had missed them for more than a week. Never would have thought of them if it hadn't been for the smell. Both their heads beat flatter'n pancakes, raped front and back and then just left there to fester and swell in all that heat. *Jesus,* he thought, remembering what it was like to take that first step across their rancid threshold.

He waited now while Burke gave instructions to a young patrolman in the yard below the porch steps. The whole thing took less than a minute. Still, it was a minute of sanity. The insanity of it all was not only what he knew he would find when he stepped inside this house; the real insanity was the fact that he loved it so. Since childhood he had never wanted to be anything but a soldier and a cop. He had been both. And once he had decided he was more likely to become a police chief than a general, his course was set for life. Now his goal was just around the corner. Old Man Toland couldn't last much longer. And a case like this one, he thought, could be just the shove I need to take that last step up.

He looked through the screen door as a man in civilian clothes walked across the front room with a Polaroid camera in his hand. Or it might be the catastrophe that knocks me clear off the ladder, he thought, and wondered why he was so apprehensive.

"Well, le's get it over with," he said.

"I ain't goin' back in there," said Burke.

"What?"

At best Lieutenant Burke was a short, fat, ugly sod of a man with a head like the old German Kaiser's. Tonight he looked really bad.

"It's the kid, Charlie. That little fucking baby." The anguish in his voice had the cutting edge of a hacksaw. "She coulda been my own gran'chile."

"Stop it, Fred. She coulda been anybody's grandchild. That's got nothing to do with your job. You're a cop an' that's all there is to it."

"I ain't goin' back in there, Charlie. I can't help it, man. I ain't like you. You got ice water in your veins. Nothin' bothers you, but I ain't got the stomach for it. I ain't goin' back in there."

"Now you listen to me—"

But Lieutenant Burke wasn't listening to anyone. He walked over to the far end of the porch and vomited into the bushes.

There was nothing for it; Tate was driven inside alone. It looked to him like a sound stage in one of those murder and mayhem atrocities his ten-year-old was always watching on TV, in spite of the million and one times he had warned Holly to keep a closer rein on the boy's viewing habits. But expecting Holly to follow through on something like that—on anything, for that matter—was about like expecting all them A-rabs suddenly to shit peanut butter instead of oil.

A half-dozen officers were already at work, performing a series of more or less mandatory tasks. In the living room the police photographer was taking pictures with all the aplomb of a jaded cameraman shooting an orgy scene on a second-rate porno set. One door opened into a hallway, another into the garishly lighted kitchen. Tate's heart reacted even before his eyes had focused on the grisly scene. His heart seemed to have jammed in his chest for an instant, then it tripped over once or twice and his pulse began to race.

A woman's body hung spraddled on the edge of the kitchen table as if it was impaled on a meathook. Her dress below the waist was saturated with blood and bits of flesh and body spoor, and her left tit was absurdly pooched up above the top of her blouse. Tate suddenly remembered an old Vietnamese grandmother he had come across spread-eagled in the back end of a rice wagon on a farm just north of the village of Bien-hoa. A bayonet and a half-dozen phallic shafts had done a pretty thorough job on that one, too. He had to swallow hard and tighten down on his stomach muscles now to keep from joining Burke on the end of the porch.

"Watch where the hell yore steppin' there, bud. Oh—sorry, Cap'n."

"It's okay, Orin. I see it." He stepped around a puddle of blood roughly the shape of the state of Florida on a road map. "I want all the body locations marked and sketched too," he said.

"We done photographed 'em, Cap'n."

"I want 'em marked and sketched too, I said. And put down some silhouettes out back for the other three."

"I just figured that since we done got our man—"

"Jesus," he sighed. He looked into the bleached eyes of one of his detectives and said, "Doc Winter must've given you a terrific grade. You must've won the book! Just what the hell makes you think the guy we got did all this damage by hisself?"

He walked carefully around the room, taking it all in, muttering to himself. "What the hell use is it sending such meatheads to school? Maybe Chester Biggs is right. College is a waste of time for these bozos... A badge and a gun and a license to hunt is all the academic credentials needed by a cop... That, and the ability to do what they're told and just let somebody else do all the thinking for 'em."

He stepped back around the pool of blood and bellowed: "I want me some blood samples too, you hear me now."

A patrolman came up on the front porch and called to him through the screen. "Cap'n Tate, sir? They's a bunch of reporters out here—"

"Well now, you just go on back an' tell that bunch of reporters to go fuck a knothole," he said without even looking at the young uniformed policeman. "An' you better keep 'em the hell out of *here* or I'll put *your* scrawny butt behind the fence."

Fucking termites, he thought. Of course he would have to talk to them sooner or later, but he would do it when he was good and ready and not because they were worried about their fucking deadlines. He could see the headlines now. Even old Chief Toland would wake up and take notice come morning when all this garbage hit the fan. He just hoped to Christ the Old Man wouldn't suddenly try to play cop himself and fuck everything up three ways to Sunday for sure.

Tate moved around the room and tried to get some fresh

air as he passed an open window. It was futile: the dank odor of blood burned in his nostrils. He had seen some pretty hairy things in his life, in Nam and with the department. But this was about the worst he had ever come across.

It was the cold calculation behind the massacre that really got to him. This thing didn't just happen. It was too soon to know the answers for sure, but he was pretty certain that this was not the escalated violence of a bungled robbery attempt. He would have the house thoroughly searched, of course, but he didn't think for a moment that anything would turn up missing. Though it was still just a hunch, he was pretty damned sure that the guy who had done this knew exactly what he was doing and why. It was a preplanned assault if Tate had ever seen one. The whole family had to go. It was an incredible act of rage and hatred, a calculated act of vengeance.

"Fred, who the hell did all this anyway?" He leaned into the window and spoke through the screen. "Fred!"

The lieutenant straightened his shoulders and sucked deeply on a cigarette about the length of a fingernail. "Don't know his name, Cap'n. Hemphill just radioed in, said it's still touch and go. An' the same goes for our boy Bubba Grooms."

"You okay, Fred?"

"Yeah, sure."

"How the hell did it happen? Who shot the bastard?"

"Don't know whether Bubba got 'im or the other fella— Billy T. Musgrove. Bubba talked a little bit 'fore he passed out. Apparently the suspect was tryin' to kill hisself when our boys arrived but had run out of bullets. They come through the front door flyin' and he threw down his Army .45 and grabbed up that old man's shotgun over there an' let 'em both have a blast right in the face."

Captain Tate shook his head angrily. "A real textbook entry, hey." Then, with a sigh, Tate asked, "Fred, where the hell is Sammy Jack? I ain't seen him yet."

Burke came back inside now, his step cautious, his gaze fixed hard on nothing, his breathing still labored. "Why, I don't expect he's even been called, Charlie. I mean, since we had it all wrapped up...we...I thought—"

"You fuckin' jackoff! I want this here place dusted for prints, man. Now you get him the hell out here faster'n I can hit a lick at a rattlesnake."

Tate was still cursing under his breath as he moved over to where the old man lay sprawled under the TV set in his blood-spattered khakis. If only I could teach these dumb rednecks at least to follow the numbers, he thought. Never mind imagination, inspiration. Hell, just the basic fundamentals of handling a crime scene. Follow the numbers, my ass, he laughed to himself. Most of these clucks couldn't count past the fingers on both hands. And Burke was far from being the worst of the lot. Why, Burke had even taken a couple of courses out at the university under John Winter. And if a guy couldn't learn the ropes under Winter then a guy just couldn't learn the ropes. Tate shuddered to think what the good professor would say about the present fiasco. The next time he asks me to lecture to his class—

His line of thought broke off as he looked down at the old man on the floor. The faded patches on his sleeves where the chevrons had been indicated the old guy had been a tech sergeant in the old World War II Army. His uniform was faded and torn, but his body was in pretty good shape from the neck down. The face was gone.

Tate stepped aside as a crime scene technician came over and began to outline the corpse on the carpet with white adhesive tape. He noticed a framed family photograph on the TV set and picked it up. There was a total of six people in the picture. He made a quick body count and came up with six victims, discounting the suspect and the two policeman. An entire family wiped out in one senseless stroke of violence.

Then he looked again at the photograph of the Cubbage family and frowned. It wasn't a professional picture. Who had handled the camera?

Tate made his way carefully into the hallway just as the medical examiner was concluding his preliminaries. At least Burke or someone had thought clearly enough to send at once for old Doc Spooner. All the victims had been placed in their sleeping bags for transportation to the morgue. All except the child.

It was the part he least wanted to see. Burke was full of shit if he thought that something like this didn't affect him, too. Hell, I'm as human as the next guy, Tate thought, grinding down on his teeth. I just don't always show it. His lungs began to burn as he watched the activity at the end of the hall.

"What about witnesses?" he called suddenly over his shoulder. "Anybody see or hear any of this goin' on?"

"A woman over next door saw what happened out in the backyard," Burke said, maintaining his distance from Tate's position in the hall. "Called in an' give Hemphill her name, believe it or not. Naomi Hooks or somethin' like that. Her bedroom window opens onto the Cubbage backyard. Said she was undressing for bed when all the commotion started. At first she said she didden pay it no attention when she spotted some guy lurkin' around in the bushes. Says the Cubbage boy used to peek in her windows sometimes, you know, an' she just figgered it was prolly him again up to some of his old tricks. So she just paid it no particular mind. But then suddenly all hell just broke loose. We still got some people over there with her, but she's in purty bad shape right now."

"Yeah, well, I want you to canvass the neighborhood, an' I want every statement you can get on my desk before ten o'clock."

As he talked the captain watched the attendants in the back of the hallway lifting the small lifeless form and working it methodically into the canvas shroud. One of the men inadvertently kicked the toy duck and it started rocking back and forth with a metallic clatter on the floor. For some reason it made the hair on the back of Tate's neck rise.

"Where is the bastard?" he said abruptly, turning back to Lieutenant Burke. "The fucker who did all this."

"He's over at Central Hospital. Looks like he was hurt purty bad too."

"Well, I'll take care of things here. You get over to the hospital an' keep me posted on that motherfucker's condition." Tate sighed. "I might as well get it over with," he told Burke as they walked onto the porch. "Before you go, send those fuckin' termites over here for a statement and a few pictures. Oh, and tell Officer White I want her to drive me down to the station in a few minutes, for her to stand by."

The lieutenant nodded and started down the steps, but Tate stopped him again before he could get clear.

"Fred. You make damn sure those doctors take good care of that fucker who did this, you hear me now. I want him alive an' healthy, sose we can burn his ass to a crisp."

# Chapter Twenty

John heard the tires crunching on the gravel drive that wound in through the trees long before he could see her car. He had been up since six, working on his book in the den, and had only emerged for his morning coffee a few minutes earlier. Sal had dropped the baby off at John's mother's and then driven Davey into Adelphi to his day nursery. John knew she was in a hurry to get back to her garage studio and work for a couple of hours before having to reclaim Cathy, but he would be damned if he could figure out why Sal was coming down that driveway like a bat out of hell.

He leaned forward anxiously in the rocking chair and was able to catch a glimpse of the red Toyota slicing down through the trees. He put down his cup and walked over to the end of the porch.

Inside, the telephone began to ring. The car skidded to a halt and Sal came out fast. "John!" she called, waving the morning newspaper, which she had fetched from the mailbox at the end of the driveway. Without knowing why, the expression on her face caused his heart to sink.

"The phone," he said and hurried inside to answer it.

When he hung up he slumped down in the big leather chair in the den, the newspaper open across his lap.

"John—? Anything new?"

John had scanned the headlines and the lurid front-page photographs, with Sal hovering anxiously over his shoulder, while he talked to Dr. Gooch, the chairman of the local chapter of the Civil Liberties Union and a sociologist at the college.

"Just a minute," John said, and phoned one of his contacts in the Police Department while scanning the lead article for any trace of identifications.

"John, *tell* me," Sal said when he hung up again, her dark eyes wide and anxious.

"Well, it's bad, of course," he sighed. "I know—I know some of the victims. They haven't publicly released the names of the family yet. But the boy—name of Sonny-Boy Cubbage—was a student of mine."

"I think I've heard you mention his name."

"And his sister was in the Nursing School."

"Oh God," Sal said, and she looked sick.

"The cops—one is already dead, the other dying. They ran into—well—" Sal was beginning to bend forward at the waist, hugging herself with both arms. "I don't know the one in the hospital. The dead cop was in my class last year."

"Oh," she whimpered and her eyes began to fill with tears. But there was no way to keep it from her. He had to get it over with.

"He was married and had three young kids," he concluded.

Clamping her hand over her mouth as she began to gag, Sal turned and ran for the bathroom with John but a few steps behind.

# Chapter Twenty-one

Captain Tate was beginning to think the goddamned phone would never stop ringing. First the mayor and then Chief Toland and then half the members of the city council, four, no, five preachers counting the black evangelist, a dozen of the fucking media termites and finally a representative of the D.A.'s office. First thing he knowed old Rapid Robert Randolph hisself would be gettin' on the horn. What with an election coming up in November that damned publicity hound could be expected to make a Roman circus out of a thing like this if he thought there was any mileage in it for him. Thank the good Lord there weren't any blacks involved in the mess or he sure would have the rabble-rousing bastard on his neck.

And this thought gave him pause to breathe a sigh of thanks for the one stroke of luck that had saved them from a real fur-flying cat-skinning Sunday-come-to-meeting: the fact that the Cubbage home was located no more and no less than sixty-five yards *inside* the city limits. Such a close shave was it that one of his boys had actually gone back out there and flat walked it off. Sixty-five yards. Just a slight tip in the other direction and the whole damned thing would've landed in Taliawiga County and right smack in the lap of old Chester Biggs.

"Jesus," Tate thought aloud. "That fuckin' hog." And he swore as the phone began to ring again.

"Yeah, this is Tate. Yes. No. Okay. Hell no, you cain't do *that*, man!" He banged down the phone and sat for a moment grinding his teeth.

He didn't know why but there was something about this case that gave him the willies. He had felt it at the crime scene the night before and he still felt it. It *seemed* cut and dried, sure. And maybe that was what was bothering him. Or was he just tired from lack of sleep? The argument with Holly after dinner—what the hell was it about *this* time?—had caused him to drink too much beer. More than three beers at a sitting always kept him out of sorts for a couple days. Why do I drink at all? I hate the goddamned stuff so. And then he thought: a wife like Holly would drive any man to drink.

The captain pried his attention away from his wife and returned his thoughts to the issue at hand. What the hell was it about this case that had him so much on edge? Suddenly he was seething with resentment. He really shouldn't be handling the case anyway. He was an administrator now, he had the whole Detective Bureau to run. But what in hell could he do—assign the Cubbage case to the likes of Fred Burke?

He actually laughed as he thought of the old fathead sitting up there on the stand telling Rapid Robert about the gory details at the scene of the crime and heaving his bourbon-laced cakes all over the dapper prosecutor's wing-tipped shoes.

As Tate shifted his gaze to the mound of exhibits wedged in among the plastic coffee cups and the doughnut crumbs littering the top of his desk, he reflected that he would do a hell of a lot better to turn the case over to one of them split tails in the cute scout uniforms like Sharon White than to rely on Fred Burke, Lieutenant of Homicide.

Tate looked at the U. S. Army holster and frowned. A woman a few houses away from the Cubbage place had discovered her son playing soldier with the holster early that morning and had turned it over to one of the uniformed men on security duty at the crime scene. Surprisingly, the fellow had instantly radioed the department and less than an hour later the evidence was on Captain Charlie's desk. Such efficiency made him feel like a red-neck Kojak. But he would have felt just a whole lot better if his crack team could have determined from the kid exactly where he had found the holster.

The lab was still working over the .45 and the shotgun and all the empty shell casings. The lab, he snorted. A kid's chemistry set would offer more to work with. But then Chief Toland didn't hold much with such newfangled notions of criminal investigation. The old bastard didn't like cars either, being more partial to horse shit than engine oil.

The guns, Tate reflected, had already been tested for prints—with negative results. A lot of smears and partials, but nothing useful. And there were no wallet or identification papers on the suspect. They had a killer in their custody with no idea who in hell he was. Was he a pro, maybe? Tate didn't think so. Why the hell would anybody want to hit the whole Cubbage family? Maybe the fucker's clothes would reveal something useful. They were still in the lab too, being processed for laundry marks or anything that might help identify the bastard.

Captain Tate opened a manila folder on the desk and began thumbing through the stack of entries that had accumulated already. He noted curiously that the grip handle of the .45 was chipped. The matching piece had not as yet turned up in or around the Cubbage house. Of course the handle might have already been broken before the killer ever arrived at the Cubbage place. The chipped piece might be an undetected clue at still another crime scene and the connection to the guy they had in custody would probably never be made.

The file presented another puzzling factor. The ammo clip for the .45 was empty. Both police officers had been hit by shotgun fire. Six people had been killed with the automatic. But the clip had a capacity load of eight rounds. He leaned back in the swivel chair and began to rub at the grimy bristles on his chin. Had the fucker known exactly how many rounds he would need? Or were there a couple of earlier victims lying around somewhere with lead weights in their brains?

Tate's attention shifted to the meat cleaver on the side of the food-stained ink blotter, and he felt his flesh begin to crawl. Jesus, the female of the species. The lab had already taken samples of the dried blood on the blade edge. It belonged to the suspect all right and besides, there was a gash a half foot deep in the guy's left shoulder according to Fred Burke's first status report from the hospital.

Other items were interesting but Tate wasn't yet convinced of their relevance to the case. For instance, a stack of dirty magazines had been found in the Cubbage boy's room and a box of raunchy color photographs of the scratchy homemade variety were discovered in the girl's closet, along with nearly a pound of prime marijuana wrapped in a plastic Baggie and rolled up in a soiled brassiere. And there were a dozen or so MDA capsules in a mason jar in the girl's bureau, along with a thick leather-bound diary in the girl's handwriting.

He didn't really know what to make of it all. He began to frown again. Of course the Cubbage girl might have been dealing for the guy and attempted to cross him. But why kill the whole family? There were a lot better and safer ways to waste the girl than a head-on attack with the whole world watching. Tate sat there rubbing his chin with thick callused fingers, wondering if one man could really have done it all.

Then he caught sight of some of the tits and ass in the packet of photographs that had been taken from the girl's room. He leaned forward and began to thumb through the stack again. His mouth was suddenly dry and a thickness was rising in his throat. Who in hell would pose for something like that? he wondered. The camera must have got *inside* for some of those shots. And Jesus, just look at 'em—black, white an' vice the versa—goin' at each other like nobody's business with daisy chains up one side an' down the other.

He felt a queasy sickness in the pit of his stomach as he

stared at the little blond girl with the black dude's tool halfway down to her stomach. How could a girl do a thing like that? Catch a white girl and a nigger like that and they both ought to be strung up to the nearest tree. He had a pretty damned good idea that the girl in that picture was the dead girl Sissie Cubbage. He couldn't be sure, the way her face was all contorted—but if it was her the little bitch got just what the hell she deserved on the back porch of that house last night.

He flipped hurriedly through the crime scene photos until he came to the one of Sissie Cubbage sprawling halfway off the edge of the back porch with her head hanging in the hydrangea bushes. What was left of her head.

The swelling in his groin now was uncomfortable against his fly. There was a hot sensation in his chest, like the fluttering of a bird's wings.

Suddenly, he was angry, furious. He slammed the file shut and reached for the phone.

Clearing the phlegm out of his throat, he dialed his home number. He would want his supper early tonight, and if Holly gave him any shit about *anything* he would punch her eyes out. But the line was busy.

# Chapter Twenty-two

**She had just come into the kitchen to get started on the** dishes. The boys were already at the ball park preparing for a Little League game later in the day. As she started for the sink the telephone stopped her in mid-stride.

If only she might let it ring.

But suppose it was Charles.

Holly took a deep breath and reached for the phone. Suppose it's *him?*

"Hello," she said weakly.

"I know he ain't home now. It's in all the papers and on the tellyvision."

"You."

There was a low soft chuckle in her ear. "Hidy do, Miz Tate."

"I told you not to call me anymore."

The chuckle sounded in her ear again. "Where are you, honey? Still in bed?"

"No, I'm in the kitchen. And I don't have time—"

"Get up on the table."

"W-what?"

"Le's do it on the table this time."

"You must be crazy!" she snapped. "I want you to leave me alone."

"I know what you want, sweetie-pie."

"No," she whispered, leaning her forehead against the cold kitchen wall. *He'll kill us if he ever finds out.*

"Holly...? You still there, sugar?"

"Yes." Her eyes were shut tight; her face was flushed and mottled, the skin of her neck stippled with red splotches.

"Watcha got on?"

"None of your damned business. Pajamas."

"Shorties?"

"Yes."

"The blue ones again?"

"I'm going to hang up now."

"What color, Holly?"

"Oh, you. Yellow. I'm wearing the yellow ones. With white lace on the edges."

"Ah, the see-throughs."

"Yes."

"I bet the crotch is soaked by now."

"You shut your filthy mouth!"

"Get up on the table, Holly."

"I *said* no."

"Do it, cunt."

"The cord won't reach."

"On the counter then. Get up on the counter top."

"I am."

"What?"

85

"I *am* on the counter top. Now you tell me." Her voice sounded as if she had swallowed a cup of gravel.

"I shoulda knowed," he chuckled. "I bet it's dripping."

"Yes," she said fiercely, drawing her knees up under her breasts. "Now *tell* me what you'd like to do!"

# Chapter Twenty-three

**John Winter was straining hard as he came up the graveled drive.** The lead-tinged sky with a hint of impending rain was deceptive. It was a hot stifling morning and he was finding it more difficult with each stride to get his breath. But still he pushed himself relentlessly.

He ran at least two miles each day, often farther, and was in excellent condition. Of course he had never smoked and had used alcohol sparingly for the last six years or so, and he actually *enjoyed* the variety of health foods to which he had become accustomed since he met Sal.

But he was punishing himself today. He knew it and so did his body. There was about a quarter mile yet to go. He ought to stop and walk it but he drove his legs on with a fierce determination. His jogging path was a homemade obstacle course winding and twisting through the trees on his property, over hills, across gullies, spanning the winding branch in at least three places. Homer said he deserved hazardous duty pay every time he completed it.

Today the course had seemed uphill in all directions. At last he came around the corner of the split rail fence that marked the beginning of the house lot, momentum alone keeping him going. His legs were beginning to drag, there was a searing pain in his chest and his eyes stung with tears.

He labored up the steep grade in front of the house, lashing himself into an all-out sprint over the final fifty yards or so, and was surprised to find Sal waiting for him at the side door.

"Are you trying to kill yourself?" she said crossly.

"What are you doing out of bed?" he gasped, barely able to manage the words.

"I'm all right now. There's a phone call for you."

"No more phone calls," he said above the roaring in his ears.

"It's somebody from the *Constitution* in Atlanta. He says it's urgent."

"To him maybe, not me," said John, leaning forward with both hands on his thighs, sucking up the arid air. "What else can I tell them, Sal? Crime is hell. Violence is awful. It hurts people. Sometimes people hurt so much they die. We really oughta do something about—"

"Okay, John."

He leaned over against the wall with both arms extended, head down, eyes on the ground. "What good does it do to solicit comments about such a thing? 'Joe Blow, prominent citizen, said this morning...' To hell with it," he said bitterly. "Tell 'em to quote somebody else."

"Well...Homer called too. He wants you to call him as soon as you get in."

"You ought to be resting, Sal, not acting as a telephone receptionist."

"John, please stop it. I'm all right now. I'm going to pick up the kids in a few minutes anyway. You pull *yourself* together. I know you're upset but I want you to stop snapping at *me*."

He looked up at the sharpness of her tone, then drew a deep settling breath. "I'm sorry. You're absolutely right, so just don't pay me any attention. But you're sure you're okay? I can pick up the kids—"

"No, I'm fine. I'll get them." She paused. "The man's still on the line, John. You really don't want to take the call...?"

"I really don't," he said.

"I'll tell him you're unavailable."

"Yeah, tell him that. That's me, all right—Unavailable Winter." He was thinking of the short shrift he had given poor Sonny-Boy Cubbage when the kid had come to him—when was it, just yesterday morning—obviously troubled, clearly in need of help and counsel.

John turned away and started to walk down toward the branch. Sal's voice stopped him when he reached the gravel path.

"John—?"

He looked back at her.

"Are you sorry?" she asked, her voice as tight as a wound spring.

"Look, I said I was." He came back a couple of steps toward her. "I didn't mean to be crabby with you, I—"

"No, I mean are you sorry that you gave all this up?"

Now *that* was a surprise. He just stood there, staring at her in stunned silence.

"Do you miss it, John? Being involved in this sort of thing personally, I mean?"

He gave her a sour look and at last found his tongue. "Sure, I miss it. About like a fella miraculously cured of cancer misses that gnawing little rat at the center of his being."

He turned away and went down to the branch to rest.

# Chapter Twenty-four

**Charlie Tate washed his hands again at the sink in the** corner of his office. Then he tried to rinse the foul taste of coffee and anger and—what?—some kind of twisted desire out of his mouth. What the hell is wrong with me? he thought, looking in the mirror above the sink. Is it me, or is it this goddamned job?

He combed his smooth blond hair, straightened his tie and stood riveted for a moment by the hard blue eyes. Was I like this all along, or have I seen too much too often? His momma used to love to say that if a man got into bed with dogs he would sure Lord get up with fleas. But what could he do about it now? Did he really want to do anything about it?

He went back to his desk and slumped down in the chair. The veins in his temples were beginning to throb with a dull ache. He needed some fresh air; he needed sleep. What the hell was wrong with him thinking in such a mixed-up way? What was special about this Cubbage case to go and get him so worked up and all? He had to pull himself back on the beam ends and fast. He had to take hold. He was the captain.

Tate knew he had never been accused of being either stupid or brilliant. Nor had he ever been thought lazy. The truth was he did a good solid workmanlike job, and he worked his ass off. He was, in short, a good cop for his time and place.

He had been with the department going on fourteen years, minus eighteen months in Vietnam before coming home with his row of chest medals bought and paid for with hard time. He had made detective after only three years on the force, sergeant after six, lieutenant just a tad before a decade, and was then jumped prematurely to captain last year after only three years in grade as a lieutenant. Though his formal education was spotty, he was a solid performer and about as honest as any man in his position could possibly be. He had been promoted to captain of detectives in the wake of a police scandal that had seen a dozen officers indicted and six of them convicted in federal court on an assortment of corruption charges involving aspects of organized crime and racketeering. And the other six *should* have been convicted.

No breath of corruption had ever touched Charlie Tate. Not without reason was he known as Pat Boone on the street. At the moment, however, he was in no mood for singing.

He looked broodingly at the file and the mound of exhibits on the desk. The porno pictures were wrapped and pushed out of reach. His reverie was jarred when the door opened and his secretary came in with a new stack of entries for the file.

"If I told you oncet I told you a hunnerd times, Maggie—"

"To knock before I enter," she said pertly, placing the sheaf of papers on top of the file. "I forgot."

She turned and left, wiggling her ample bottom in the too-tight skirt. As she closed the door behind her, she knocked cutely on the other side.

"One of these days—" he said aloud, and let the thought fall of its own weight.

He sat up straight in his chair and picked up the stack of papers she had dropped on the file. It was time he started behaving like a good cop.

When he finished reading, Tate closed the file and began to rub at the bridge of his nose. The preliminary report was about what he had expected. So far there were few surprises. Probably there would be none. The itch at the back of his neck was nothing more than his customary paranoid rash. The case would be straightforward right down the line and that was all there was to it.

He quickly reviewed in his mind the state of the case at the moment. They had the car now. It had been parked only a short distance from the scene of the crime. There was a letter in the glove compartment addressed to someone by the name of Eddie. It was signed Sissie. The text of the letter was short and to the point.

*Dear Eddie:*

*I hope you are okay by now. It wouldn't do to tell you what we had in mind. You never would have agreed. It's best this way. Don't try to see me no more cause it ain't no use I can tell you that right now. You oughta go off to Calif. like you was always talking about only it ain't no use to try to get me to come along.*

*Bye,*

*Sissie*

Eddie *who?* wondered Tate. Too bad the recipient had thrown away the envelope. Was Eddie the guy they had in the hospital? Did the car belong to him? Since it bore an Illinois license plate the car was probably stolen. An inquiry regarding registration had been telexed to the Illinois Motor Vehicle Bureau.

So far there had been no luck in the print department. Nothing on the weapons, and the few identifiable "lifts" they had secured from the crime scene all belonged to members of the murdered family or to an investigating police officer.

One of the lab boys was at that moment working over the vehicle.

Tate took a sip of the cold bitter coffee from a Styrofoam cup on his desk and grimaced as though he were drinking poison. At least the goddamned phone had stopped ringing, he thought. But now the silence was beginning to make him nervous. He still hadn't entirely adjusted to the quiet of his own private office. The only noise in the room was the catarrhic rattle of the window air conditioner behind his desk. Sometimes the blamed thing got to clattering so loud he had to turn it off while talking on the phone.

Absently, he picked up the phone and dialed his home number again.

His inner sanctum wasn't much to look at either, he reflected, glancing around the room as he completed dialing. Drab gray walls peeling like a bad sunburn, a matching pair of filing cabinets, a scrofulous leather sofa taken as graft from a used furniture dealer by the former occupant of the office, who now resided in a sparsely furnished room in the Atlanta penitentiary, and a pair of straight chairs positioned in front of his big metal desk. Outside the only window in the room was a splendid view of a water tower with the advertising slogan of a local feed store emblazoned across its bulk.

He slammed the phone down as the number signaled busy, again. Theirs was a private line so it had to be Holly. Her folks were visiting relatives over in Arkansas and wouldn't be back thank goodness for at least another week, so he wondered who in hell she could be talking to for so long anyway. When he got home to supper he would give her hell for tying up the line all morning long.

There was a hasty knock on the door, and Burke blustered into the office with a look on his face that prompted Charlie to shift mental gears immediately.

"Okay, Fred," he said, beating the lieutenant to the punch, "I reckon you better give it to me nice 'n' easy now."

"You ain't gonna care to hear this even a little bit, Cap'n. It seems that there guy didden wipe out the whole Cubbage fambly after all."

"Oh?"

Burke plunged right on for a change. "The prints from the lab done come back, Charlie. Five of them people were Cubbages all right. But the sixth victim, that there slob with his shriveled little peter hanging outa his pants on the back porch—? His name's Elton Pittman."

"Pittman? You mean that whore's kid, the one who lives out there by the mill on the old Atlanta highway? The one Chester Biggs is supposed to be knocking it off with?"

"Tha's the one awright. The boy just got outa the Illinois state pen a few weeks ago. A drug bust of some kind or other. We ain't got all the details—"

"Then who the hell's missing, Fred? Which one of the Cubbage clan missed out on this here little shindig last night an' where the hell is he now?"

"The daddy's the one, name of L. G. Cubbage. People call him Shortstride. He's a salesman, been out on the road some five or six days now an' don't know a blessed thing about this here a-trocity involvin' his fambly. One of our boys is just now bringin' him in."

Tate leaned back in his chair, took another sip of the wretched coffee and shook himself like a wet dog. He searched methodically through a stack of photographs from the crime scene until he came up with the family portrait that had so intrigued him when he had first examined it last night in the living room of the Cubbage home.

He looked up at Fred Burke and said, "So he don't know nothin' about it, huh?"

# Chapter Twenty-five

**Josie Fletcher had never been more frightened of any-**thing in her entire life. Not even that time back when there was all that trouble about her man, a ruckus that she never did rightly come to understand, not even in all these years since he had been off an' gone. Had it not been for Colonel Stokes, God rest his soul—Mr. Homer's daddy—she had no idea in the world what her an' her young'uns would have done to make out on their own during such tryin' times. An' all these years they never let her down—checks ever' month in the mail just as regular as the rising sun. Mr. Homer, who was just as fine and saintly as his daddy, sent them after the colonel died. Why, the girl was *rich*. Plumb rich. She could go to any college in America, maybe even somewhere over there in Europe iffen she thought it would be best for her kind. Josie had never asked Colonel Stokes why he taken such good care of Ellie an' he ain't never said the first word to her about it 'cept to tell her the money would be a-comin' an' for her to put it in a bank account for Elmarie an' leave it there till the day she growed up an' needed it fo' college an' all.

Josie began to rock a little faster and to hug herself a little tighter as her thoughts played numbly back over all the hours she'd been sittin' an' waitin' an' prayin' that her baby girl would soon come a-walkin' up them front steps, limp an' all, an' throw herself safely into her old momma's waitin' arms.

"Where *is* she?" Josie groaned aloud and then began to croon: "Swing low, sweet chariot, comin' fo' to carry me home..."

Ellie had been seen standing on a street corner after school the day before, waiting for a ride from her boyfriend, Marvin Watts. Marvin had left work at the sawmill around three o'clock. Neither of them had been seen or heard from since.

Marvin's folks said they prolly done run off somewhere together an' got married. Josie Fletcher knew her daughter better than that.

"Swing low, sweet chariot..."

# Chapter Twenty-six

Just before noon, the door to Captain Tate's office burst open suddenly and a man shot angrily across the room like an arrow out of a bow, aimed directly at the Captain of Detectives.

"Now I wanta know just what the hell is goin' on here, mister."

Charlie looked up with a surprised blink. Had he blinked twice he might have missed the guy. Even all swollen up and red in the face with righteous indignation the way he was, he was no bigger'n a minute, Tate thought, and repressed an urge to laugh. But he would soon learn that L. G. Cubbage was no laughing matter.

Before he could say anything the guy was at his throat like an angry ferret.

"You gonna tell me who you are an' why that nigger brung me down here or am I gonna have to raise me some hell?"

Charlie held his temper and nodded toward one of the straight chairs. "Sit down, Mr. Cubbage, and let me explain—"

"I don't wanta sit down, man. I been on the road for days. I'm hot 'n' tard an' I come home an' finds me a big ol' nigger as black as you please standin' on my doorstep wearin' a badge 'n' gun an' the burrheaded bastard won't even let me in my own house!"

"Yes, well, I'm sorry as I can be about all that. I'm Captain Tate and I'll try to make this as painless—"

"An' then the sumbitch packs me off down here in a squad car just like I'm some sort of low-down criminal, embarrassin' me like that right out in front of all my neightbors an' all—"

"If you'll just calm down for a minute—"

"I wanta see the chief. I wanta see Old Man Toland an' I wanta see him now." Suddenly Cubbage scowled and cocked his oversized head to one side. "Say, has this got somethin' to do with that gal of mine, is she in some kind of trouble again?" His face was so red now it looked like a boil that needed lancing. "Are you gonna tell me or am I gonna have to go to my friend the mayor?"

Tate sighed, reached into the file and drew out one of the photographs of the crime scene. "I'm going to tell you, Mr. Cubbage. But I really do think you oughta sit the hell down."

But the little bantam rooster was still ranting and raving. "I don't have to take this here kind of treatment, you know. Not from you or that shoeshine boy in the bus driver's uniform. I pay your salary, you know—"

"You don't pay me much," Tate said, but the man wasn't listening.

"—while all you guys do is sit around on your duffs while niggers an' criminals run around takin' over the whole country—"

Captain Tate slammed his fist down on the desk and stood up.

"Sit down, Cubbage, before I knock you down."

# Chapter Twenty-seven

"Nobody knows the trouble I've seen..."

Josie Fletcher had not moved out of the rocking chair beside the front window for hours. She wanted to be right there the moment that Elmarie came limping down the dirt road and up the front steps onto the porch. She was coming soon. She had to come. Soon.

"...Nobody knows but Jesus."

# Chapter Twenty-eight

**Captain Tate almost missed him in the blink of an eye.** One moment the little runt was sitting out on the edge of his chair, his beady little eyes dilated and hard bright, and the next he was on his knees in front of the desk.

"Hey now—" Tate began and then watched as Cubbage's tumid head bounced off the edge of the metal desk. The photograph fluttered into the air as Cubbage slipped to the floor and rolled over with a great whooshing sound like that of a dying swan on the bank of a millpond. He lay there spread-eagled with his eyes rolled back in his head and his mouth wide open.

Charlie sighed, leaned around the edge of the desk and retrieved the gruesome color photograph that had finally stopped the man's mouth, and put it with the other crime scene photos on the desk. Then Tate buzzed his secretary and summoned a couple of detectives to lend a hand.

When they entered the room he said, "See what you can do to help the little fucker," and then shouted through the open door for Maggie to bring him another cup of coffee and a handful of aspirin.

# Chapter Twenty-nine

**Normally, Lamar Stick did not go home for his noon meal.** But as he was leaving for work that morning Slideen had run out to the truck in one of her flimsy nighties to remind him that she had the afternoon off from the mill. "I reckon I'll just come on back home 'n' have me a few beers 'n' some pizza pie," she had said all husky-throated, "an' just lay around the trailer all day."

Lamar had carried a thickness in his chest so troublesome he had been unable to concentrate on his work all morning. On his last job at old Nellie Bascomb's house he had become so distracted that he managed to kick three of his best goldurned wrenches into the well while working on her waterlogged pump. And of course he was so angered by his own carelessness that he had to take it out on somebody, so naturally he had turned on his weak-minded helper and cussed ol' Watermelon up one side and down the other. Then he left the sullen ol' darky to retrieve the wrenches and said he was just goin' on home to his dinner.

Now he turned his battered truck onto the dirt road that bounded John Winter's property and rattled along just ahead of the billowing trail of red dust. He had a good two and a half miles to go to his little patch of scrub property down back of the old Horse Lot Branch that crossed the Winter acres over on the back side.

As he passed the Winter driveway he hocked up a big old slimy goober and let it fly out the window to smack upside the Winter mailbox.

The laughter that rattled around up in the top of his head

sounded like a handful of nickels rolling about in an empty bucket. His nose began to run and he sniffed it back up, wiping at it a couple of times with the back of his bony hand. He had no sleeve to use, since he was wearing no shirt, not even a T-shirt under his cotton overalls.

People often remarked how aptly named Lamar Stick was. He was as skinny as a rake handle and could be twice as mean when stepped on. Of course he wasn't considered right bright by most folks, and no one would trust him for a minute. He was tall and about as common-looking as a soybean, with ears that stood out on the side of his head. His hair looked like limp seaweed and the first three fingers of his left hand were missing beyond the big knuckle. All things considered, he was not untypical of the lowest-class white man of Taliawiga County.

The Sticks had lived for only the past six months or so on a half acre of land that Lamar had managed to buy with the proceeds of a whiplash suit down in Forsyth. He had put two hundred dollars on the purchase price of the land and the rest of his settlement award against the cost of a new secondhand trailer.

Not that the money went half as far as people seemed to think, he thought to himself as he cut the steering wheel sharply, attempting to hit the old hound dog that had run suddenly out of the woods yapping at his truck wheels. Not when a fella had a family of seven mouths to feed, including an infant still at her momma's tit and a drooling old fool of a mother-in-law with pinecones in her head.

Stick detested the Winter family with a blinding passion. He began to curse his neighbors under his breath as he took one final shot at the dog and almost ran the truck into the ditch on the side of the road.

"Goddurned sumbitch!" he gasped, fighting the wheel with both hands flying. "Rotten bastards." His eyes were on the thick stand of Winter trees now, the way a starving man might leer at a seven-course meal a few feet out of his reach.

It just wasn't fair, he told himself, moving the truck into the middle of the rutted dirt road. A man with family obligations like his needed more room than a puny half acre could provide. With more land he could have a proper garden, he could have a pigsty, a milk cow and plenty of space for his chicken coops. Then he could sell his surplus crops and milk to the farmer's market in Macon or maybe up in Atlanta and with his profits he could buy some more land and become a respectable farmer with a fine house and some money in the bank. Why, he might even buy hisself some of them shares of stock in one of them big ol' Northern companies up in New Yawk or De-troit. Shore! That's what he'd do, buy hisself some company stock.

The sense of pride in ownership and wealth that had lit his gaunt features just as suddenly went slack now upon the realization that such a dream would never come true, and he had the Winter family more than anyone else to blame for it. They refused to sell him even so much as an acre, despite the fact they hardly did a gol-durned thing with all that fine land. He had tried to make a deal with the old lady, but she wouldn't hardly give him the time of day. It made the hair stand on the back of his neck when he thought of how the moth-eaten old bitch had practically threatened to have him arrested if he ever came pestering her again up to her front door.

Lamar bounced on the seat and laughed conspiratorially. As iffen Chester Biggs would let anything like that happen to his good ol' buddy. Nosiree, ol' Chester had taken good care of Lamar Stick the last year or so. Ever since I done that little job for him involvin' that there uppity nigger preacher that come down here a-tryin' to stir up trouble in our community.

The sound of Lamar's laughter turned ugly. Flecks of spittle stuck in the whiskers on his pointed chin. That's one ol' burrhead won't be causin' folks in Taliawiga County no more trouble, he thought. He won't be causin' nobody no trouble *no*wheres from now on. His red muddy eyes narrowed into slits. He thought again of the smelly-assed Winter witch. A few old rags, some kerosene and a match would take care of her one of these here hot summer nights.

And that fancy son wadden a whole lot better than the old woman, he reflected, for all his soft ways and smart talk. There was still the look of one of them there aristocrats behind his eyeballs that said he would just as soon sic the dogs on you as look at you. What it all come down to was that Lamar Stick and his kind wadden good enough to do business with such grand folks as the Winters.

He knew one damn thing though. He sure as shootin' wouldn't mind doin' a little piece of business with that wife of John's. Even his Slideen didn't have nothin' to compare with that squaw-looking Winter woman in the tit department. He remembered one day he was in the Winter woods, checking on some of his rabbit snares. She was working in the yard in a pair of shorts and a halter no bigger'n it had to be. Thinking she was alone, she had stepped up on the back steps, rinsed the dirt off her feet with a hose and then pulled off her sweaty clothes before going inside. Lamar had scrunched down on the ground behind a tree stump and flogged himself silly.

Now the itch behind his fly had him twisting on the seat, and he hocked up another goober and spat out the window again as he turned the truck into his rutted driveway. A great glob of wet phlegm splattered up against the Sears, Roebuck HOME SWEET HOME plaque mounted on a fence post. "Aw, Godamighty," he whined, watching as the spittle began to drip down over the golden letters.

But as soon as he saw Slideen's cowlike face appear in the bedroom window he forgot all his miseries, suddenly remembering why he had come home for dinner in the first place. He even forgot about Sally Winter's big ol' tits.

He entered the trailer without a sideways glance at the lump of a woman watching a TV soap opera in the front room. He didn't have to worry none about her; she probably hadn't even noticed him. In any case, she couldn't remember anything more than ten or fifteen minutes. She prolly didn't even know Slideen was to home, he thought, grabbing a can of beer as he passed the kitchen. He paused to look in the first bedroom where the baby was sleeping in her crib, and then stopped in the bathroom. He had difficulty pissing with his half-swollen dick and didn't bother stuffing it back inside his overalls.

At the far end of the trailer he slid back the door to the girl's bedroom and stepped inside.

"Where's yore ma, gal?"

"At th' mill, where you reckon?"

"An' the others?"

"Be home from school around four like always." She was smiling at him out of her broad freckled face like an alley cat in heat. "You got plenty of time."

He felt a flushing sensation in his loins. His dick was about a foot long and throbbing now and felt as thick as the beer can dripping moisture in his other hand. Slideen had not missed the look on his face or the weapon he was holding in his hand. She slid the sheet down over her naked body. Then she moved into one of those poses like the models used in those girlie magazines she hid for him under her mattress.

100

She began to stroke between her legs with her fat stubby fingers, thinking about the new pair of shoes she wanted, or maybe a fancy blouse to go with the new skirt he had bought her last week; and she needed some perfume.

Lamar watched with hot bulging eyes and little wheezing noises in his throat as she worked at the hair-covered little hole until it began to look about like one of his fresh-dug wells slashed out of the raw red Georgia clay. He tilted the beer can to his mouth and emptied half of its contents in one long noisy gulp.

Slideen was getting bored with the delay. She removed the two fingers of her right hand and looking her old man straight in the eye, she stuck them in her mouth and began to suck.

Lamar reacted, as she knew he would, like a maddened bull. His face exploded like a punched boil. He threw the beer can at his daughter, bouncing it off her shoulder, raising an angry whelp on her freckled skin. She was still laughing and sucking on her fingers as he began frantically to tear at the snaps on his overalls.

"Whore," he was shouting. "Goddam dirty little whore," as he went over the foot of the bed after the object of his lust: the flesh of his own loins, the blood of her mother's womb.

# Chapter Thirty

Shortly after one, John Winter pulled his white VW Rabbit into the red brick driveway curving between the trees and lawns in front of the Stokes mansion. It was an immense white-fronted house set back perhaps a hundred yards off the old two-laned oak-shrouded Atlanta wagon road. The only wagons that used the wonderful old residential street were of the Cadillac, Oldsmobile and Pontiac variety. Much of Adelphi's old landed and commercial gentry lived along this half-mile strip popularly—or derisively—called Millionaires' Road by the locals of Taliawiga County.

The house was a combination of three main sections. The first and tallest was the original construction, built by Homer's great-grandfather in the 1850s. The two smaller sections on either side, miniature replicas of the center portion, had not been added until Homer's grandfather came into possession of the house in the 1870s. Of course Homer's daddy—known in the family as Big Homer because he was *big*—had made any number of improvements and even structural changes over the years of his stewardship, but basically the old house was the same as it had been from its inception.

Except for the novelty of its dual entrances. Above the terrace there were wide mahogany double doors, which opened into a central foyer that was in its turn divided by a wrought-iron rail separating the left side of the house from the right. The railing was a late addition, having been installed somewhere around the summer of 1962. Homer's mother lived in the left wing of the house, Homer in the right wing. As far as any outsider was aware, the two had not spoken a word to each other since the summer of 1961.

Around the side of the great house John spotted a barefoot black boy in jeans washing Homer's Concorde-like Olds, laboring in the hot sun under the supervisory watchfulness of a small plaster black boy planted in the grass nearby with a fishing pole over his shoulder. His Rabbit would easily fit in the trunk of Homer's massive chariot, John thought, slamming the tin-sheeted door of his car and starting up the brick pathway leading around to the front of the house.

He had scarcely reached the terrace steps below the soaring columns that rose to a railed gallery high above, when the solid oak double doors opened and a black manservant in a gleaming white jacket greeted him with warmth and evident sincerity.

"I saw you coming, Mr. John. It's mighty good to see you again, suh. It's been too long since we had your company in this ol' house. An' how is the missus an' the chil'ren?"

"Hello, Dut. It's good to see you. My wife and kids are just fine, thanks."

"And Miz Ida Belle? Your momma been having any more trouble with that cantankerous knee of hers?"

"Momma is gonna have *trouble* all the days of her life, Dut. You know that."

The old man chuckled and said, "You come on in, Mr. John. We're lettin' out all the cool air."

As the tall, portly, graying black man stepped aside to permit his passage, John lightly placed his hand on the servant's shoulder and pressed it warmly. "It *has* been a long time," he sighed, looking around quickly at the fine old house that he had known almost as well as his own in his youth. "Doesn't seem to have changed much."

"Nosuh. Some things don't never change."

John looked at the old man for a moment, then said, "Most things *do* change, Dut."

The black man cocked his grizzled old head. "Depends on the perspective, don't it, suh?" and closed the doors.

Inside, the house was shadowy and cool in spite of the absence of air conditioning. No one but a Stokes had ever resided under its roof in a position of ownership. For almost a hundred and thirty years, without exception, war or no wars, personal ecstasy or tragedy piled upon tragedy, the cool night air had been preserved by closing the shades at the first light of dawn. And for the last seventy some-odd years Dut had without fail overseen that household task. And *that* was tradition, thought John; *that* was loyalty.

"Junior is waiting on the gallery," Dut said, leading the way up the curving mahogany staircase on Homer's side of the iron railing.

Dut was the only person in the world who referred to Homer Stokes as Junior, to his face as well as to others. John had no idea what Homer thought of the custom, if he ever thought of it at all. A feeling of sadness weighed heavily on John as they climbed the broad carpeted stairs. There had been so much happiness in this house, so much music and laughter and just downright fun. The early morning departures for the hunting and fishing trips with Homer, his daddy, John and his grandpa, and of course the omnipresent Dut. And there was Miz Theolene—or Miss Leenie, as they all called her—waiting upon their return with fresh hot biscuits and jam, strong coffee and bourbon for the men, hot chocolate or milk for the boys. And there were parties and picnics, and when they were older, dances and after-the-ball-game wakes or celebrations. Whatever, there was always a spirit of excitement and anticipation at what the next day might bring.

And then, one day, suddenly, without rhyme or reason, it

was all over. It wasn't just the normal progression of events. John left in the fall for the university and Homer had been sent early in the summer to the Sorbonne in Paris; but it was over before that. By the time they both came home again Big Homer was dead, Papa Hightower was dying and Miss Leenie was a walking automaton, sullen, remote and—insofar as her only son was concerned—forever uncommunicative.

"How's Miss Leenie?" John asked at the top of the stairs.

Dut paused on the landing. "About the same, Mr. John. She's just about the same."

"I don't suppose..."

"Nosuh," said Dut, sadly. "She won't see nobody."

"I don't mean to pry, Dut..."

"You are just like one of the family, Mr. John. Nothin' you say or do could ever be considered as pryin'."

"Thanks, Dut. What I mean is..." He lowered his voice. "Is it true...all these years...?"

"Not a word, Mr. John. Not a single solitary word."

There was no mistaking the anguish in Dut's fine old eyes. He started to turn away but John stopped him with his hand on his sleeve.

"But *why,* Dut? Surely, whatever it was, after all these years..."

Dut looked at him for a long moment, heavy with thought; then he shook his head, slowly, but with finality. John knew better than to press him further. Somehow the old man's honor was involved.

"Well," John said, starting down the long corridor toward the gallery, "I might as well go find out why Homer sent for me in such a cloak-and-dagger fashion. At least I'll get a good lunch out of it."

Homer Stokes was waiting on the gallery, slouched down in a deep cushioned rattan chair, a pink-tinted aperitif held loosely in the bony fingers of one hand, his beloved meerschaum in the other. At John's approach he cradled the pipe in a black onyx ashtray and rose to shake hands.

"John. How good to see you. I'm so glad you could come."

They always shook hands. They had been friends all their lives and still shook hands each time they met, often after having just seen each other the day before.

"Okay, Homer. Out with it," John said without preamble. "What the hell's this all about?"

Homer smiled. "Dut, please bring our guest an aperitif—his usual, I expect."

"Vermouth cassis, Mr. John?"

"I reckon," he nodded. "Yes, that'll be fine, Dut," accepting the fact that he was being sandbagged by a pair of professionals.

"Take the settee, John. It's quite the most comfortable spot on the gallery."

"I'll have to take your word for it," said John, settling down into the soft comfortable cushions. "None of this stuff"—looking around the gallery—"was here when I..."

He stopped as Homer seemed almost to wince at his words. He let the observation hang there incomplete, but there was no way to cover it over now.

"Yes, it's been a long time," said Homer, resuming his seat and reaching for his pipe. "We don't have many guests nowadays..."

Homer, too, simply let his words hang.

"Almos' *none*," said Dut, mixing John's drink at a sideboard behind the luncheon table.

"Yes, well, thank you, Dut. When you have done with the drinks you may see to our lunch. I'm sure that John is famished by this time of day."

The old man brought their drinks over on a silver tray, the first for John, a "freshener," as he called it, for Homer. His gnarled old hands were steady, John noticed, his dark face as impassive as a wall.

Then he stepped back rigidly, the empty tray behind his back, and said, "If they's nothin' else, Junior, I'll just go on downstairs an' see to the food."

He didn't wait for an answer.

John smiled at Dut's exit. "So he's still got you by the tail after all these years."

"That old boy will see us *all* on the right path yet."

"I reckon that's about what he promised your daddy to do. And we both know Dut's never gone back on a promise in his whole life."

"Uhm, yes, well," Homer said, a trifle uncomfortable, and then raised his glass. "Cheers."

"Oh yeah, sure. It's one hell of a cheerful day we've got, ain't it. The Lord God's in His heaven and all's just right and dandy with the world."

"John," Homer sighed. "Let's at least have our lunch before we spoil everything."

"You *said* it was urgent, Homer."

"Believe me, my friend. It is just that."

"Then let's—"

"Have lunch first."

For just an instant John suspected, without knowing why, that perhaps someone else was coming to lunch. But when he looked at the small oblong table beside them, which was covered with a spotless white damask tablecloth, he saw it was set for two.

When Sal had seen Homer in front of the courthouse the previous day she had said he was wearing one of his impeccably tailored Savile Row suits imported from London. But you never could tell what kind of apparel you were liable to find Homer regaled in at any given moment. John recalled having unexpectedly met him outside a restaurant one night in the New Orleans French Quarter. Homer was wearing a black velvet suit, a black cashmere cape and a black *fin de siècle* hat with a broad floppy brim in which he looked more or less like an abandoned Abraham Lincoln in quasi-drag. They were with different sets of friends and had only greeted each other in passing—pausing long enough, of course, for the long-standing ritual of shaking hands.

Today his friend was cast in another role entirely. He presented an incongruous sight in this lavish Gone-with-the-Wind setting. The view from the gallery was spectacular. The breeze was soft and sultry, not as yet poisoned by the approaching furnace-like heat of midsummer. There was a delicate aroma of dogwood and sweet olive blossoms in the air. Homer had always been an outdoor man, an adventurer. Awkward in such sporting activities as golf and tennis, he was an avid hunter, angler, canoeist and long-distance walker. He usually wore a year-round tan and now, having only recently returned from a two-week fishing trip in the Bahamas, his skin was about the color of a highly buffed cordovan shoe. On the return trip, he had spent half a day in Miami's teeming Cuban *barrio* and had come home with half a dozen *guayabera* shirts, one of which he was wearing now, with starched khaki shorts and a pair of heavy leather sandals. His hands, John noticed again, were as big as feet, his feet huge. His arms, deeply tanned, were as lean and tightly muscled as those of a Taliawiga plowhand.

"All right, I know that look," said Homer with a rueful grin. "I give up. There's no way to put this off until we've had our lunch." He paused, shook his head and set his pipe on the table. "It's a dreadful business, of course. Simply dreadful. Sal said you were acquainted with one of the officers, I believe."

"The one who died, yes. And I knew the Cubbage boy, too."

"Students, I gather?"

"Yes," he nodded. "But apparently I didn't teach them very well, did I?"

"You're not a training officer, John."

There was no reply. For a few moments they sipped their drinks in silence. Somehow the incongruity of the moment was heightened by the splendid view from the shaded gallery. The front lawn was studded with graceful oaks, maples and a row of pink-blossomed dogwoods along the roadfront. To the right of the house—on Homer's side—stood a towering magnolia tree that would assuredly have to be cut down in a few years' time, due to its threatening size.

"I might as well tell you," Homer finally said, noting his friend's deepening gloom. "The other policeman is not yet out of the woods either. I talked with the hospital adminstrator a while ago. The lad has suffered major liver impairment and a severe spinal trauma. He's expected to live, barring unforeseen complications. But apparently he will be paralyzed from the waist down."

"Jesus, what a rotten break," said John. "What about the suspect?"

"Bad shape, still touch and go. No one knows who he is yet, or where he comes from, or what his motive was for such a monstrous act. Or if they do know, they aren't saying."

"Who's in charge of the investigation?"

"Charlie Tate is handling it himself."

John nodded. "It could be a hell of a lot worse."

"It certainly could. It might have been Chester Biggs."

"Jesus!"

"Do you realize just how close the Cubbage house is to the county line?"

"We must remember to be thankful for the happy aspects of murder and mayhem in Taliawiga County," John said sourly.

Homer nodded, paused, cleared his throat. "John, I must tell you. There's more to this thing than meets the eye."

"There usually is," John said. "But how does it concern me?"

"It may very well concern us all before it's over and done."

John put down his glass. "Are you going to tell me or not?"

Homer sighed and reached for his pipe. John could not resist the mental image of a harassed Prime Minister about to drop the ax on a long and faithful retainer. Though he had no idea what was coming, he had the distinct feeling that it would somehow involve himself in one of Homer's quixotic social crusades.

"I'm waiting," John prompted.

Homer gestured with both hands. "Let me put it this way, John. Adelphi is a typical Southern town, no different from a thousand others. But what one sees on the surface is one thing. What is lurking beneath the waterline is quite another."

"Homer—"

"Don't you see, man? We are facing bad weather ahead, and we'd best be running the storm warnings up."

"Have you brought me here for a bloody weather report?" It helped to break the tension and they both enjoyed a good chuckle.

"I'm just coming to the point."

"I wish you would move a little faster than this year's economic recovery."

But Homer didn't smile this time. "John, we've not had an incident quite like this in many years. One can't be entirely certain how our people will react."

"What do you mean?" John leaned back in his seat, stroking his moustache pensively. "Are you talking about mob violence or something?"

"Who can say? The temptation to act out the small-town Southern tradition might just be too strong to resist. This is an existential land, man. We've always wanted to be a little different down here in the South, and by God we *are* different."

"And proud of it," John said sourly.

"That's right. You take that church incident down in Plains just after Jimmy's election. A quaint bit of local color with which to entertain the public at large. And that nut who banged his car into the Klan rally a few weeks later."

"Not to mention the attempt to gun down that born-again porno fellow up near Atlanta," said John, taking up the litany.

"Exactly. And don't think for a moment that we don't have precisely the same sort of ingredients for violent mischief right here in Adelphi."

John shook his head doubtfully. "I don't know, Homer. Apparently the police have the killer. And without the race issue, or sex, I don't see—"

"Politics."

"What?"

"Politics... power... money."

"Homer, what the hell are you driving at?" John demanded.

His host looked at his watch, rather anxiously, thought John, who was completely mystified by now. What the hell was the man up to?

"I've talked with Judge Harbuck, John."

"You've been busy," he said, almost sarcastically.

"The judge is going to appoint Bobcat Tribble to represent the suspect.

"Oh boy."

"And Robert Randolph is already preparing to go before the grand jury to seek a first degree murder indictment."

John shrugged. "They don't call him Rapid Robert for nothing."

"He's also going to file for the congressional seat being vacated in the fall by old man Joyner."

John whistled sharply. "A three-ring circus in the making if ever there was one."

Homer looked at his watch again. For some reason John began to experience a sinking sensation in the pit of his stomach.

"Homer, what the hell are you up to?"

"We're going to stop it," he said, slapping the table with his open palm. "We're not going to permit a three-ring circus."

"I don't see what the hell we or anyone else can do about it."

"I'll tell you what we can do, John. A special prosecutor. It's the only answer." He consulted his watch a third time and stood up. Dut came onto the gallery with a telephone and plugged it into a wall jack. "I've already discussed it with the governor," Homer added, moving toward the phone. "He should be calling us just about... now."

"'Us,' my ass!" John exclaimed, leaping to his feet just as the phone began to ring.

# Chapter Thirty-one

**Ida Belle put in a lot of duty hours behind the lace** curtain picture window in her living room, a lot of sitting and rocking, a lot of watching and waiting. John had once joked that she spent so much time watching the comings and goings on the road in front of her house that she ought to start charging a toll for its use. Ida Belle didn't think it was funny. She didn't laugh. She couldn't even remember the last time she had had a real good laugh. She only felt like laughing when she was around Davey, which wasn't often—and she knew good and well what the reason for that was and just where the blame had to lie.

She watched their comings and goings at the window because it was the only way in the world she had of knowing what was going on, since they never *told* her anything. And she knew who was to blame for that, too. They never came to see her unless they wanted something. They only let her see her precious grandchildren at all because it was cheaper to use her than to pay a baby-sitter from out to the university.

At the sound of another vehicle on the road, she leaned forward in her antique rocking chair, anticipating the car's approach. She had a clear view in both directions across a gently sloping flower-studded lawn. A gravel driveway led in a straight line from the front door out to the road, bordered on both sides by a measured row of flowering dogwood trees that were the envy of Taliawiga County.

The house itself—small by country standards and by Ida Belle's—was a one-story antique brick affair, consisting of-two bedrooms and a bath, a narrow screened breezeway on the back side of the house and a combination kitchen-dining room and living room arrangement. The sleeping quarters were snug and fully carpeted, the living quarters paneled from floor to ceiling and lined with custom-built bookcases and kitchen cabinets. There was a rock fireplace against the back wall that eliminated the need for winter fuel. It was a cozy comfortable room, hated by its unwilling owner.

Ida Belle leaned back in her chair with disappointment and a touch of pique as old man Tuttle creaked by in front of the house in a vintage Chevrolet. She had hoped, of course, that it might be John coming back from town. He had no call to go off and leave those children down there in the woods at a time like this. Anything might happen with murderers roaming loose about the county every which way and him traipsing off on who knows what kind of a fool errand out at that old university. I *told* their mother to leave those babies up here with me, she thought.

*But no, she wouldn't do that. She won't do nothin' she thinks might please me. An' especially not where Davey is concerned.*

Ida Belle's body shook visibly as she experienced the conflicting emotions of love and hate that tore at her heart when she thought of her beloved grandson and his pernicious mother. She saw Davey as the only hope of redeeming her relationship with her own son; and she clearly perceived the child's mother as the primary obstacle to such promise. She despised the woman with such a passion it shook her like a virulent fever in her blood.

*She robbed me of my own boy an' now she's working to take away my precious Davey.*

Again the sound of a car out front drew her attention. She felt her heart leap and her pulse began to race. *Maybe it's John coming back. Maybe he'll stop. Maybe...* She leaned back in her chair with renewed disappointment as Ruby Stick turned her old rattletrap of a car onto Horse Creek Road. Ida Belle had seen that fool husband of Ruby's pass in his truck a while earlier. He seldom went home to lunch. And Ruby had left work early. What was going on down there in that Tobacco Road pigsty? she wondered. Lord knows, I have enough to worry about with all those killings in town.

Why in the world did I ever let them talk me into selling my nice house in town to move out here to this isolated little hut to have my throat cut open and to be raped by some smelly nigra, not that they would care even a whit. And to think my own son after all I've done and suffered for him could treat me in such a way.

Ida Belle knew who was to blame. Make no mistake about it: I know. The bitch. The jealous selfish grasping halfbreed—she's the one to bring such divisiveness into our once happy relationship. Oh Godamighty when I saw her get out of that car with the babe in her arms didn't I just *know* what she had gone and done to my boy. How *could* Buddy-Boy have been so stupid and weak-kneed as to let such a woman get her poisonous hooks into him in such a way? As God is my witness I've never seen a boy as good as my Buddy change so fast in such ways as what happened to him when he fell under the spell of that woman. To think that he would go and choose such a woman to be the mother of his children, *my* grandchildren, with the love of such a fine Christian girl like Rachel Pettigrew his for only the asking.

Ida Belle's eyes suddenly puddled, and she covered her heart with the palm of her hand as if it were an open wound. She had loved her son with the extravagant passion not unusual in one who has been disappointed by the adult love in her life. The care and attention she had lavished upon him had been obsessive in the extreme. And being the romantic soul that she was, seeing only what she wanted to see, indeed, what she could *bear* to see, she had no idea how much her darling son had resented her cloying behavior, nor the slightest idea how embarrassed he had been by her eccentricities in front of his peers.

No one could *ever* have convinced Ida Belle Winter that the primary inspiration to John's athletic prowess was not a natural love of sport at all. Rather, achievement in athletics was to her son's undeveloped mind the only means by which he might fashion an escape from his mother's oppressive coddling. It was a memorable day to mother and son alike when at last he went off to the state university on a football scholarship.

After his departure Ida Belle's grief was boundless. Her only consolation was the weekly letter from him; her only hope that he would see how much she missed him and return home to stay. He could attend college in Adelphi and their lives would be as they were meant to be. But with the exception of holidays, John had never come home again. Until...

*Oh God,* her anguish all but shrieked against the inside

of her skull, how could he have done this to me...it could not have been more cruelly aimed had he pierced a spear through my grieving heart. To think he'd had the gall to bring that woman home and set her down in Papa's own dear house and had they actually expected me to *condone* their sick behavior!

She began to rock back and forth, as a shroud of depression settled over her head like a wet woolen blanket.

It's *my* fault. All my own fault. No one else to blame, no, *I'm* the one allowed the Winter blood into the purity of the Hightower family line. Tainted, unwanted, Yankee blood. The look of shock and grief on dear Papa's face. And Momma's silent everlasting rebuke. *My* shame, *my* guilt, not John's.

She lowered her face into her hands as the sound of Moses's lawnmower began to splutter in the backyard. She neither saw nor heard John's car as it passed.

# Chapter Thirty-two

"It's possible, Fred. Ennything's *possible* where the female of the species is concerned."

"He's a mean liddle bastard, I can tell you that. I got some friends go to the same church. They say Cubbage is as mean as a snake."

"And what do they say about the woman?"

Fred Burke shook his big head and shrugged his beefy shoulders. "Well now, Gladys Sudash warn't no swinger. Ugly as homemade soap all her life. Old man Sudash kept her pretty close to home just in case some fast-talkin' dude got to seein' dollar signs on her chest 'stead them there liddle bitty titties."

"So naturally the first chance she got—"

Burke nodded. "So old L. G. wormed his way into the honey pot with both eyes on the old man's money pot."

"An' ever'body lived happily ever after," said Charlie. "In a pig's ass."

"The old man kept the lid on his bank account a hell of a lot tighter than he managed to guard liddle Happy Bottom's underpanties."

"What's your point, Fred?" The captain left his chair, walked to the sink in the corner and washed his hands again.

"The point is, Charlie, that ol' L. G. Cubbage sure as hell ain't no Prince Charmin', now is he? Iffen Gladys dropped them pants as a girl for a jerk like Shortstride, then what's to say she wouldn't do it again for somebody else?"

"Nothin' says she wouldn't," Tate said, drying his hands on a paper towel. "So who you got in mind? Your informants got any ideas who the jock is this time around?"

The light seemed to go out of Burke's beady eyes. "Well...not yet, Charlie. It's really just a theory—"

"Bullshit, Fred. You wastin' my time with rumors and innuendos when you oughta be out gettin' me some relevant evidence."

"Aw, Charlie, shoot. There *ain't* no more evidence. We done turned up about all—"

"Jesus," Tate sighed. He took out a pocket fingernail file and began to clean under the tips of his nails. "You remember that McArdle broad some six or eight years ago, the one lived over in Jones County?"

The lieutenant began to scratch the back of his bull neck, frowning as he searched laboriously about in his sparsely populated memory bank.

"Ain't she the one"—he finally began—"who murdered her husband in order to collect on the poor bastard's life insurance?"

"No, she's the one who hired someone *else* to kill her husband and make it look like an accident sose she could collect on the poor bastard's life insurance."

"Oh sure. Now I remember. Hey, Charlie, an' you think mebbe—"

"I don't *think* ennything, Fred. Not yet." He moved back over to the desk. "I want me some facts, Lieutenant. Then I'll decide what I *think*."

Tate rummaged through a stack of photographs, dug one out and slid it across to Burke. The lieutenant scarcely glanced at it and his face lit up like a boil.

"Charlie, I..." He pushed back his chair and began to rise.

Tate leaned across the desk and reclaimed the photograph. The pose was of Gladys Cubbage suspended in death on the kitchen table. The dried blood looked like someone had poured brown barbecue sauce all over her pussy.

"Probably not insurance," Tate mused, as if talking only to himself. "But that there furniture store where he works—it was owned by old man Sudash, wasn't it." It was not a question. "When the old boy croaked a few years ago his whole estate come to his daughter Gladys. And Gladys Cubbage née Sudash"—he looked at the photo again—"she passed on last night right up there on her kitchen table."

The look on Burke's face revealed that he had at last come into the picture. "An' you think mebbe—" he began, only to be cut off abruptly by his captain.

"I told you, Fred. I don't think ennything. Now get the hell out of here an' put a couple boys on this angle right now."

When the door closed he stared for a moment at the photo of the woman's obliterated pelvis, then sat down. He rummaged through the stack again and came out with a picture of Sissie. The whole side of her face was gone, but one perfect little tit was hanging out of her shirt and her shorts were riding up so high they were lining her slit. He began to sweat on his forehead as he felt his erection pushing against his fly.

This has got to stop, Tate thought savagely as he reached for the phone. And if Holly has got the fucking line tied up again there'll be hell to pay when I get home.

# Chapter Thirty-three

The waning sun was tangled in a nest of treetops. Thick stands of pine stretched away from the Interstate on both sides as far as the eye could see. It had looked like rain all afternoon. They passed beneath an overhead bridge from which a young black boy dangled a homemade sign that read: PEECHES 2 MILES.

As the Toyota moved on toward Atlanta, holding the fifty-five-mile speed limit against the horde of state troopers that had taken to the Interstates for the summer infestation of tourists migrating to Florida, Sal worried about John's grimly sustained silence. She couldn't help wondering if he was stunned into silence by the thought that what he was now being asked to do was in effect a retreat to almost identical circumstances that had induced him to go away some six and a half years before.

How could they ask him to do such a thing? What right have they to interfere in our lives again? Especially Homer. Above all, he ought to know better.

Sal looked at her husband, willing him to speak. She thought she knew all of his moods. But she had never seen him quite like this. After he finished relating the gist of his conversation with Homer and the phone call from Governor Barrow, John had hardly spoken a dozen words. Though it had been his idea to leave the children with his mother and take a drive, he seemed now to resent being there.

Or am I imagining things? If only he would *say* something. But she wasn't imagining his anguish. That was genuine enough. Either way, they both realized that his decision was bound to have lasting implications on their relationship and their lives. He was being driven into a confrontation that was not of his making and he seemed to feel that she and Homer and the governor were forcing a decision upon him.

Although he had not said so, she had the instinctive feeling that John was going to relent to the political pressure of the moment and accept the appointment as special prosecutor. She was suddenly angry. It was Homer, she thought, who had struck the unkindest blow.

*A man who does not live up to his potential, John, is not only a failure in life; he is a disgrace to his people.*

Such sage advice from a man as useless and uncommitted as Homer Stokes. A millionaire who owned a bank he didn't manage, a newspaper he didn't edit, a cattle ranch he didn't oversee. No wife, no children, no profession—no reason for being.

Her anger dissipated as suddenly as it had flared. Perhaps *that* was why Homer had urged John with such fervor to accept this challenge, to use all of his talents to their fullest extent.

And now what would John do? His hands were clasped tightly on the wheel, his eyes fixed unmoving on the road ahead. She knew the primary reason for the depth of his anguish. He was concerned for her welfare. If he decided to accept the job, how would it affect her? She had suspected for some time now that many of John's major decisions had been determined by his concern for her stability. Had he really quit his job and taken her off to Europe only because he thought she needed a change. Had he brought her home again after Davey was born because he believed she needed a more stable environment?

She leaned her head back on the seat rest and closed her eyes. God, what a mess I must have been.

At that moment John reached out and took her hand. It was so like him, she thought, to sense her unspoken need. He was always there for her, like some huge immovable rock upon which she could kneel to calm her fears. And now, perhaps, for the first time, he needs *me*.

She felt a sudden rush of heat in her blood. She wished she could throw her arms around his neck and just hang on for dear life. But who would be saving whom? She wished they could stop somewhere. She could smell the coming rain in the air; it would be lovely to stop in the rain. But the mood, the timing, was all wrong. Later. Tonight. It started raining as if a tap had been abruptly opened, and she wished it would rain all night.

"John," she said, squeezing his hand. "Are you listening?"

"Hmmm."

"Honey, I don't want you to decide this thing because of me."

He turned and looked at her for the first time in many miles. The expression on his face was indecipherable.

"At least," she amended, "not entirely because of me. You have to do what you feel is best for us all. I don't know what's going to happen, I don't guess anyone does. But I do know one thing. I... I can never be happy, nor will the children be well cared for, if you aren't doing what makes you happy."

"Jesus, Sal. You sound like Homer."

"I'm talking for me, not Homer. Look, if you want to be a teacher, that's fine. But if you want to practice law again," she began, her face tightly set, her hand clasping his, "—if you *want* to accept this job..."

"Sal"— his expression and tone betrayed his incredulity— "are you saying you think I ought to *accept* the governor's appointment?"

"I'm saying that if you *want* to take the job—"

"Then the decision is all mine," he said flatly. "As usual."

She looked at him in astonishment. "John, you're the one..." She let her words taper off. She had to, she didn't know what to say. What did he mean, saying such a thing? And the look on his face. If he was trying to say that he wanted her to share fully in the decision, it would amount to a fundamental change in their relationship. From the moment she had announced "I can paint *anywhere*," such decisions had been primarily his concern.

What is he trying to do now—make me into a full partner? Or is it—incredible thought—is it his way of trying to shift some of the responsibility for what is going to happen onto me?

Does he really want this job? Maybe—maybe he's afraid of it. Maybe he's not thinking of my welfare at all—maybe he's using me as an excuse to avoid doing something he's afraid to attempt.

It was the harshest, unkindest thought she had ever had toward him. And she was shaken by it.

"John—"

The rain was pouring in torrents now, and there were chunks of hail bouncing off the roof. Vehicles were stopping on the side of the highway until visibility cleared. John pulled over and stopped under a bridge and the sudden silence was deafening.

"Oh, John, hold me."

She was in his arms. Safe, snug, secure. But somehow it was different. She couldn't take back her thoughts. Already this thing in their midst had begun to change them.

# Chapter Thirty-four

**Gordon Joyner was too intent on watching the roadway** on his side of the divided highway even to notice the red Toyota parked under the bridge on the other side. Gordon had spent the previous night and all of this day in Atlanta, so preoccupied with his own activities that he had been no more than vaguely aware of some sort of violent crime that had occurred down home in his part of the state the night before.

Now as he plunged southward through the heavy rain in his lavish Eldorado, he snapped on the radio to catch the hourly news report. The sky was looking pretty dark and suspicious all around and he didn't want to be driving into a wall of tornadoes with no advance warning.

Since it was a few minutes before the hour, Gordon reduced the radio's volume and let his mind wander below the level of the music that fused discordantly with the blower of the powerful air conditioner behind the dash. He was bone-weary, but in a comforting, satisfying way. There was no longer any doubt that he was going to receive financial assistance from the Atlanta people in his bid for his father's seat in Congress.

He smiled as he considered the simple quid pro quo of the situation. A new bank charter for his friends; the guaranteed election of a new U. S. congressman.

Gordon began to laugh as he anticipated the expression on the old bastard's face when he laid the words on him at dinner later in the evening. "Daddy," he would say, "I just thought you oughta know. I'm gonna run for your seat in November an' by God, I'm gonna win."

It was almost time for the news and he turned up the volume. He wouldn't tell the old man until after supper. The first person he would tell would be Sissie. He hoped to hell she would be waiting for him at the office. He wanted another score with which to celebrate. And he wanted Sissie on her knees between his legs again.

My praying mantis, he laughed.

He was still grinning when the news announcer's mellifluous voice penetrated his fantasy with the identity of the local family that had been so brutally murdered in Adelphi.

The name Cubbage seemed to come at him from the dashboard like a flying missile.

# Chapter Thirty-five

**Charlie Tate hustled down the back stairs to the basement** laboratory, such as it was, arriving just slightly out of breath. Conrad Peavyhouse had said on the phone: "Cap'n, I think I'd like to give you this 'un straight acrost the table."

Tate caught his breath now, as he always did upon contact with the smell of the Forensic Medicine Department, and hurried across the room to the coroner's cubbyhole.

"Okay, Doc. Now what the hell you bein' so all-fired cagey about ennyhow?"

"We got us an ident from Washin'ton a few minutes ago," the coroner said, moving sideways toward his cluttered desk like a freckle-faced crab. "Didden have nothin' on file here, an' wadden nothin' over to the sheriff's neither," he continued. "Then we telexed the state boys in Atlanta an' come up with a blank there too."

"Jesus Christ, Peavyhouse! You gonna tell me what the hell—"

"The FBI give us the whol' works," he said, picking up a telex sheet from among the clutter on the desk. He began to read in a monotone. "James, Edward Talmadge. Age twenty-four. Born Dothan, Alabama. Veteran, Vietnam, eighteen months. Wounded in action, lavishly decorated, honorably discharged. Last known residence Chicago, Illinois."

Peavyhouse dropped the telex sheet on the desk, removed his rimless spectacles and stared at Tate.

"You got me the hell down here for a routine background with all the work I got on my desk?" But he was only making noises, hoping against hope. He knew Peavyhouse better than that. And suddenly in that instant, even before the coroner could drop his little bomb, Tate knew exactly what item had been omitted from the background information.

"Jumpin' Jehosaphat. You ain't gonna tell me—"

"Tha's right, Charlie. The fuckin' kid's a nigra."

# Chapter Thirty-six

Even as Josie Fletcher continued her rocking chair vigil—"Swing Low, Sweet Chariot"—at the window overlooking the front porch, her daughter Ellie was whispering another prayer.

"Please, Lord, help me now, please. Don't let me panic. I can't see a thing and I'm scared to death of the dark all the scary little sounds and all. I wonder if there's rats here. Or snakes. *O God*. I wonder why that man went and did a thing like this. I can hear the water dripping somewhere must be an underground spring or something. I know I'm underground it's so cold must be a cave or something but it's so *dark*. Is Marvin all right, Lord? Please. Don't let there be no rats in here, Lord, and no snakes. My momma must be so afraid and worried don't let her suffer, Lord, you reckon anybody'll ever find me here? Maybe no one's even looking for us. We heard the shot and we thought it was the sheriff at first, caught us spoonin'; no tellin' what he would've made us do from the stories I heard at school. My head sure hurts, Lord. Where the man hit me after he run me down in the woods. If only I'd made Marvin carry me straight home. But I was so upset because of that man in the car—was it the same man I wonder? I don't know I didn't look at him on the street in front of Miz Maddie's place. He must have known all about this place before I don't think it was the same man so big and strong like an ox my head and jaw too and the pain in my chest. Those things he said, Lord, I never heard such dirty talk. Why me, Lord? Why me, and Marvin too did You really let that man go and kill my Marvin? I think

You did, Lord. I think maybe I'm gonna die too but I wish You wouldn't let me, it'll hurt poor Momma so. I have no idea how many hours it's been or days even. Will I ever get out? I don't think so. Rats and snakes and little crawling bugs. *O God.*"

# Chapter Thirty-seven

"No, Homer. I just don't see it that way. This doesn't change a thing as far as I'm concerned."

The phone had been ringing when they walked into the house. Sal carried Cathy to her crib and maneuvered Davey into his bed already half asleep while John answered it. She returned to the doorway, her dark eyes alert and apprehensive, watching and listening intently for any clue as to the kind of pressure Homer was now using on John to gain his agreement to accept the governor's appointment. The evening ride had helped clear the air between them, but nothing had been decided. Or if John had made up his mind, he had not as yet told her.

"Of course I understand the implications," he was saying, his voice firm, his eyes on her with a steady gaze of reassurance. "It's a chilly situation—yes—I know how the governor must be taking it. No, I don't. I'm sorry, Homer. I've made up my mind."

Sal caught her breath. Their eyes met and locked, the anxiety stretched out between them like a clothesline. She didn't know what to think...ever since his ourtburst back there in the car...what did any of it mean?

"I just don't think this is something I want to get involved in," he said, smiling thinly at the look of relief that passed over his wife's face. "I know that, in the larger sense, of course. But I don't want to be personally involved. I'm not the man for the job, Homer. For a variety of reasons." He put out his arm as Sal crossed the room and leaned against him with her head momentarily on his shoulder. "No, I won't reconsider, Homer. Thank you. Thank you for your confidence, but my decision is final. Well, it's up to you what you tell the governor."

When he hung up, they embraced so tightly she could scarcely breathe.

# Chapter Thirty-eight

As darkness settled over Adelphi that evening an unspoken tension hovered about the houses throughout Taliawiga County, white and black alike. No one as yet attempted to match words to mood. It was too soon, the facts were still too unsubstantial, the emotions too skittish and unsettled. No one knew precisely what to make of the rumors that had begun to circulate about the county in the late afternoon. People would have to chew things over, think on it, sleep on it. Then they would make the appropriate response.

Only one man in Taliawiga County already knew exactly what he felt about the entire affair. He knew also precisely what he intended to do about it.

More than once had it been said that L. G. Cubbage was as paradoxical as a snake. One moment calm and indolent, the next lashing out with angry venom at the nearest victim. Most people who knew him simply put such contrariness down to the fact that he was a pig-headed ornery sonofabitch. Not one person in the whole world understood the true source of L. G.'s biliousness.

What had really twisted L. G.'s mind and heart beyond repair was a deep-seated frustration that was impossible to ameliorate inasmuch as his dilemma was entirely due to the fact that he had been born poor white trash, and runtish in stature.

All his life L. G. Cubbage had longed passionately for wealth, social position and longer legs. Nor was he an idle dreamer. He read the stock market reports with his breakfast every morning, at home or on the road. He studied the niceties of corporate structure and modern business practice. He never listened to inside "tipsters" such as barbers, waiters and hotel porters. He subscribed to Standard & Poor's, read it every night at home and on the road. He investigated the companies he was interested in, their management record, the quality of their competitors in the field, their earnings and their potential for growth. He kept abreast of his tax position at all times in order to know when to buy and sell to the best advantage. At various periods in his life he had painstakingly maintained a journal of the share purchases he would have made had he enjoyed the use of sufficient funds for the purpose. The irony of his bookkeeping labors was that had the entries actually represented real transactions of buy-and-sell, Cubbage would presently have been a wealthy man.

His rise in social stature over the years had not much exceeded his increase in financial gain. He had been employed throughout most of his married life by his father-in-law in what amounted to a condition of bondage. Only in the last year, since the old man's death, had matters improved even in the slightest. But he still lived in a lower-middle-class neighborhood, drove a five-year-old automobile and maintained a savings account with exactly one hundred and seventy-nine dollars accumulating interest at an annual return that wouldn't buy him a good cigar. And even though he had finally become a deacon in the First Church of Christ, Revised, he was fully aware that his elevation had come solely as a result of his marriage and his persistence rather than as the sincere desire of his fellow members to welcome him to their select group in the bosom of Christ.

But the core of his persistent intractableness was his lifelong obsession with the enhancement of his runtish physical stature. As a boy he had worked out religiously with barbells and pulleys; as a young man he had consumed a pound of liver for lunch day in and week out; and as an adult he had quaffed such a variety of blood tonics that a quart of his blood might well have been expected to power a diesel engine. Over the years he had even tried stretching exercises involving a variety of complicated and semi-lethal apparatuses that had served no purpose other than to leave his stunted legs in a state of perpetual scarring, exceeded only by the abrasions and contusions of his malformed psyche.

Needless to say, as the result of such a dedicated regime he was as strong as an ox. Many an overbearing bully had discovered this unexpected strength to his immediate discomfort. But if L. G. was even aware of this Herculean byproduct of his quest, much less impressed by it, the true fruit of his labors greeted him each day with his first confrontation with the morning mirror. However irrational the fleeting hope, he never approached that first look without half expecting to find in the reflection a tall splendid-looking fellow in a white linen suit, with a full head of dark wavy hair, the rugged sun-scorched skin tightly stretched over a rawboned frame, and an expensive cheroot clenched in the corner of a strong sensuous mouth.

Alas, neither Rhett Butler nor a pale facsimile ever greeted him in the non-magical looking glass. All he ever saw was the pale blotchy skin, the pinkish thinning hair and the bright blue eyes behind the white stubby lashes peeking above the lower rim of the bathroom mirror frame. Old man Sudash had been fond of saying, at the drop of anyone's hat, that his runted son-in-law was the spitting image of a Van Gogh self-portrait executed during the famous artist's last days of terminal madness. Though L. G. had no idea who in the world the fella was or even what he looked like, he knew damned good and well that old man Sudash was making his daughter's husband out to be a horse's behind. When the old bastard's liquor-rotted liver finally played out on him, L. G. Cubbage was the first and happiest of the pallbearers to throw a handful of thick Georgia clay in the dearly departed's face.

But now, thought Cubbage, as he squatted on the toilet with the tips of his toes stretched to the floor—now that the old bastard is dead and gone these last twelve months, and now that my own miserable family has gone to claim their reward, I'll show the good folks of Taliawiga County the true size and worth of L. G. Cubbage!

He leaned sharply forward with his elbows on his knees, craning his neck to see into Naomi Hicks's bathroom window across the narrow corridor between their houses. It must have been her night off from the checkout counter over to the Handy Andy, 'cause he had seen her come up in her noisy old car some ten or fifteen minutes before. He had been sitting on the toilet ever since, hoping she might go in and take another bath with the light on. She always left the curtain up, too, just like she did in her bedroom whenever Andy Joe wadden home.

L. G.'s mouth went dry as her bathroom door opened across the way, light spilling in from the bedroom beside it, and Naomi Hicks came in naked.

"Oh sweet Jesus," L. G. gasped in a whispery little swoon, and he began to struggle frantically with his belt buckle as she turned on the light and started the water. When she straightened he could see her from her neck down to her knees. The hair on her pussy was as red and thick as a burning bush. As she bent over again to adjust the water, he pushed his pants down around his ankles and got down on his knees beside the window.

So many things were going to be different in his life from now on. And one of these days Naomi Hicks and the whole blessed county would sit up and take notice of L. G. Cubbage. He was going to be somebody, amount to something. He'd show 'em. Why, before I'm finished the name of L. G. Cubbage might just be as well known all over the world as that of Lester Maddox hisself.

L. G. began to flog himself as Naomi sprinkled bath suds into the tub and then bent over to stir the water with her hand. His tongue was between his teeth and his head was jammed halfway into the window. He could see it all now... He would go into the world and have his say. A martyr to the time and place in which he had lived, worked and suffered. A common man of the people, he would wear his losses like a badge of honor for all to see. And even though the identity of the warped fiend who had cleft him of his family and delivered him unto his fate was still as yet unestablished, it was in the name of the Good and Almighty Jehovah that the lacerated soul of L. G. Cubbage cried out for vengeance.

Kneeling there in the blood-scented house of his private travail, watching the woman with searing eyes and aching guts as she anointed her pink supple flesh and then submerged her naked body into the sudsy waters of life, Cubbage knew full well that his course was set, his destiny determined once and for all. The Lord God was speaking to the people in these bitter days through this His servant's personal woe. The Lord would have vengeance. Law and order would be established in the land and the Lord's Word would be the Rule. It was God's command that justice be done, and L. G. Cubbage would be His instrument of delivery.

He began to bleat and gasp in disbelief and horror as Andy Joe entered the bathroom opposite with an enormous erection and went down into the tub with Naomi.

# PART THREE

# Chapter Thirty-nine

"**Have you** *read* **this bloody claptrap?**" Homer Stokes demanded, as John finished his second cup of morning coffee and pushed back from the table.

"Almost curdled my ham 'n' grits and redeye gravy, Homer. You really oughta *do* something about that scandal sheet."

"You know I never interfere with the operation of the paper. And certainly not with its editorial content."

Homer picked up the Sunday morning edition of the Adelphi *Oracle* and stabbed an accusatory finger at the black-bordered editorial on the front page.

"Can't you *see* what they're up to?" he demanded, almost shrilly. He was wearing one of his safari suits, olive drab in color, and John couldn't help thinking how theatrical he looked. A pipe-smoking Abraham Lincoln on the Serengeti plain.

"Of course I see," John said, and started for the front porch with Homer a few steps behind.

"Well what the devil are you going to do about it?"

"I'm going fishing," said John, kneeling on the porch to inspect the equipment in his metal box of fishing tackle. He was dressed in his customary fishing wear, sneakers, jeans and cotton work shirt. Davey was in the bedroom with Sal, getting dressed. Few Sunday mornings in summer found the Winter men anywhere but the pond by nine o'clock.

"For God's sake, man. Just listen to this rubbish." Homer began to quote from the editorial. "'The entire county is saddened by the senseless slaughter of seven innocent law-abiding citizens, while even now an eighth unfortunate victim—a much-decorated veteran of the Adelphi Police Department—lies on the edge of death under the watchfully anguished eye—'"

"Who in the world wrote *that* little gem?" John scoffed. "'Watchfully anguished eye,'" he snorted and busied himself with a plastic box of fishhooks.

"'...under the watchfully anguished eye of his grieving wife and their three little babies,'" Homer continued. "'These tragic deaths have stunned Taliawiga County like no other crime in recent memory.'"

"Come on, Homer. I know the damned thing by heart. Jesus. Innocent law-abiding citizens. Alton Pittman and Sissie Cubbage."

"And here's the worst part," said Homer, with genuine indignation. "'Although the motive for such an unpardonable act of savagery is as yet undetermined, a suspect is already under police custody in the county hospital. He was wounded in a blazing gun battle at the scene of the crime and is reported to be in critical condition after lengthy surgery.' Now get this...'Little is known of this culprit's identity, other than his name, age and race.'"

"Color *that* red flag black and take the sheets off the beds, Ma—the Klan is gonna ride again, Colonel, suh."

"It makes me sick to my stomach, John, it really does," Homer said, and he did look ill. "And just listen to this cheap shot. 'What *is* known'"—he continued from the editorial—"'is that the deed of which this Eddie James stands accused is so heinous that when his guilt has been duly established in a proper court of law his just punishment *must* of necessity be in conformity with the magnitude of the crime.'"

"Not *if* his guilt is established," said John, rising. "*When*. Due process is gonna cover Dixie like the dew when these old merchants of justice take to horse again." He picked up the box of tackle and started down the wooden stairs, talking over his shoulder. "I bet nickels to a doughnut those old boys down at Reidsville are dusting off that four-legged frying pan even as we stand here talking."

Homer was following him down the steps so intently that when John abruptly stopped he collided with him.

"I think you're right, John," he said, backing up a step. "It may be a trifle premature, but I tell you, I see it coming. The dance of death is cranking up again. It started in Florida with that Spenkelink chap and now, by God, it's coming home to the sovereign state of Georgia."

John turned, almost angrily. "So what the hell do you want *me* to do about it?" he demanded.

"I want you to try to stop it."

"You try to stop it."

"I don't have the credentials, you have."

"You own the *Oracle*. Use it."

"John, you know I'm not a newspaperman."

"Yeah, well I'm not a lawyer anymore either."

"Nonsense. You're just marking time and you know it. You're not going to play gentleman farmer and write scholarly tomes for the rest of your life, I don't care *what* you say."

"And I don't care what *you* say. I'm not getting involved in this thing."

"You *are* involved, my friend. We all are."

"I'm going fishing." He looked up toward the bedroom window. "Davey!" he called, almost certain that he'd seen Sal's face in the window for a fleeting moment.

"John, listen to me—"

"No."

"The governor called again this morning—"

"Tell him to call someone else."

"He wants you."

"Bullshit," he said sharply. "*You* put him up to this."

"John, you can't run away from your reputation. Your experience, your talent, your capacities are well known beyond the borders of Taliawiga County."

"Now who's talking rubbish?" He cupped his hands over his mouth and shouted, "C'mon, Davey-O!"

John started down across the front yard toward the branch. Homer stopped him.

"If you turn your back on this challenge, John, you might as well pull the switch on that boy."

"You sonofabitch!" John said, whirling around and retracing his steps. His face was white, his lips drained of color. He looked as if he might strike his friend. "Don't you lay this on me!" he growled. "I won't take this kind of shit, Homer, not even from you."

Homer put his hand gently on John's shoulder. "I'm sorry, John. It's the way it is. There is no one else."

"What the hell are you talking about? How can *I* help by prosecuting the bastard? What he needs is a good defense lawyer. You people aren't after me to defend him—you want me to prosecute the case."

"Anybody can defend him, John. In fact, he has one of the best."

"The Wild Man of Taliawiga County."

Homer smiled thinly. "Tribble will do as good a job as anyone could do."

"So he's in good hands then." John tried to turn away but Homer kept hold of his shoulder.

"It's not the defense attorney, John. The crucial factor lies in the character of the prosecutor. You're the only lawyer in Taliawiga County who has the nerve, as well as the principle, to resist the pressure to turn this into a crusade for capital punishment."

They stared at each other for a long moment. The hundreds of talks they had had over the years concerning such matters as death, crime, sin, government power, the goodness versus the mendacity of the state—all this, and more—seemed to coagulate with the heavy summer heat that hung between them now.

"You can't run away from it, John," Homer said finally, softly. "Everything you've ever done, thought, experienced, has prepared you for this moment, here and now, in your own backyard." He paused, almost let it go, then added, "It's your duty, John. Your responsibility. Don't run away from it, man. Running will get you nowhere. I ought to know," he said, with deep feeling, his dark eyes hard and shining in the brightness. He waved a pesky gnat out of his face and cleared his throat brusquely. "Make your life count for something, John. Before it's too late."

They were silent for another moment. Then the screen door banged open and Davey exploded onto the porch. They looked up and saw Sal standing in the doorway with Cathy in her arms.

"Hey, Dad! All *right!* C'mon, ol' Dad! Le's *go!*"

The boy galloped off across the lawn, heading for the pond.

John turned back and shook his head. "You're wrong, Homer. There goes my duty, man." He gestured after Davey, then looked up on the porch at Sal and the baby. "There's my responsibility."

He walked swiftly down the sloping lawn.

# Chapter Forty

Homer knew what he was talking about; the dance had begun in earnest. From the moment Charlie Tate had called a press conference on Saturday morning to announce the name and race of the assailant, public and official desire for retribution and vengeance had intensified incredibly. Front-page news articles, lead editorials, letters to the editor and TV news shots were enthralled by the case.

The Cubbage family funeral on Monday afternoon became a three-ring circus. The announcement concerning the identity of Eddie James and his race had propelled L. G. Cubbage into the throes of rabid hysteria. From that moment he began calling press conferences to deliver ringing harangues on law and order; he took to the pulpit to sermonize on sin and debauchery; and he traversed the streets and highways, the back alleys and the nooks and crannies of Taliawiga County crying his woe day and night and offering himself as some sort of avenging angel.

At the funeral the Reverend Pinkie Washburn had scarcely concluded the benediction before old L. G. had hold of the nearest television mike and was making yet another impassioned plea for a moral reawakening in the land, a call for a return to the old values and standards (unspecified), a renewal of man's faith in the Almighty and a commitment to Jesus Christ as Lord and Savior of all—and for a rigorous reactivation of capital punishment in order to stem the alien tide of lawless violence that was sweeping across the nation.

The next morning he went down to the courthouse and

filed his application as a candidate for mayor in the fall election.

That same evening, like a jack-in-a-box, District Attorney Robert Randolph leaped to his feet at the dais of a civic club dinner at the Adelphi Holiday Inn and bellowed out the ritual law-and-order sentiments with such impassioned vigor that he made poor L. G. Cubbage seem like a boy scout selling cotton candy at a down-home NRA barbecue.

"Fire can only be fought with fire," Randolph railed in a peroration that was more smoke than blaze. "Justice, if it's to be of any social effectiveness whatsoever, must be swift, certain and harsh. These criminals out there marauding up and down our land are like animals. Hungry, man-eatin' tigers. To stop a hungry man-eatin' tiger you don't try to reason with it, ladies an' gennelmun. You *kill* it."

Every man and woman in the room was standing, applauding, cheering, and more than a few had tears streaming down their flushed cheeks. At least one of the half-dozen black waiters in the banquet hall at the moment set down his tray of dirty dishes and edged his way over to a side exit.

"Thank you, friends, one an' all. Thank you," Randolph purred, raising his arms in a Billy Graham gesture of benediction. "I'll say only this in closing an' then I'll say no more." He paused dramatically, arms still in the air, waiting as the silence came down over the crowd like a curtain. "The death penalty in such cases as this atrocity that has befallen our good community is not only justified, it is absolutely *necessary*, if civilized society is to survive this heathen onslaught upon our revered way of life."

"You tell it like it is, Brother Robert."

"Amen."

"And as long as *I* am your district attorney," he intoned in a quavering voice, his hand groping about above his head now as if he was searching for a light cord, "I will fight with all my strength and with all my unswerving dedication, and with all the power of my noble office, to uphold the law of this land and the right of you good citizens to be safe and secure in the sanctity of your homes!"

The editorial in the *Oracle* the next morning came out foursquare in favor of his law-and-order point of view and in strident support of Randolph's quest for re-election in November.

# Chapter Forty-one

The funeral service for the slain patrolman Billy T. Musgrove the next day was even more fraught with incendiary potential. Like the Cubbage production, it too was a fully covered media event, presided over by the eloquent and flamboyant pastor of the First Church of the Redeemer, the Reverend Hardy Bass. The deceased's grieving widow, their three children, two sets of grandparents, nine or ten aunts and uncles, and, according to one reporter's head count, forty-six cousins and an unlimited number of their offspring and relatives by marriage and near-marriage, sat in stunned attendance in the relentless summer heat.

The Musgrove family sat on the right side of the coffin on hard folding chairs. On the left sat the entire off-duty force of Adelphi policemen, resplendent and sweaty in their formal dress blue uniforms, some making their silent prayers to whatever gods they were on speaking terms with, others sitting quietly in stunned grief and wonder at the swiftness and senselessness of the deed that had robbed them of their friend and colleague, while still others whispered together and fretted in the distressing heat, pulled at their soiled collars, picked their noses, tugged at their creeping jockey shorts and hoped to hell they would make it home in time for a little sleep before going on duty.

In the front row of the police section sat the mayor, two members of the city council, Chief Toland (who fell asleep each time he closed his eyes in an affectation of prayer), Captain Charles Tate and his pretty wife Holly, and the president of the local chapter of the Benevolent Association of Police Officers and his blowsy girlfriend. And, of course, District Attorney Robert Randolph was so visible that an outsider might have thought the ceremony had been staged in his honor.

The response from the general community was remarkable. Friends, neighbors, concerned citizens, curiosity ghouls, all came out to pay their respects and to demean the reality of death in just about equal proportions.

There were fewer than half a dozen people in attendance at the burial of Elton Pittman an hour later; no newsmen, no cameras, no mourners. Lucy Pittman didn't shed so much as a public tear.

# Chapter Forty-two

**The square in downtown Adelphi is dominated by the** two-story brick turn-of-the-century courthouse, the basement of which is given over to the police of Taliawiga County.

An argument had erupted in the corridor in front of the sheriff's office and was beginning to attract a crowd of spectators. A tall husky black man with bloodshot eyes and the lobe of his left ear missing was on the verge of getting his skull cracked open by an enormous police billy club.

"Now you lissen t'me, boy. I'm gonna give you just about five seconds to *vanish* or I'm a-gonna award you a two-week vacation out at the county work camp."

"I want yo' to see to things *now*," the black man insisted. "I wanta know what's done happened to my boy. It's been more'n twenny-four hours now—"

"I *said* we'll look into it, Watts," the deputy growled, and began to weigh the club menacingly in his hands. "So iffen you don' get on along home now an' leave us be—"

"I wanta talk to the sheriff."

"Hah. You gonna talk to the sheriff awl right. Iffen you able to talk to ennybody."

The deputy started toward the black man, ready to do business. The crowd in the corridor began to separate.

The deputy took another step, raised the billy club and then froze. The black man, standing his ground, was hunched slightly over to one side as if already attempting to ward off the blow.

"Put the goddamn club down, Tyler."

Everyone in the corridor looked at the massive man in the straw Stetson standing in the doorway. The gold star on his chest was the size of a pie plate and the black leather belt around his enormous waist looked like an elephant's cinch. He was wearing faded khakis and logger's boots.

"Lissen, Sheriff—"

"You lissen, you dumb Cracker sonofabitch. Put down that club and stand easy."

The deputy did as he was told, and the crowd breathed a collective sigh of relief. Without moving from the doorway Sheriff Biggs waved his hand at the spectators and they began to move away.

He glared at the deputy and said in a voice that was only barely audible, "What th' hell you tryin' to do—start a race riot?"

"Sheriff, this here nigger—"

"Shut up, Tyler."

"He come in here a-throwin' his weight around...third time today—"

"I said for you to shut up. I said it twicet. I have to say it again I'm gonna shove that billy club up yore ass."

A black boy in jeans and a T-shirt standing beside the stairs began to giggle. Biggs looked at him and winked.

"Now what's this all about?" Biggs asked, turning to the black man, still without raising his voice above a conversational level.

"My boy, Sheriff, suh...like I done told the deputy here—three times—he gone an' disappeared."

"What you mean, disappeared?"

"Tha's it, Sheriff. He lef' work soon yesterday afternoon

to pick his girlfrien' up at school, an' they ain't been seen hide nor hair of since."

Biggs put a hand in his pocket and came out with a set of car keys. "Mebbe they run off together, Tooney."

"Nosuh, Sheriff, suh. My boy he ain't that kinda boy."

"Which one of your boys is it, Tooney?"

"Marvin, suh."

"Works over to Pettigrew Lumber Company?"

"Yessuh, tha's the one."

Sheriff Biggs chuckled. "He's the type all right, Tooney."

"Nosuh, I swear, Sheriff—"

"Who's the gal?"

"Uh, that liddle Fletcher girl. Elmarie."

"Josie Fletcher's girl?"

"Yessuh, tha's the one."

Chester Biggs stuck out his bottom lip thoughtfully. *"She shore ain't the kind,"* he mused, then turned to the now subdued deputy. "Josie been in about this, Tyler?"

"Ain't seen hide nor hair of her, Sheriff."

"Then get somebody the hell out there to see if she knows where her girl is."

"But, Sheriff—"

"One more time, Tyler, an' that club's goin' right up yore ass. Thick end first." He turned back to Watts and said, "C'mon, Tooney. I'll walk you out."

When he had assured the black man they would do what they could to find his son, Sheriff Biggs waddled out to his parking slot in front of the courthouse and wedged his incredible bulk in behind the wheel of his cruiser. He started the engine and hit the car radio. As soon as the dispatcher came on the air, he said, "Be out to the MacAtee place iffen you need me, Wally."

It was not much of an exaggeration for Chester Biggs to assert—as he occasionally did—that he owned Taliawiga County lock, stock and barrel. The mayor of Adelphi was in one hip pocket, the county judge in another. And scattered throughout the rumpled recesses of his oversized clothing was an assortment of city and county officials and so-called solid citizens from the private sector.

Reciprocity. That was the core of Chester's philosophy of life. "Do unto me an' I'll do you right. Do me wrong an' I'll eat yore face off." For an unlettered grammar school dropout, the Biggs philosophy had insinuated itself more deeply into the fabric of Adelphi's social structure than had Plato's attitudes into Athens' some years before. The sheriff's influence had undergone a curious evolution. When he had first made his move toward the courthouse—having crawled up unexpectedly out of the swamp, Biggs's detractors privately joked—no one had really taken him seriously. A man as fat and grotesque in appearance as Chester Biggs *couldn't* be taken seriously, people had said. But that was almost fifteen years ago. Few people failed to take him seriously today, though he was just as fat and grotesque as ever.

The green and white sedan pulled around the square and turned on Main Street as Biggs headed out toward the old Atlanta wagon road. It looked like rain up toward the northern edge of the county.

The one thing that people had failed to notice about Chester, even as a boy, was that he was not as stupid as he looked. Persuaded perhaps by custom, people seemed to think that because he was inordinately fat he was also jolly and not very bright. Although Chester Biggs laughed a lot and on occasion could be possessed of a down-home cracker-barrel humor, he didn't have a jolly bone in his gargantuan body. And though he might *look* stupid, what with his pink ham of a face, his sausage-like fingers and his ridiculous waddling gait, he was in truth about as dumb as a silver-tailed fox at large in a country henhouse; and he was every bit as mean and low-down in the bargain.

The bedrock of Chester's strength was just about evenly distributed between the white and black elements of the county. According to the latest census the population was more or less evenly divided between the races. Most voters, black and white alike, cast their ballots for Chester Biggs with regularity. It was really a simple matter and Biggs, being anything but simple, had figured it out long ago. Whites wanted nigras kept in their places, while blacks had been encouraged to want houses that didn't leak, food on the table, easy credit and shiny new cars in their front yards. One way or another, Chester Biggs saw to it that, within an acceptable margin of error, both factions *thought* they were getting what they wanted. In return, the sheriff got what he wanted: votes.

Grunting with the exertion now, he managed to turn the car onto Millionaires' Row. It had looked like rain earlier but the wind seemed to have shifted now and moved the heavier, darker clouds over to the northwest. It was hot and muggy though, and he could feel the sweat pouring down the crevice between his buttocks. His brow suddenly wrinkled with the discomfort of his thoughts as he neared the Stokes mansion.

What the hell was this here talk about Josie Fletcher's girl supposed to be missing? He hadn't had the first contact with the woman in more years than he could remember; he wouldn't even recognize the girl if he was to meet her on the street. Fact was, the way he remembered Josie was more likely the way her daughter looked now. At that moment his eye caught sight of a movement up on the gallery of the Stokes mansion, and he ducked his head down to see out of the window as he passed in front of the house.

It was the old lady, sure enough. Miss Leenie. He hadn't seen her in a coon's age. But he sure remembered the last time he had seen her. There she stood, like a ghost in the kitchen pantry, listening to every word her husband was saying. I saw her and she knew I saw her, thought Chester, and in that split second we made our bargain: I wouldn't tell on her iffen she wouldn't tell on me.

Biggs shook his head and began to suck loudly on his yellowing teeth. He wondered if the bargain had been worth it.

About a mile down the road, he suddenly said aloud, "I don't know about *her;* it sure as hell has been for *me.*"

He pulled the sedan into the long circular driveway in front of Miz Aimee MacAtee's crumbling antebellum monstrosity of a house. Some people said it still had a quiet, sad dignity about it; to Chester's way of thinking, it was a wreck. Just like its owner and occupant.

Jesus, what a funny farm, he thought, cutting the engine and leaning his bulk back against the seat for a moment. Half the old women in Taliawiga County seemed to have bats in their belfries. And the richer they were, the screwier they seemed to be. More often than not having something to do with a wayward husband or a problem son. It was just one more reason he considered himself fortunate never to have gotten involved with any wife and family of his own.

Yessiree, he thought, a real funny farm. He sat a moment longer, his beefy fingers drumming tonelessly on top of the dashboard. He had been preoccupied all day with thoughts of Sissie Cubbage. Not really too surprising, the way the little cunt was carrying on. But the circumstances were a mite perplexing. What the hell was she doin', messing around with the likes of Elton Pittman? Chester didn't even know they were acquainted. Besides, he thought Alton was still in prison up in Illinois somewhere. Why hadn't Lucy told him her boy was back in town? I'll have to go by 'n' see her this evening, he thought; see how she's taking it. Prolly hasn't missed a trick all day, he chuckled.

He sighed, squirmed around and struggled to reach the door handle. Having the Cubbage gal out of the way was probably a blessing in disguise, though. If ever a cunt smelled like trouble that kid was it. Of course it presented him with something of a minor problem in logistics, but he could take care of that soon enough. But one thing was sure: no cunt this time. This time he would just get hisself a supply source up in Atlanta and let it go at that. Send somebody like, say, ol' Lamar Stick to Atlanta for the pickup an' stay the hell out of it hisself. Then he would never have to worry about anybody like Sissie Cubbage again. He sure as hell wouldn't have to worry about Lamar Stick.

This little task with Miz Aimee was the last of his daily chores and then he would get down to some serious business. What he had to do, and real soon, was get a handle on things. He didn't like not knowing what was going on in his county. Sissie and Alton Pittman; Lucy withholding information; who in hell that skunk in the hospital was who had wasted the Cubbage family.

If only the goddamn house had just been a few feet over the county line, he thought, as he struggled to get his massive legs out of the car. Well, it didn't really matter all that much. He might not be running the investigation, but he had his pipelines into the P.D. and there wouldn't be much that he wouldn't know about almost as soon as it happened.

He began to chuckle as he pulled himself to his feet and started slowly up the flagstone walk. His armpits were soaked with perspiration. He might even find a way to put the screws to ol' Charlie Tate, he thought.

The door opened as Chester approached the porch and a black man in a white coat appeared behind the screen door.

"Hidy-do, Jeeter. Kindly tell Miz Aimee I'd like to please talk with her a minute or two iffen she can spare the time."

"Atternoon, Sheriff. Miz Aimee has just come up from her nap, but I'm sure she will be pleased to see you. Won't you come on in the house?"

Biggs quickly examined the old servant's face to see if he was being made fun of. It was like looking into a plastic mask with a pair of lizard's eyes behind the narrow slits. With the help of the guardrail on the steps, the sheriff pulled himself up on the porch and paused for a deep breath. "I'll jes' set out here on the porch an' rock a spell," he rasped. "You run along now an' tell yore missus I'm here."

The sheriff waddled down the long porch to a large reinforced rocking chair and eased his heavy bulk down between the sturdy arms. He had always suspected the old lady of having installed the chair solely to accommodate his periodic visits. Folding his meaty fingers over his huge belly now, he began to think of Jeeter. Bright, talked real good, carried hisself just right. Head smooth and black as an eight ball.

Biggs was sure that the old darky had been jabbing at him with that won't-you-come-in-the-house routine. Smooth as molasses, to be sure; but a jab in the belly all the same. Chester would just have to see iffen there wadden a little sumpin' might be done to improve the feller's attitude. Mebbe like havin' Lamar Stick an' one or two of his associates pay the old boy a liddle visit. Biggs was beginning to smile. Just to make certain Jeeter didden go 'n' get hisself too all-fired uppity atter all these years of knowin' his place 'n' all.

His thoughts were interrupted by his hostess, who came out onto the porch. He was scarcely able to begin the courtesy of rising before she had settled herself upright on a cushioned rattan fan chair beside a huge potted fern.

"'Scuse me for not risin', Miz Aimee. I seem to be movin' a tad slower than usual today. I reckon it's the weather, don't you? Lord knows it's hotter'n a bluetail bitch done run a swamp coon up a pine tree."

The old lady didn't bat an eye. Sat her chair as rigidly as if rigor mortis had already set in, staring with unfocused eyes into the middle distance beyond the porch. "It has most assuredly been verra warum, Sheriff. Jeeter will be along in jes' a minute now with a cool refreshment."

When she talked her mouth moved scarcely more than a ventriloquist's, and her voice was as dainty as the squeak of a little mouse. Biggs couldn't help admiring the old girl, at least up to a point. Her appearance was a combination of contradictions. Though her tiny voice and precious ways gave one the impression of smallness, she was actually quite tall. Her round fleshy face with the bright pinpoint eyes drew one's attention away from the long spare skeleton that seemed to move only with the assistance of a polished hickory cane.

Biggs suddenly found himself imagining what it would

have been like to have been such a woman's son. To come home from college on vacation, perhaps, or back from his law office at the end of a long satisfying day. Just to rock and sip refreshment and sit on the front porch in idle conversation until dinnertime. But it never seemed to work out like that somehow. Either you didn't have a grand old mother like Miz Aimee or you did and the relationship got all poisoned up some way, as in the case of such community stalwarts as Homer Stokes, Buford Pope out to the sawmill, poor sad ol' Harvey Wildersham and even John Winter. From stories he had heard, ol' Doc Winter's Momma sure Lord had a few bats flyin' around loose in her belfry too. Chester decided on balance he was probably better off with the slatternly old swamp bitch that had dropped him in a backyard shed in between her pots of boiling laundry.

Suddenly he was no longer smiling. Without turning his head, he looked at the old woman out of the corner of his eyes with a scythe-like expression. Of course old Jeeter had been jabbing him. In all the years he had been involved with the old girl, she had never once invited him inside the house.

When Jeeter came onto the porch with a serving tray bearing a pitcher of iced tea, a pair of tall ice-frosted tea glasses and all the makings, neither his mistress nor her guest ever looked at him.

"I must say, Miz Aimee, you sure are lookin' fine," Chester said. "I don't see how you always look so fresh and alert the way you drive yo'self with all them civic duties an' all."

No response. The old lady just sat there, hands folded in her lap, staring into the yard. She had been a beautiful young woman, Chester recalled. He remembered her well. She was still a comely woman, entering her eighth decade. But the once luxuriant hair had given way to a tightly curled wig, the eyes were weak and vapid behind rimless spectacles and her fingers were beginning to swell with signs of creeping arthritis.

"I reckon it's the long afternoon naps, for one thing. You reckon iffen I was to try...naw," he said, "I jes' ain't got the time for no daytime nappin'. No tellin' what all might break loose in this here county iffen I was to jes' lay down 'n' go to sleep. 'Sides, it's too blessed hot over to my place to sleep much day or night, I can tell you."

If Miz Aimee or Jeeter either one was listening, they showed no evidence of it. Chester watched now as Jeeter poured the tea and arranged the sprigs of mint around the lip of each glass accordingly. He noticed the tattered edges of the old man's serving jacket and the threadbare elbows. With all the old lady's money, why didn't she buy Jeeter a new coat? Fix him up like ol' what's his name down to the Stokes mansion. Why didn't she fix up her house an' make it look like something again? All the money in the world an' she goes an' lives like a washerwoman.

He looked at her as Jeeter passed around the drinks. There was a scented lace handkerchief tucked just inside the loose bodice of Miz Aimee's thin cotton dress. Her chest looked to Biggs to be as flat as an ironing board. He had always found it hard to picture the old woman in the act of screwing. Of course he always tried; Chester Biggs had made it a lifelong practice to try to work out in his mind how people he knew went through their sexual exercises. Was Charlie Tate's wife frigid and a lesbian to boot? And what was the truth behind all those stories about John Winter's chesty Choctaw wife in her wild days up in Atlanta? Sal Winter in particular was one of Chester's fantasy favorites, same as John's little girlfriend—whatshername?—used to be afore John went off an' found hisself this fine piece he brought back home. There sure Lord wasn't much that the human anatomy could do that he hadn't pictured Sal Winter doing over the last three years or so she had been in Taliawiga County. Rachel, the little Pettigrew girl, that was the gal's name used to be so sweet on John Winter. Chester used to keep a real close eye on her, the way she sashayed around town so high 'n' mighty but was no better'n she ought to be accordin' to half a dozen young bucks who used to take her out to the old quarry road after John went off and left her. What in the world had happened to sweet little Rachel, he wondered. Seems like I heard tell of her not too long ago, a year or so mebbe, somethin' about her marryin' some no-acount an' going on over to New Orleans to live. Ol' man Pettigrew—he chuckled—must've plumb split a gut when his precious little darlin' up 'n' hightailed it away from Taliawiga County.

What Biggs liked so much about his relationship with Lucy Pittman was that she knew almost as much about the perversities of the citizens of Taliawiga County as did he. It was Lucy, for example, who had first tipped him off about Lamar Stick and that there girl of his; Lamar had been in his pocket ever since. And Jasper Sands, the banker, delightin' to have his toes sucked by Lucy while she squatted over his face. With Lucy's help, Chester hadn't had an unpaid campaign debt or an overdrawn personal check in more than five years.

Biggs examined the barren waste of Miz Aimee's concave chest. For Miz Aimee's was a story that always gave Chester pleasure to contemplate. Her husband had died young and Miz Aimee thereafter controlled the family fortune with an iron hand. Her son was in his thirties before he convinced the tight-fisted old girl to loosen the purse strings so that he might go into business for himself. She did and he did, with a vengeance. He promptly sold off all his holdings to a business competitor of his mother's, married a slattern from the wrong side of the tracks, moved to California and was never heard of again. The old woman, according to local legend, had never since mentioned his name to a living soul.

Sheriff Biggs was chuckling audibly as Jeeter inquired of his stiff-backed mistress: "Will they be anything else, ma'am?"

"That will be all, Jeeter," she said. "Thank you."

She hadn't touched her own drink and sat rigid in the increasing heat of the afternoon while Chester drained his glass of tea in one long gulp. Then he smacked his lips appreciatively and said, "Miz Aimee, you gotta do somethin' about them fuckin' shacks out on the Row."

The old woman neither flinched nor so much as blinked her eyes.

"Now I realize you charge them people a mere pittance," he said. "An' I know maintenance costs is goin' sky-high. But them people got rights too, Miz Aimee. They's citizens jes' like the rest of us." He grinned like a direct descendant of one of the Founding Fathers. "An' they votes, Miz Aimee."

"Sheriff Biggs," she said in the soft cultured voice for which she was so well known, "I have absolutely no knowledge of such matters, as you are very well aware. So far as anything *I* know those houses are in excellent living condition. If there *are* any complaints, however, and if there are any merits to such complaints, you have only to pursue the matter with my solicitors."

Biggs stopped rocking and set his glass down on the floor beside the chair. He heaved his bulk out of the chair and had moved toward the stairs before her voice could stop him.

"Chester!"

He paused, without turning, and waited.

"Please," she whimpered. *"Please."*

He turned with a contented grunt and waddled back over to her chair. The grande dame was gone. A withered old hag sat slumped like a bag of soiled laundry in the rattan chair. Her head was bowed, her hands trembling over a lace handkerchief knotted tightly in her lap.

Chester Biggs took a deep wheezing breath as he stood over her, and worked a pair of fat fingers into his grimy shirt pocket. He said, "Please is jes' a whole lot better, Miz Aimee," as he withdrew a cellophane package of white powder and dropped it contemptuously in her lap. "And you get yore people out there an' you fix them fuckin' shacks, you hear me now."

As he passed the front door, he jerked the screen open and said to Jeeter, who was cowering against the wall, "Help the smelly ol' bitch into the house, nigger."

# Chapter Forty-three

**Judge Harbuck looked up from a stack of paperwork** and smiled at his old childhood buddy, Bobcat Tribble. "C'mon in, Cat. Have a seat an' a cup of coffee while I push a little more of this paper out of the way."

Judge Horace Harbuck was one of the most efficient men in the state judiciary. There was no cleaner, more organized docket in the state of Georgia than his; recent state and federal rules pertaining to speedy trials were already established precedents in Harbuck's jurisdiction. People said that such efficiency assuredly had something to do with the pattern of his background experiences. He was captain of the local high school football team the year they won the state championship. He was captain of the Georgia Tech team the year they won the Sugar Bowl. And he was captain of a company of 82nd Airborne paratroopers the year they helped win a war in Europe. He just didn't know how to do things any other way. He organized, he followed the rules and he usually came out on top.

Tribble shuffled on into the judge's chambers and sat down on an aging leather sofa while Harbuck's secretary fixed their coffee in a little alcove off the main office.

Bobcat looked his usual eccentric self. He was wearing his standard summer uniform of rumpled linen suit and Panama hat with a soiled sweatband, which he balanced on the crown of his knobby knee. Although short in stature, flabby and pasty white, Tribble was obviously a man of latent physical strength. His thinning hair and scraggly beard resembled sweat-soaked moss, and his beady blue eyes were magnified to the size of painted Easter eggs by the powerful bifocals that prevented him from walking in front of cars.

Incongruously, Tribble was by reputation a legendary hunter. He had acquired his nickname at age seven when he had bagged his first and only bobcat with his granddaddy's shotgun. Though he had never hunted again or killed a living thing larger than a mosquito (he was unqualified for war because of his weak eyes and the flattest pair of feet in Georgia), his reputation as a woodsman was imperishable.

He also had a reputation of another sort. For most of his adult life he had enjoyed the dubious honor of being Taliawiga County's number-one eccentric. There were drunks, perverts, wife-beaters and whoremongers a-plenty throughout the populace, but they didn't rank with Bobcat Tribble according to most county folks. He was Taliawiga County's homegrown, genuine bluestockinged aristocrat-turned-rabble-rouser. He was, in short, a "nigger lover."

Tribble's "peculiar" tendencies had exhibited themselves in childhood by an obsessive identification with the outsider, the underdog and the underprivileged. The girl with braces on her teeth, the boy violinists and, of course, the blacks. As far as the latter were concerned, his allegiance to his black playmates was unshakable. Though consigned by parents, custom and law to separate and highly unequal schools, he obstinately would not sever his relationships with his black brothers and sisters. His distraught parents could only hope and pray that matriculation at a fine private university would correct this perverse defect in his character. Tribble had other ideas. He attended a formally all-black university, graduated with a degree in political science, read law for two years in the county law library, sat for the bar examination and passed with flying colors. He nailed up his shingle on the wall above the pharmacy in Adelphi and had functioned as the unwanted conscience of Taliawiga County ever since.

In his tight, orderly hand—a close approximation of the Latin script he had learned as a child from his schoolteacher mother—Horace Harbuck signed an order denying a motion to vacate sentence filed the previous day by Butts County lawyer Peter Paul Poag. He placed the order on top of the neat stack of documents in the out box, picked up his coffee cup and looked across his desk at Tribble.

"You had a chance to talk to that boy yet?"

"Naw, cain't nobody get near him yet. Doc Whipple says iddle be a few more days 'fore ennybody can say whether he'll live or die."

Judge Harbuck lit a short cigar. "The moment he opens his eyes, Cat... I want you there like his good strong arm."

He inhaled on the cigar, twirling it slowly, thoughtfully between two fingers. Gray smoke swirled up around his face and neat blond head like a river mist, so that only the bright blue eyes burned through.

"That boy may be a mad-dog killer just like everybody says," the judge continued from behind the wall of smoke. "But we'll be havin' no lynching here in Taliawiga County, legal or otherwise."

"Tell *that* to old Blood 'n' Guts down the hall."

"Randolph's just makin' political hay while the sun's shining," Harbuck said, dismissing the district attorney with a flick of cigar ash.

"Ain't they all," said Tribble. "It's June June June—an' political fever's bustin' out all over."

Harbuck nodded and made a scoffing little sound high up in his nasal passage. "That conniving little runt, Cubbage!"

"You know 'im, Judge?"

"Shortstride?" He shrugged. "Know of him, mostly. He was a defendant once, some years back; on a defaulted promissory note, I think it was. Old man Sudash picked it up for him. And, of course, he used to prosecute all the collection accounts for the old man's store. Mean as a snake," said the judge. "Never been worth nothin' in my estimation, an' never will."

"May damn well be the next mayor of our beloved home town," said Tribble, and clumsily dripped coffee on his pantsleg.

Judge Harbuck smiled faintly. "That confirms it. A man

149

with no more ambition than that will never amount to a hill of beans."

Tribble smiled in his beard, flashing an uneven line of yellow teeth. He sipped his coffee and then shook his leonine head thoughtfully.

"Judge, this here town ain't no better'n it oughta be, an' don't you fergit it. You been readin' them editorials an' watchin' the TV. An' you just oughta *hear* some of the vicious things our good citizens have been suggesting to me ever since you appointed me to represent this poor feller."

"I'm not going to discuss the case with you, Cat. But I will say that this is precisely one of the reasons I appointed you. Nobody else hereabouts could stand up to the sort of battering this case is going to generate.

"Let's put it this way," the judge continued. "There's no tellin' what those yokels over to the P.D. may have already done to incur the wrath of the Supreme Court. It's too late to help any of that now. But we damn sure aren't gonna botch this thing up here in the judicial process."

Tribble finished his coffee and began to stroke his unkempt beard. "I dunno, Horace. There's still Rapid Robert to contend with."

Judge Harbuck stood up and came around the desk. "You let me worry about the district attorney," he said, indicating that the interview was concluded. "You take care of your client."

As Tribble moved into the hall, the judge stopped him.

"One more thing, Cat. I have a pretty good idea what you're thinking about this case. I've put up with a lot of those wild-eyed radical antics of yours over the years, for old times' sake, and because I generally hold with a citizen's right to espouse what he believes in."

Tribble grinned through his scraggly beard like a hungry shark.

"But there'll be none of your political or social posturings in my courtroom. This is a criminal trial, old buddy, and that's *all* it is. Either the boy's guilty or he ain't." He stuck the cigar between his teeth and said, "You try to get cute with me an' I'll come down on you like a ton of bricks."

# Chapter Forty-four

**John Winter was reading the morning paper. Again.**
And Homer had just phoned to tell him that the case was beginning to be more prominently displayed in the Atlanta papers too. Locally, the noon TV news reported that the surgeon who had operated on Eddie James had announced he expected the suspect to recover sufficiently in the coming weeks to assist his court-appointed defense attorney in the preparation of his case. The doctor said he saw no reason the judicial process should not begin to move ahead accordingly.

The phone rang again and while Sal cleared the lunch dishes, John answered the call in the den.

"Do you know what that scoundrel has done now?" It was Homer Stokes again.

"He murdered his surgeon and the entire on-duty staff of the county hospital."

"Not the suspect, John. That demented idiot that the good people of Taliawiga County so proudly call their district attorney. He's bypassed the grand jury altogether and filed a direct information. Murder One."

John sighed. "Well, they don't call him Rapid Robert for nothing."

"I say, John, can he *do* that?" asked Homer. "I mean, is it—legal?"

"He can do it," John said. "It may be slightly unprincipled, but it's legal all right."

"Bloody fascist," Homer mumbled.

"Naw, just a real sharp down-home politician, man. Don't you see? He can't take any chances. The doctor says he *thinks* the suspect will live. He *thinks* he'll be able to assist Tribble in his defense. But Randolph has to be *sure* that he gets his position on the record and before the voting public."

"Yes, I see. This way..."

"If anything should go wrong, if Eddie James should die unexpectedly, or if for some reason he is unable or unfit to stand trial, Randolph has already come down on the side of law and order, mother and country, and death by burning to all who violate the laws of our enlightened society."

There was a brief pause. Then Homer said, "The man's a menace. He *has* to be stopped."

"So long, Homer," John said, and hung up.

He rejoined Sal in the kitchen and helped her put away the last of the dishes. For a moment or two they avoided eye contact. Then they looked at each other and John shrugged, licking a dab of catsup off his finger.

"Homer," he said.

"I'm beginning to get jealous."

He smiled, related the contents of Homer's message.

"Can he do that?"

"You sound like Homer. It's perfectly legal."

"It shouldn't be. One man shouldn't have that much power. Certainly not a man like Robert Randolph."

"What's the difference," John said dryly. "The grand jury's nothing but a rubber stamp for Rapid Robert anyway. The results would have been the same, Sal. It was only a little faster this way."

She shook her head adamantly. "It's wrong. Randolph can't know what happened inside that house yet. How can he be so sure of the facts, that it was first-degree murder rather than second-degree, or maybe even—I don't know—manslaughter?"

John shook his head. He poured a quantity of dish powder into the soap tray and closed the door to the dishwasher. "Well, the D.A. can ask for what he wants."

Sal went to the living room and waited while John activated the dishwasher. When he joined her she asked, "You going back to the university this afternoon?"

"No, I can't get any work done over there. Not with all this ruckus going on. I'll just hang around the den and do a little work on the manuscript."

"I'm going out to the barn and paint for an hour or so while the kids are napping." She was already wearing her studio clothes: hacked-off denim jeans, one of John's T-shirts,

152

with her hair down her back in a single plaited ponytail; and she was barefooted..

"Okay," said John. "But don't forget, I'm taking Davey to the pool around five."

He started for the den and her voice stopped him at the door.

"What's going to happen, John? To that boy in the hospital, I mean."

He looked at her for a moment. "They're going to try him in a month or so. He'll be convicted and then in due course they'll kill him."

He closed the door when he went inside the den.

John worked at the typewriter for some twenty minutes before admitting to himself that what he was writing was worthless. He snatched the sheet of paper out of the roller, balled it up and tossed it into the wastebasket.

Though he felt it was a stupid thing to do at four o'clock in the afternoon, John went to the bar in the corner and mixed a drink. Vodka and tonic on the rocks. Moving across to the large picture window beside the fireplace, he stood for a long moment staring across the hillside into the woods.

He loved to stand at this window like that, barefooted, his feet buried in the deep shag carpet, reaching out occasionally to stroke his hand over the cool rough texture of the stone fireplace beside him. It was this fireplace and the other one in the living room that symbolized for him the memory of his grandfather. These stones *were* old Flood Hightower: hard, crusty, imperishable. The old man was dead, but he was not gone.

A man wasn't gone, thought John, as long as memory survived. And Flood Hightower would survive as long as John Winter lived. Soon it would be time to tell Davey about his great-grandfather. How his own father had come from England and met and married a Shropshire girl on the boat over, and how Flood was born the following year on this very piece of land and how it had always been his and a part of him so that now, even as it was John's and a part of him, one day it would belong to Davey and Cathy and their children and they would belong to the land for time unending.

He was standing now with arms outstretched, both hands open and widespread, pressed firmly against the gritty stone slabs, his drink abandoned, his thoughts turned inward, reaching, digging, deeply searching for the nexus between then and now.

The decision to return had not been an easy one. This land had been his birthright and his torment.

He had gone off with Sal to Europe not as a tourist, not as an expatriate in quest of a salubrious clime, but as a seeker in search of his own personal place in the sun.

Three years later, the arc had turned. The road to *There* had come to look like the road *Home*. And so, he had brought his family back to Georgia. So far it had been a good decision.

# Chapter Forty-five

"It's a pleasure to make your acquaintance, John. I've heard a lot of fine things about you. The governor sends his warmest regards."

Harry Downs was a dumpling of a man. Pink-haired, red-faced and freckled. He dressed like a used-car salesman and was about as sharp as the tusk of a wild boar. John had heard enough about the man not to be misled by his benign appearance. A lawyer, a businessman and a self-made millionaire—now Downs was a professional politician. He knew everything about Georgia politics and everyone engaged in the sorry business. He had been the governor's right-hand man for the last ten years. It was said in political circles that he had made Barrow a state senator, then a governor, and would make his man President in a few years' time, after the public had forgotten and forgiven the state of Georgia for sending them a previous occupant of that august office, a most unfavorite son indeed.

Downs extended his pudgy hand as he came into the

sunken living room with Homer Stokes trailing a step or two behind. John shook hands, not altogether unfriendly, and motioned the two men to a seat.

"Ah, what a lovely room," Downs said to Sal, as she returned with a fresh pot of coffee and the necessary accoutrements on a pewter serving tray. "And such a magnificent fireplace."

Sal smiled and began to pass around the cups and saucers, while John took orders for drinks. A whisky for the governor's aide, brandy for Sal, Homer and himself.

"What a fascinating painting," Harry Downs remarked, indicating the striking abstract of blues and blacks and yellows that graced the widest wall in the room. "Something you picked up in Europe? Or New York?"

"It's one of Sal's," Homer said, holding his cup while Sal poured.

"Oh yes, I do remember now. Some years back...you had established quite a reputation in Atlanta..."

"I was known in some circles for my artistic expression too," Sal said with a straight face.

Her little joke was only momentarily lost on Downs. Then he smiled, remembering his hostess's activist participation. But he didn't respond; he was here to win friends and influence people. He looked at Sal a moment longer and then back to the painting. "It's incredibly—powerful. That slashing use of black is...well, I don't really know enough about abstract art to adequately express myself."

"But you know what you like," smiled Sal as she poured for him.

"Exactly."

John came over from the sideboard with the drinks. "Like Justice Stewart in his Supreme Court ruling on pornography."

Downs looked up and laughed. "Yes. I may not be able to define it, but I know it when I see it."

They talked of generalities for a few moments. Then the old pro got down to business.

"I do appreciate your allowing me to visit with you on such short notice."

John nodded. "You're welcome anytime, Harry. But in this particular instance, it won't do you any good." He looked sharply at Homer. "I told both of you on the phone—"

"Yes, I know you did. Your position is clear, your reasoning unassailable and your refusal sufficiently Shermanesque to impress even me."

"Then why have you come?"

He gestured with both palms turned up. "To get you to change your mind, of course."

Everyone laughed and settled back in a relaxed mood. Any tension that might have been felt was relieved by the easy rapport they had so quickly established. It was, in fact, the only thing that bothered John. He already knew instinctively that he was going to like the guy.

"You know what that skunk in the D.A.'s office will try to do with this case?"

"Of course," said John.

"Well, the governor has no intention of letting him get away with it. He's not going to allow Randolph the freedom of riding all over the hills of middle Georgia at the head of a legal lynch mob. And he damn sure isn't going to let the bastard come galloping into the capital like a white knight on a law-and-order charger when the governor's term is up next year."

John set aside his coffee and picked up his brandy snifter and commenced swirling it. "Look, Harry. I've been over all of this with Homer."

"He needs you, John. The governor really *needs* you with him in this thing."

John almost laughed at the man's sudden affectation of Lyndon Johnson sincerity. "Maybe so," John replied. "But I don't need him or it, and I want no part of it."

"Why is it so important that John be the one to handle this? Surely, there are other lawyers?"

Harry Downs turned to Sal. "There are other lawyers, of course. But none as qualified as your husband for this particular case, at this particular time, in this particular location. Randolph will make a mockery out of the trial. And we can't send in an outsider."

"Why not?"

"Countians wouldn't respond well to that, Sal," John said. "You've lived here long enough to understand the attitude toward outsiders."

"Yes, haven't I though," she said sourly. "That old-fashioned down home hospitality to one and all."

Homer said, "An outsider as special prosecutor would be strung up alongside the James boy. At least figuratively speaking."

"But why?" Sal demanded obstinately. "Surely if the boy is convicted—if he's guilty, that is—"

"It isn't just the conviction, Sal. If that was all there was to it..." Harry Downs allowed his voice to trail off and then emptied his glass in a long draft.

John took his glass across the room for a refill, listening as Downs continued.

"I don't know if Homer has told you, but Governor Barrow is playing for very high stakes in the coming year. As you know"—he took a deep breath, accepted the replenished drink from his host—"a governor cannot succeed himself in the state of Georgia. Clyde has decided to launch a crusade to repeal the capital punishment statute." He nodded to John. "More than that, really. He plans to reorganize the entire criminal justice system. The capital punishment issue is just one of many aspects of the program. A very important aspect, of course; perhaps the single most important thing he will ever try to accomplish."

He paused. No one spoke.

"Think of it," he said. "Here is a chance for a man to make a significant contribution to the advance of civilization. He does not have to concern himself with votes or with re-election to office. For the first time in years he can run entirely on his conscience and on his intellect. Both—his conscience and his brain—tell him that capital punishment is useless as a deterrent to crime, that it is unworthy of a civilized government, and that quite probably it is unethical, immoral and unconstitutional as well."

Again there was silence in the room.

Finally Homer said, "Just look at the scenario for tragedy, John. Randolph, Cubbage, Charlie Tate. And God help us if Chester Biggs gets involved in some direct way. And you know he will, John. You *know* he will."

John shook his head. "Not to mention Bobcat Tribble," he said dully.

"God, yes. It will be a travesty, John. Taliawiga County will be a disgrace before the world. And a boy is going to *die*."

John flinched. "A lot of others have already died," he said sharply. "And chances are, this fellow James is responsible. One life in return for six or eight or so... I don't know, maybe the odds aren't so disproportionate after all."

"You don't mean that," Homer said gently.

"I suppose not," John sighed.

"Anyway," said Harry Downs, "it's not for a bunch of lynch-crazy cretins to decide."

"That's right. Nor shall they. Even if James *is* convicted, it's still up to the governor whether he lives or dies."

Downs shook his head judiciously and said, "Not this governor, my friend. You know how long the appellate process takes. Clyde won't be in office when that hot little item drops in the hopper." Downs paused, leaning forward tensely. "Besides, John—that's not the extent of the issue. The process itself can be every bit as destructive as the final result."

The phone began to ring and Homer said, "Harry's right, John. You know he is," as Sal went to the kitchen to answer the phone.

There was a long silence.

"It's the governor," she said, returning to the room. Her tanned face was pale and drawn, her eyes glittering with anticipation. "He wants to talk to Harry."

Harry went briskly to the kitchen. John rose as Sal crossed the room, and they embraced.

Downs returned and said, "He wants to talk to you."

Sal said, "John...?"

"Don't worry, honey." He tried a reassuring smile but lost it.

"Wait," she said, and he stopped at the door. "I think you've got to take the appointment," she sighed.

"What?"

"Oh, I say!" Homer exclaimed, jumping to his feet.

John kept his eyes locked on Sal, waiting.

"It's the only way," she said, softly. "Don't you see? You're the only one who can stop this madness from happening here. Everybody says you're the only one."

"You really don't know what you're saying." John went back and took her by the shoulders, more roughly than he had intended. "You can't hold up under a thing like this, Sal. And what about the kids—"

"Don't you *dare* do that!" she snapped, her dark eyes flashing. "Don't you dare use me and the children as an excuse. Not again, not this time."

He looked as if she had slapped him. "What are you—saying?"

"I'm saying that this time you've got to stand and fight for what you believe in. You talk about this sort of evil in our midst, you write about it, and lecture about it...now you've got to *do* something about it." She moved closer to him and said, "You can't use me and the children as an excuse not to face up to your responsibilities. And these are *your* people, honey. You're responsible for them. And if they're wrong—and they *are*—you've got to make them see that they're wrong."

Now it was her turn to take *him* by the shoulders.

"Don't you see?" she asked, imploring him with her eyes as well as her voice. "If you can see that justice is done, and keep these people from lynching this boy at the same time, then you've got to do it. At least you've got to *try*."

He looked at her for a very long time, astonishment mingled with love and pride and pity; pity because he knew very well that she didn't even begin to comprehend what she had let herself in for.

"Well, that was quite a speech," he said finally, softly, and a trifle sadly. Then he took her in his arms and kissed the top of her head.

Vaguely, he heard the voice of Harry Downs in the kitchen.

"He can't come to the phone right now, Governor. But everything's all right; he'll do it. You can put out the announcement anytime you like."

# Chapter Forty-six

Governor Clyde Barrow issued the statement concerning the appointment of a special prosecutor the next morning, less than an hour after Bobcat Tribble's press conference on the steps of the Taliawiga County Courthouse.

Newsmen were smirking as they made notes and ground away with their cameras while Tribble issued his statement. "I have been appointed by the court to represent Mr. Eddie James in the charges brought against him by direct information upon the initiative of District Attorney Randolph."

He took a deep, rather weary breath and resettled his

rumpled white linen suit coat over his hunched shoulders. "I did not seek this appointment," he continued, gazing with intense sincerity into the glare of the television cameras. "I do not desire to bear this burden. But I will not shirk from my sacred duty." He paused for effect and then said with devout conviction, "I *will* represent Eddie James. I will do my duty in the face of whatever opposition arises. Due process will have its unyielding spokesman. Whether justice will prevail is the province of the trial court, the criminal justice system of our state, and the citizens of our community."

Tribble's performance was soon overshadowed, however, by the furor raised in response to the governor's subsequent announcement of John Winter's appointment.

Aaron Goetz was having his coffee break with Danny Telander in the back room of the hardware store when the radio announcer's mellifluous voice broke into the sequence of their World Series predictions and a jarring note caught Aaron's ear.

"Hey, Sophie. Turn that volume up a little, will ya, darlin'."

His wife reached for the radio on the shelf behind the sales counter.

"...shortly after nine o'clock this morning. John Winter, a former Assistant U. S. Attorney in Atlanta, currently a professor of criminal justice at Adelphi University, has been named special prosecutor. The governor said..."

"My God! Didja hear *that?*" said Aaron, advancing upon the vicinity of the radio, his blue eyes wide with astonishment, his soft mane of wavy white hair agitated by such sudden exertion. *"John Winter."*

"I thought he was off in Yurrop or some such," said Telander.

"Been back three years or more now, Danny."

"Lord, don't time fly?"

At the corner of Main Street and First Avenue a man jumped out of a car in the middle of the intersection and ran shouting toward Mayor Tittle, who was drinking a Coca-Cola in the shade of a Confederate war memorial.

The mayor spilled Coke on his tie, dropped the bottle in the grass and loped off toward the courthouse.

"Jesus!" Gordon Joyner was having his hair cut and jumped so hard when the announcer read the news that Doc Sample almost nicked his ear.

"Good Lord," exclaimed Matthew Grit, reclining in the next chair awaiting his turn under the scissors, "just you wait'll ol' Rapid Robert hears tell of *this* piece of news."

Around the room some of the men began to chuckle. Others shook their heads in dumb wonder and clucked their tongues against the roofs of their mouths. Rufus Anderson, the shoeshine boy, kept his head down and his eyes fixed firmly on the job at hand.

Lamar Stick, on his way back to the trailer for a meeting with Slideen, snapped off the radio, looked over at the Winterland and said, "Prick."

In his walnut paneled office at Pettigrew Lumber Company Orin Pettigrew picked up the telephone and placed a direct call to his daughter in New Orleans. He wanted Rachel to hear the latest news about John Winter from him rather than from some meddling town gossip.

"Have you heard the news?" asked the Chief Assistant U.S. Attorney in Atlanta, rushing into his scowling boss's office.

"The deceitful sonofabitch!" snarled Thurlow Wheems, slamming his fist on the desk so hard it knocked a basket of mail onto the floor. "Both of 'em. The bastards. Wouldn't come back to work for me. Oh, no. But he'll work for that lily-livered milquetoast simpleton in the governor's office."

"What do we do now?" asked the assistant. "How does this affect—"

"It doesn't affect our plans one goddamn bit. Not a bit!" exclaimed Wheems. The natural darkness of his face had deepened with his anger to the blackness of a thundercloud. He got up and went to the window overlooking the city. From his office in the Federal Building he could see the top of the gold dome of the state capitol. "I'll still be sitting in that chair two years from now... and our friend John Winter will rue the day he ever fucked with me."

"That kooky wife of his probably egged him into it."

Wheems turned in a fury. "I should have crushed her myself, when I had the chance. Fuckin' whore." He began to pace the room. "Bleeding heart, social misfits. I'll show them. I'll show 'em all. Fuckin' Clyde Barrow too."

He spun sharply around and bumped into a cigarette stand, knocking it over and spilling ash on the carpet. "I *will* be the next governor," he said. "And anybody—*anybody*—who is not with me is against me!"

\* \* \*

The lead story on the noon television report was given over to John Winter's appointment. There was no live interview as yet with the new special prosecutor, but the local channel anchorman was giving a brief biographical résumé of the appointee as Robert Randolph stood in the motel lobby with a crowd of assistants and hangers-on, watching in stunned disbelief.

"...football star at the University of Georgia, an army officer and an Assistant U. S. Attorney in Atlanta during the explosive turmoil of the sixties. Winter is reported to have prosecuted more than a hundred serious felonies in those days, while losing merely a handful. Governor Barrow expressed his confidence that the prosecution of the suspect in the recent Cubbage murders will be handled with efficiency, thoroughness and an absolute observance of fair play and due process."

"I don't believe it," muttered Randolph.

"...Governor Barrow emphasized that the appointment of a special prosecutor in no way reflects upon the integrity or the capabilities of the elected district attorney in Taliawiga County."

"Hah! The sonofabitch."

"...he further pointed out, however, that in such cases involving such a heinous crime, when emotions and passions might well be expected to run at fever pitch, that even the mere suggestion of political considerations involved in the criminal justice process must be scrupulously avoided."

"What the hell would *that* mealymouthed two-faced bastard know about scruples?" said Randolph.

"What are we going to do, Bob?"

He turned to his assistant and said, "What I always do. Fight fire with fire."

He started for the banquet room at the end of the corridor, but stopped halfway to the door, straightened his tie and took a deep breath. Randolph was an imposing figure. Six feet four, lean and mean. He looked the part of the ex-fighting Marine that he was. Korea veteran, highly decorated, wounded. He had a reputation as a fighter, never backed down and was most dangerous when under attack. He turned to his assistant again, asked, "Who the hell we talkin' to t'day?"

"Why, uh, the middle Georgia chapter of the Lions Club International."

Randolph grinned his wide toothpaste ad smile. "Perfect. Just watch this old boy beard alla' those lions in their own den." He looked back down the corridor at the face on the TV screen. It was a picture of John Winter. "Take my forum away from me, will they? All they've succeeded in doing is kicking me out of the courthouse. They ain't no way they gonna keep me off the streets, an' tha's where this old war's gonna be won."

# Chapter Forty-seven

"I apologize for all this covert cops and robbers rigamarole, Dean. But it really is necessary in order to evade the—termites of the press, as Captain Tate calls them."

John went to the window of Homer's seldom-used office in the bank and peered out from behind the heavy damask drapery. John had held a press conference concerning his appointment, and in order to avoid the reporters afterward, had slipped out a basement door of the courthouse and walked as fast as he could without attracting attention over to the back entrance of the People's Bank. It was after closing hour and Homer himself had met John at the door.

"We've got to quit meeting like this," John had joked, and Homer replied, "Upstairs, the coast is clear. Dean Witcomb's already here. I called him for you."

Even under those circumstances, Dean Witcomb was as deferential as ever.

"Don't apologize in the least," he said nervously, perspiring above his collar and tie. As usual, he was impeccably groomed. John had wanted to talk with him before the announcement but it just had not worked out that way. The dean had been stunned by the appointment, and among the faculty and students, no one was talking about anything else.

"It's all very exciting, I must say. A background in sixteenth-century literature doesn't exactly prepare one for such down-to-earth hard-core realism."

"I don't know," John said, turning from the window. "Half of this country's clandestine services are administered by fellows with academic backgrounds not too dissimilar from your own."

"Oh?" Witcomb was genuinely surprised, and, thought John, more than a little flattered.

"Cecil, this is important or I wouldn't have imposed on you this way," he said.

"Please, John. If there is anything I can do to help. Anything at all..."

"There is. You can run interference for me with the Old Man. I just don't have the time, Cecil. This mess I've gone and got myself in will take every minute of my time and all of my energies for the next few weeks."

"Oh? I didn't realize..."

"There is no part-time approach to this sort of thing, Cecil. But I want you to assure President Reed that I have made arrangements to have my classes covered, and my final exam is already prepared. I'll need a leave of absence, of course. For the remainder of the summer session."

"Goodness. Surely not...for the whole summer?"

"At best," said John. "I'll accept whatever pay cut you or the president or the trustees suggest."

"Well, I see no need for...I mean...I don't think..."

"I think they will," John smiled. He rose, drawing the dean to his feet also, and led him toward the great mahogany double doors that opened into the paneled corridor. "I just want you to make sure the president understands my position. As soon as this thing is over, I expect to be right back in the classroom."

"Surely not in the classroom, John. After our little talk the other day..."

"Cecil, this just isn't the time. Besides, I think you will find the situation is somewhat changed."

"I...I don't know what you mean," the dean said, perplexed, as John opened the door and a uniformed security guard immediately hove to attention at his station across the corridor.

"Well, let's just table the subject for the time being, okay?" Before the dean could respond, John signaled to the security guard. "Would you please see Dean Witcomb out, Sam. And then come straight back here, if you will, and help me with a couple of important matters."

"Yes sir!"

"Thank you for coming, Cecil. I'll be in touch."

\*   \*   \*

"What the hell you doin' with all these boxes?" Robert Randolph asked the captain of detectives.

"Your replacement wants 'em ready in a separate office, by eight o'clock tonight," Tate replied.

"My replacement, your ass," the D.A. grumbled, lighting a cigarette and shaking out the match flame will ill-concealed chagrin. "And he wants me, Lieutenant Burke and every detective who's worked directly on the case to be standing by."

Randolph shrugged. He had made his estimation of the situation but saw no reason to share his deductions with the likes of Charlie Tate. He knew he could trust Charlie only up to a point. Straight Arrow, as he was derisively called on the street and in the department, would not play politics with a case. At least not for someone else. Certainly not for Randolph. Still, Tate could be useful, if handled properly. "Typical file review. Nothing more sinister than that. What I want you to do, Charlie, is keep me posted. I mean every time that professor dots an *i* or crosses a *t* I want to know!"

"John Winter may not approve of that little administrative wrinkle," said Charlie Tate. "You know, he's pretty much of a stickler for rules and regulations, due process an' things like that."

"Look, Charlie. What that ivory-tower egghead don't know ain't gonna hurt you or me. Right?"

"You're the district attorney."

"Damn right I am. And this is still *my* county. Le's don't too many of us forget that liddle ol' fact." Randolph grinned crookedly and slapped the captain of detectives on the shoulder.

# Chapter Forty-eight

**The room was approximately 9 x 12, situated at the end** of the corridor within easy walking distance of Captain Tate's office on the second floor of the new City Hall Building. There was a large metal table, the top of which was cigarette-scarred, cut and marked over every square inch of its surface. There were five hard-backed folding chairs ranged around the table, and three Publix cardboard boxes stacked on one end. John Winter smiled at the Spartan accommodations, thanked Lieutenant Burke and said that he would call when he was ready to confer or if he was in need of assistance.

John closed the door, removed the jacket of his seersucker suit, loosened his tie and rolled his sleeves up to his elbows.

It was five minutes past eight when he opened the first box.

At eight-thirty he asked Lieutenant Burke for a yellow legal pad.

At nine-fifteen a secretary brought him an unrequested cup of black coffee on a serving tray with cream and sugar on the side.

At ten-twenty John asked Lieutenant Burke to send for Captain Tate, Sergeant Martinez and patrolman Grover Binns. He also invited Burke to join them.

Captain Tate arrived last, almost certainly on purpose. His glance shifted quickly from the boxes on the floor to the yellow legal pad on the table, to the cup of untouched coffee. He looked at John Winter, who was leaning against the wall in one corner of the room, his arms folded across his chest.

"Have you had a chance...I mean..." Tate just didn't know where to go with it, so he left it there.

"Have a seat, Captain."

Charlie Tate sat down, looked at Burke and the two officers, and then at the legal pad again. Page one was covered with notes and he had a good idea that a couple more were too. He cleared his throat.

"Well, Doc. I, uh, hope you found everything you, uh, needed."

John smiled thinly. "Not exactly everything, Captain." He turned to Lieutenant Burke. "Lieutenant, am I to understand that you were the ranking officer in charge of the crime scene until Captain Tate's arrival?"

In view of Fred Burke's reaction, John Winter might just as well have said something like "So you're the ignorant sonofabitch who's responsible for this fiasco," for the lieutenant was literally speechless with fright.

"Well...I...I..."

"That's right," said Captain Tate. "Fred was the man in charge until I got out to the house."

John looked at the patrolman. "And you, patrolman Binns, you were the first man on the scene after your two fellow officers had been hit."

"Yes sir."

Next he looked at Sergeant Martinez. "You were the first detective to reach the scene." The sergeant nodded his assent and John said, "You spent most of your time next door attempting to interview Naomi Hicks."

"I *did* interview her," said Martinez.

John sat down and moved the legal pad closer to his position. He picked up his ballpoint pen and, reading down the page, occasionally made a check mark in the ruled margin, underlined a word or two or circled a phrase here and there. Then he lifted the page and repeated the process on the next page of notes. The whole thing took about a minute and a half during which nothing was said. Patrolman Binns coughed nervously, Martinez yawned, Burke stared at the table and Captain Tate cleared his throat again.

Finally John Winter looked up, sighed thoughtfully and removed his horn-rimmed reading glasses. "That's all for tonight," he said. "But I'll want to talk with each one of you first thing in the morning."

They all stood up, except John and Captain Tate.

"Uh, Dr. Winter, sir." It was Sergeant Martinez. "Begging your pardon, sir. But I have to be on duty in the morning at—"

"I want you all in my office at eight o'clock sharp. Eight o'clock, my office, in the courthouse, third floor."

Captain Tate said, "What office, Doc? I mean, you don't have—"

"Just ask at the information desk, fellas. I'll leave the office number at the desk. Goodnight, and thanks for coming."

When they were gone John turned to Tate and said, "Do you call this an investigation?"

"We got the skunk that done it, ain't we?"

"I don't know, man. I don't know whether you've got him or not."

"What the hell you talking about?"

"I'm talking about evidence, Charlie. What you have accomplished so far is an arrest of a suspected murderer and a premature information—"

"Don't hang *that* one on me," snapped Charlie.

"Neither the arrest nor the information has any evidentiary value—I'm sure you are aware of that."

"Look, we have the gun and a ballistics match—"

"What you *have,* Charlie, are a bunch of dead bodies, a gun that killed most of them, and a suspect."

"It's *his* gun!"

"Prove it."

"He carried the fucking thing in there—"

"Prove it."

"Aw, f'Pete's sake, Doc. This here ain't Criminal Investigation 210. I mean, what the hell, man—"

"What the hell is right. What the hell is going on here? You have damned little of evidentiary value, Charlie. Let me tell you a little story." John got up and walked to the end of the table. He put his foot up on a chair and leaned a forearm across his knee.

"Eddie James was hitchhiking on the Interstate one day," he began. "A motorist stopped for him and a little while later they drove into Adelphi. The guy was a perfect stranger, see. Eddie had never met him before. He said he had to stop by a friend's house before continuing the journey. So he drove out to the Cubbage place, got out and went around back. Eddie waited in the car, a little puzzled but not really concerned. And then he heard a shot ring out from behind the house.

"Well now, Eddie's first inclination was to drive away, but the guy had taken the car keys with him. Another shot rang out and then another, and Eddie jumped out of the car and started to bolt for it. But there was the guy who'd picked him up, pointing an army .45 right at him. He forced Eddie around behind the house, up on the porch and into the kitchen.

"That's when Eddie caught the meat cleaver in the shoulder. His companion blasted Gladys Cubbage and prodded Eddie into the living room. The old man cut loose with one side of the double-barreled shotgun and ripped part of Eddie's arm away. His companion got the old soldier right in the face. Eddie, dazed and bleeding from multiple wounds, was down on the floor now, when the man pumped his last round into poor little Layde Cubbage. Then he walked over, wiped the gun handle on his shirt, clamped it in Eddie's hand and said, 'Thanks, sucker.'

"As the man started to leave, a patrol car drew up in front of the house with lights flashing and siren blaring. Calmly, this dude picks up the old soldier's shotgun and steps over to the far side of the darkened room. When the two idiot police officers burst through the front door with their service revolvers blazing the man calmly lets them have it dead-on with a shotgun blast. Then he drops the shotgun in Eddie's lap, walks out to his car and drives away."

John suddenly stopped talking.

Tate was looking at him with his mouth half open, transfixed as if he was a cobra mesmerized before its tamer.

Finally, Tate licked his lips with a couple of sweeps of his tongue and said, "Shit, Doc. You don't expect me to swaller a fuckin' harebrained tale like that."

"Of course not," said John. "But it doesn't matter about you one way or the other. It's what the *jury* will swallow by the time Bobcat Tribble gets through telling 'em *his* story that counts."

Tate sat there with both arms hanging by his side. "Jesus H. Christ," he muttered.

"Right," said John, and he walked over to the door and opened it. "Get somebody to load those boxes for me into my car."

"What? Why, hell no," Tate said, jumping to his feet. "You cain't do that."

"The hell I can't. *I'll* conduct the investigation from now on, Charlie. We'll run it out of my office over at the courthouse. I want two of your best investigators assigned directly to me. You will coordinate matters here in the P.D."

John called Lieutenant Burke and ordered him to get someone to carry the boxes down to his car.

Tate went past him in the corridor like a bowling ball.

"Hey, Charlie?"

The captain stopped down at the end of the hall, at the door to his office.

"See you at eight sharp," John said. Then he cocked his head to one side and grinned affably. "Just a point of curiosity, Cap'n. What kind of grade *did* I give you in Criminal Investigation 210?"

# Chapter Forty-nine

"It's just hard to believe that such a rich, educated and prominent fella can be such a regular hog at bottom, now ain't it though?"

Sheriff Biggs was sprawled on the sofa, his sweaty face yet a mite flushed, his corpulent legs extended with his booted heels resting upon a flimsy coffee table. His fly was still unzipped.

"Jasper's a nice man, Chester. He don't never hurt nobody," said Lucy Pittman, hanging his freshly rinsed handkerchief over a metal coat hanger to dry. She had already closed the curtain over the two-way mirror and washed out his soiled handkerchief, and now she came over to kneel beside him with a washbasin of warm soapy water and a thick washcloth.

"It'd sure law hurt the holy hell out of that wife 'n' daughter of his iffen they was to get wind of the old boy's perverted toe-suckin' ways," the sheriff allowed sleepily.

"But they ain't got no business ever learnin' any such thing," she said, carefully lifting and soaping his flaccid penis. Chester merely chuckled, leaned his head back on the sofa and closed his eyes as she wrapped his fat little joint in the warm cloth, squeezing the bulk of it in the palm of her hand. He lay unmoving for some moments, breathing phlegmatically like a beached whale in a soft summer mist.

Chester was a man of few and simple pleasures. Food, television baseball, politics and—as he called it—policing. Sex in any active sense had not been one of his numbered pleasures for nearly two decades. Not since his inordinate love of food had rendered any such prurient interest futile if not downright absurd. Since he had discovered Lucy Pittman, however, and brought her under his protective wing, porno films and magazines imported from Memphis and Atlanta had taken a back seat to voyeuristic delights framed within the rectangle of the two-way mirror on Lucy's bedroom wall.

Not only had it served to relieve him of any sexual anxieties that he might otherwise have suffered, it helped him no end in keeping a firm grip on more than a few leading citizens of Taliawiga County. Biggs often joked with Lucy that he obtained more useful information on this side of her bedroom mirror than he got from an identical mirror in one of the interrogation rooms at the Sheriff's Department.

With this thought in mind, he half opened one eye and said, "So you can just take all that there talk about leavin' an' put it right straight out of yore mind. You hear me now?"

Lucy zipped his fly, rose and set the basin on a nearby lampstand. "I'm scared, Chester. I can't help it." She dug into the pocket robe for a cigarette. "This here thing with Elton has done spooked me somethin' awful."

"Oughta be damn glad to be shut of the goddam ape," Biggs snorted.

"Oh I *am*. Jesus, I can't tell you what it's like just to know..." She inhaled deeply and trapped the acrid smoke in her lungs. "But it's all this other stuff, Chester," she said with a burst of smoke issuing from her face. "I mean, what the hell was the fool up to this time?"

"Who knows? The kid was a goddamn buffoon. If only I'd knowed..." He opened both eyes this time and raised his head a half inch to look at her. "The next time you keep somethin' important from me—anything—well now, we got that all sorted out, ain't we, darlin'?"

She nodded and anxiously went to work on the cigarette again. "But...but Chester...what if they trace everything back to *me?*"

"Hell, they ain't got nothin' on you, girl."

"It's *my* gun, Chester!"

"But they ain't no records to say so, now is they?"

She shook her head. "No. I don't even remember where I got it. I know they warn't no paperwork though."

"So you're home free," he said, closing his eyes again and lowering his head.

"But what was it *doing* there?" she almost shrieked. "How could someone have found *my* gun in the gutter in front of the Cubbage house?"

Chester Biggs shrugged and began to scratch at his testicles. "You said Elton had yore car all that afternoon and part of the night. All that stuff you found in the back end—TVs, toasters, fans an' what have you." He chuckled dryly. "The ol' boy was just planning to open up a liddle business, don't you see. Now Lucy, stop yore worryin'. It's all nice and simple, really. Elton was pullin' a lot of jobs around the county, prolly tryin' to get hold of a bit of travelin' money. He was usin' yore car. An' yore gun. Okay. You know what a clumsy nincompoop he was. The gun was in the car when he went over to the Cubbage place, an' the fool kicked it out accidentally or somethin'."

He laughed, dropped his big heavy feet to the floor and pulled into a sitting position.

"Tate an' all those assholes over to the P.D. just stompin' around all over the place. Just stompin' around, an' there lays what mighta been an important piece of evidence right out in the front yard." He began to guffaw. "An' a civilian has to go 'n' find it for 'em!"

"But the *car*, Chester." Lucy was pacing up and down the room in front of him. She stopped abruptly and waved the cigarette in the air like a boy's lighted sparkler. "The car wadden *there*."

He sighed. "Look, I don't know yet, Lucy. I just don't know." He got laboriously to his feet and began to yawn. "But I'm gonna find out. Chances are he went to the Cubbage house, left with the car and then came back on foot."

"Why?"

"I don't know, goddammit! I didn't know he even knew the

Cubbage slut. Maybe he didn't. Coulda been somethin' to do with the brother. Or maybe he was just casing the place. Hell, I don't know," he said, walking over to the handkerchief on the coat hanger. "You reckon this here thing's dry by now?"

"I s'pose." She took his handkerchief off the hanger and folded it for him. "Sure you don't wanta stay the night?" Lucy asked, walking with him to the door. "I don't have anybody else booked. I always cancel out when I know you're comin'."

"Sure you do, honey. You know who butters yore bread."

He opened her robe abruptly to the waist, watching avidly as the two enormous breasts tumbled free. "You know, ol' girl—when I was a kid I used to roll watermelons off 'a trucks that warn't half as big 'n' juicy as them tits 'a yourn."

He pinched a nipple hard enough to make her wince and said, "Now you just get all them there travel plans out of yore head, you hear me now. I been taking purty good care of you for more years than I can remember offhand. I ain't gonna let no fools come interfering with my way of doin' things now. I'll get to the bottom of all this, an' I'll see to it that it don't have nothin' to do with you."

He waddled on out to the police cruiser and drove away.

Lucy Pittman closed the door, watched out the window until his car was out of sight and then raised the shade up and down three times.

Moments later a figure rushed out of the bushes across the street and hurried furtively up on the front porch. She let him in and bolted the door.

Down the block, with the nose of the cruiser barely visible and the lights extinguished, Chester Biggs sat watching as the shoddy little drama unfolded down the street.

"Cancels all her bookings on my nights," he said aloud, laughing. It wasn't a pretty laugh.

He wondered who the dude in the bushes was tonight. Good thing it wasn't wintertime. The poor guy would freeze his pecker off.

He cranked the engine, hit the light switch and turned into the intersection away from Lucy Pittman's house. Maybe six years was long enough, he thought. Maybe their relationship was getting stale. Maybe he oughta encourage her to hit the road after all, and import some little chippie in from oh, say, N'Awlins maybe. Something younger, cleaner, fresher. Lucy was getting a little long in the tooth, no two ways about it.

"God, but what a pair of titties," he said, turned on the siren and floored the accelerator just for the simple hell of it. Wadden he the cock of Taliawiga County, sure enough? Mr. Big. Big Chester Biggs. Always had been, always would be.

He put back his head and came out with a Rebel yell to beat the band.

# Chapter Fifty

**John Winter heard the muffled wail of the siren out on** the highway, pushed back the file and removed his reading glasses. Taking a deep breath, he rubbed his eyes and then began to rotate his head on the stem of his neck. His lower back ached too. He had been at his desk for hours. He didn't know what time it was but had heard the clock strike two some while ago.

Might as well go on to bed, he thought wearily. What's the point in going through any of this again? He had sifted through every piece of evidence the P.D. possessed, read every file, investigative report and interview sheet time and again. He picked up a glossy eight-by-ten photograph at random—this one of the Pittman boy, sprawled over the end of the back porch—and stared at it with vague detachment.

What was the connection between Elton Pittman and the Cubbage family, he wondered. It had to be Sissie.

He put the photo down and picked up the girl's diary. He thumbed his way to the last few pages and just let his eyes skim lightly over the girlish scrawl. After a few moments he gave it up. Sissie's handwriting was atrocious, her spelling disgraceful. The teachers and administrators who had passed her out of high school were felons in their own right.

In addition to the poor penmanship, she had apparently used some sort of code of her own devising that, although it may have simplified her work, made it tedious going indeed for the uninitiated. Of course she had never intended her creative efforts to see the light of publication.

Still, some parts of the recitation were clear enough. Certainly the last few paragraphs referred to Elton Pittman. The subject of her scathing remarks was alternately identified as A.P., the Dummy, the Albino, Apo and the Idiot. John was pretty certain from the part of the text that he could make out that the references were to a single individual.

He took up the book and glanced over the lines still again. "The Albino has really put his foot in it this time. Jesus, the creep ought to rilly be locked up for good. If they katch his ass this time they'll burne it to a crispe." Then there was something about him being "scared shitless" of Sissie's old man. She hadn't wanted to see Elton. She had smoked with Gordie and just wanted to "fuck off around the house." But Apo had raised hell on the phone, he was really in a panic and she had been afraid he might do something crazy that would rub off on her.

Apparently, after Elton had been with her for an hour or so he had panicked at the thought of her old man coming home unexpectedly and finding his old lady's car outside. So he had taken the car home and then returned on foot some while later in such a panic that Sissie thought she might have to dope him to calm him down. He had lost his gun. His mother's gun, actually. It was in the car and when he got home it was gone. He wanted Sissie to help him find the gun.

"The dum fucker has rilly gone and done it," she wrote. "He's wasted a dude and kidnaped his girl frind—all for a meesely five bucks."

John looked up and stared across the room, his gaze falling somewhere in the middle distance. What dude? What girl? If only Sissie had finished the entry.

"If he's kaused any truble for me," she concluded, "I'll kill the basterd myself."

John got up and walked around his huge desk. He was stiff and sore all over. He began stretching his arms high up over his head. Then he went to the fireplace and leaned over with his arms extended, palms spread against the great rock slabs, and did a few pushouts.

What the hell have I stumbled on, he thought, recalling some of the names in earlier sections of Sissie's diary. Not everything was encoded. And many of the names she had devised were so transparent as to be useless. In the context, Gordie almost had to be Gordon Joyner. A regular customer for pot and cocaine. Sissie was dealing dope? Maybe that's why she was killed. And sex? Sissie Cubbage and Gordon Joyner? Though he had no idea who the Cop's Wife might be, John was sure that the Big Man references could only apply to Chester Biggs.

"Sissie Cubbage and *Chester Biggs?*" he said aloud, and went back to the desk.

He rifled the stack of porno pictures taken from the girl's bedroom and pulled out a photograph of Sissie on her knees with a man's penis in her mouth. John had no doubt that the man's gargantuan khaki-covered belly belonged to Biggs. But his head had been purposely lopped off the picture. Why?

And where was the matching part of the photograph? "Where the hell are the negatives?" He found at least ten more photographs of men in sexual attitudes in which the male faces had been mutilated beyond recognition. A few of the mutilations even involved the faces of women in the company of other women.

Not that Sissie herself was always identifiable. But John could tell her from the shape of her body, the style of her hair, the protected flatness of her bosom. She had been an awfully busy little girl. No wonder she didn't have enough time for school.

But what the hell did it all mean? What was she up to? If only he had time to figure out the whole diary. The file reflected that no one in the P.D. had done so yet. Apparently Charlie Tate had not deemed it interesting enough to give it more than a cursory glance.

As the grandfather clock struck three John closed the diary and pushed his chair away from the desk. He had been appointed to prosecute a fellow named Eddie James. So far, a review of the case materials cast Eddie James as one of the least interesting characters in a drama that seemed about to expand to a cast of thousands.

He would certainly prosecute Eddie James if the evidence warranted it. But he was beginning to have the feeling that the list of indictable defendants yet to be developed would simply dwarf the James involvement by comparison.

# Chapter Fifty-one

**Only one assistant district attorney was on the premises** when John arrived at Superior Court. A young fellow named Peoples, recently out of law school. He recognized John immediately, reacting to his unexpected appearance as if he were Leon Jaworski or some such giant-killer come to stem the tide of a small-town Dixiegate.

The eager Peoples helped John carry the boxes into the new office and then made himself conveniently scarce.

At eight o'clock, as ordered, Captain Tate, Lieutenant Burke, Sergeant Martinez and patrolman Binns appeared in the corridor outside his door.

John took them one at a time in accordance with their rank, beginning with Binns and working up. He grilled them until they were dizzy. By the time he finished—it was ten-fifteen—he knew far more about the status of the investigation than they did in combination.

"So what's next?"

John looked across the desk at Captain Tate with a thoughtful expression. He was wondering how far he could trust him. Not far enough, he finally decided. He would have to play his cards pretty close to his chest. He was also wondering if one of the entries in Sissie's diary could possibly have referred to Charlie's wife.

"We hit the streets," John said, rising. "I want Burke to

cover the hospital, give me regular reports on the condition of the suspect and patrolman Grooms. As soon as the doctor says they're able to talk, I want to be informed."

Tate got up as John came around the desk, and they walked to the door.

"I want Sergeant Martinez to sit down with Cubbage and get his life's history. I mean from A to Z."

"Shortstride? Why hell, Doc—"

"From A to Z, Charlie."

"You thinkin' about insurance, maybe? Hell, I already thought of that. Had Burke check 'im out. He's clean. Nothin' to collect on." Tate opened the door for John, and said, "Course now, there's the estate itself."

"From old man Sudash, you mean?"

"Yep. It ain't nothin' to sneeze at, an that's for sure. The old man left almost everything to his daughter. Now Shortstride has the works." He paused. "Still an' all, I'm purty sure he's in the clear."

Although it was not what John had had in mind, he was curious about the way the captain's thought processes worked. "On what do you base your conclusion?" he asked.

"Well, he really was out of town on business. We checked his movements for the whole week. He's clean, I tell you. An' besides, I saw his face when I showed him that photograph." He shook his head. "Nosireebob, he didden know nothin' about it."

John nodded. "I'm inclined to agree."

Tate looked surprised. "You are? Then what—?"

"I still want him checked out. I want to know all about his travels, not just during that week, but in the two or three months preceding the murders." He paused, then said, "And I'm gonna have to have a couple of your people assigned to me for the duration."

"Who you got in mind?"

"You can pick 'em. I want someone assigned to do a job on the Pittman boy. I mean the whole works. Criminal record, family history—"

"Hell, surely you know his momma is that there old whore that Chester Biggs—"

"I know about Lucy Pittman," John said. "But I want a complete dossier on them both. Particularly the charge Elton was last locked up on. Where? How long was he there, when did he get out and where did he go when he got out? And most importantly, what was his connection with the Cubbage girl? When did they meet? Where?"

Captain Tate walked off a couple of steps and then turned back. "I wonder if maybe they's ennything else you want done?"

"As a matter of fact, there is," said John, smiling. "You handle the background on Eddie James."

"But we already—"

"I want it *all*, Charlie—a complete biography from cradle to..."

"Yeah, tha's purty likely where he's headed awright. One way or another."

John ignored the captain's lack of subtlety. "I'll handle Sissie Cubbage myself. But I want some help. There's a former student of mine, Officer White—I want her assigned directly to me."

"White? The split tail?" Tate was genuinely surprised.

"Have her report to me here at the office, oh, say about one o'clock."

"You want me to have a bed an' some beer 'n' pretzels sent up too?"

John said coldly, "Let's get cracking, Captain. There's work to do. You can talk the fool on your own time."

# Chapter Fifty-two

**L. G. Cubbage pulled himself up to his full height of a** tall midget, took a deep breath and launched into a rousing climax.

"How long, how long, my friends, will we allow this evil cancer in our midst to deepen and grow? How long will we permit these alien spirits to abuse the very foundations of our country's glorious history? Spit upon our flag, dishonor all our values and debase our precious women an' children—How long?"

"What'd he say?"

"Don' rightly know, son; but don't he say it good?"

The crowd was neither large nor vociferous. But they and L. G. Cubbage were kindred spirits. He was not good at it yet, inarticulate and totally unaccustomed to the limelight. He could not yet whip up a crowd to a frenzy; in fact, they still laughed at him rather more than they cheered him. But there was a difference. Now they laughed to his face rather than behind his back. That was a marked improvement and Cubbage instinctively responded to their good will.

"How long," he continued to rail, "will we stand for all this sin an' debauchery in our land? What has happened to us, this land of milk 'n' honey, of strength and pride, that we used to love so much we were willing to fight an' die for it?"

The crowd was gradually settling down a little, to hone in on what it was he was trying to say. Somehow, he was beginning to strike a responsive chord in their collective breast.

After all, ol' Lester was down and out. George Wallace was an embittered cripple in a wheelchair, frozen in the present by the glories of the past and the tormenting void of an empty future.

Talmadge had been stripped of his powers by the sanctimonious hypocrites up in Dee Cee, fanned up like a pack of hungry wolves by the vituperation of a woman scorned.

But maybe, just maybe, beat the hope in the breast of such as these, a new leader had been sent to pick up their tattered flag. To rally them around a Sacred Cause.

"Crime and sin," Cubbage shouted in a rasping voice. "Sin and crime!"

Sheriff Biggs looked at the old farmer with the heavy-lidded gaze of a wary turtle.

"Rufus, you sure you ain't been on the sauce agin an' tha's all there is to this here tale?"

"Nosireebob, Sheriff. I'm tellin' the flat-out truth an' you better believe it, man." The bewhiskered old man in the bib overalls was about as fidgety as a cat looking for a spot to crap in. "Lyin' right out there in the ditch big as you please," he insisted.

"Dead?"

"Daid as a big ol' field rat."

"Shot?"

"Right in the haid."

"Didja move the body? Touch it?"

"Shoot. Man, what you talk? I ain't goin' *near* no dead nigger, no sir."

"You get close enough to see who he was?"

"Didden have to git clost. I know 'im good as I know ennybody. Ol' Tooney's boy, tha's who it was. The biggest one."

"Tooney Watts?" For the first time since the old farmer had come in Biggs looked interested. He had been interested almost from the moment the old man had started talking; he just hadn't shown it. Now he *looked* interested. "Marvin Watts? That the boy you talkin' about?"

"Tha's the one. Works out to ol' Pettigrew's place. Delivered lumber to my house a passel of times. I know 'im good as ennyone. Brought me a load of two-by-fours no more'n a month ago. Right out to my house."

Biggs pulled laboriously out of his chair and reached for his hat. "Back in the woods you say, over toward the river?"

"Yep. Went in there lookin' for a stray calf or I never woulda found 'im. It's purty thick an' tangled an' you can believe that awright." Rufus followed the sheriff to the door, saying, "What you reckon he was doin' back in there, Sheriff? Workin' a still mebbe? You reckon he had him an' ol' still back in them thickets?"

Sheriff Biggs spoke to the dispatcher. "Have a couple patrols meet me out by Hightower Road. Rufus'll go with me an' direct us on in."

As Biggs went into the lobby he spotted Charlie Tate and Sergeant Martinez huddling over by one of the exits. It didn't take a crime expert to determine that the Police Department's captain of homicide was purely pissed. As Biggs passed, he said, "You boys need enny help, you just let me know," and waddled down the stairs into the glaring sunlight.

At his car, Biggs paused to catch his breath. He opened the door, and Rufus walked around to the other side.

"He alone, Ruf?"

"Wha's 'at, Sheriff?"

"The nigger alone out there in the woods?"

The old farmer was taken aback. "Fur as I know he was," he said, and pulled a plug of tobacco out of his side pocket.

"Sho he was alone. Stretched out in that there ditch with a bunch've rotten leaves over 'im like a dead field rat."

"Warn't no nigger gal with him then?"

"Gal?" said the farmer, beginning to gnaw at the tobacco plug. "I didden see no nigger gal. What the hell you talkin' about, Chester?"

Murder, thought Biggs, wedging his bulk into the front seat. I'm damn well talkin' about some more murderin', right here in Taliawiga County.

Starting the engine, he looked up at a third-floor window in the courthouse, and saw John Winter looking down.

# Chapter Fifty-three

**Eddie James was staring at the closed door. He had** heard their voices outside. Sentries on duty around the clock. Where am I? Where have they taken me? He swallowed hard on his ragged throat. Are the nightmares real? Shredded flesh, mangled limbs, vomit in the dust. Blood, tissue, bone and muscle. Senses dull. Anesthesia; scopolamine? Name, rank and serial number.

When the door opened and the nurse bustled in, he closed his eyes.

In the darkness, the images began to rise...

# Chapter Fifty-four

**The afternoon editorial read in part:** "But the larger issue for Taliawiga County is, Why? Why has this atrocity happened here? This is not New York or Atlanta, Detroit or Houston. Have we somehow in recent years unknowingly helped to create the kind of climate in which such an abomination might be expected to occur? Do we all share in the guilt of the perpetrator of this heinous offense? Have we turned our faces away from the values that once made our nation good and strong and great in the eyes of law-abiding peoples everywhere? Is it perhaps time to return our trust to the old verities? There are those among us who are calling for such a rebirth in this moment of self-examination and challenge. Will such voices be heeded?"

John Winter put down the paper as the door opened.

"Hi, Sharon. Come on in."

"Gosh, I'm sorry it took so long," she said, breathlessly. "It was my day off. I took my son up to High Falls for an outing." She was wearing jeans, a tight pullover blouse and tennis sneakers. She saw his glance and said, "I came straight over as soon as Mom—"

"It's perfectly all right, Sharon. Have a seat."

She sat down on the edge of the chair, with her arms folded on the desk. John smiled. All she needed was a stack of textbooks. It had been over a year since her graduation, and she still looked like anything but a policewoman—a secretary, a bank teller, a wife and mother. At twenty-three, she was a fine figure of a young woman. And she wanted to be a cop. She had graduated number one in her college class, number one in her class at the Police Academy, and had been the first female to break the barrier in middle Georgia. "Breaking and entering," Charlie Tate had called it. It had been anything but easy for her. No one wanted her: not Toland, not Tate, not the wives of her fellow officers. It got so bad that the patrol commander had to assign her to ride only with bachelor partners. Of course the wives' fears were groundless. The only man on the force who had overtly tried anything was left crawling around in agony on his hands and knees for some twenty minutes in the back alley of a hock shop over on Main Street.

"How's the boy?" John asked. "Doin' okay?"

"Growing like a weed. He still talks about you." She lowered her eyes and blushed slightly.

"Next to his mom, Joey was about the smartest kid who ever came to my classes."

"I wish...well, I miss school."

John said, "I miss you too, Sharon. You were a fine student and a good friend."

"I don't know what I would have done without you. Probably never finished school. Certainly wouldn't have made it with the P.D."

He shook his head. "All I did was listen, Sharon. You had the answers within yourself. All you had to do was talk them out."

"You did more than listen, John." She looked him directly in the eye, so intently that it almost formed a tangible connection between them. She took a deep breath and said, "You saved my life. And I'll always love you for it."

Her blue eyes were like rain puddles, and a tic was jumping furiously on her left cheek.

"There it goes again," he said, breaking the ice, and they began to laugh. "Quickly now, and then let's get down to business," he said. "Is Joe Don giving you any more trouble?"

She shook her head. "Not since you got the child support order amended. He pays through the Support Division every month like clockwork."

"Good. And your mother?"

"Better. I'm hoping my sister will soon come to stay with her, and then Joey and I can get a little apartment of our own. I love her but—"

"She's a mother," said John, and they both laughed.

"Sal and the kids?"

"Oh, fine. Fine."

"It was a terrible shock about Billy Musgrove. It's hard to believe, even now," she said. "We started at the university together, went through the academy together, trained on the same shift together."

"I'm damned glad you didn't die together," said John.

"You taught the Cubbage boy too, didn't you?"

John nodded sadly. "He came to me for help the other day, too. But I wasn't able to draw him out enough to help."

"I...I don't understand."

"Maybe you will, as soon as you've completed the assignment I have for you."

"Assignment? Me?"

"Didn't they tell you what this hurry-up call is all about? You've been relieved from patrol duty. You're assigned directly to me for the duration of this case."

"Oh, John." She was clearly elated.

"I have to have people I can trust, Sharon. I haven't exactly been welcomed with open arms around here, you know." He grimaced sourly.

"I can imagine. But I'm so proud of you. I was so excited by the announcement, and now this. What's the job, boss? Whatever it is, I'm your man."

"Well, you're my kind of man," John laughed, reaching for Sissie's diary. "You may just be the most important fellow in this entire investigation."

He handed her the diary and said, "It's back to school for you. Master this material and I'll give you an A+ and a Phi Beta Kappa key to boot."

She took the book, perplexed, and thumbed through it hastily.

"I don't understand...?"

He looked at his watch and stood up. "Jesus, the time," he said. "I've got to be in court first thing in the morning."

John went around the desk and Sharon rose to meet him. The top of her blond head barely reached his shoulders. Her breasts, small, hard and straight, pointed directly at him. The thrust of her nipples dented the fabric of her bra and blouse.

"It's a diary, Sharon. Sissie Cubbage's diary. I've only scanned it, but I think it tells one hellofa story. It's in a code of some sort, pretty superficial from what I've seen."

"And you want *me* to break it?"

"Right down the middle. Translate all the coded passages and give me a written report on every single item that might bear in any way on the investigation." He put his arm around her shoulder and walked her to the door. "But most importantly, I want all the uncoded passages placed in context so that I can see for myself what she was up to. And, make a list of every individual that figures in the text—*every* one, no matter how highly placed—and the corresponding page or pages on which the references appear."

They didn't open the door. "And, Sharon, I don't have to tell you—"

"No, you don't," she said. "It's strictly confidential."

"Tell no one what you're doing. No one. The chief, Charlie Tate, Bob Randolph—no one. You report directly and only to me."

"Gotcha, boss. Hell, I wish that was the story of my whole life."

He smiled, took her by the shoulders and kissed her gently on the forehead.

"Get out of here," he said. "You've destroyed enough marriages in the P.D. You leave the special prosecutor's family alone."

She laughed and left.

And John went back to his desk. It was after ten, but he had a few more matters to review before going home.

# Chapter Fifty-five

**"Is he home?"**
"He left an hour ago."
"Doesn't he *ever* sleep?"
"Not with me."

Homer laughed, then said, "I wonder if he's heard the news?"

"What news?"

"The latest murder in Taliawiga County, that's bloody what news."

"Good Lord. Homer, what—"

"Sheriff Biggs announced it this morning. One of our local boys was found dead, in the woods, not too far from your place—point of fact. He was murdered."

Sal went cold all over; her knees were on the point of buckling. She sat down at John's desk in the den, her gaze fixed on a photograph of Eddie James on the front page of the Adelphi *Oracle*.

"Who was it?" she asked weakly.

"A black boy named Marvin Watts. Works in Orin Pettigrew's lumber mill. He'd been dead for over a week. The thing is," said Homer, pausing, "everyone thinks that he was most likely killed by the same chap they're holding for the Cubbage murders."

"Oh, no. And now John—"

"He may very well have this one dumped in his lap in addition. Only this time, he'll be working with Chester Biggs."

Though they talked for a few moments longer, Sal remembered little else that was said. She sat there with the blood pushing through her veins like ice water. Chester Biggs was the embodiment of all that she feared and hated of uniformed authority. She had confronted so many of his kind during the civil rights and antiwar struggles. She was young then, with no responsibilities. No husband and children to consider. She could spend a night or a week in jail, absorb an occasional crack on the head from a police nightstick. Reputation meant nothing. Ending discrimination and the war meant everything. But then, John became her everything.

Now, she had other responsibilities to consider. She cared as much as ever; it was just that her role in life had changed. She viewed her world from a different vantage point.

She looked at the photograph of Eddie James again—the young handsome face, the dark soulful eyes—and wondered about John's commitment to the task of saving his life. Seven human beings; men, women and an innocent child. And now perhaps another victim. *Should* his life be spared? Did he deserve to live when so many others had died at his hand?

She caught herself. *If* he is guilty, that is. Suppose...just suppose the boy is innocent. She didn't think he was, it wasn't likely; but what if he was innocent?

They *had* made the right decision. There was no other way. If the boy was guilty of the horrible offense with which he was charged, then he had to be put away. It was up to John to prove his guilt and to convict him. It was also up to John to save the boy from any mob.

She folded the paper over—a futile gesture—and abruptly left the room.

John Winter entered the courtroom on the third floor of the old brick courthouse on the square in Adelphi. It was not yet ten o'clock and he was already a weary man. He had slept little more than four hours, had breakfasted on coffee and Danish rolls for the umpteenth morning in a row. The pace was already beginning to tell on him. He wasn't used to that sort of unrelieved strain. In the old days he often tried jury cases week in and week out; but that was more than six years ago. The easy bohemian life in Europe and the gentility of college and country routine had softened him.

Sharon White had hit him with the news of Chester Biggs's announcement concerning the Watts boy, and Captain Tate had informed him that there had been a girl with Watts who was probably dead too. Biggs thought, and so did Tate, that Eddie James was the murderer.

John hadn't had time to go into the reasoning behind the conclusions of Tate and Biggs, but he had a sinking feeling in his stomach that told him they were *almost* right in their reading of events. Eddie James probably was connected in some way, but John didn't think he was the killer of Marvin Watts. John had isolated another suspect for that dubious honor.

"Mawnin', Counselor."

"Good morning, Anson."

The doddering old bailiff courteously opened the mahogany gate and held it for John to pass through the bar.

"Good to see you in the courtroom again, if you don't mind my saying so."

"Thank you, Anson."

"Yo' ol' gran'daddy Flood would be mighty proud of you, John."

John looked at the old man and smiled warmly. But he wasn't at all sure that Anson was right. *Would Papa be pleased? Would he be proud, in view of my motives for what I'm trying to do?*

"Go get 'um, John," said another, young freckle-faced bailiff whose brother had attended the university with John.

"Hello, Frank. How's Joe Bob doing?"

"Good, John. Said to wish you good luck." He moved a step closer and lowered his voice. "Said tell you if you need enny help just to say the word. There's plenty 'a people'd help you git that nigger one way or the other."

John looked at him coldly and moved on over to the prosecution table. He opened his briefcase and took out his court file. As he scanned the grounds of Tribble's first motion, he was aware of the courtroom filling with spectators beyond the bar.

A couple of reporters and a cameraman tried to finesse an entry but the bailiffs effectively barred their way. There were no windows in the big double doors but the next time they were pushed open to allow a spectator in, John caught a glimpse of Bobcat Tribble holding forth in the corridor.

A few of the spectators nodded in his direction, a woman smiled and more than a few waved their support. A large segment of Taliawiga County had turned out to observe as justice took its course.

The same bunch, and more, would turn out to watch the boy dangle at the end of a rope or fry in the chair. *Vultures,* thought John, *or dedicated citizenry?*

Tribble bustled down the aisle in his white rumpled suit. He looked like Charles Laughton's idea of Charles Laughton portraying a Southern defense lawyer.

"Hidy, Mr. Prosecutor. You doin' awright?"

"Good mornin', Cat. Haven't seen you in a coon's age."

"Watch them racial slurs there, Counselor, or you'll find yo'ownself settin' up there in the dock."

John smiled and watched with as much fascination as the tittering spectators as Tribble shuffled over to the defense table and began to unwind his briefcase. It was the sort of receptacle from which one expected little four-legged rodents to scamper out when opened.

Anson brought the assemblage to its feet as Judge Harbuck strode briskly into the room, his black flowing robes as neat as his well-pressed hair, his right hand covering his heart.

"I pledge allegiance to the flag of the United States..."

The judge sat down in the oversized swivel chair, banged the gavel and instructed the clerk to call the first case.

"The State of Georgia vs. Eddie James!"

"What says the People?"

John stood and said, "Ready, Your Honor."

"And what says the attorney for the defendant?"

Tribble half rose, as if the effort was tearing his poor body loose at the seams, and replied, "The Defense is ready, Your Honor."

Judge Harbuck smiled thinly and said, "Then I suggest we get on with it, gentlemen."

John remained on his feet. "Your Honor, if it please the Court, we are here this morning on a host of routine defense motions—"

*"Routine?"* roared Tribble, coming to his feet like a goosed duck. "I wish to assure this honorable Court here an' now that the motions filed in behalf of my client are ennything but *routine*," he continued in a voice compounded of equal portions of anger, wounded pride and righteous indignation. "Indeed, it is with profound sincerity and—"

"Yes, Counselor," Judge Harbuck interposed. "That will do quite nicely, your objection is well taken." He turned to John and said affably, "Does the Prosecution have any objection to omitting the use of the offending word 'routine'? If not, the Court will reserve ruling on this matter and give the Prosecution leave to continue. If the Prosecution objects, I will order the word stricken from the record."

John bit back a smile, did not dare meet Judge Harbuck's puckish gaze, and said, "The State willingly withdraws the use of the word 'routine,' Your Honor, and apologizes to the Court and to learned counsel for the defense—"

"Yes, yes," said Harbuck with a wave of the gavel and a scowl to soften the titters sweeping through the courtroom.

John took a look at Bobcat Tribble and sighed. The ordeal had begun.

Two and a half hours later, Tribble was still afoot, offering his final comments in support of his fourth—or was it fifth?—motion of the day. John really couldn't remember.

Thus far Judge Harbuck had "routinely" denied a defense motion to dismiss the information, along with a motion to suppress any and all physical evidence as having been obtained without a valid search warrant. Harbuck's position was that all such evidence had been gathered incidental to an arrest and was therefore not tainted. Not so, argued Tribble, especially insofar as the search of the defendant's car the day *after* the arrest. Harbuck granted Tribble leave to appeal the issue and Tribble assured His Honor that he would do exactly that.

The Court granted the defendant's motion to produce and a motion for more definite statement. John agreed to furnish the defense with a list of state's witnesses, insofar as they were known, immediately after the hearing. The Court also granted Tribble's motion for a bill of particulars.

The only surprise was that Tribble had not filed a motion for a change of venue, as he might have been expected to do, basing it on the grounds that Eddie James could not be assured of a fair trial in Taliawiga County due to the level of adverse publicity and inflammatory feelings that already existed throughout the jurisdiction of the Court.

But he had filed a motion for a psychiatric examination, and was at this moment arguing his position with eloquence and passion before the Court.

Both of which emotions were misplaced, thought John from his seat at the prosecution table. Hell, he wasn't going to offer any strenuous objection. He wanted to know the state of the defendant's mind as much as Tribble did. And even if he objected, Harbuck was sure to grant the motion anyhow. What the hell was Tribble getting so worked up for?

As if I didn't know, thought John sourly. He turned slightly and looked out across the bar, at the rapt faces in the audience, the moving pencils of the newsmen, even the quick slashing movements of a courtroom sketch artist who had already sniffed a whiff of national notoriety about this case. Tribble was playing to the gallery, thought John.

But *why?* What the hell was his motive? There was no *need* to turn this case into a circus and make Taliawiga County a national disgrace in the bargain. What was motivating Tribble; was it something more than his congenital disagreeableness and his innate antipathy to the American criminal justice system?

Suddenly John remembered Sissie's diary. Jesus, is *that* it? Was Tribble mentioned? He racked his brain, but couldn't remember any entry that might have pertained to the lawyer. Could Tribble be functioning in this case primarily out of personal motives of self-interest, perhaps even self-survival?

John watched him now with cold objectivity as he gesticulated before the bench.

"...and I would represent unto this honorable Court that in order to even approximate a semblance of fair play and due process, a comprehensive psychiatric examination must be ordered, so that the Court can have clear and convincing evidence before it of the state of mind of the defendant, now and at the time of the commission of the crime. And as His Honor is well aware—"

"Yes, I am," Judge Harbuck said softly, but was apparently resigned to hearing out the garrulous advocate.

"...there ain't a qualified psychiatrist within thirty or forty miles of here, let alone in Taliawiga County itself. I therefore respectfully request that the Court in its wisdom order that the accused be removed from the county hospital and transported to the state mental institution in Milledgeville for the appropriate Court-ordered examinations."

What the *hell*, thought John. He's running the risk—if he *wants* a show trial in court, that is—of having his client certified incompetent to stand trial, if those head doctors get him over at Milledgeville.

Tribble took a deep breath and was about to launch into a renewed oration, but Judge Harbuck moved quickly to cut him off. "What says the State, Mr. Prosecutor?"

John rose and said, "The State has no objection, Your Honor."

There was a heavy silence in the courtroom. Tribble turned sharply and stared at John with ill-concealed surprise. Judge Harbuck didn't bat an eye, but was silent for a moment longer than was called for. He sat hunched forward over the bench, staring intently at the two attorneys. Then he said, "Counsel approach the bench."

Both attorneys started for the raised platform in front of the judge's dais. A whisper of muted conversation swept around the courtroom, tolerated for the moment by Judge Harbuck.

"What the hell are you two bastards up to?" Harbuck asked, leaning so far down over the bench John could smell the odor of Certs on his breath.

"Your Honor, the State has no objection to a determination of the defendant's state of mind. Indeed, it is equally as important to the People to know if this defendant is capable of assisting his defense counsel—"

"You let *me* worry about the rights and legal defenses of

my client, Mr. Winter." Tribble was so swollen with anger and thwarted purpose that he looked as if he might strike the special prosecutor.

"Now listen to me, boys. I had a lousy breakfast this morning, anticipating this confrontation with you birds. But Roseanne is havin' blackeyed peas, biscuits an' ham at home, an' if you fuckers spoil my lunch as well..."

Both attorneys backed away from the dais and took their respective positions across from each other.

"The Court will take the defendant's motion for psychiatric examination under advisement and reserve ruling."

"Your Honor, sir. If it please the Court..." Tribble was on his feet with a long bony finger in the air.

"It does *not* please the Court, Mr. Tribble."

"Your Honor, it is manifestly unfair to deprive a defendant of the benefit of every doubt, when not only are his health and well-being at stake, but his very life as well. If the Court will only do its duty and reconsider—"

Harbuck banged the gavel and fire flashed in his thin blue eyes. "The Court will do its duty, Mr. Tribble. Of that you may rest assured." Though he said nothing further, the look he gave the chastened attorney encouraged Tribble to resume his seat and hold his peace.

The Court was adjourned for lunch and Tribble was swarmed over by newsmen in the corridor.

John Winter was confronted by a steely-eyed district attorney as he tried to get into the men's room.

"What the devil are you up to?" Randolph demanded, tight-lipped and white with indignation.

"Mornin', Bob. Things goin' all right with you fellas down the hall?"

Randolph followed him into the men's room like a shadow.

"I asked you a question, Winter. What the hell you think you're doin' in there?"

"I'm getting ready to take a piss," said John. "Only I never can get started when some red-eyed dude is breathing down my neck like one of those queens over at the Greyhound station."

Randolph stepped sharply back from the urinal, flushed redly about the cheeks and then stammered back to the attack.

"Why didn't you resist that damned motion? You *want* that commie shyster to get James over to the state hospital an' get 'im certified?"

John flushed, zipped and moved over to the lavatory to wash his hands.

"Don't you see what he's tryin' to do? He wants to beat your ears back before you ever get in the ring." Randolph moved up close again and said, "You let that slimy bastard get certified an' slip off the hook, Winter, an' I'll see to it that *your* ass winds up in the sling."

John wiped his hands on a paper towel, said, "Fuck off, Randolph" and handed the district attorney the soiled towel as he left the room.

# Chapter Fifty-six

**"But why the deuce *didn't* you object?" Homer asked** across the dinner table, laughing at the thought of Taliawiga County's eminently flappable district attorney standing in the men's room with egg on his face.

Both John and Sal had been surprised when Homer had showed up for supper that night with a bottle of wine and a sack of fresh-picked muscadine grapes. Sal had been so agitated by their phone conversation that morning that she had forgotten all about having invited him to supper. It was merely coincidental that John happened to have come home to eat for a change.

John told them all about the hearing on the motions that morning in court, and about Randolph's brazen behavior in the washroom.

"Why, John?" Homer asked again.

"For two reasons," said John, pouring himself a second cup of after-dinner coffee. "First, I'm just as anxious as Cat to determine the mental condition of Eddie James. I certainly haven't been able to make any determination so far. I haven't even had an opportunity to interview the guy I'm prosecuting."

"He's still in critical condition then?"

"That's just it—he isn't. He's been off the critical list for a couple of days now." He reached for a piece of cheese and Sal passed him a dish of sliced apple. "At least the doctors say there's little chance of his not pulling through physically. Mentally and emotionally, well, that's something else."

"Is he conscious?" asked Sal, sipping from her glass of claret that Homer had brought along for the meal.

"Apparently so," John shrugged. "At least the doctors say they *think* he is aware of his surroundings. The trouble is, he just stares at them. When they can get him to open his eyes at all."

"Might he be faking?" asked Homer.

"He certainly might be. That's one of the reasons I don't object to having him examined by a qualified psychiatrist. I have to *know* if he's faking or not. If he is, he goes to trial. If not, if he really *is* mentally disabled, to the point of incompetency, then there can be no prosecution."

"Good Lord," said Homer. "I shouldn't like being in your boots if you have to stand up and announce to the good citizens of Taliawiga County that James does not even have to go to trial, let alone to the electric chair."

John looked at Homer with just a touch of pique in his expression. "No, you wouldn't like that, would you," he said with a thin smile. "But you didn't mind putting those boots on my feet, did you? Whether they fit or not."

"Now, John"—but Homer was a trifle uncomfortable— "there is no one is this county better qualified to handle such a sticky situation than yourself."

"Homer, I never cease to be amazed by the consistency with which you exercise your poor judgment."

They laughed and the tenseness of the moment was dissipated.

Sal nibbled at a piece of cheese and asked, "Just exactly what determines whether Eddie James—or any defendant— is competent to stand trial."

John sipped his coffee and paused thoughtfully. "In the state of Georgia, as in most states today," he began slowly, "the matter of sanity is considered to be a legal rather than a medical question. Doctors know better than to call a person insane, for then they would also have to determine who is

195

sane. They have quite enough difficulties with their profession as it is."

"But how can the law—or judges—make medical decisions—"

"They don't. They make *legal* decisions. The test used is whether the person accused of a crime has the mental capacity to understand the difference between right and wrong. If he does, he is legally sane. If not, he is legally insane."

"But that's too simplistic," she protested.

He smiled. "There's nothing simplistic in trying to implement it, I can assure you. Now wait, let me finish. In order to find a person guilty of a crime it must be established—by the prosecution—that the accused was legally sane at the time he committed the crime. Not free from mental flaw, mind you. But merely that he could in fact distinguish between right and wrong."

"At the time he committed the offense," Homer emphasized.

"That's right. He had to understand that what he was doing was wrong."

"Did Eddie James know—"

"I haven't the slightest idea," said John, anticipating her question. "That's what I have to find out."

Homer said, "Go on, John. There's more, isn't there?"

John nodded. "If Eddie James was legally insane at the time he committed the murders—*if* he is the perpetrator of the crime, of course—he cannot now be tried for those murders. And to complicate matters even further," he said, reaching for a handful of green seedless grapes, "if Eddie James was sane at the time he killed all those people, but he is determined to be legally insane now, today, here, he still cannot be tried for the murders."

"My God," said Sal.

"The law cannot put an insane defendant on trial," said John. "Not even if he was sane when he committed the crime."

"Then Eddie James may never be tried?"

John nodded to his wife. "It's possible."

"He may even go free," opined Homer.

John hesitated a bit longer before saying, "That's possible too."

"How?" demanded Sal. "How?"

"If he was sane when he committed the crime but is insane

now, he can't be tried. But if he is treated and his sanity is restored, he can then be put on trial for the original crime."

"How long...how many years?"

"There's no statute of limitation," said John. "But now, if Eddie James was legally insane when he committed the crime, he cannot be tried, or rather, he cannot be *convicted* of the crime now or at any time in the future."

There was a long silence.

"Oh, John. That's...that's monstrous. I've never *heard* of such a thing," she said. "It makes no sense. I don't know exactly where or how, but somehow the system, the entire legal system, is...is..."

"Isn't it though?" said John, reaching for the wine.

"And that's what you think Tribble is up to?" asked Homer. "He intends to have his client certified insane, either then or now, preferably then, so that the chap may simply walk free."

John didn't answer. He wasn't sure of his answer in any case. Was that what Tribble was up to? Or did he have something else in mind?

"You said two reasons," Sal reminded John. "Two reasons you didn't object to the motion this morning."

"Oh yes. The desire to know in order to make my determination as to how the State is to proceed. And secondly, it wasn't necessary to object."

"How so?" asked Homer.

"Judge Harbuck isn't going to grant that motion. Not the part about removing the defendant to Milledgeville at least. The law, you see, doesn't require a psychiatric examination. It specifies a medical examination to determine an accused's competency."

"I begin to see your thinking," said Homer.

"Harbuck will appoint a team of doctors to examine Eddie James and that will be the end of it. We don't have any psychiatrists in and around Adelphi, but we have a sufficient number of medical doctors."

"But how do you *know* the judge will do what you are suggesting?"

John smiled at Sal and said, "Hon, Horace Harbuck was born and raised in Taliawiga County fifty some-odd years ago. He went to school here, then to college down in Macon and on to law school up in Athens. He was in turn a Cub Scout, a Boy Scout, a Christian and a Democrat. He's a thirty-third-degree Mason and was a paratrooper in World War II.

He has been mayor of Adelphi twice, district attorney for eight years, and he's gonna be judge of the Superior Court here for the rest of his unnatural life."

Homer laughed, and Sal said, a little sharply, "I don't see—"

"Honey, Horace Harbuck has played the game by the rules his entire life. The judge not only believes in the game, Sal, he believes in the rules too. Throw away the rulebook and the game unravels at the seams."

John refilled all of their cups and said, "Let's get out of these hardbacked chairs," and stood up.

"And you?" Sal asked without rising. "Are *you* going to play the game by the rules?"

He stared at her for a moment. Her deeply tanned face shone like a burnished copper plate in the soft dining room light.

"I'm going to do my best to see that justice is done, Sal. And I am going to *try* to prevent the further taking of human life. I will use the rules to help achieve this end. I *may* bend the rules a little, if necessary."

She looked up at him and then over at Homer, who had also risen with his cup and saucer. "Some friend," she said pointedly at Homer.

As they walked into the living room the topic of conversation shifted to the murder of the Watts boy, and Homer asked John if anyone knew anything about the identification of the teenaged girl who had supposedly disappeared some days ago with the boy.

John hesitated a moment, then said, "It's Josie Fletcher's daughter Ellie."

"Oh my God," Homer exclaimed, and knocked over his cup.

# PART FOUR

# Chapter Fifty-seven

**Not since the late Elvis Presley's motorcade had broken** down on its way from the Atlanta airport to the Macon Coliseum had Taliawiga County experienced so much concentrated excitement.

Rumors were already building. Some said that the killings at the Cubbage house hadn't accounted for all the murders in the county that night, or thereabouts. There were even suggestions that Eddie James might not have been operating entirely on his own. It was known that a black youth had been killed around the same time of the deaths at the Cubbage house. Ballistics had not matched up the murder weapons but there was thought to be some sort of connection between the two crimes. And there was something about a black girl missing for the last week or so. She had been seen getting into a truck with the boy the day they both disappeared.

Meanwhile, Judge Harbuck issued his order on Bobcat Tribble's motion for a psychiatric examination of Eddie James. He denied the motion as it was worded, refusing to allow the wounded prisoner to be transferred to the state mental institution in Milledgeville for the desired examinations. But he included in the order the appointment of Dr. Whipple and two other county physicians, charging them with the duty of examining Eddie James on behalf of the Court. They were given ten days in which to report their findings as to whether or not, in their medical opinion, the suspect was competent to assist his counsel in the preparation of his defense and to stand trial.

The reaction to the ruling was mixed. Though most people didn't understand the legal niceties underlying the substance of the motion in the first place, they were pretty certain that Horace Harbuck had done the right thing. In their minds, he had been doing the right thing for so many years that they weren't about to start second-guessing him now. And since the whole issue had been raised by Bobcat Tribble, most people were disposed to look at it with a deal of skepticism from the outset. After all, Bobcat was—well—everybody knew what he was like.

There were those, however, who thought the judge should have just let 'em take the rascal on over to Milledgeville so the county could have been shut of the whole mess once and for all. Eddie James certainly wouldn't have been the first one to go behind those gates and not be heard of again. On the other hand, you never could tell about those head doctors over at the mental institution. They had been known to do some pretty weird things over there. A lot of people thought it was the doctors who really ought to be locked up so they couldn't do any harm to the public at large. Suppose they had come up with some kind of voodoo hocus-pocus that caused the murdering bastard to be set loose? It was gonna be hard enough to swallow, folks said, when Bobcat Tribble started all that communistic drivel about social repression and how poor Eddie James was just a downtrodden abused black boy whose murderous actions had been forced upon him by an uncaring white social order. Why, old Tribble might even try to make the murdering coward into a freedom fighter of some sort.

But Taliawiga County could deal with Bobcat Tribble. They could handle the likes of Eddie James too. That's what the law was for. Judge Harbuck, Chester Biggs and John Winter could be counted on to see things right. Oh, they would do it fair and square all right. They would give the boy justice, accord him all the trappings of due process. They would try him, convict him and would burn him in the electric chair down in Reidsville. Bobcat Tribble and a horde of bleeding hearts around the country would weep and wail, gnash their teeth and pull their hair, slobbering about how dastardly was such a murderous act at the hands of the all-powerful state. But, as usual, the bleeding hearts were full of shit, most countians agreed. There would be hundreds, thousands of Americans willing to step up and pull the fatal switch. And Taliawiga County, folks said, boastfully, pridefully, would not be lacking in its full complement of representatives.

\* \* \*

It was late afternoon before Bobcat Tribble got back from Forsyth. He had spent most of the afternoon arguing his ass off in Judge Hickey's courtroom on the third floor of the Bibb County Courthouse. In the end his client, a nineteen-year-old black girl, went to the penitentiary for shotgunning her stepfather while the man drunkenly attempted to rape the girl's ten-year-old sister.

"Twenty years!" exclaimed Tribble's secretary when he called his office on the phone.

"The old bastard was furious. Here he not only had the chance to sentence a defendant to the electric chair, but the culprit was a woman to boot. And we'd snatched the opportunity right out from under him."

"The sonofabitch."

"Ain't that the holy truth. Lissen, Rita—enny of those people come down from Atlanta yet?"

Jesus, he thought. He'd told everyone to gather at his house around five-thirty. He didn't care much about the others, but wondered if the young dude would come. He'd better; his role just might be crucial to the whole operation.

"Well, go on an' close the office," he said, "an' get over to my house. I'll be along directly—soon's I stop by the hospital an' see if ol' Doc Whipple'll let me talk to the James boy."

"You heard about Judge Harbuck's ruling?"

"Everybody in town tol' me about it."

"I got a stack more of them hate letters."

"Wallpaper the reception room with 'em for all I give a shit."

He hung up, left the phone booth and got back in the VW beetle just as it started to rain.

Tribble was drenched by the time he made it from the parking lot into the hospital.

"Well, for heaven's sake," sniffed the elderly receptionist. "You're gittin' it all *over* the place."

"Miss Mary, it ain't like I can just sponge it up, now is it, dear?"

"Go on back," she said with about as much sociability as a spent hypodermic needle. "He's waitin' for you an' said to send you on back as soon as you got here."

Doc Whipple was sitting behind his desk, looking at a patient's file. The doctor looked up and said, " 'Bout time you got here. You think I ain't got nothin' better to do—"

"Doc, it's a real pleasure to see you too," Tribble grinned.

"Jesus, Cat. You look like somethin' a drunken old whore might come draggin' in off the waterfront down Savannah way."

"Speakin' of drunken ol' whores—"

"Mind your manners when talkin' to yore elders, son. But it was a hell of a party, Cat. You shoulda been there."

"I heard she was such a dog—"

"Drove a stake through her heart, an' left her bayin' at the moon."

When old Doc Whipple laughed he looked and sounded like a constipated weasel. He was making one hell of a noise as he came up from behind the desk and clapped Tribble on the shoulder.

"You can see the boy," he said. "But it ain't gonna do you a bit of good."

"Nothin' yet?"

"Don't even tell nobody when he wants to piss."

"When you an' the other two ghouls gonna examine him for the Court?"

"I examine him every day. I don't need no goddamn court order to tell me when to examine a patient of mine."

"Then you already made a determination?"

Whipple grinned. "You be in court on Friday mornin' an' you'll be one of the first to know."

"Doc, I al'ays said you was a scholar an' a gennelman. I mean it, one of nature's first-class specimens. Sometimes you can be a first-class prick too."

Whipple laughed so hard he described a tight circle in the corridor, like a speedboat with a broken rudder.

"You really got your hands full this time, you know. They say that John Winter's dynamite in the courtroom."

"Well, I sure hope he don't blow us all up."

Doc Whipple dropped off at the nearest intersection, leaving Bobcat to introduce himself to the guard on duty. His visit had been arranged and approved by the special prosecutor's office.

The first sight of his celebrated client in the flesh was a shock Bobcat hadn't anticipated. He didn't look at all like the photograph the news media had been using via the courtesy of the U. S. Army. He was lying in bed propped up on a pair of pillows with a fresh white sheet draped over his body. His complexion was not nearly as dark as the media photograph indicated. And he looked younger than Tribble had expected. He was a handsome boy, there was no question about that. He had a smooth coppertone complexion, dark wavy hair and soft lustrous black eyes.

Unfocused, disturbing eyes, thought Tribble.

It was the eyes that got you. They didn't blink or turn away; but they didn't *see* you. The boy lay there wrapped in the sheet like a mummy, staring at Tribble, saying nothing and, as far as Tribble could discern, hearing nothing that was said to him. It was an unnerving experience.

Tribble tried to talk to him, glanced questioningly at the nurse on the other side of the bed. She merely shrugged and gave her attention to the patient's pulse. Still, Tribble went through the whole rigamarole. He told Eddie James who and what he was, and what he was doing there; how Judge Harbuck had appointed him to represent James and promised to protect his rights to the best of his ability. Then he told him what he had done so far, about the motions he had filed and why he had wanted them and the way in which Judge Harbuck had ruled.

None of this appeared to matter a hill of beans to Eddie James. He just lay there and if there was a spark of comprehension in his eyes, or one of fear, Tribble could not detect it. He told Eddie how much he needed his assistance in order to prepare his defense, and then he leaned forward and said close to his ear, "An' just in case you're fakin' this whole thing, lemme give you a little piece of advice. It won't work. Shape up an' help me prepare your defense or they gonna burn yo' ass to a crisp."

# Chapter Fifty-eight

Sal emerged from the bathroom with her hair and body wrapped in towels. John was lying naked in bed, his body covered by a light sheet. His hands were folded behind his head and his eyes were closed, but he was not yet asleep. It was earlier than they customarily retired—much earlier than John had been coming to bed since taking on the special prosecutor's assignment. But he had had a particularly wearisome day and expected another like it tomorrow, and so had decided to get a full night's rest for a change.

Sal looked at him in the soft bedroom light, and her heart went out to him. She knew how tired physically and how emotionally drained he was after his difficult interview that afternoon with Josie Fletcher. While they ate a light supper John had told Sal about the condition in which he had found the Fletcher woman. Josie was absolutely shattered by events. Her last ray of rational hope had been dashed with the discovery of Marvin Watts's body in the woods. She knew that her daughter Ellie had gone off with the boy the afternoon of her disappearance. Biggs had already told her that old Miss Maddie Yates had seen Ellie getting into the boy's pickup truck, just after another man in a car had apparently attempted to accost the frightened girl at the edge of the road in front of the old lady's house.

Both Sheriff Biggs and John had tried to determine from Josie who the man might have been; but Josie would only say that her daughter was a good girl and had no male friends other than Marvin Watts. She looked at their photographs of Eddie James and shook her head without recognition.

John remembered Josie Fletcher from the old days, but really had not given her much thought over the years. And although he must have seen Elmarie around town on a number of occasions, he was really not aware of what she looked like until he got Josie to produce a color photograph of the girl. He had seen her, many times. And so had Sal. She was a pretty girl, quiet and well-mannered, and she walked with something of a limp. One leg was shorter than the other, Sheriff Biggs had said.

As far as John knew, Homer had had no contact with any of the Fletchers since Josie had left the employ of his family in the summer Homer went away to college. Sal, of course, had insisted upon an explanation of Homer's strange behavior the previous night when John had disclosed the identity of the missing girl. John didn't really know the whole story himself—or so he said—but told her what he knew, and Sal filled in the rest with the gossip that she had picked up in bits and pieces over the years.

As a young girl Josie had worked for the Stokes family for most of Homer's teenaged years. She was married to a young fellow named Jesse Fletcher and they had a four-year-old son named Otha. Some sort of undisclosed incident had occurred during the summer following Homer's graduation from high school. Josie was forced to leave her position with the Stokes family and go to work in the kitchen of a local restaurant. Josie's equally young husband—who had been employed by Colonel Stokes to tend the grounds and the family motorcars—had also left his position and was never seen or heard from again. Homer was packed off to Europe and did not return home until after his graduation from the Sorbonne four years later. Homer had never volunteered any information to John, and John had never inquired.

Of course tongues wagged, the county being what it was. John had heard it all, Sal enough to get the gist of the way countians felt about one of their leading citizens. Some people said that old Colonel Stokes had caught Jesse Fletcher with his hand in the petty cash box; others opined that it was Jesse who had detected in young Homer a pair of straying hands.

In any case, Jesse left for parts unknown, Homer went to Paris and Josie gave birth to a daughter seven months later. In due course, newer, riper scandals materialized and the "incident" at the Stokes mansion began to pale, although it was never forgotten. Certainly no one paid the slightest attention when Josie gave birth to a daughter about five years later without benefit of a new husband. Such things happened in the black community right and left. So, although nobody cared one way or the other about Josie's babies being born out of wedlock, when they thought about her oldest daughter, Elmarie, most people usually got around to remembering the peculiar circumstances attending her birth, and there was always at least one outspoken soul in each such gathering who would boldly come out and say what all of them knew and believed: that Homer Stokes was sure Lord the gal's natural father.

"Is it true, John?" Sal had asked at the dinner table over their coffee and peaches. "Is Homer really that girl's father?"

"Jesus, Sal. Who can say? I've heard the rumor, sure. But he's never indicated anything to me about it one way or another."

"Now that I think about it, I heard Orin Pettigrew's wife say something about it one day at a tea party at the country club."

"Yeah, I remember Rachel talking about it, too, on occasion. Seems as how if that kind of scandal about the Stokeses was true, it somehow made the Pettigrews a little grander."

"Rachel Pettigrew." Sal made a face.

"Meow," he said, passing her the cream.

"Not at all. If you can let me live down *my* life, I suppose I can handle that prissy little piece of Southern insipidness."

"Touché," he said as she poured a measure of cream on her peaches. Then she began to laugh. "What's so funny?"

"The joke might be on this entire county," Sal had said. "Suppose its richest, most powerful and cultured citizen was the father of three—not one, mind you, but all three—of Josie Fletcher's kids."

"What the hell, Sal. *Anything's* possible."

Sal asked about Josie Fletcher's oldest son. He was something of a mystery.

Otha Fletcher had left Adelphi the year before John and Sal had returned from Europe. Only a teenager, Otha had left school in the middle of his senior year, gone to Atlanta, then on to Birmingham and then either to Detroit or Chicago, no one was really certain. He had not left Adelphi under the best of circumstances. Always a hothead, Otha had been in trouble of one kind or another since his boyhood. His difficulties had increased as he got older, and he eventually became the closest thing that Adelphi had to a black radical.

Once, a couple of years back, a photograph of the Reverend Ralph Abernathy and a group of the late Martin Luther King's followers had appeared in an Atlanta newspaper in conjunction with a memorial ceremony for the slain civil rights leader. There, in the background, just behind Abernathy's shoulder, was none other than Taliawiga County's Otha Fletcher. It was the first he had been heard of so far as anyone knew. Even Josie had never received so much as a postcard from him since the day he had left town.

Sal closed the bathroom door now, unwrapped the towel around her head and began to dry her hair briskly.

"You look like Tanya the jungle girl," he said when she straightened up, her long hair wild and tangled round her face and shoulders.

"I thought you were asleep."

"Just resting my eyes."

"That's probably what Rip Van Winkle said. You were snoring to beat the band."

He smiled, breathing deeply as he plumped up the pillows beneath his head. "That's quite a tan you're getting for so early in the summer."

"Yard work," she said, and began combing the tangles out of her hair.

"I'm sorry I haven't been around, Sal."

"I understand."

He sighed. "If only I could say it will soon be over."

"Can you tell yet—?"

"No, it's too soon."

"Everybody's on your side."

"Are they now?"

"It's all anyone talks about. In the stores, at the gas station, on the street. And Ida Belle and her friends can't even *think* about anything else."

"Good Lord. I can imagine that bunch."

"Have you stopped by to see your mother since all of this started?"

"Sal, I've been so damned busy."

"I know you're busy. But you know what she's like, honey. You better make time to see her once in a while, or you'll have more trouble on your hands."

He sighed again. "I suppose so. The last thing I need right now is for her to pitch one of her spells."

Sal laughed and put down the brush. "She says if you don't get that murderer put away—if he gets out on the streets again—she and Irma Tidwell are just going to pick up and move away."

John snorted and scratched his belly through the sheet. "Where they goin'? Up to Atlanta, or over to New Orleans, maybe, where it's safe?"

Sal put down her brush, went over to sit on the edge of the bed.

"Will they let Eddie James out again? What if the doctors say he was crazy when he did it but he's sane now?"

"He better get out of this county fast."

"You said the other night—"

"I told you what all the options are. I have no idea yet whether the boy's sane or not."

"Will Tribble accept whatever Doc Whipple and the others say?"

John thought about it for a moment before answering. "I don't know, Sal. I'm not quite sure what Cat's up to yet. He lost on his attempt to get Eddie over to Milledgeville, but he might still try to get a couple of those psychiatrists brought in here."

"Can he do that?"

"You can do anything if you can get a judge to listen to you. Cat will try everything in the book, and a hell of a lot of things that aren't in anybody's book."

"But if Doc Whipple—"

"I don't care how many times they say the boy's sane, Cat can always find a couple psychiatrists *somewhere* to say he's nutty as a fruitcake."

"Maybe he is."

John shrugged. "And maybe he is."

After a moment's pause, Sal said, "And if he is, you really won't prosecute him?"

"You can't prosecute a crazy man, Sal. I don't care what he's done. At least you can't do it legally."

She put her hand on John's thigh. Her face was tense, her voice suddenly apprehensive. "If you were to do that," she said, "they would turn on you, wouldn't they? Like Homer said? If you don't prosecute Eddie James—even if you just let him keep his life—those people out there—*your* people—are going to turn on you?"

"Just like a pack of hungry sharks on one of its own kind," he said.

Sal shivered and tightened her grip on his thigh. "Is it my fault, John? Have I made you do the wrong thing?"

He covered her hand with his and said gently, "We did the only thing we could do, honey. And now we'll just have to ride it out."

"Maybe you could—"

"No way. Quit and run? Uh uh. We're in it now, up to our eyeballs. And we stay until the job's done."

"And then?"

He shook his head. "That's too far away. Right now I've gotta worry about tomorrow."

# Chapter Fifty-nine

"So you're Otha Fletcher."

The young man nodded. He was tall, blue-black, thin, and something in his eye said he was mean when pushed. He wore a goatee, a simple gold chain necklace, jeans and a flowery shirt. The clothing *seemed* simple, but was stylishly expensive. Otha was something of a dude, but that didn't mean he wasn't tough as a claw hammer, thought Tribble.

"We were beginning to think you weren't coming."

"I had a few stops to make. Includin' a courtesy call on my momma."

"How is she taking it?" Tribble asked, walking the new arrival into the crowded room.

"She wouldn't lemme in," he shrugged.

Tribble started to respond but the boy's manner said that was all there was to it, so he let it drop. For the moment. Animosity between mother and son might be a problem later that would have to be forestalled somehow. But first things first.

"C'mon in an' meet some people."

There were more than a dozen people in the big sparsely furnished living room. Mostly white, mostly middle-aged. Everyone had a drink; a lot of red wine seemed to be going down. And one couple could be seen through French doors standing on a terrace in the moonlight, sharing a joint while engaged in earnest conversation.

Tribble's secretary Rita, a black woman in her early twenties, had done a good job with the food and drink. A mound of fried chicken, a baked ham, a variety of salads, pies and cookies. Everyone seemed to be well fed and contented by the time Otha Fletcher arrived.

Tribble introduced Otha around the room. These were the money people, the influential people. At least these were the people who knew how to get to the money, how to push the right buttons. Aaron Goetz and his wife Sophie had already kicked in a pretty penny or two. A doctor's wife from over in Macon was on hand and Tribble knew damn good and well she had her checkbook in her purse.

Harvey O'Brien, a sociology professor at the university, was ready, willing and able to raise a student phalanx to hit the sidewalks at the snap of a finger. And one of the SCLC's experienced ramrods had come down from Atlanta to lend his expertise to the preliminary negotiations. But best of all, thought Tribble, was the presence of Ronnie Bell, an associate of Orson Vine, the millionaire genius of direct-mail fund solicitation from over in Alabama. Vine ran his Southern Poverty Law Center from his Mobile estate, using his brains and fortune in the support of worthy causes involving the nation's down-and-outers. In response to a recent late-night call from Bobcat Tribble, Vine had agreed to consult with him on the problem of raising sufficient monies to fund a Free Eddie James Committee.

"An' how long you reckon you're gonna be able to stall the prosecution from gettin' this here case into high gear?"

Tribble scratched his belly and straddled a straight chair in front of Ronnie Bell, while Aaron Goetz began to bring Otha Fletcher up to date on the latest information available concerning his sister's disappearance.

"Tha's a good question, Ronnie. I almost shit in my pants when that damned college professor didden even object to my motion."

"But the judge turned you down anyway?"

"He did an' he didn't. It would have taken *weeks* to get a

decision out of those shrinks over to the state hospital. Plenty of time." He shook his head and brushed his moustache out of his mouth. "But these local fellas, now tha's somethin' else. Why, I got a pretty good idea that ol' Doc Whipple has done made up his mind."

"So?"

"So if he says Eddie James is nuts, the other two will say the same thing. An' if they go in there as early as Friday of this week and tell the judge our boy is too far gone to stand trial—why, there ain't gonna *be* no trial."

Ronnie Bell looked him straight in the eye and said, "Congratulations, Counselor. You've won almost without a shot being fired."

Tribble just sat there, looking at the visitor in his home; Bobcat looked like a worried old stud bull chewing its cud.

"Tha's just the trouble, Bell. An' we durn sure can't let that happen, now can we?"

The wife of the Macon doctor barged in. "But Cat—donchew all *wanna* win?"

Half turning, he said, "Of course we want to win, Betty Ann. We just don't want to win so goddamn *fast*."

"I...I don't understand."

Bell said, "There's more to this than the defense of Eddie James, ma'am. There's the question of capital punishment in general, and who is going to be the next governor of the state of Georgia."

"My goodness gracious. Why I never..."

"This case could make or break it for the capital punishment crowd—for or against. Governor Barrow's reputation and his future in politics are at stake."

"And then there's Thurlow Wheems."

Bell looked at Tribble. "There's always Thurlow Wheems."

"And Robert Randolph."

"We don't know that much about him."

"You will, if this case turns out wrong."

Bell paused for a thoughtful sip of his whisky. "Okay, so what next? What if Hobarth—"

"Harbuck. It's Horace Harbuck."

"What if Judge Harbuck says he's nuts?"

Tribble sighed. "Well, we might decide to emphasize the girl's case. It's not as good, but..."

"Chester Biggs."

Tribble smiled. "Right on, brother. He's a natural. Paramount Pictures couldn't cast a better Southern heavy."

212

"I don' under*stand*," said Betty Ann, her face close enough to Tribble's beard now to tickle her nose.

"It'll all come clear in the wash, honey. You just be patient now an' trust ol' Cat, you hear."

Bell said, "Of course Harbuck *may* play right into your hands."

"Yeah, an' he may bite into my ass like it was a plug of his favorite chewin' t'bacco."

"Tough?"

"Like a corncob with razor blades in it."

"Still..."

"He might," agreed Tribble. "He just might do it. Then we'd have all the time in the world."

"Uhm. How much money do you want?"

"As much as I can get."

"A hundred...two hundred thousand?"

"At least."

"Goodness gracious," hissed Betty Ann. "I never in my whole life heard of such a thing."

More than an hour had elapsed before Bobcat was able to engage Otha Fletcher in a private conversation.

"You met everybody?"

He shrugged.

"Any questions?"

"What's in it for me?"

"I tol' you on the phone. Same thing's in it for us. Publicity. You use yours for your own purposes an' we'll do the same."

"What are yours, man? You a commie?"

Tribble bristled but held his temper. "My family has roots as deep and as old as yours, Fletcher."

The black man grinned, pleased to have rattled his host's cage. "Mebbe they came over on different boats at the same time together. You reckon it was worse on a slaver or a prison ship?"

Tribble looked at him for a long moment; then he grinned. "Seems like you always was an ornery cuss, Otha. I remember people sayin' you never would make much of a house nigger no matter how much you got polished up."

"I remember you too, Cat. People use to say—"

"Are we gonna stop this afore we start throwin' punches?"

Otha grinned and his teeth sparked like piano keys. "I don't throw punches, Boss. I *cut*."

"And *I* shoot. Fast and straight. You come back to this

213

here town an' fuck with me, nigger, an' I'll blow your balls off."

They glared at each other in the half-light. It was either cut and shoot or do business with the enemy. It was clear to each that they hated each other's guts—a clash of style and philosophy having nothing to do with race. But the necessity of expediency rasped in Tribble's voice as he said, "It's up to you, Otha. You know what we've got to do, and you know we don't have much time to do it in. Now you're either with us or you're not. Which is it?"

Otha Fletcher grinned and said, "Man, what you think I come all this way for? Now let's hear what you got in mind."

# Chapter Sixty

**The telephone rang the next afternoon in John Winter's** makeshift office. He was reviewing Bobcat Tribble's latest barrage of motions, and cursing Robert Randolph for having jumped the gun with a direct information against Eddie James. Such a course was at least a month premature in view of the preliminary status of the investigation.

John reached absently for the phone, then came alertly to attention at the sound of her voice. "Where are you? Well, stay there and I'll be right over." He stood up and said, "Where then? Yes, I know it. I'm on my way right now. Hold tight."

He hung up and started for the door. She sounded terrified. It didn't make sense. What did she mean, don't tell anyone where he was going? Or whom he was meeting, or why?

* * *

As he turned off the Interstate at the High Falls exit John felt more than a little foolish. For the last forty minutes or so he had been acting as if he were a paranoid American spy in the desolate Hungarian countryside. It was hard to believe that such evasive action was truly necessary right here in his own native Georgia.

He turned into the paved entrance leading to the High Falls parking lot. He didn't park though; instead he slowed his speed to a crawl, looking for her behind every car and tree.

Suppose she didn't show? What if—what if her fears were after all well founded? He knew he hadn't been followed; or if anyone had tried, he was positive that he had successfully taken evasive action. But what if—and then he saw her.

She stepped out from behind a giant oak tree on a grassy hill, and waved, threw down her cigarette and then came running down toward his car. Wearing jeans and a simple blouse, she carried no purse, but had a booksize package tucked under her arm like a football.

John attempted a smile. He lost it the moment he saw her anxious face framed in the window.

"Sharon, for Pete's sake...?"

"Not here, John," she said, jumping in the car. "Drive." She almost gave herself a whiplash, the way she continually jerked her head around on her neck.

"Honey, what the hell's going on? Look, relax. There's nobody—"

"You don't know that, John. It could be anybody. I tell you, they've got me under surveillance. And I think my phone is tapped."

"Who the hell is they?"

"And I know they broke into my house last night."

"*Who* did? Sharon, who the devil is *they?*"

"I don't know," she said and began to cry.

"Hey." He looked quickly in the mirror, found a peaceful spot with no other cars within twenty yards and parked. "Come here now," he said, putting his arms around her. "Take it easy. Take it easy, honey."

She wept against his chest for a few moments, the package on the seat between them. John could look down over the rolling grassy hillside to the magnificent falls a thousand yards below, and see the families picnicking in the grass, tossing Frisbies and footballs, and the few older kids fishing off the rocky shoals along the riverbed.

Didn't any of them look very menacing, he thought.

"Okay," he said finally, handing her his handkerchief and moving her back against the seat. "Now what the hell is this all about?"

"Oh, John," she said, dabbing at her eyes and then blowing and wiping her nose. "This thing is dynamite, man." She shoved the package at him and said, "Here, take this damned thing and then go back to the office and announce to the whole stinking world that Sharon White has been relieved of her duties and has nothing further to do with this case."

She was about to cry again. John wanted to laugh at her rampant paranoia, but he couldn't; she was too damned sincere.

He started to open the package but she stopped him.

"Not now," she said. "It's too long, too complicated. Besides I don't want to be involved anymore. John, I know what you're thinking—"

"No, you don't," he said gently.

"You think I'm a coward. Behaving like a typical woman under pressure, not like a cop." She snapped at him with her eyes; there was real fear there. "Well, I *am* a woman. I'm a mother, too. I can't take the chance, not with my son's welfare, maybe even his life at stake."

"Of course you can't, Sharon. I understand that. No one will think any the less of you." He took her by the shoulders. "But you've got to tell me what you're talking about. I can't begin to help you—until you tell me what you're afraid of."

She stared at him for a moment, then searched the surroundings with anxious jerks of her head and eyes. She looked back at him and said, "It's all in the diary, John. At least enough to send this county up in smoke, and maybe you and me and our families with it."

She could see the incredulity in his face. "Just read it, John. I've outlined it in narrative form. Then I indexed everything, every reference to...just read it. And then *do* something. Read it and tell me what to do."

"But I don't see why—"

"They *know*, John! *That's* why. They know that I've read the diary. Somebody knows what is in it, or some of it. And now they know *I* know."

John nodded. "Last night—what happened?"

"Every night I've been working in our den. Just a little study really, on the street side of the house. It has windows, anybody could see me. God, I wish I had a cigarette. Every other night I've left the diary in my desk, locked in a drawer, when I went to bed."

She paused and swallowed hard; telling about it was like reliving the terror.

"You're such a goddamn health nut. Don't you have any cigarettes in here, in the glove compartment, anywhere?"

"Sorry. Go on," he said. "The other nights you locked the diary in the desk drawer."

She nodded and began to chew at her lips. "Last night, though, I took it with me to my room. I slept with it under my pillow. I...I'd cracked the code entirely, I knew the whole story. At least—enough to get myself killed."

He reached out and took her hand reassuringly. "Go on."

"This morning Momma woke me in a tizzy. We'd had a burglary. A window was broken on the screen porch, there were footprints in the flower beds outside...outside the den and under my bedroom window."

"Didn't you hear anything?"

She shook her head. "Joey did though. At least he thinks he did. I can't say for sure, you know kids."

"Was anything missing?"

"Sure. Enough to make it look like a burglary. Some silverware, a radio and a mantel clock."

"Maybe—"

"Maybe *nothing*, John." Her eyes were big as saucers. "The den had been searched. I mean *searched*, and the lock on the desk drawer was broken."

"Jesus," he whispered.

"Suppose—suppose they'd come to my room looking for it. I had it with me, right there under my pillow." She wasn't crying now, but she was shaking all over. "I can't take this, John. I just can't take it."

"Of course you can't," he said, patting her hand. "It's all right now. Don't worry."

"I typed it all up this morning, the whole narrative. Then I called you. Please, John. *Please* tell me what to do." She was on the verge of tears again.

John cranked the engine and slid the gear into reverse. "You come on home with me," he said. "Stay with us until I've read your report and can figure what to do."

"I can't leave Momma and my son."

"Nobody will hurt them."

"We can't be sure. We can't be sure of *anything*."

He drove over to her car and sat for a moment with the motor idling.

"I'll get one of the officers to stay at your place around the clock."

"No!"

"Why not?"

"That's the last thing I can do. I can't trust *any* of them. *None* of them. And neither can you, John. My God, don't you *see?* Everything you're doing as special prosecutor is leaking."

"What makes you think—"

"How do you suppose anyone knew I was working on Sissie's diary?"

John thought about that for a moment. It was probably true enough; no doubt everything he did was reported to Randolph and Chester Biggs. Or was Charlie Tate behind it all?

"Don't worry, I'll get somebody we can trust. I'll talk to the governor, we'll get some outsiders to come down and give us a hand."

"I don't *want* anybody in my house!" She was really on the verge of hysterics now. "I just want to be relieved from this case so they'll leave me alone."

He looked at her and shook his head compassionately. "Honey, you know if all of what you suspect is true, it just won't work that way."

"Oh God," she whispered. "What are we going to do?"

"We've got to beat them, Sharon. There *is* no other way now."

# Chapter Sixty-one

**Chester Biggs went on home to supper, stopping only** long enough to pick up a box of Kentucky Fried Chicken and a six-pack of his favorite beer. By the time he got his clothes off and settled down on the living room sofa in his undershorts with the bucket of chicken and two cans of Bud on the coffee table it was only a little after five.

With sweat pouring down his face and neck, he felt as if he were on the verge of heatstroke. It had been years since he had been so physically exhausted. Not that he had actually participated in the search; but he had been on the go all day directing the operation. He had gone as far as he could go, considering the terrain; then he had just had to hunker down and send the others on ahead. Even so, his forearms were laced with briar scratches and his calves felt as if the muscles had been twisted into knots, soaked in kerosene and set on fire.

And all for nothing. No sign of the little Fletcher gal nowhere. The search party had combed the wooded area in which the body of the Watts boy had been found, but to no purpose. They discovered two abandoned stills, a stolen car about ten years old, a young calf freshly dead and down by the river enough beer cans, whisky bottles, used rubbers and discarded Kotex pads to rival a weekend cleanup haul at one of the sorority houses at the university.

But no sign of Ellie Fletcher, dead or alive.

Still, that wasn't his biggest worry at the moment. What he had to do now was figure out just what in hell he was gonna do about John Winter.

He had some heavy thinking to do for sure; that fuckin' schoolteacher was gettin' too close for comfort, Chester told himself as he reached for the bucket of chicken.

Gnawing on a crispy drumstick, he wondered why in hell the professor had gone all the way up to High Falls to meet with that little split tail from the Police Department.

He also wondered if that fool Stick had just plumb overlooked the dead girl's diary when he searched through Sharon White's den the night before. Is that what Sharon and the professor were talking about—Sissie's diary?

Biggs had thrown a conniption fit when his source in the D.A.'s office told him about the existence of a diary in the dead girl's own hand. What in God's name had the cunt been trying to do? He had almost yanked his hair out at the idea that she might have mentioned *his* name. It was unlikely, of course; but she *might* have.

His heart actually began to flutter in his chest now. If there was *anything* in that diary that might in any way connect him with Sissie Cubbage he would—what, *kill* her? Jesus, how could a thing like this have happened?

He had to get himself under control; he had to think calmly. How much did Winter know? *He* was the key to everything. Sharon White could be handled, one way or another. But John Winter. Jesus, how did you *handle* a guy like John Winter?

Chester opened a can of beer, consumed nearly half of it in one gigantic gulp and then rubbed the cold wet can against his throbbing temples.

That's what I gotta do, he thought; get me a handle on ol' John Winter.

Everybody had a soft spot, Chester believed. All you had to do was find it.

John Winter was one of those *new* men of the South you was always hearin' an' readin' about, whatever the hell that meant. But he had always seemed more like a duck out of water to Chester than anything else. The boy just didn't seem to know whether he was fish or fowl. Was he gonna take his place in his community and uphold the traditions of his people, or was he gonna turn tail and run? He come from good stock, the best, and Chester was fully aware of that. They didn't come no finer than old man Hightower, and his grandson could go wherever he wanted and roll in the mud with any kind of people and it wouldn't change the blood that was flowing in his veins. He was a Hightower and that was all there was to it.

Chester finished his beer and began to remember the old man. Unlettered, self-made, strong as an ox and brave as a bull. Best cotton man in Taliawiga County, and nobody's inferior when it come to politics. Of course he never held any public office himself. But along with Homer Stokes's daddy and gran'daddy, old Flood Hightower sure Lord controlled the political life of Taliawiga County. But the Stokeses for all their excess money and hifalutin' ways couldn't hold a candle to old Flood's personal magnetism. When you come right down to it, the Stokeses just weren't in the same league. Even today, Homer wasn't worth a bucket of hot spit compared to John Winter. Still, it was the Stokes influence nowadays that carried more weight in the county. The power of the Hightowers had passed with the death of old Flood.

Chester finished the beer and opened another as he remembered the good old days. The Stokeses delivered the city vote, while Flood Hightower controlled the county ballot. They used to come from all over the state—the Talmadges, Walter F. George, Ellis Arnold, Brother Carl Vinson—to pay homage to the Stokes/Hightower coalition.

Neither John Winter nor Homer Stokes had so much as lifted a hand to carry on where the old boys had left off. Winter had turned into an ivory tower dreamer and Homer Stokes was a bleeding-heart dilettante that wouldn't amount to nothin' in the long run. It was only the size of Homer's bank account that made a difference between the two.

Chester thought wistfully for a moment what it would have been like for him to have been born a Hightower or a Stokes. With all the back-alley-field-rutting shenanigans goin' on all these years in Taliawiga County, why in the name of God couldn't his own mother have been a little more selective about who she dropped her pants for?

His thoughts focused now on Homer Stokes. Chester knew where *his* soft spot was located well enough; he knew exactly what it was. As he began to chuckle the layers of blubber around his thighs, belly and neck started to oscillate like waves at sea. What would they think, the good folk of Taliawiga County, if they knew what *I* know about our hifalutin' la-dee-da number-one citizen?

Chester began to laugh now as he reached out a greasy hand for another piece of chicken.

But it wasn't Homer that concerned him at the moment—

especially now that the news about Josie's girl had hit the fan. It was John Winter that Chester had to consider. It was just possible that the sonofabitch had come down out of the ivory tower with a vengeance.

The one blot on Winter's reputation—up until his marriage to that Indian with the big ol' tits 'n' ass—had been his momma's sudden marriage to an uneducated sharp-talking, fast-stepping salesman from Toledo, Ohio. Chester began to chuckle again. Yessiree, he thought, remembering how ol' Ida Belle had run off with the fella when she was just a senior in high school and didn't set foot back in Taliawiga County for six long years.

Chester could still remember the way John had looked—skinny, sad-eyed and fatherless. Ida Belle's husband—so the story went around the county—had died a hero's death in France in the war, which, if the truth be told, didn't amount to a hill of beans with the folk of Taliawiga County. He coulda been a regular John Wayne for all they cared. After all, the man *was* a Yankee and there was no two ways about it.

John's father was a tall, skinny, sandy-haired feller, the best Chester could remember—but after Ida Belle had been home a few years, it was almost as if the man Frank Winter had never even existed. In fact, people were soon claiming that there really had been no such person as Frank Winter at all, that John had had no earthly father, Ida Belle no assistance in the making of her precious son; the *second* immaculate conception had honored one of Taliawiga's own home-town girls. Anyway, John was raised and schooled by his granddaddy. Never on any occasion were the circumstances of his birth and those six years referred to, so far as Chester had ever been able to ascertain. And over the years people watched uncomprehendingly as the boy's pretty mother became a withdrawn hysterical neurotic, frightened of her own shadow almost to the point of immobility.

Chester knew John's life story backward and forward insofar as it was rooted at home in Taliawiga County. He didn't know much at all about him up in Atlanta, Washington and Europe. He had done a little digging though, close to home. It wasn't too hard to run down more than a little dirt concerning John's hippie wife, Sal Massingale, as she was called back in those days. Sort of a poor man's Joan Baez or that there Fonda gal, thought Chester.

What Chester had learned was that Sal was a painter with a reputation for "expressing herself in powerful melancholy images"—whatever the hell *that* meant—and the authorities had once marked her for serious criminal indictments as a result of her antiwar activities toward the latter part of the Nixon administration. Biggs hadn't been able to learn why she wasn't prosecuted, nor exactly how John Winter had hooked up with her.

Ruined Winter's career though, according to what people said. Got pushed out of the U. S. Attorney's office and wound up slogging along in the streets for a while right in among all those niggers and commie rabble-rousers. It was enough to make ol' Flood Hightower turn over in his grave, thought Chester.

And yet now here was the boy all of a sudden right back on center stage again. The governor had thought well enough of him to enlist his aid. He wondered what Barrow's connection was with John Winter. Both eggheads, both bleeding-heart liberals and both friends of Homer Stokes.

And there it was!

It hit him all of a sudden like a fist between the eyes.

He jumped so hard he sloshed cold beer out of the can onto his flabby milk-white thigh. That was John Winter's weak spot. Homer Stokes!

Jesus H. Christ, it was so simple. They were boyhood friends, had remained friends all of their lives. Surely Winter would not stand by and watch as Homer's life and reputation were destroyed before his eyes. Still, he would bide his time...Homer would be Biggs's ace in the hole. Who else could get to Winter?

The sheriff finished off the drumstick and the can of beer, grinning all over his greasy face. It was so simple. He crushed the beer can in his hand, dropped it on the floor and reached for the telephone.

As he dialed, he scratched avidly at the heat rash beneath his lumpy testicles.

"Lamar?" he said, belching into the mouthpiece. "Get yo' ass over here. Now."

# Chapter Sixty-two

**Shortly after six o'clock John Winter found his family** at the supper table. "I wasn't sure whether you would make it home to eat," Sal said, raising her face for his hasty kiss.

"I didn't," he said, picking up a hot buttered biscuit and heading for the den. "I'll eat later."

"Hey, Dad. I went fishin' with Moses t'day—"

John closed the door to the den and crossed to his desk. He dropped the package on the desk, went to the bar and mixed a heavy scotch and water.

He needed a stunner. Though he hadn't read the contents of Sharon's report line for line, he had glanced quickly over the pages. It was explosive, absolutely incredible material.

He had kept the diary and Sharon's report with him every moment he was in the courthouse. When he had returned to his office, he had checked his phone messages, glanced over a couple of investigative reports that had come in during his absence—nothing much save for a pretty thorough background dossier on Elton Pittman that had been assembled by Sergeant Martinez. Then he had called Charlie Tate to inquire about any new developments.

The doctors had announced that Eddie James was definitely out of the woods physically. But there was no change in his mental condition. Then John had told his secretary he was going home early—six o'clock—but would be in the office before eight the next morning.

The last thing he had done was glance at his phone messages again. One in particular: Rachel Pettigrew. The return number was a county number; her father's, as he recalled from distant memory. What the devil was *she* doing back in town, he wondered; and what does she want with me? He had left the office without returning the call.

Settling into the swivel chair behind his desk in the den, drink in hand, John fastened his attention onto Sharon White's report.

Nothing had ever astonished John more than the contents of Sissie's diary and the implications that it contained. Not the incredible revelations concerning the Watergate imbroglio, nor the Georgia banker's scandal, not even the revelations regarding his own father that he had learned quite by chance while serving in the Justice Department in Washington, D.C., had caused him to react as strongly.

He looked at the typewritten report on the desk beside the closed diary and grimaced as if he were physically ill.

For some reason none of those other times had shaken him in the same way as these revelations, which sliced so intimately and deeply into the total fabric of his life, his existence, his home community.

"My God," he groaned. "What am I to do with this garbage?"

His head was ringing. He needed food. Sal had brought in a cold plate earlier, taken one look at his face and withdrawn. He looked at the food on the tray now with unseeing eyes.

I'll have to talk to them, he thought. All of them. His mind went racing ahead. I have subpoena power, I'll have to use it. So many of them won't talk voluntarily. Good Lord! Chester Biggs...the mayor's wife...all those good Christian people in their Sunday finery, their Bibles and prayer books in their dirty hands. Miz Aimee, for heaven's sake, and Councilman Scrugg's daughter. And good Godamighty, Gordon Joyner! Was this why the old man had decided not to run for re-election to Congress after all these years? Does he *know*?

Suddenly John could hear the man's soft syrupy voice on the hot line from the White House: "Well, my goodness gracious, Professor. What in the world is goin' on down home?"

John's chest was beginning to tighten. His head was spinning and he thought he might start to hyperventilate.

And that little sawed-off prick, he thought, suddenly furious in his unwanted knowledge. That vicious little prick! If any of them had to go down, he would see to it that L. G. Cubbage would be first on the list.

But Cubbage wouldn't lack for company. So many of these stouthearted proponents of justice would have to stand in the dock and receive justice. John began to laugh; not a happy laugh; a dry hollow sound that carried no mirth, excised no anxiety.

So they wanted to burn Eddie James, did they? Sadist ...mad dog...fiend. No-good nigger bastard. Make the land safe for decent white folk.

John rose slowly, leaning momentarily with both hands braced on either side of the neatly typed report. It's all there, he thought. Enough to blow the whole case out of the water; enough to blow Taliawiga County to kingdom come.

But could he use it; could he do it?

He owed it to Eddie James to save the boy's life. He owed it to Tribble and the Court to reveal information favorable to the defense and to produce evidence of undetected crime that was in his possession.

He cursed aloud and began to pace the floor.

He *had* to do his duty.

He was *obligated* to protect an emotionally and mentally unwell defendant from a legal lynch mob, yes. But his duty was more complicated than that. Who ever said all moral and ethical issues were either black or white, or if they aren't they *ought* to be?

He stopped pacing, turned to the bar and mixed another drink. Then he clapped the glass down on the Formica bartop and stalked over to the window. Peering into the darkness, he caught only his own reflection staring back from the darkened glass.

He hadn't thought of that day in the woods since the day it had occurred, so many years ago; and yet he remembered every nuance of the scene as if it were being played now for the first time on the other side of this magic mirror.

"Why stay in Georgia? Why not come North with me?"

"I don't think so, Homer. I'm not the Harvard type."

"What type is that?"

"Your type."

"Then what type are you—Rodney Redneck of Tobacco Road?"

"The truth is, I just can't afford it, Homer. I have my scholarship, I'll be satisfied at the university."

"John, if it's just the money, you know that Daddy—"

"And you know I won't take it."

226

"I know you won't. Old man Pettigrew has been trying to give you some of his for the last four years."

"His money and his daughter."

"Tell me something, John. This may be our last good talk for years to come. What do you really want most out of life?"

"My independence, I suppose."

"It takes a lot of money for that."

"No, it doesn't."

"I suppose you're right. It all depends on the man. You don't have much money, and you don't need much. I have money I can't count, and still I need more."

"You've really got a problem, Homer."

"I'm serious, John. I have all this money and there's no apparent end to it in sight. But do you know what I would give my last nickel for?"

"No, what?"

"To be like you."

John turned abruptly away from the window. After all these years and we've come to this. Will Homer talk to me? Will he come in voluntarily and talk to me?

Or will he have to be subpoenaed?

It was after one o'clock when John emerged from the den, soul-sickened and weary unto the bone, and started along the darkened hallway toward the bathroom.

With his hand on the knob he was startled by Sal's sudden cries from the bedroom. "No!" she shrieked, as he rushed into the room. "God no, *don't!*"

"Sal...honey...it's all right."

He snapped on the light and hurried over to the bed. He found her sitting bolt upright, wild-eyed, both arms up in front of her face as if to ward off a hail of blows, or perhaps some insupportable vision of horror.

He took her naked body in his arms and began to caress her hair and neck and shoulders.

"It's all right, sugar. It was only a bad dream. You're okay now. I'm here."

"Oh God, it was awful," she gasped, her face against his chest.

"Tell me about it, quickly, before you forget—so it'll never come back again."

He could feel her trembling against him as he lay back on the bed and held her closely across his chest. He stroked her hair and kissed the top of her head. She pressed her body against him and clutched his arm so intently that her fingernails cut into his flesh.

"It was horrible, John. I've never been so frightened. It was so—*real*. There were dozens of them, hundreds maybe. Nothing but vague smeary faces with their reaching arms and hands. I didn't recognize any of the faces, but I knew everyone in the mob. I knew them all. We were on a racing train or a rocket, I'm not sure which. You, me and the kids. And they were reaching for us...screaming, shouting, hurling stones and obscenities and rotten fruit. And they were grabbing at our arms and hair and flesh as the train roared by their position...and suddenly you were gone. They had you! I could see just for a split second as your naked thrashing body disappeared on a sea of grasping hands and arms. And then the train or the rocket or whatever roared away and suddenly their hands were at us again. I was trying to protect Davey and Cathy with my body—I could hear their terrified screams—and then they were just suddenly gone. I couldn't see them anywhere, I couldn't hear them cry anymore; they were just gone. I was alone. You were all gone and the mob focused all its hatred and anger upon me. It was awful, John. They were screaming and cursing and spitting at me and then I could feel their hands..."

Instead of talking, John reached up and turned out the light and resettled her in his arms. She lay like a wounded bird with her ear over his troubled heartbeat far into the night.

Owls screeched, whippoorwills mourned inconsolably and foxes hunted lithely through the woods on padded feet.

# Chapter Sixty-three

**Otha Fletcher called a press conference the next morning.** A crowd gathered in the early sun on the courthouse lawn. Otha was standing about halfway up on the steps, and a sheriff's deputy was positioned in the doorway above him with his booted feet spread and his beefy arms folded across his khaki chest.

Things couldn't have been better staged by a Hollywood film director, thought Robert Tribble, observing the action down in the square from his office window above the pharmacy. Only thing could have improved on this scene, he thought, was to have ol' Chester Biggs himself standing up there in that doorway like Genghis Khan II. But the old bag of shit had better sense than that. It would take more than a little mouthing off in the Southern sunshine by a hometown watermelon eater to smoke Chester out into the open.

But it's a beginning, he thought. We'll get him on the line. He'll bite.

And the timing will be just about right; not too soon, not too late to catch the rising tide. Support was beginning to generate in quarters far and wide. People were coming down from all directions, sensing another big case in the making.

Soon Tribble would have to establish a regular operations center to coordinate matters. And they would be needing more living space; already his house, big as it was, was overcrowded. Vacationing students were beginning to return to Adelphi. Soon he would be pitching tents in his backyard to accommodate the overflow.

And that was one aspect of recent developments that troubled him. The kids would be of considerable assistance in the coming weeks, but in these numbers you couldn't hope to control them. There was no telling what some of them might get up to. Boozing, doping, sex. If Biggs decided to make it rough—*when* Biggs decided to make it rough—he might try to get at Tribble through the kids. They were vulnerable; Biggs knew it, and Tribble knew it. But he had no alternative; he had to use them. They would be the shock troops when he moved his operation from defense to offense.

"Lord, Lord. Just give us enough time," he said aloud. "An' Your humble servant will be ever so grateful."

"You blaspheming again, boss?"

"Prayin', honey chile. Liftin' mine eyes an' my voice unto the Lord, in prayer an' supplication."

"I'm not gonna stan' too close to you, sose when the lightning strikes..."

"Come here, chile, an' watch this. Watch this and learn how it's done."

Rita Mays crossed the threadbare carpet and stood at the window beside her employer. She had been with Tribble for three years, and she worshiped him. But she didn't understand him.

"What's gonna happen, Cat? Do you know?"

"I reckon I can guess," he said. "Look, *look* at that goddamned movie star." He chuckled as Otha Fletcher leaned down over the stair railing and patted a pretty black girl on top of the head. "He's good, no doubt about it. Next thing you know he'll be signing autographs. He's got star quality, though. Charisma, as they say. An' he projects well."

"He's mean as a snake," said Rita. "Yo' turn your back an' he'll sink his fangs in your ass."

Tribble looked at her sharply. "He been messin' around with you, girl?"

"Shoot. He messes with anything in skirts. But he ain't gettin' his dirty black hand in *my* cookie jar."

Laughing, Tribble put his arm around her shoulder and hugged her to his side.

"Good girl," he said. "You stay away from his kind, Rita. His kind ain't for you. We gotta use him occasionally, but we don't have to like him."

She looked up at him, and put her arm lightly around his flabby waist. In the sunshine slanting in through the window her golden brown face glowed.

"Why do you do this, Cat? Tell me. Why do you help us like this an' make yore own people hate you so?"

For a time he didn't answer, he just stared down at the milling scene below.

"Cat...?"

"Somebody's gotta do it," he said finally. "It might as well be me."

"But *why?*"

"Because the system stinks," he said flatly. "It's rotten at the core, and it has to come down."

"Are you really—like some of them people are always sayin'—a communist?"

Tribble laughed. "Sweet Jesus, I'd be one of the first to go against the wall iffen the commies ever took us over. Rita, these people are *scared*—scared shitless. They know their system is rotting out from under them. They just don't know what to *do* about it. So they figure if they hide their heads in the sand iddle all just go away. Of course it won't. They got to pull their heads out of the sand and face it. Someday they just gotta face up to things as they really are."

"In the meantime they gonna nail your *scrawny* white ass up on the courthouse door."

"Maybe," he smiled. "But I'll be gettin' some of them first."

Rita looked down to the courtyard and pointed to Otha. "An' *he's* gonna help?"

"He'll help all right. Believe it or not, even Otha Fletcher will help. Right now, he's helpin' to buy us some time, an' tha's what we need most. Time. We ain't got us a national case yet. We got the ingredients for it. But we gotta get the kind of national exposure that's gonna get us the money—the New York money, the Washington, D.C., money, the Philadelphia and Atlanta money. *Then* and only then will we have us a national case. And only with a national case, with officials an' everybody down here feelin' that the whole goddamn *world* is watchin' us, will we be able to chip us off a little piece of this goddamned stinking system an' strike a blow for freedom."

"...and it didn't take em' long, did it?" Otha was saying in a high-pitched strident voice. "Nosireebob. City, county and state...cops in every color uniform you can think of. Even ol' Shadow Barrow done come out of the depths of the governor's mansion and appointed himself a special prosecutor. Why, the next thing you know, the President hisself will up an' send in the FBI, the CIA and the whole U. S. military establishment."

Otha paused dramatically for a moment, and struck one of his most practiced poses. He did look more than a little like an actor winding up for another Academy Award performance, thought Tribble, what with his cultivated little chin whiskers, his denim pants and jacket, his smooth dark chest bare almost to his navel.

"All this, mind you, to help convict and execute a black man, sick and wounded, already in custody, helpless and absolutely beyond any danger of escape or further threat to this here community.

"But—what is the government of the United States doing about the cold-blooded murder of a young black boy in this community, or about the disappearance of that boy's little girlfriend? What is the state of Georgia doin' about *this* crime? Where is the governor now, his state investigators and his oh-so-special prosecutor?

"Where are the local police, in particular the highest elected police official of Taliawiga County, Sheriff Chester 'the Bigot' Biggs?"

Blacks in the crowd began to shout their wary encouragement. Some whites were starting to mutter and many of the earlier catcalls and jibes were turning nastier. And the crowd was swelling in numbers. District Attorney Robert Randolph watched attentively from an upstairs window; L. G. Cubbage stood across the street in front of Grant's mercantile store, in company with a half dozen or so of his newfound admirers; and in the back row of the crowd, below the courthouse steps, Lamar Stick clenched the claw hammer in his hand.

"...and I have a right, a constitutional right as a citizen of this county, to *demand* of the police authorities that they does somethin' about the disappearance of Ellie Fletcher. My sister is a good, decent girl, my mother a fine law-abiding Christian woman, and they *deserves* the assistance an' cooperation of this here—"

The rock struck Otha Fletcher just under the left eye, splitting open the flesh along his cheekbone and splattering blood into the crowd below. Otha gasped, clutched his face and fell back on the steps. Women began to scream as more rocks and eggs came from a variety of well-orchestrated sources. Men were cursing, running this way and that, and wildly throwing punches. And the television cameras were rolling.

A black man got kicked in the balls, a white girl fell down and was stomped on. The deputy at the top of the stairs ran down with his club flying in the direction of the nearest black faces, and a squad of deputies came roaring around from the side of the building. Lamar Stick, aiming for the center of a black man's head, misdirected the path of his swing—mostly due to nervous excitement—and hit the strapping fellow a glancing blow on the shoulder.

The man squatted halfway to the ground in agony, grasping his shoulder with both hands. Then he looked up and caught sight of Lamar Stick backing away through the boiling crowd. The man came up with rage in his eyes and Lamar turned and bolted for his truck.

Tribble winced as he saw a club-wielding deputy working on a teenaged black boy who was down on the grass with his head between his arms and his knees up under his chin.

"There it goes," he told his secretary, standing beside him at the window, clutching his waist, her dark face blanched bone white. "It'll go national now, Rita. God help us, it'll go around the *world* before it stops now."

"My God," the girl cried. "Oh my God."

Lamar had run so hard and fast that he scarcely knew where he was. His vision was spinning, his heart ramming against his chest hard enough to crack his ribs. He had been unable to make it to his truck in time; that wounded gorilla had been all over him.

God, it scared him almost to death, even now, just to think about it. If the bastard had got a hold of him that sure Lord would have been the end of Lamar Stick. Goddamn animal had hands like a pair of ice tongs, he thought.

Jesus, what an idea. Look around this place. Old man Littlejohn's abandoned icehouse. How the hell did I get in here? If that ape corners me in this place... Lamar's heart leaped into his throat as the wooden window shutter was suddenly slammed back from the outside against his head.

He felt the rusty latch slice jaggedly into his forehead and screeched like a wounded owl, but he couldn't fall, couldn't run, couldn't *move*, caught as he was by the fellow's vise-like grip on his forearm. Oh Jesus Lord, the pain! Another second and his arm would be mashed to a pulp.

But the fuckin' gorilla didn't want his arm, he wanted his

life. It was all happening so quick. Jesus, God. The man jerked him halfway through the window, and had him by the throat now. Lamar could see the rage in his oily eyes, smell the foul stench of liquor on his breath; he was gasping for his own breath now, on the verge of extinction when the dull crunching sound registered in his brain.

Once, twice, three times he heard it before the man's grip on his throat loosened.

The next thing Lamar knew he was on the ground, gasping for breath, his hands at his ravaged throat. He was on the verge of vomiting, as much from fright as anything. The crotch of his pants was soaking wet. He winced as a door opened and a dark shadowy figure rushed in with the blinding light and swooped down over his cowering body.

"C'mon, c'mon. Git up before some more of 'em sees us. Jesus H. Christ, they runnin' wild out there." They could hear the distant sounds of shouting and screaming, the blaring of car horns and the wailing sirens, mostly coming from the direction of the courthouse square.

"Who...what...?" Lamar couldn't talk, his vocal cords felt like knotted strands of rope.

"I saw 'im chasin' you...got here soon's I could. Jesus, that was a close call. Fuckin' bastard was strong as an ape."

L. G. Cubbage helped Lamar to his feet. Then they went out the side door of the dilapidated icehouse, pausing for only a moment to get their bearings.

"C'mon, I got a car about a block from here," said Cubbage.

"Is he...?"

"Naw, he ain't dead. I didden have time enough to kill the nigger bastard."

Cubbage went over to the crumpled black man and picked up Lamar's claw hammer, which was lying beside the body. The man began to moan, and tried to rise. "Here, you better not leave this in case somebody might try to trace it."

Cubbage handed Stick the hammer and they started off across the narrow alley beside the icehouse. Up at the far end of the alley a fire engine suddenly raced by, its siren screeching.

Lamar stopped, and went back to where the man had pulled himself up on one elbow. He was looking up into the sun with unfocused eyes. He couldn't even see it coming.

"Made me piss in my pants," Stick said, and smashed the man's nose all over his face.

# Chapter Sixty-four

**A nine o'clock curfew was clamped on Adelphi that evening,** and Chester Biggs put out the word through the county to stay the hell off the roads.

But it wasn't going to work, not that easily, not now. The lid was off and it couldn't be clamped back on again by a few government proclamations. Too much had happened in too short a time span; Taliawiga County had never seen the likes of it.

The square in Adelphi looked like a battle zone. State troopers, sheriff's deputies and city policemen were on guard patrol in roughly concentric rings throughout the city and county. City police were most visible in Adelphi proper, the deputies were stationed in the countryside and the troopers were patrolling the state and federal highways that cross-hatched the county.

On the square in Adelphi windows were broken, a parking meter in front of the Citizens Bank was bent like a pretzel and the courthouse lawn was so littered with debris that it resembled the aftermath of a political rally or a rock concert.

The toll in human misery was considerably more alarming. Otha Fletcher's wound had been more serious in appearance and implication than in actuality. The rock bruised the cheekbone and made a cut that required a half-dozen stitches to close, but he was in and out of the hospital in less than an hour.

Others were not so fortunate. A girl of sixteen sustained a broken leg. An elderly farmwoman watching the melee from a feedstore across the street suffered a coronary and was in critical condition in the intensive care unit in the Community Hospital in Macon; her family had refused to allow her to be treated at the county hospital in Adelphi.

Two sheriff's deputies had been injured; one man was struck in the face by a brick, and another was severely bitten on the ankle by a black woman while the deputy flailed away at her husband with his billy club.

And in late afternoon a passing motorist had discovered the unconscious body of a middle-aged black man lying in an alley out by the old abandoned icehouse. He had been smashed in the face repeatedly by an unidentified blunt instrument and was in critical condition over at the county hospital.

The most far-reaching of the day's calamitous events had, however, resulted from the unwitting actions of Special Prosecutor Winter.

Early that morning, before any of the troubles had begun, John Winter had driven up to Atlanta to see the governor. Though he hadn't revealed the extent of the information that he now possessed by way of Sharon White's explication of Sissie Cubbage's diary, he had informed the governor that he had uncovered sufficient evidence to justify a suspension of the prosecution of Eddie James until all of the new leads could be thoroughly investigated and analyzed.

"But what'll that do to your case?" Clyde Barrow had asked, sitting in his shirt sleeves behind the big mahogany desk in the den at the governor's mansion. "I'm no lawyer, John, but won't that run you afoul of all these new court rules about speedy trials and what have you?"

"It's a chance we'll have to take, Governor. Maybe the defense counsel will even waive the right to speedy trial."

"Will Tribble *do* that?"

"Who knows *what* that guy'll do? But it's possible that he might. He's filed a half-dozen motions already; I'm sure he's got a dozen more to serve in the next couple of weeks. He needs to do a lot of discovery and he may want the time. He may even ask for a continuance, which would almost automatically operate as a waiver of the speedy trial rule."

"What's the time limit—a hundred sixty days?"

"One eighty. But there's still time to simply dismiss the case—nol pross—without prejudice, and then when we've got all our ducks in line start all over with an indictment."

"And that's not double jeopardy?"

"Not at this point. Not if you nol pross soon enough."

"And that's what you want to do?"

"Well, I'm not completely sure about that yet. But I do want to slow things down until my investigation is completed. Then I'll make the decision about whether to go ahead with the prosecution of Eddie James, and on what basis."

"You mean it's really possible that you might not prosecute at all? You have evidence other than the mental considerations...?"

"Governor, I'd really rather not—"

"Yes, yes. I know. The confidentiality of the Court and all that blather. *I'm* the guy that appointed you, man."

"And the reason you appointed me—so you said at the time—was because you believed that I would handle the job with all the integrity—"

"C'mon, Winter—did I *really* gargle with all that mouthwash?"

In the last analysis, however, Governor Barrow had acceded to John's refusal to reveal any further information pending the completion of his investigation. Actually, John had given the governor two alternatives: accept his terms and he would continue as special prosecutor, reject them and he would resign.

A few minutes before Otha Fletcher's news conference had begun in Adelphi, John had announced in Atlanta his intention to suspend the prosecution of Eddie James pending further investigation.

At first the announcement went almost unnoticed. By nightfall, however, the implications of John's position had begun to seep through the cracks in the wall of mass preoccupation that had attended what was now locally known as the "courthouse riot."

Taliawiga County was a seething hive of contradiction and conspiracy.

"You reckon the bastard's gonna die?"

"I don't know, but I doubt it. You know what they say about a nigger's head."

"I hit 'im purty hard though."

"You did that all right."

"Black sonofabitch should've let me be."

"Damn right he should've. What the hell are things comin' to when niggers got no respect for white folks no more? Can you imagine—big black ape chokin' a white man in broad open daylight. *Chokin'* 'im."

"I can imagine it. I was *there*."

"Jesus, Lamar. You shoulda seen it. He had you flappin' around up in the air like a rag doll."

"Strong as a fuckin' ape," said Stick, rubbing gently with his fingers at the bruise marks on his throat. It hurt to swallow his beer, but he finished off the contents of his can anyway. "I can't tell you how good it made me feel to smash that ape's face in," he said, and his eyes brightened with the memory. "Jesus!"

"Here, have another beer. I know what you mean." Cubbage shook his head admiringly. "You sure Lord cracked him a couple good ones." He pushed another cold beer at Stick.

"Thanks," he said, then added thoughtfully, "Course you'd softened 'im up a good bit with those licks of yourn."

"Well, ain't nobody ever gonna know nothin' about how it happened 'cept you an' me. Right?"

"You can say that again, Mr. Mayor."

The two men looked at each other over their beers in the half-darkened room. They watched each other and held their counsel for a time while they sipped can after can of beer.

Finally Lamar Stick belched, cleared his throat and said, "Is this where it happened?"

Cubbage looked at him quizzically.

"All the killings? Is this where the nigger murdered all yore fambly?"

L.G.'s voice hardened. "Right where you're settin'."

"Jesus," Stick whispered, looking around the shadowy living room. He licked at his lips and darted a glance at Cubbage. "You don't reckon... I mean, could you...?"

"C'mon," Cubbage said, rising. "I'll show you."

The tour ended on the back porch where the initial carnage had begun.

"Imagine it," said Stick, breathless and shiny-eyed, "yore whole fambly."

"An' right over there, my gal Sissie. Found her lyin' right there, half in the bushes, half her purty head blown plumb off."

"Jesus," Stick said again, as Cubbage walked over to the end of the porch.

L.G. wasn't inspecting the bushes, though. He wasn't even thinking about Sissie. He was looking at the darkened bedroom window at Naomi Hicks's house. Apparently she was still up in the front part of the house. It was early, she wouldn't take a bath yet until it was time to get ready for bed. She was probably watching TV for a while. L.G. hoped she would wait until he got rid of Stick. He knew damned good and well she knew he was watching her now. The last week or so she had been more brazen than ever.

If only, he thought... If only there was some way; if only Naomi would *say* something.

"Say, you all right there, Shortstride? You lookin' kinda funny like."

Cubbage whirled on Stick and almost hit him. "Don't you never call me that again! You understand?"

Stick moved back a step and almost fell off the porch. "Well, hey now, I didden mean nothin' by it," he said. "It's what everbody... I mean, shoot, man..."

"Ever call me that again an' I'll...I'll..."

"Call you Mr. Mayor to yore face iffen tha's what yo' wants."

Cubbage glowered at him a moment longer and then went inside. Back in the living room he said, "I got work to do, Lamar. C'mon, I'll give you a ride home."

"I ain't goin' home. I got work to do, too."

Cubbage looked at him quizzically. "What kinda work?"

"I gotta get me another nigger."

# Chapter Sixty-five

Governor Barrow sent down his right-hand man, again, in the company of two plainclothes state troopers, for an on-the-spot investigation of conditions in Taliawiga County. It was the intention of Harry Downs to deal with John Winter as his contact man rather than with any of the elected officials.

That night, after supper, they left one of the troopers as a guard at Winter's house and the other trooper drove John and Harry Downs around the county in their unmarked police sedan.

The county seemed fairly quiet but the tension in Adelphi was palpable. Especially in the black quarter. Although the place was all but deserted on the outside due to the curfew restrictions, inside the houses were seething with resentment and fearful uncertainty.

That afternoon a black group—something called Blacks for Democratic Action, a group that was non-existent earlier in the morning—had called for an evening protest march in response to the racist behavior of the authorities and the white citizens of Taliawiga County for instigating the morning's "courthouse riot." A white citizens' council of some sort—also previously non-existent in the county—had immediately announced its intention of mounting a counter-demonstration. That was when the authorities decided upon the curfew measures. Now, both sides were poised to march and counterdemonstrate the following morning at eleven o'clock.

"What you reckon'll happen if they do meet out there on the streets tomorrow?"

"No idea," John said over his shoulder. "Another gunfight at the O.K. Corral, for all I know."

Harry Downs was sitting comfortably in the back seat of the sedan in a semi-sprawl, and John was up front with the red-haired driver from the state patrol. The driver was a lean wiry young man of about thirty or so with shoulder muscles like hickory knots and the strong rough-skinned hands of a woodsman. His name was Jim Darden and John was impressed with the man's competence behind the wheel.

"You can't predict how your own people will act?"

"Sure I can," John said, again without turning his head. "But I'd probably be wrong. Just as wrong as I would have been if asked whether I thought a thing like this would happen in Taliawiga County in this day and time." He shook his head. "It's beyond figuring now."

They went slowly past City Hall on their way down to the square. The lights were on in the mayor's office and in the city council's chambers. Around in back, the Police Department was lit up on all three floors, uniformed officers coming and going with unceasing regularity. Police vehicles were pulled up all along the street. Curfew violators and other offenders were led to the booking station with their hands cuffed behind their backs; most were young and male and black.

Near the corner a policeman about to re-enter his vehicle and resume patrolling looked at them with curiosity over the hood of his blue-and-white as they passed on down the street. John figured they would be seeing him again in the not too distant future.

The square was all but deserted save for the presence of policemen. There were lights in a few commercial establishments and a carpenter on a ladder was busily boarding up the front window of the Citizens Bank. John asked Jim Darden to pull around by the People's Bank so that he could see whether Homer's office was occupied. It was dark.

John had phoned the bank and the house late that afternoon, asking to speak with Homer. His secretary and his house servant both promised to have Homer return John's call. So far he hadn't.

They turned onto Main Street and started out toward Shad Row. Suddenly a blue-and-white pulled up sharply behind them with its red dome light flashing. "Uh oh," said Darden, as the two policemen got out of the car and cautiously approached on either side of the unmarked state vehicle. Both cops had their hands poised on their gun handles.

"Please get out of the car and face the rear," said the cop on the driver's side. It was the same cop that had spotted them driving past the station house.

John said, "It's okay, they'll recognize me," and pulled the door latch.

As he stepped out of the car he found himself eyeballing the business end of a Magnum .357 in the hand of a very nervous and overwrought young policeman.

"Whoa," he said quietly, slowing his movement and stepping completely free of the car, his empty hands clearly visible. "Easy now, lad. I'm John Winter—"

"Put that goddamn cannon away," snapped the officer on the other side of the car. He had recognized John the moment John began to identify himself. He hurried around the car, pushed the younger officer aside and said, "This is Dr. Winter, the special prosecutor, you idiot."

"Oh, Jesus. I didn't know. I mean..."

"No harm done," said John, and he noticed two other police vehicles drawing near in front and behind their position.

The older officer had noticed them too. "Get on the horn

and call off the dogs," he said. As the young man went back to the patrol car, the older man came up to John. "You better be careful, sir—ridin' around in an unmarked car with a couple of strangers. Things are really tense out here tonight."

"I just found out how tense."

"He ain't the first guy to draw down tonight, I can tell you that. And it ain't only the rookies what's shook up."

"It doesn't seem all that bad," said John.

"I know. That's what's so damned misleadin' about it all. It's the quietness. It's unnatural. Somethin's building an' I don't think anybody knows what it means. We ain't used to this kind of thing here an' it's gettin' to us."

"Yeah, well listen, we were heading out toward the Row—"

"Jesus, Doc. I wouldn't do that."

"Have you had any trouble out there?"

"Not yet, nothin' bad anyways," he said, as the two other blue-and-whites cruised slowly by their position, their occupants carefully scrutinizing John Winter and the two strangers in the parked car as they passed. "We've had a couple minor fires," he was saying, "a few passing cars have been egged. An' there was a report of some brief sniper fire, but nothin' come of it that I know of."

"Well, we'll be careful, officer. But I do want to take a look for myself all the same."

John started to get in the car but the policeman stopped him. "Uh, say, Doc. Could you, ah, vouch for these two gentlemen, sir? I mean, we're supposed to check on all strangers and, ah..."

"These men are from the governor's office, sent down as his special representatives to report directly back to him as to conditions in Taliawiga County."

"Oh, well sure...fine. It's just that we, ah, have to do this. I'll have to see their, ah, identification."

"Is this really necessary?" Harry Downs asked from the back seat. "We have work to do."

"I'm sorry, sir. But yes, sir, it really is necessary, sir."

"John—"

"I think you ought to show your identification, Harry. The man has his orders; he's only doing his job, and doing it well."

The police officer looked at John Winter with obvious relief and gratitude, and then he stepped over to the car to check their identification.

"Thanks, Dr. Winter," he said when he was done. "Now you be careful out there, you hear. I'll put it on the radio that you're on the road. Any trouble, you just give us a holler."

When they were moving again Harry Downs said, "I almost shit in my pants when I saw the length of that barrel shining in the headlights."

"You just ought to take a sniff of *my* pants, ol' buddy." John took a deep draft of fresh air in his lungs. "That damned thing looked like the Holland Tunnel."

They turned onto the Row and moved slowly along the narrow street. Most summer nights the Row was jammed with moving cars and people. Music would be blaring from the open doors and windows, men and women would be laughing and shouting throughout the neighborhood, youngsters would be skating on the sidewalks, playing softball in the streets, running to and fro. And there would be the occasional tavern fight; a cutting, perhaps, even a shooting now and again.

But not this night. The Row looked like a movie set after the klieg lights were turned off and all the performers had gone home. A few men had ventured onto their porches, but no farther. Occasionally a child would break the stillness of the night with a shriek of alarm, probably frightened by the unnaturalness of such quiet at this time of night.

The air was hot and muggy. With the car windows rolled down and the air conditioner not in use, the men were soon sweating uncomfortably. Harry Downs was already talking about calling it a night. "That guy was right," he said. "There ain't nothing goin' on down here tonight."

"Too soon to say," John noted. "They might just be working up their courage."

"They got a lot of that," said Darden, "if they come out in face of these odds. This place looks like an armed camp."

"This place *is* an armed camp," said John. "And what you see is only a portion of it. The smallest portion at that."

"I don't know," said Downs. "Maybe the authorities will be able to defuse the whole thing. It seems peaceful enough to me."

"The authorities," said John, looking out the window as they passed the darkened home of Josie Fletcher. "Chester Biggs, you mean?"

When he had come out to see Josie earlier in the week, it was the first time John had been to the Row since high school days. Dut had been in the habit of bringing John and

Homer to the Row from the time they were little kids. By high school age they knew almost every family in the Row. Certainly everyone knew them. In his days of football stardom John had even had his own fan club that came up from the Row to Athens on Saturdays for the home games.

Tonight, he wasn't sure if it was safe for him to walk down the Row unprotected.

"Well, we can't do this all night," John said. "Let's go out to the Holiday Inn for some coffee."

"Le's go for some gin," said Harry Downs as Darden turned the car out of the black enclave and started out toward the highway.

Since police cars were everywhere, they had to be careful, but it had to be done. Lamar Stick didn't dare screw up on an assignment given to him by Chester Biggs.

Just as they turned off County Road 301 where it crossed the entrance ramp leading up onto the Interstate, they met another car with its blinking flasher indicating a turn onto the ramp. All six men in the car held their breath until they made sure that the other car wasn't a police vehicle.

It was too dark for the occupants of either vehicle to recognize any of the occupants of the other; only Lamar and John Winter would have recognized each other in any case. The two cars slowed their speed as they passed and then each proceeded on its separate mission.

John Winter and his companions went for a coffee break while they waited to see whether the events of the night would heat up. Lamar Stick and his associates were bound and determined to stoke the fires for them.

Earlier, when Lamar had related the nature of his association with Chester Biggs over the years, he was surprised and pleased to find in L. G. Cubbage a kindred spirit. Though Cubbage was unable because of his political aspirations to participate actively in the "schooling" of Otha Fletcher, he was not without his usefulness. He had immediately got on the phone and within minutes had lined up assistance and crucial information.

To teach Otha Fletcher anything would require swift action; Cubbage had learned from an inside source close to Bobcat Tribble's operation that Otha was calling it quits. He had had enough. Try as they might, Tribble and the others could not talk Otha into staying. He was scared and that was all there was to it. He was leaving Taliawiga County without delay.

The informant had said Otha was driving a white Camaro and would in all likelihood be alone; everyone else in the Tribble camp was disgusted with him. But Stick didn't care whether he was alone or with an army, he had to be stopped. Chester hadn't just said run him out of town. He had said whup him and run him out. And that's what Lamar had to do. Thanks to L. G. Cubbage he had a chance.

They crouched like alley cats in the bushes beside the road with their car lights out. Only the driver remained in the car, bolt upright, his hand alertly on the ignition switch. Lamar and the others waited on their haunches, watching the rutted gravel driveway that led to and from the Tribble property a couple of hundred yards off the macadam road.

"Here it comes!"

Almost an hour had passed. The white Camaro came blistering up the driveway and began to slide from side to side as the driver pumped the brakes and fought with the wheel to hold the vehicle on the uncertain path.

Stick's driver had waited until the last possible instant; then he hit the lights and the ignition and shot forward into the mouth of the driveway, effectively blocking the Camaro's exit.

The boy was a real demolition derby expert. His timing was so perfect the two cars barely touched; certainly no damage was done. But as Otha was fighting his way back down off the steering wheel, with a huge goose egg on his forehead from a crack against the windshield, the doors on both sides were jerked open and he was pulled out by a beefy pair of hijackers, one of whom beat him into a state of unconsciousness with a series of brass-knuckled punches to the head.

The two cars then raced together down the narrow county road for a mile or so, turned off on an unmarked dirt path into the woods and disappeared in the darkness.

The sheriff's patrol responsible for that particular area of the county had been called back by the dispatcher to await a special assignment from the sheriff. At the moment Otha Fletcher was having his balls crunched, they were still waiting.

# Chapter Sixty-six

"Get over here, John. And I mean *fast.*"

Doc Whipple's voice sounded in his ear as if it were three o'clock in the morning. John looked at the illuminated dial of his wristwatch on the nightstand.

"Jesus, Doc. It's three o'clock in the morning," he said.

"It's later than that, Mr. Special Prosecutor, an' you better get your tail over here by the time I hang up this tellyphone."

John sat for a moment on the side of the bed, rubbing his weary eyes.

"John...?"

"Go on back to sleep, honey."

"What time is it?"

"Early."

The grandfather clock began to strike the hour in the hall. "John, for heaven's sake, it's only three o'clock."

"That was Doc Whipple on the phone. They need me over at the hospital."

"Why? What's happened?"

"I don't know. That's why I have to go." He got up and began to dress in the dark.

"It seems like you just got to bed."

"I did."

She snapped on the light. "Don't go," she said.

"I have to," he said, scarcely pausing to glance over at her. She raised up on the pillows and her breasts tumbled free from the sheet as it slid down around her waist. John sat on the bed and began putting on his shoes.

"When will you be home?"

"I don't know, hon.".

"In time for breakfast?"

"I don't know, Sal." He snapped at her in his haste to get away, but he turned, instantly contrite. He put his hand on her arm and said, "I'm sorry. I don't mean to be such a bear. Look, I'll try. To get back for breakfast, I mean."

He leaned over and kissed her shoulder. "But don't count on it," he added. "It's gonna be a hellofa day."

"Aren't they all," she said glumly.

He got up but didn't leave at once. He wanted to try to make it up to her, to say the right thing. "Listen, you be careful, hear? Keep Davey close to home. And don't you come into town, for anything. Steve Hines will be with you all day; it's already arranged."

"That's great," she said coldly. "Maybe I ought to invite good reliable ol' Steve Hines in here for the rest of the night as well."

She snapped off the light and rolled over with her back to him. She seldom cried anymore, but he had the feeling she would cry tonight. He stood in the darkness for a moment, wanting to say something, unable to find the words.

He shut the door softly and left.


The county hospital appeared to be under attack. Armed and uniformed policemen were everywhere. The parking lot looked like the police motor pool immediately prior to the launching of a major raid.

Ten to twenty police vehicles of one denomination or another were on the scene, many with their dome lights flashing still, so that the whole exterior of the hospital was bathed in a pulsating redness.

John rushed across the parking lot outside the emergency room almost on the run. Nearby police radios squawking terse commands chased him across the concrete apron. A clutch of policemen at the door stood aside for him as he passed. Their voices followed him inside but the only words he was able to decipher were "Bet ya ten to one he wishes he'd stuck to classrooms by now."

Doc Whipple had left word for John to be sent straight to his office.

Captain Tate and Lieutenant Burke were sitting in the visitors' lounge as he brushed through the waiting room. He heard Charlie Tate call out to him but didn't stop. Doc Whipple had said *now*.

Whipple was conferring with an intern and a pair of harried nurses when John arrived. "Just a minute, John," he said briskly, and then issued a few more instructions to his associates. They left in a hurry and he turned to John.

"Lay it on me easy, Doc. Please."

"There ain't no easy way, boy. So brace yore shoulders. It's Otha Fletcher."

"Otha? What—?"

"They nearly killed him, son."

"What!"

"That's it. Don't ask me who *they* is. Otha ain't talkin'. He come in a couple hours ago. Walkin' iffen yo' can believe it, an' holdin' his nuts with his hands."

"Jesus. Is he—is he gonna make it?"

"He's gonna live. But he ain't gonna *make* it enny time soon."

"Doc, this is incredible."

"Ain't it though."

"Is the word out yet?"

"The cops know all about it."

"Probably—" He stopped.

"Yeah, you better learn to watch yore mouth."

John said, "Is that all you can tell me? That he's gonna live?"

"That's about it. And that's something that wasn't to be taken for granted, in view of the shape he was in." He walked John to the door. "They'd worked him over pretty good, John. Face was a mess. His right arm was broken. Three ribs were cracked. An' then they busted his nuts. Prolly while he was still conscious, or I miss my guess."

John went outside and met Charlie Tate in the corridor.

"What's it all about, Charlie?"

"I'm not sure. All those folks up at Tribble's swear the guy was leavin', pullin' out, headin' back to Atlanta."

"Then somebody didn't want him to go."

"Like who?"

"The Tribble bunch, for starters."

"You don't think—"

"I don't know. What else you got?"

"Not much. He left Cat's place around eleven-thirty, driving his white Camaro. That's the last anybody saw of him till he turned up here around one o'clock or so."

"Somebody saw him."

"Yeah, well—"

248

"And he just showed up here at the hospital, driving his sports car and holding his balls?"

"Tha's about it. Bleedin' like a stuck pig." He chuckled harshly. "Tha's purty apt, now ain't it?"

They stared at each other until Lieutenant Burke hustled up, saying, "Cap'n, one of the boys just called in. They want you back at headquarters right away. They's an FBI agent from Macon over there askin' a whole lot 'a questions."

"Jesus H. Christ!"

"It had to happen, Charlie. This whole thing is a natural for the Bureau and the civil rights people." John took a deep ragged breath. "If we don't get matters cleaned up pretty damned soon now, Taliawiga County's gonna go national sure as hell."

A few minutes later they all left the hospital on their separate destinations. No one had even thought to ask about Eddie James.

While John Winter and Captain Tate were talking at the hospital, Josie Fletcher was rocking stolidly in the parlor of her home on Shad Row. She was singing in the early morning darkness.

> *Swing low, sweet chariot,*
> *Comin fo' to carry me home...*
> *Swing low, sweet chariot,*
> *Comin' fo' to carry me home.*

Josie, for one, knew a little something about her son's recent activities. She had been rocking beside the parlor window, crooning, praying, grieving, waiting for her daughter to come home. The way she had been waiting for her Ellie to come home ever since...

> *I looked over Jordan and what did I see*
> *Comin' fo' to carrry me home...*

Her heart had lurched in her chest as the white Camaro came sliding down the street with its lights off and stopped in front of the house.

It was dark, she couldn't see much. But she heard a door open and there was a thumping sound, like something heavy hitting the ground. She didn't stop rocking.

>*A band of angels*
>*Comin' atter me...*

A pickup truck had pulled up alongside the car, its ragged engine coughing in the silence, and a figure ran from the car to the truck. The man jumped up over the tailgate and the truck sped away with a screech of its tires.

>*Swing low, sweet chariot,*
>*Comin' fo' to carry me home.*

The thing on the ground had begun to move. Slowly, laboriously, it had made its way across the yard and up to the front steps. It was hurt bad. It moved like a wounded animal, dragging its agony along behind like a broken shadow. As it came up the steps and slithered across the porch, Josie could tell that most of its bones had been crushed inside its skin.

"Momma," the thing had said, scratching and tugging weakly at the bottom of the latched screen door. "Momma, please..."

>*Swing low, sweet chariot,*
>*Comin' fo' to carry me home.*

Finally, Otha had dragged himself back across the porch, down the stairs and out to the car. As the Camaro moved slowly down the street, Josie's high-pitched wail had shattered the morning breeze.

# Chapter Sixty-seven

Early the next morning John and Judge Harbuck met in the courthouse corridor on their way to their respective offices.

"Boy, oh boy," the judge said, and all John could do was shrug silently as Harbuck entered his chambers.

Judge Harbuck's was not the first such reaction of the day. At breakfast Sal had said, "Do you have any idea what you're doing to *them?*" John looked at the kids, but before he could answer her the phone rang. *"You* take this one," she said coldly. "These are your people, not mine. *You* listen to what your friends and neighbors are saying about you and your family."

After breakfast, John had run in the woods for ten or fifteen minutes, hoping to calm his thoughts and nerves. The hate calls had become so ugly and numerous that they had had to leave the phone off the hook. On his way back to the house John stopped in the garden for a few words with Moses Minnow.

"How are you this mornin', Moses?"

"Tolerable, Mistuh Jawn."

*"Look* at me, Moses."

The old Negro dutifully stopped his chopping and raised his dark milky eyes.

"What should I do, Moses? What would Papa have done?"

Moses shook his bald shiny head, squinting against the morning sun. "Nothin' like this coulda happened in yo' gran'daddy's day."

"Is it my fault? Am I just making things worse?"

The hooded old eyes never wavered. "Yo' fault, an' people lak yo'. White an' black. All you folks of this here so-called New South." He shook his head. "Mistuh Flood, well now, he jus' wouldn't have nothin' to do with it."

Moses turned his narrow crooked back and started chopping his way down the long row of beans.

John went into his den with a second cup of coffee and Sissie's diary. He read over Sharon White's report one more time; he felt as if he knew it by heart now. His head was spinning in confusion. There was so much to do, so many details to attend to. There was nothing simple about blackmail involving an entire county. One thing was certain though; before the day was over he would have his talk with Homer Stokes.

John had no sooner settled behind his cluttered desk in the courthouse with the morning newspaper spread before him, than the district attorney was hovering about like a hungry vulture.

"Well boy, it's done hit the fan now, all soft and soggy."

"It sure looks that way," John admitted.

"What you intend to do about it?"

"Duck?"

Randolph laughed; he was unable to refrain from gloating. "Man, you ain't got nowhere to hide."

John shrugged. "Well, I reckon I'd better start digging then. If you'll excuse me..."

Randolph nodded toward the headlines. "*They* ain't gonna excuse you. No way, Professor." He went over to the door and paused with his hand on the knob. "Only place for you is back up there in that ivory tower. I suggest you start climbing real soon."

"I have a suggestion for you too, Randolph."

But he was gone, laughing, before John could deliver it.

"Bastard!" exclaimed John, pounding his fist on the desk beside the *Oracle*. One of the headlines came screaming up at him: SPECIAL PROSECUTOR DECLINES TO PROSECUTE.

A photo of Eddie James was captioned: Mass Murderer to Escape Trial?

A second boldface headline read: COURTHOUSE RIOT NOT SPONTANEOUS.

On the right-hand side of the page the lead article read in part: *Special Prosecutor John Winter yesterday abruptly announced his intention to suspend the prosecution of suspected mass killer Eddie James pending further investigation.*

*Winter revealed no details concerning his decision. He said he could not discuss specifics of the case pending completion of the investigation. He gave no indication as to when he expected that to be.*

On the left side of the front page the lead article recounted the details of the melee on the courthouse lawn, branding Otha Fletcher, black activist, the instigator. An accompanying photograph showed a white girl down on the grass surrounded by a mob of enraged—or terrified—blacks.

The front page of the Metro section carried a photograph of L. G. Cubbage haranguing a men's club on the subject of law and order and swearing to "kick him some ass" if the good people of Adelphi saw fit to elect him their next mayor.

The lead editorial took John to task for interfering with the orderly process of justice.

*Apparently the special prosecutor has decided to take the law into his own hands. Appointed by Governor Barrow to see justice done, he has decided to suspend the operation of the justice machinery. It is well and good to be fair in dealing with persons accused of criminality. It is likewise important to defend the rights of innocent victims of crime, their families and the community at large. A defendant's rights must never be allowed to supersede the rights of the public. The governor should instruct his special appointee to do his duty or resign.*

"Idiots," said John aloud, reaching for the intercom. "Miz Nellie—would you please locate Captain Tate for me?"

"He's right here, Dr. Winter. Waitin' to see you."

"Send him in."

"And Dr. Cecil Witcomb has been trying—"

"Oh no. I don't have time for him."

"He says it's very urgent. He was really upset...said he must at least talk with you by phone."

"Oh, all right. When Captain Tate leaves, get the dean on the line."

The door opened and Charlie Tate entered, wearing army boots and fatigues with the insignia stripped off.

"Somebody giving a war, Charlie?"

Tate laughed. "Before the day's over that might not be such a farfetched notion. Naw," he said, drawing up a straight chair. "Another search party's gonna hit the woods again today. Be back in time for this afternoon's demonstrations."

"You better. All hell may break loose out there."

"I reckon you heard some of the Klansmen are beginning to trickle in?"

"Oh, Lord."

"Down from the Atlanta area. A few from Memphis, an' a couple from over Montgomery way."

"That's all we need. The Klan and SCLC butting heads."

"The black folks are beginning to call this Otha Fletcher Day."

"What ever happened to Eddie James?"

"The forgotten man," said Tate dryly.

"You don't reckon many of the local folks—"

"Hell, John, you know they're *here*. I don't know how many, but it don't take many. Look at that ball-bustin' orgy out there last night—"

"You think the Klan was behind it?"

"It don't matter. It was Klan mentality. Prolly some of the local boys done the work—you know, any one of them swamp Crackers we got runnin' loose around the county. But I reckon some of the Klansmen were behind it, eggin' 'em on."

"Any leads yet?"

"Not really. But they'll start talkin' it around out in the boondocks. Can't keep their mouths shut about a thing like this for long. Meanwhile—"

"Meanwhile it's gonna blow up in our faces."

Tate smiled. "Mostly yours, I'd say."

"Thanks," John said. "I needed that."

"Just callin' a spade a spade," said Tate, rising.

"Not around here you better not." They laughed and John stopped him before he reached the door. "Wait a minute, Charlie. I want to show you something."

He took a county map out of a drawer and spread it on the desk as Tate came back across the room. "Up here," John said, pointing with his pencil, "in the area back behind the falls. I want you to concentrate on this area real hard."

"Why the hell way up there? That's nowhere near where the boy was found," Tate said, scowling over the area of the map John had indicated.

John picked up the map and folded it. "You look up there anyway. And look good. Foot by foot if you have to till you find that girl."

"And what am I supposed to tell Chester? This is his baby, you know. I'm surprised he even lets me and any of my boys help in the search."

"Tell Biggs anything you want. Only get some people up in that High Falls area. If he won't cooperate, pull your own men into a team and run an independent search."

Tate raised an eyebrow and whistled.

"If you're afraid of Biggs, I'll just have to—"

"Up yours, Professor."

John smiled as Tate started for the door. The captain stopped abruptly and turned around.

"What the hell makes you think she's way up there?" he asked.

John hesitated for a moment. He needed to trust *someone*. He *thought* Tate was clean, but he wasn't sure. He decided to keep the contents of the diary to himself a bit longer.

"I really don't have time right now, Charlie." John went to the door and opened it. "Just humor me, and I'll fill you in later. Miz Nellie—get Dean Witcomb on the phone now, please."

John eased Captain Tate out the door and shut it against his quizzical expression. He didn't really have an answer for him anyway. The diary didn't exactly *say* that was where Ellie Fletcher would be found. Sissie had known where the girl was: there was no doubt about that; but the entry was just short of spelling it out. He closed his eyes and there it was. On the last page of the diary, in the girl's childish scrawl, that entry more slapdash than usual.

*The ape has gone and done it this time.*
*He's really done it. He's been stashing his loot*
*for weeks up in that old cave of his neer*
*the Falls. But who the hells gonna fence this*
*here package for him?*

The phone rang. John rubbed his tired eyes and reached for it.

"Hello? Yes, Cecil. Yes I am, very busy. No, I don't see how..."

But in the end John had given in. Dean Witcomb had sounded on the verge of hysteria. And of course John's curiosity was instantly piqued when the dean had said that what he had to discuss directly concerned John's role as special prosecutor.

Jesus, he thought, getting into his car outside; what the hell could Cecil have to do with any of this? *Don't tell me Cecil Witcomb was involved with Sissie Cubbage!*

\* \* \*

Cecil Witcomb would have to wait. John had made another appointment that had to be attended to without any further procrastination. He took the two-lane country road southward out of Adelphi and drove into the country toward the old Macon highway.

I haven't driven out this way in—God, how many years *has* it been? There was a time, he thought, when I might have driven the entire route wearing a blindfold without so much as scraping a fender. Today he was having to work his way along with the caution of a traveler in a foreign land.

It all seemed so different, somehow. So much—so much more *condensed* than he had always remembered it. He had felt the same way about the old homestead the first time he had returned to it after a long absence. Now he was having to grope his way along another once beloved and familiar path. Much had changed during his years away from home. And yet, did anything fundamental ever really change? In places or people?

The confused feelings he still harbored about his home county made no sense at all. At least no lasting sense. One moment he thought he understood it, he had got a handle on it at last, and the paradox was solved. The next moment it was all gone. Why did he love it so, in spite of the gloom and pessimism that so often dogged him?

He almost passed the turnoff, marked after all these years by the squat fieldstone pillars that stood like bookends on either side of the open gate. He backed up some twenty yards or so, and turned off the highway onto the graveled path.

There's a madness on this land, he thought, no doubt about it. Papa knew it even back in the old days. He warned me about it, in his way. But there is another face to it. Papa knew that too, and I know it now. I would hate to have to explain it, though, he thought as he negotiated the graceful curves along the oak-lined driveway. It's such a slow, easy land. Some say dull, but it's not so. It's simply Nature's way down here. Even the seasons rotate with style and grace; there's a gentle dignity in the passage from one time of life to another.

Catching sight of the bright splash of flowering shrubs that studded the intervals between the great oaks, John was reminded of some of Sal's paintings done in Italy when her palette was as bright and gay as her mood. If only... but her vision was laboring in a different season now, and they would simply have to wait.

At the next turn in the drive, about a thousand yards off the highway—he used to know the distance *exactly*—he slowed the car and came to a halt. Some things never changed. He caught his breath again, as he had always done, each time he approached the stately old house. Homer Stokes and Miz Aimee MacAtee might have more money, but nobody else had *this*. Only one family had ever owned Oak Grove.

The house, a weathered old colonial structure of the Georgian period, stood like an architectural miracle on a gradual rise surrounded by a parklike setting of bucolic peace and serenity. The lawn was alive with magnolia trees, oaks, weeping willows and rows upon rows of flowering camellias and azaleas.

John sat there for a long breathless moment, scarcely aware of his own disordered thoughts. I suppose this is what I love, merely knowing in my soul that such a place as this exists. *This* is the South; my South. This is the way it *ought* to be. Not that other; *this*. He was smiling. But just *try* to explain it. Jonquils and forsythia blooming the whole year round...deep-starred nights and piny woods that whisper in the gentle breeze. Ham and grits and redeye gravy...and that soft satin sheen on strong black coffee. It's good, man. It's really good.

It's why I came home, he thought. *This* is what drew me back, always has and always will. Abandon all this? Shaded country lanes...berries in the fields...the magnolia with their delicate ivory blossoms and leaf of tender jade...the clean sweet smell of honeysuckle on a quiet summer eve?

Not me. Not again. Not ever again.

*This* is the land I know, and love, and grieve for. This is not a land of hate and cowardice.

As he pulled up the circular drive and stopped in front of the house beneath the enormous white columns, he thought, And all this could have been mine.

# Chapter Sixty-eight

"Hello, Rachel."

"I wasn't sure you'd come."

"I was afraid not to." He tried a smile but she was having none of it. He followed her to the small informal parlor across the hall from the grand salon which was reserved for state occasions. Ordinarily a servant would have shown him the way, but this confrontation had obviously been stage-managed down to the last detail.

But was it a confrontation? She had phoned him at the office. *You wouldn't return my calls. I had to catch you at work. I want you to come to see me today, John. I know what you are doing. Come to Oak Grove today, or I'll blow your whole scheme out of the water!*

A confrontation, he thought, stepping down into the spacious paneled room. Something else that hasn't changed, he thought, looking around at the familiar appointments. Then he looked closely at Rachel. On the other hand...

"You haven't changed a bit," Rachel said, and it was almost an accusation.

"And you...look every bit as lovely—"

"Bullshit."

He refused to show his surprise. She was facing him from in front of the cold fireplace, standing with her hands on her hips beneath the enormous painting of her great-grandfather. She, too, was wearing riding breeches and boots and John was surprised that, unlike the old man, she was not carrying a leather riding crop. It would have been appropriate for her to slash him across the cheek. He fought back a smile. Her pose and the entire stage setting was *that* theatrical.

But he didn't dare laugh. She wasn't carrying a whip, but from the glint in her eyes he wouldn't be at all surprised to discover the hard way that she had a loaded derringer in her pocket.

"Rachel, I'm really very busy..."

"You certainly *are*. The question is, just what the hell do you think you're doing?"

"I beg your pardon?"

"And well you should. Mine and a lot of other people's. But you aren't going to get off that easy."

"Okay, Rachel. Get it off your chest. I've come all the way out here, so you might as well tell me what the hell you're talking about."

She really did look for a moment as if she wanted to hit him. And John knew that he wouldn't be the first man she had hit in the years since he had last seen her.

He remembered that day five—no, six—years ago. She had come up to Atlanta to make one last effort. All her life she seemed to have been trying to persuade him to marry her. All through high school, on weekends and vacations during his college years. And when he had gone off to the Army without marrying her, that had been the last straw. *One* of the last straws. But sweet Jesus, he thought, and all the latter-day saints: why Tommy Endicott? That wasn't marriage on the rebound; it wasn't even a respectable double dribble.

John never did learn much about the second husband. Homer had always hinted, only half in jest, that the fellow had been two-thirds round the bend when Rachel got him and she had pushed him the rest of the way.

But this third merry-go-round with Buster Carnes was something else again. From the little John knew about Buster—which was more than enough to suit him—he could imagine that the bottom line of their relationship read something like Do Unto Me Before You Get Yours.

Rachel was a tough bird, all right. But it was the instability that made her so dangerous. He had sensed it when they were kids; now she might as well have it painted red on her forehead—DANGER: EXPLOSIVES. It was in the eyes, the set of the jaw, the attitude of her bloated body. Now that wasn't true; she wasn't bloated. Any other woman would be pleased and proud to have a body like Rachel's. It was her character, her personality, her soul that was bloated.

"Who are you trying to get back at? Me, Daddy, Chester Biggs? The whole goddamned county!"

Shocked, he said again, "Rachel, I don't know what the hell you're talking about."

She looked at him with loathing. "How could a man that I..."

She turned abruptly and leaned her head against the oak mantel. John went to her and put his hands on her shoulders. She jumped as if he had goosed her with a fire poker.

"Don't touch me!"

Her eyes filled with tears and she began to cry. Her mouth and jaw were slack and he could see the hard living in the lines beside her nose and eyes. He could also smell the odor of whisky on her breath.

"Rachel, sit down. Here"—he took her by the arm—"sit down and tell me exactly—"

"Not *there!*" she snapped venomously, and jerked her arm out of his grasp. She moved away from the sofa as if it were a bed of quicksand.

He stared at her for a moment, unable to make the connection. Why not the sofa? And then, finally, he remembered. The night of the junior prom. Jesus, how many years ago had it been? And here she was acting like the morning after again. But there had been no similar histrionics after all the other nights, he recalled. Perhaps, he thought, because the first time had produced such unpromising results.

He crossed over to her now and they settled into a pair of Georgian armchairs that he seemed to recall had some slight history of their own.

"I want to know"—she spoke coldly and directly—"if it is Daddy you are after, and if it is, what you intend to do."

He shook his head and tried again to deflect her line of thought. "Rachel, I swear to you—I'm not interested in your father."

"I know about the diary!" She almost screamed it at him. Then she lowered her voice and said through clenched teeth, "I *know* about the goddamned diary."

John was stunned. His mouth open, staring, he sat back in his chair, speechless, watching her cry. Finally, he leaned forward again and took both her hands in his. This time she did not recoil at his touch.

"*How* do you know about the diary, Rachel?"

"You tell me what you're going to do about Daddy—"

"Tell me what you know, Rachel—and how you know it—or I won't discuss any of this with you at all."

"Promise—"

"I can promise nothing," he said. "Now tell me."

She stared at him with exactly the same look of defiance that she had used when they were young. But the resolve was no longer intact; the willfulness had long since broken down. Her imperious nature had crumbled against the craggy face of an unobedient world. John hated even to speculate upon what her present life must be like; and that of her husband.

So much about her seemed the same. He watched her closely as she lit a cigarette and exhaled avidly. The tall stately figure; the neat blond hair that had transcended so many fashion changes over the years; the haughty, imperious voice and manner. But there were subtle differences too. What had gone wrong? There had to be more to it than a lost love. A woman with any character at all could have risen above such a disappointment.

"My daddy," she said, almost mechanically, "is a good and decent man."

As her father was neither good nor particularly decent, and since John had no idea where she was going with this line of thought, he decided to withhold comment altogether.

Rachel tried again. "He's never been anything but good to you. He would have given you the world. He didn't want you for me half as much as he wanted you for himself. You would have been the son he could never have... it would have been the culmination of all his dreams. But no, you couldn't see it that way. You had to—"

"Rachel," he said gently, "we've been all over this. A long time ago. Let's not go through it again. Things just didn't work out, honey. I went my way, you went yours."

"Hah. This time around I got a drunken brute that isn't fit to live with pigs, and you got yourself a—"

He looked her directly in the eyes. "I don't know anything about your situation, Rachel. But I got the woman I love."

She recoiled as if he had slapped her. "Thanks, you bastard. I really needed that."

He stood up. "I'm sorry, Rachel, I shouldn't have come. This isn't—"

"Are you gonna prosecute Daddy?"

He just looked at her.

"Are you trying to *destroy* him?"

He sat down again, waiting.

"Chester says—" She stopped.

"Go on," he said cautiously.

"You have the girl's diary. You have the little slut's diary and you know all about—" Again she stopped.

Sissie Cubbage and Orin Pettigrew? John racked his brain for an entry in the diary or an item in Sharon White's report that might tie into all this. But there was nothing.

"He...he doesn't even remember how it started. Just once or twice in the beginning. And then, little by little, it somehow became a regular thing."

No wonder Orin was acting so skittish the other day when they met in front of the bank. Jesus. No wonder he had sent for Rachel to come home. But what did it all add up to?

John's heart was hammering as he waited, forcing himself to hold his tongue and just let it unfold. The accursed diary was like a Pandora's box that opened on all four sides.

"He didn't think it was so bad...not at the time. No one seemed to be getting hurt. It was even—sort of a public service—in a way. It would have cost the county a lot more to send them to prison."

Prison? What the hell was she talking about? Who was *them?* "That's one way of looking at it," John said noncommittally.

"That's what Chester said. That's how he got him started—the big bag of shit." She lowered her voice and her eyes were like snake's eyes. "I hope you do get *that* sonofabitch. I hope he *rots* in jail."

"How long—? I mean..." He couldn't push too hard or he'd blow it.

"Oh—for years," she said. "Instead of sending them to work camps, he would turn them over to Daddy for work in the lumber yards and in the forests. Nobody ever complained. They would rather work for Daddy than go to jail."

I'll be damned, thought John. I'll just be damned. But he still couldn't remember anyplace in Sissie's diary where any of this might have been mentioned. "And the payoff—?" he prompted.

"Campaign contributions mostly. Chester has never wanted for a dime all these years."

"When did he tip your father off—about the diary?"

"I don't know. A few days ago...a week maybe. Daddy's been acting like a crazy man ever since."

"What exactly did Chester tell him?"

"That you were out to get them. All of them. That you'd always hated this place...that like your momma, you always thought you were better than the people of Taliawiga County. Chester said—that was why you wouldn't marry me. The Hightowers were too good for us."

"And you believe that crap?"

"I don't know what I believe anymore. Oh, John! What are you going to *do*? About Daddy, I mean? Don't you see—a scandal like this will destroy him."

He shook his head, got up, walked across the room. He turned and looked at her. "I don't know," he said. It was true; he really didn't know. It was so sudden, so unexpected. "I just don't know, Rachel."

She stood up. She looked like a block of ice.

"I'll do anything you say. You once cared for me, John. I know you did. If the memory of that means anything at all..."

"The law doesn't work that way, Rachel. Or at least it shouldn't."

"Fuck the law!" she said furiously. "I'm talking about my daddy's life, his sanity and our family reputation." She crossed over to him, talking as she walked. "I said I'll do anything. I mean it—*anything*. I'm no little Southern titmouse, you know. I never was. My life—it's not been a pretty affair. All these creeps I married on the rebound—oh well, never mind all that."

"Rachel—"

"Listen to me, John. I'm begging you. Is that what you want. Do you want me to crawl?" She dropped suddenly to her knees. "Is this how you want me—on my knees? What else can I do, John? Tell me. Order me. Is this what you want—?"

She slid forward on her knees and reached abruptly for his fly.

"Rachel! Get up!"

He stepped back, grabbed her by the shoulders and jerked her to her feet. Her hands were fumbling still with his zipper.

"Stop it," he said, pushing her roughly away from him. She stumbled over a mahogany footstool and went sprawling onto the floor. And in that instant, it dawned on him how much liquor she must already have consumed in order to screw up her courage for this revolting scene.

He went to her and tried to help her up. She threw her arms around his neck and pulled him down on top of her. She kissed wildly at his mouth and he felt her tongue swiping wetly across his lips; the taste of the booze on her breath was stale and acrid. "Rachel—" She was clutching at him with her legs too, and suddenly she ripped open her blouse. She was braless. As her soft creamy breasts spilled over his arms, the flashbulbs began to pop one after the other all around them.

"Okay, let 'im go," a sudden voice barked, and a big booted foot pushed John over on his side.

He raised on his elbow, Rachel beside him with her breasts bared, and the explosion of another series of flashbulbs blinded him for a moment.

"Get up, cunt—an' get yo'self dressed."

Rachel scrambled to her feet, looked at John with an expression that he would puzzle over for the rest of his life. Fear, hatred, remorse—vengeance? Then she folded her torn blouse over her naked breasts and ran from the room.

John sat with his arms folded across his knees looking up at Chester Biggs. The sheriff nodded at the two cameramen and they quickly left the room. Orin Pettigrew hung limply in the doorway like a skeleton on a hook, shaking in his limbs as if he had the palsy. His eyes said it all. *We had to do it, John. He made us. There was no other way.* John looked at the two men, not with anger or hatred, but with utter contempt. Pettigrew couldn't face him. He backed out of the room and closed the door.

"Well, John—I reckon you see how it is."

John looked up at Biggs and smiled. "I reckon I do."

Biggs reached his big hand down and John pulled himself to his feet. Biggs began to chuckle. "You two looked just like you used to in the back seat of ol' Orin's Packard. Only that liddle ol' gal shore has done some fillin' out in the lung department."

"You know, Chester, if you weren't an old man—"

"You'd risk throwin' a punch at me, hey boy? Jesus," he chuckled, "I just bet you would." He turned the footstool upright with his boot and said, "Now lookahere, John. All you gotta do is use a liddle common sense an' that there Hollywood business ain't gonna mean a thing."

"Chester, you know damn good and well there's nothing in that diary about Orin Pettigrew."

"I didn't reckon there was," Biggs admitted.

"But Orin didn't know any better," said John.

264

"Orin's a good ol' boy, iffen ever there was one."

John started for the door.

"Now John, wait up a minnit. Okay, I admit, I don't know exactly what yore up to. An' I don't know just what's in that there diary. But I know what that Cubbage cunt was like, so I can make a purty good educated guess."

"How can a semi-illiterate like you make an educated determination about anything?"

"Now John. Le's don't be so goddamned abusive, you hear me now. Iffen we gonna work together—"

"What the hell are you talking about?"

The sheriff waddled over to him. "I don't wanta fight you, John. Never have. You an' me could make a real fine team. Like I say, I ain't shore what yore up to yet. But I've seen this sort of thing before. You just been waitin' to make yore move. Mebbe you ain't even decided yet, I don't know. District attorney...Congress...a judgeship. That what you aiming for, to sit on the bench? Well, it don't matter much which office you pick. You cooperate with me, John, an' it's yours. Whatever you want."

He put his hand on John's shoulder and grinned conspiratorially. "I'll furnish the votes, Orin the money, and Rachel will even throw in a liddle—"

John hit him. Just one time, in the sternum. He went down in a whoosh of rancid air.

# Chapter Sixty-nine

To say that John was shaken would be an understatement. He remembered absolutely nothing about the drive back from Oak Grove to Adelphi. In fact, he had forgotten his luncheon appointment with Cecil Witcomb. He was almost at the courthouse when he remembered, and had to drive back out onto University Road to the Country Kitchen. The restaurant was located only three miles from the campus and Dean Witcomb was already waiting when John arrived.

"Sorry I'm late, Cecil. It's been one of those days."

"It's all right, John. I've only just arrived. Something to drink?"

"No, if I get started I'm afraid I won't stop for a month. I think I'll just have black coffee."

"Are you all right?"

"What? Oh, I'm fine. Just up to my eyeballs in quicksand, that's all."

Dean Witcomb smiled nervously. "I know the feeling," he said. "That's what I want to talk to you about."

John looked at him, his guard momentarily down, and said, "Cecil, don't tell me you were involved with that little pit viper, too."

The immediate questioning look that crossed the dean's face gave John the first real pleasure he had known all day. He knew intuitively that Witcomb was not involved with Sissie's diary.

"I don't understand," said Cecil.

"I'm glad you don't," said John, and determined not to be so careless again. "Now what is it you wanted to see me about? I don't mean to rush you but I really don't have much time. You said it was about the investigation."

"That's right. This investigation is going to spoil everything, John."

He sounded so petulant John thought for a moment he might cry. But at that moment the waitress arrived with her pad and pencil poised. Both men ordered the businessman's special, and Cecil Witcomb ordered iced tea while John asked for coffee.

"What do you mean, Cecil? How does the investigation affect you?"

"It affects me, it affects you, it affects the university. John, it affects us all."

"Well now, Cecil. Of course I know the whole community is involved in one way or another—"

"No, no, that's not what I mean. John, the trustees have been meeting almost weekly concerning your involvement in this case."

"What the hell have they go to do—"

"John, do you remember when I talked to you some weeks ago about your future status at the university?"

"Of course."

"Well, I didn't tell you the whole story."

John leaned back in his seat and smiled. "Cecil, that's the story of my life lately."

"I'm sorry, but I just wasn't at liberty at the time to indicate to you just what sort of, ah, plans were actually under way."

"And now you are?"

"Now I have to, in view of your involvement in this Cubbage matter." He paused, added sugar to his iced tea and took a long bracing swallow.

"John, I wanted you to take over as chairman of the division, that's very true. But there was more to it than that. I—we—wanted you to serve in that capacity only for a short period of time. A year, two at most. As you are well aware, President Reed is on the verge of retirement. Enforced retirement, if not voluntary. As a matter of fact, the way he's been carrying on lately concerning your involvement in this case, a number of the trustees are beginning to think that there is no better time than the present to start shoving him along."

"Adelphi University without Wendell Reed," said John, almost as if thinking aloud. "It's hard to imagine."

"Yes, I know what you mean. That's why it's so difficult for us to do what we know has to be done. John, the man has to go. It's not just that he is approaching senility. It's worse than that. I'm sure you know how dependent he is upon alcohol. It has been getting worse every year. He is becoming an embarrassment to the university and to the community. One of these days he is going to do something that will seriously damage us all." He paused. "And now with this Cubbage case inspiring so much—passion. Well, you know how reactionary he is."

John nodded.

The dean glanced warily over his shoulder. "He has been speaking out quite often lately, on law-and-order themes. He's attended numerous functions with Mr. Randolph. We're afraid he'll do something rash like—endorse capital punishment."

"And openly support L. G. Cubbage," John laughed.

"My God. Don't laugh about such a thing. It's not at all beyond the realm of possibility."

John shrugged, and took a sip of coffee. "I still don't see what any of this has to do with me."

Cecil took a deep breath, stared at him for a long moment and then said, "We want you to take his place."

John couldn't have been more surprised if Cecil had started tearing his clothes off and wrapping his arms and legs around him the way Rachel Pettigrew had. He looked at the dean as if he had absolutely taken leave of his senses.

"Have you absolutely taken leave of your senses?"

"I know it comes as something of a shock—"

"Shock? Listen, Cecil, I'm not up to this. I've had more of this kind of thing in one day than my nervous system can handle. Me, replace Wendell Reed? *Me,* president of Adelphi University?"

"That's what we had planned. The trustees and I."

"You're all just crazy."

"No, we think it's a very sound notion. At least, we did think so."

"Even if I were interested, even if it were possible—what about yourself?"

"I will be the university's provost."

"Second in command to me?"

"Not exactly. At least I don't see it that way. And neither do the trustees. Now that I've had ample opportunity to explain the arrangement to them as I envision it."

"You mean this was all your idea?"

"Mostly, yes."

"Elevating me to the presidency, when everybody anticipated that you would take over if the old man stepped aside, or died?"

"John, I can't run a university. I am aware of my limitations, and so are the trustees. I don't even *want* to run a university. It has taken me a long time to accept this fact. My wife still has not quite come to accept it. I simply do not want the responsibilities of running Adelphi University, or any other institution of higher learning."

"What do you want, Cecil?"

"I want to stay here in Adelphi, with the university. My future is here. I feel a part of this community now, and I don't want to leave. But I can't stay as president. I have neither the temperament nor the talent to serve as chief executive. I do have the capacity to administer the academic side of a university, and that is what I have proposed to the trustees. That you run Adelphi, with responsibility for the financial aspects of the institution, the fund raising, the plant and campus development programs, the new acquisitions, the public relations and political necessities of life. Those are the things in which you would excel, John. You are a trained attorney, an experienced administrator, an adept politician. And you are a man with local roots that sink deep in the community."

John laughed ruefully. "Cecil, an awful lot of people in this community are chopping at those roots right now in order to sever them entirely."

"I know, John. That's exactly what is troubling us. That's why we are so upset with the manner in which this case is developing. It is on the verge of ruining everything that we had planned. And that is why we want to strongly urge you to step down."

John stared at him without breaking eye contact until Cecil looked away.

"You want me to quit as special prosecutor," he said slowly. "Or else I can't have the job as president of the university?"

"I hate to put it like that, John. But yes, that's what we want. Not only can you not have the job as president, I'm afraid you will not have the job as chairman of the division. Nor will you be able to return to the university as a classroom professor."

"All or nothing?"

"I'm afraid so. It pains me to have to say this... there ought to be some better way..."

"There certainly ought to be, Cecil, but there never is."

The waitress arrived with their lunches. John had just got the meat loaf salted to his liking when the proprietor came to the table with a manner that immediately spelled trouble to John's experienced eye.

"Mr. Winter, there's an urgent phone call for you at the desk."

John sighed and put down his fork. "Thanks, Popeye. I'll be right along."

He was gone only a moment. When he returned his face was white as paper. He placed some bills on the table and said, "Sorry, Cecil. I've gotta rush."

"Oh dear. What about—"

"Forget it, Cecil. I'm not your boy. Look for somebody else."

"John, we don't *want* anybody else."

John looked at him for a brief moment. "After today, you probably will."

Lieutenant Fred Burke was leaning against a pine tree in the woods with his head between his outstretched arms. He had just vomited in the pine straw and was not at all certain that there was not more of the same yet to come.

"Lieutenant...?"

"Leave me be," Burke gasped. Oh God, he was thinking, if Charlie hears about me gettin' sick again...

The patrolman went back over to the mouth of the cave, joining the other three officers as they smoked their cigarettes and filled their lungs with fresh air.

"Jesus," he said, "I don't wanta go back in there."

"Le's send Burke," said one of the men. They all laughed mirthlessly.

They could scarcely hear the officer shouting from above the ridge, the roar of the nearby falls was so loud. But he was excited about something.

"I'm goin' down to the car and radio in to the captain," Burke said, licking his lips with his crusted tongue.

"You ain't got nothin' new to tell 'im, Fred," said one of the men.

"He has now," said the officer, who had been making his way down from the ridge above their position. "Take a look at this."

He handed the object to Fred Burke and the lieutenant abruptly succumbed to a fit.

John found Charlie Tate waiting in the office. The whole courthouse was abuzz with activity and tension.

"You were right about the location, Doc."

"The falls?"

"Yeah, but we never would have found her in a year of lookin' day by day."

"Then how—"

"A coupla kids were messin' around back upriver above the falls. Old-timers around there say there are caves like the one we found all up and down the river. Two kids about ten or twelve years old were just messin' around back in there and happened to stumble on it. On the girl's tomb. And that's what it was, Doc. A goddamn tomb."

"They found her then? The girl, Ellie Fletcher?"

"Well now," said Tate evasively. "Maybe we have an' maybe we haven't."

John went over and sat down behind his desk. "Tell me about it."

"Well, it's the damnedest place you ever did see. Whoever done this—and he must be one hell of a character, I can tell you that—but he was no spur o' the moment operator. The goddamn place is like an apartment. I mean he had everything in there—appliances, hardware, guns, ammunition, yard machinery, furniture—everything but the kitchen sink. And there may be that too. I'm not sure. A toaster and a half a dozen electric coffeepots—"

"Sounds like a bloody warehouse."

"That's about the size of it. It's all stolen stuff, Doc. Some of it we were able to trace immediately. The guy has really been operatin' this territory, stashin' the stuff away until he could make a big run up to Atlanta and fence the load in one or two trips."

"And the girl? What about the girl, Charlie?"

"She was there, no question about it. The girl was there."

"Was?"

"Yeah, well...there were plenty of signs, see. Bits and pieces of clothing, blood splattered...a shoe...bones."

"Bones?" John felt his hair stand on end.

Tate nodded. "Doc, somethin' got to her. She was tied up, gagged too, I think. There were pieces of rope and strands of adhesive tape—"

"Bones, you said?"

"I dunno—wild dogs...a pack of wild boars...coons an' field rats. Who knows?"

"But you're sure—?"

"They're human bones, we're sure of that. Ellie Fletcher—well, we'll see. One of the searchers found a—foot—and leg, up to the knee joint—not far from the cave."

"Oh Jesus," said John, and a rictus of pain twisted his face. "In the cave—?"

"Not much. Just bits and pieces. Whatever got to her was big, see. Carried her away and just...just et her up."

John got up and for a moment looked as if he might leave the office. He opened the window behind his desk and inhaled the thick sultry air. It didn't help.

He turned around and sat down again. "Go on," he said stoically.

"The girl had a gimp leg, if you recall. We've got Doc

Peavyhouse workin' on it. If it's the right foot...well, and the search teams are still workin' the woods around the falls."

"Is the sheriff's office cooperating?"

"They are now. This mornin' it was nothin' doin'. I put a team of our own boys up in the falls area, like you said. The kids that found the cave reported to us 'cause we were closer to hand."

John shook his head. "The poor kid," he mused aloud. "What a way to die." He shivered. "God, it must have been horrible." He stared at the floor for a moment and then snapped out of it. "Who's in charge out there?"

"Burke was."

"What do you mean—was?"

"He got sick or somethin'. One of our boys radioed in and said they were takin' him to the emergency room."

John looked at his watch, drew a deep breath and leaned way back in his chair. "Your timing was perfect, Charlie. Just think what those sonsofbitches will do with this little piece of information at this afternoon's demonstration."

"You said to find her, John. We were just followin' orders."

# Chapter Seventy

A group of five men sat drinking beer around the kitchen table in the Cubbage house. Their mood was one of strained gaiety. The underlying tension stretched tightly around the table from man to man, belying the jocularity of their conversation.

"You reckon them burrheads will actually come out marchin' in broad daylight?"

"I reckon they meant what they said."

"Never knowed a nigger yet could even spell the truth, let alone tell it."

"They'll be there, all right. But us ol' boys'll make sure they get a right hot reception. Now how's about passin' me another one 'a them beers."

Cubbage came suddenly into the room, his eyes bright with excitement. "He's comin', boys. The man hisself is comin'!"

The men at the table looked up at him and one of them said, "Alvin Boyle is comin' to Taliawiga County?"

"None other," Cubbage nodded. "Him an' his party done hit Atlanta twenny minnits ago. They on their way down right this minute."

One of the other men said, "Shi-i-t! Now there's gonna be some hot times in the ol' town, an' that's the Lord's truth."

Another said, "L.G., iffen you ain't the most surprisin' sumbitch this side a Jehosaphat! Who'd a thunk a guy like you would even *know* a hot dog like Alvin Boyle?"

"We's just like two peas in a pod," Cubbage said with pride. "More'n a year now, we been gettin' together ever' time I went out on the road."

"You been plantin' enny of them firecrackers yo'self?"

Cubbage looked at the man conspiratorially. "Tha's for me to know an' the fuckin' FBI to find out."

Everybody laughed and guzzled their beer.

Cubbage said, "Okay, boys. Get a move on. You got work to do. Le's start spreadin' the word—the man's a-comin'."

The five men quickly finished off their beers and piled out of the house, filled with purpose and determination.

Cubbage waited until the last man had driven away and then began to prance and strut around in the front room. He crossed over to the side window and peered between the slats of the venetian blinds. He couldn't tell if anyone was home. It was hard to see much of anything in the daytime anyway. He would like to get a look at Naomi now. His blood was already churning in his veins; he could hardly believe so much had happened in so short a time and that he, L. G. Cubbage, was responsible for much of it.

Alvin Boyle, he thought, moving back from the window. The big leagues come to Taliawiga County. And all because I bought me a couple of beers in a Memphis tavern one night last year. Even Sheriff Biggs didn't swing such power as to have Alvin Boyle come at his beck and call. He wondered if Boyle would actually do any of the jobs himself. Probably not. That was too risky. Boyle was too well known. More than likely he was just coming down to supervise things, to get things set up. He would be back in Atlanta, maybe even Birmingham, by the time any action took place. They would never be able to pin anything on Alvin Boyle.

Cubbage began to laugh. No one would even *try* to pin anything on him in Taliawiga County. Certainly not Sheriff Biggs. Cubbage went down the hallway to a door at the back side of the house. Taking a key out of his pocket, he unlocked the heavy padlock on the door. He opened the door, reached inside and snapped on a lightswitch. Downstairs in the unfinished storm cellar, he looked happily about the concrete room. It was his pride and joy. He had played hell to keep the family from nosing around, especially after Sonny-Boy had got that wild hair about wanting another bathroom built. But he didn't have to worry about Sonny-Boy no more; he didn't have to worry about none of them, thanks to that nigger sonofabitch over to the hospital.

On the wall to his right, rows of rifle racks stretched from floor to ceiling, and there were stacks of ammunition crates, gunpowder and even hand grenades on the floor. Across the room the wall was lined with handguns of one kind or another. Cubbage kept the crates of TNT and nitroglycerin under separate lock and key in a cabinet at the back of the cellar.

As he looked around the lighted room, his chest seemed to swell like that of a pouter pigeon. Alvin Boyle would be mighty proud of this fledgling arsenal, he thought. He had come a long way in less than a year, since that lucky night of discovery up in Memphis. But it ain't nearly enough, he thought. It's only a beginning, and there's a lot more where this come from. Lamar Stick and some of the other boys were as good a bunch of professional thieves as you could find anywhere in the state. That is, if you wanted to call such as that thieving. Cubbage, just like Alvin Boyle and the other members of the Society of Christian Soldiers, U.S.A., didn't think of it like that at all. He was doing the only thing possible for a patriotic American in this day and time. He was preparing to protect himself and his community from the horde of communists, niggers, Jews and Arabs that were conspiratorially planning to take over the world.

They might take the world, he thought, digging excitedly at his genitals, but they damn sure wouldn't take Taliawiga County without one hell of a battle royal.

Just give me another year, he thought, and I'll be ready. Then let 'em come. Just let 'em come an' try it. I won't be alone neither. In another year I'll have me a regular Society workshop, training an' educating a whole army of men an' women. Becoming the next mayor of Adelphi was only one rung on the ladder of personal success and power that L. G. Cubbage was constructing.

He wanted to be mayor, all right. But he wanted more. He wanted the respect and admiration of men like Alvin Boyle. Of course Boyle himself didn't operate with this kind of firepower, L.G. thought. Boyle was an undercover, after-dark, hit-and-run man. But he was the best goddamn contract bomber in the South, maybe in the whole friggin' country. Schools, churches, houses, cars—you name it, Alvin Boyle could blow it into smithereens, or have it blown.

No, Cubbage would have to use the likes of Alvin Boyle, but that wasn't goin' to be L.G.'s own personal style. He had longer-range plans in mind. When he was elected mayor of Adelphi, he would really make his move. He wanted more than a personal arsenal. He wanted an armed city, an armed county, an armed state. He would begin as mayor, move on to the county commission and then maybe shoot for the governor's chair. It was not out of the question. If ol' Lester could pull it off, so could he. And then they could all just stand back and watch his smoke.

Cubbage went back upstairs, flipped off the light, closed the door and replaced the lock.

He looked at his watch. It was after two. His eyes were burning with excitement. Time to go to work.

# Chapter Seventy-one

"And there seems to be a civil rights confrontation in the making reminiscent of the 1960s throughout the South." The television commentator, a stringer from one of the major networks down from Atlanta, was speaking on the courthouse lawn for the benefit of the camera and the state at large. "But officials here in Adelphi—white officials—contend that the city is just caught between two warring adversaries: the Ku Klux Klan and the Southern Christian Leadership Conference.

"Black demonstration leaders brand such contentions as nonsense. Black leaders claim the city is racist to its core, that the impending confrontation is a matter of justice and civil rights.

"Earlier this morning a clash between two reputed Klansmen and a black demonstrator resulted in a minor confrontation involving sticks, stones and at least one knife that officials fear was only a preview of what is yet to come in this sleepy Southern town of about twenty thousand citizens."

A few blocks away at City Hall the mayor sounded like a man who was about to bestow a blue ribbon on Adelphi as Small Town, U.S.A., 1979.

"It's the outsiders," Furman Tittle was saying. "If they'd get out of here and leave us alone, leave us to our business, everything would be all right. Looka here. This is a good town, a fine town. The people hereabouts are the salt of the earth. Sure, there's a history of some little racial conflict in this area, like there is all over the South. It all come about with integration back in the early sixties. We didn't want it then. We couldn't help it. We were born that way, we were raised that way. Our mommas and our papas told us that's the way it always had been, the way it should be, and it was up to us to keep it that way. All over the South we had white people standing in courthouse doors, blocking little black children's way into the schoolhouse, padlocking churches and public swimmin' pools. We had all that and we were wrong. We were fightin' a losin' cause and just didn't know it. But after the war was over, after we'd lost and integration done come to us, why, lo and behold, we come to find out we were a hell of a lot better off losing than continuing on with the same stagnating policies of segregation and all that went with it."

There was no stopping the wall-eyed old boy once he got his hand on the microphone.

"All them segregated racist places up North oughta pay a little attention to our experience down here. They shore could learn somethin'. We've had less trouble since we become what you might say totally integrated, and that's the way we intend to keep it. That is, if all these durn rabble-rousing troublemakers from here, there and yonder would just stay the hell away from us and leave us be. We don't want the Klansmen and we don't want the black militants. As mayor I'm gonna do everything in my power to see that this kind of outside agitation—"

He almost jumped out of his seersucker pants when a handyman on a ladder suddenly dropped a half-dozen light bulbs onto the parquet floor.

Conditions were just about right for the confrontation that any well-intentioned person hoped to avoid. Rumor was spreading throughout the county like a contagious disease. Elmarie Fletcher, the little black girl who had been missing, had been found out in the woods sexually abused, physically mutilated and brutally murdered. The police had made no public announcements as to who was responsible, but there was no question that it was a white man and that he was a resident of Taliawiga County. A black man who had been injured in the riot the day before had regained consciousness and told police investigators that he thought he could identify the two whites who had beat him in the head with a claw hammer. Doctors said that Otha Fletcher was going to survive his beating at the hands of a bunch of white racist agitators, but he would be in no condition to cooperate with police for some days yet to come. The murder suspect, Eddie

James, lay in his hospital bed wrapped in a sheet, staring at the ceiling.

By three o'clock two lines of blacks, numbering around three hundred, began their orderly march from Shad Row toward the heart of the city, ostensibly in support of the Committee for the Defense of Eddie James. Perhaps a dozen or so whites, mostly strangers and out-of-towners, were mingled with the marchers. A police sedan led the group toward the courthouse. Another police vehicle trailed the group, and uniformed foot patrolmen walked beside the marchers all the way into the city.

Massed on the back side of the courthouse lawn, awaiting the approach of the marchers, stood a cluster of about thirty uniformed Klansmen. There were no firearms visible, but a few rough-hewn clubs were in evidence, and there was a small stockpile of rocks concealed behind a row of hibiscus plants beside the red brick steps at the rear of the courthouse.

It took the blacks nearly an hour to make it to the courthouse. A replacement for Otha Fletcher had been sent down from Atlanta to serve as their spokesman. He stepped forward to make his proclamation to the county fathers, to the state viewers and, he hoped, to the nation at large via the television cameras.

Whatever he had to say, however, was lost in the moment. Was it sniper fire, a police gunshot or merely a motorcycle backfiring? Afterward no one was able really to say. Whatever it was, it sent the horde that had gathered in the square into a frenzy of mass hysteria that even the television cameras could not keep pace with.

"How bad is it?"

"It's bad. And it's gonna get worse before the night is over," John said as he entered the house. "It's like a war out there, Sal. Street fighting, hand-to-hand combat, sniper fire, bombings. Jesus, talk about an explosion! Thank God the place was empty. At least the cops *think* it was. It was that nice old Baptist church down on Elm Street. The one that had the prayer breakfast this morning. The preacher had called for an end to these hostilities, for all outsiders of both races to go home and leave Taliawiga County to its own problems."

"And the church was blown up?"

"Blew the holy hell out of it about five o'clock this afternoon. Didn't you hear it? God, I thought it could be heard all over the county. Blew out windows in nearby buildings...shook the hell out of the courthouse and City Hall...and sent people runnin' through the streets claiming that the blacks had brought in airplanes and were droppin' bombs on the city!"

John almost laughed at such an idiotic notion. But the seriousness of the situation forbade laughter. Also, he was too tired to laugh. He just wanted to have a bite to eat and get a little rest before going back out again.

"You're not *really* going back out there, are you?" asked Sal, following him back to the bedroom.

"I have to, honey. I have to see what's going on for myself. I have to advise the governor—"

"That's what Harry Downs is supposed to be here for."

"That's right, and I've gotta help him. I'm sorry, Sal. I don't want to go back out there. But right now, it's my job. It's my duty."

She looked at him and said, "What about us? What about your family? Don't you owe a duty to us too?"

He stripped off his shirt and stuffed it into the laundry basket. "Sal, that's unfair as hell," he said. "You really shouldn't do this to me. Not at a time like this."

He could tell from the look on her face that his words had hit home. She didn't really want to be nagging him. It was simply that she was afraid. He went over to her and put his hands on her arms.

"Listen, hon. What I want you to do is to go up and get the kids, and bring Momma too, and then come on back down here and stay for the night. I'm going out for a while with Harry Downs and Jim Darden. Steve Hines will stay here and all of you will be perfectly all right. I'll check back with you by phone, and I'll get home as early as I can. Now, honey, that's just the best I can do under these circumstances."

She didn't say anything else. The fear was still in her eyes, but she shut them tightly and put her face against his chest. She wrapped her arms tightly around his waist. John kissed the top of her head and held her to him for a long time.

# Chapter Seventy-two

Taliawiga County had not seen such a night since Sherman's march to the sea. Although the streets were mostly deserted, save for policemen and their vehicles, the soft summer night was redolent with police sirens, the Klaxon call of fire engines racing from one side of town to the other and the squawking sound of the police dispatcher attempting to handle the steady flow of help and assistance calls that were flooding the airways.

Fortunately, the mayor had been successful in obtaining a court order from a federal judge in Atlanta banning any further street demonstrations. The order served at least to take the mobs off the streets. Now the task was to control the variety of hit-and-run attackers striking at random throughout the county. Groups of blacks or whites would suddenly dart out from shadowy hiding places, throwing rocks, bottles and eggs at passing automobiles, and then vanish just as suddenly into the darkness. A cross was burned on the football field of the local high school and the participants melted away into the crowds of gaping neighbors before the police could effect any identifications or apprehensions. Numerous injuries had been sustained throughout the evening, most as a result of flying missiles such as bricks, rocks and bottles. The hospital emergency room was doing a brisk business, and so were the booking desks at police headquarters and the Sheriff's Department.

The most frightening aspect of the evening was the rumors of sporadic sniper fire.

"I've seen worse than this in Atlanta," Harry Downs commented from the back seat of the car.

John turned and looked at him. "This isn't Atlanta."

"Maybe it won't be so bad after all," said Downs.

"Maybe the sun won't rise tomorrow morning," John answered.

Just before midnight, a police cruiser came across a robbery in progress about a half mile outside the enclave of Shad Row. The police dispatcher sent three vehicles to render assistance. By the time Jim Darden could drive John and Downs there, the encounter was well under way.

The first policeman on the scene interrupted the burglary of a closed liquor store even while it was in progress. There were two blacks involved, both under twenty years of age. One surrendered readily and was put face down on the ground and handcuffed; the other made a run for it. One of the policemen dropped the fleeing boy with a round from his .38 special. Fortunately it only tore into the fleshy part of the boy's thigh rather than into his back or brain. In any case, the shooting, the screaming, the cursing and the arrival of more police vehicles and an ambulance drew a crowd in spite of the curfew.

A group of blacks, no more than twenty-five in number, had gathered near the liquor store. They had first contented themselves with shouts of obscenities and accusations of police brutality, but as the group of whites began to swell across the street from them, the confrontation began to turn uglier. When the first Klansman showed up in more or less full regalia, including a wooden club about four feet in length, some of the blacks began throwing rocks and bottles into the gathering.

Police quickly formed a riot squad between the groups to keep them separated, but when a policeman took a brick in the head, it was obvious that the line would soon be broken. By this time at least fifty police officers had moved in and begun making arrests, which were running at least three to one against the blacks. Most were charged with failing to obey a police order, and a few with disturbing the peace.

Sheriff Biggs had sent out the word to his men: arrest every robed Klansman on the streets upon sight. "The last thing we need right now," he had told one of his chief deputies, "is a bunch of those goddamn moronic goons runnin' about on the loose."

Harry Downs was leaning over the front seat of the car, staring hard out the window. "You think there's enough cops here to do the job?"

"There's enough cops here to start World War III," John said.

"We could always ask the governor for the National Guard."

"We could always do that," John said sarcastically. "If we didn't have any better sense."

"Well, what the hell *are* we gonna do? Just sit here and watch all this?"

"That's exactly what we're gonna do, Harry. That's what we're paid to do. We don't have any authority to do anything else. The local police are in charge of this."

"Oh Jesus. And Chester Biggs?"

"That's right, Chester Biggs. And the Adelphi P.D. And the state patrol. We've got to wait first and see if they can handle things. And I'll tell you one thing right now—I think you give Chester Biggs too little credit. Don't get me wrong. He's not exactly what you call a civil libertarian. But he's not your ordinary Cracker bigot either. What he does, he does for definite reasons. I'll bet you ten to one he has a reason not to want all of this to blow up. If anybody can diffuse the situation, it's Chester. If he can't do it, it can't be done. Then and only then will we need the governor and his National Guard."

Photographers were scampering all around the intersection now. The flashes of their cameras jarred the already garishly lighted scene. The flashing dome lights of the many police vehicles threw a surrealistic patina over everything. John noticed one cameraman slip on the edge of the curb. He went down on one knee, wincing as a rock bounced off his shoulder. Across the street John saw a pair of beefy deputies hustling a Klansman off to a patrol vehicle parked around the corner. He wondered how quickly the fellow would be out on bond and back on the street.

Suddenly another call for assistance rang out on the police radio. This time it was a fire on the other side of town in a white district. John recognized the location and name. It was an all-night coin-operated laundry. By the time Jim Darden got them there, the place was burning to beat the band.

"Jesus, *look* at that," said Downs.

Police cars were all around and two fire engines had pulled up at both sides of the burning building. But none of the pumpers were working. And the only firemen John could see were scrunched down behind their fire trucks completely immobile for the moment. A couple of police cars flashed their spotlight beams all around the buildings in the vicinity. At first John thought they might be looking for evidence of the fire having spread to other buildings. Then it dawned on him. They were looking for snipers.

After some five or six minutes, when no further shooting had materialized, the firemen came reluctantly to the job at hand. They quickly got their hoses attached and trained on the burning building. It was not a massive fire and the blaze died down rather quickly under the heavy spray of water. Soon the old concrete building was filled with a thick billowing smoke.

"Well, I've had enough," said Harry Downs. "Let's go home. Let's make our report to the governor now."

John looked at Darden. The driver hadn't said anything. John knew what he was thinking. Darden was a professional, a good cop. He knew they needed to see firsthand what was going on if they were going to be of any use to the governor.

Downs was lighting a cigarette, saying, "Jesus, I could use a drink," at the very instant of impact.

The safety glass of the rear windshield shattered and the noise inside the car was deafening. The first shot had pierced the windshield and slammed into the steel of the door just behind the driver. The entire car jerked with the shock of impact. Instinctively, Darden stomped on the accelerator. The car lurched forward and sideswiped a parked car on the opposite side of the narrow road.

The second shot banged against the exterior of the car in a dull punching sound. The bullet struck flat metal with such velocity that the car's back end was shifted sideways, again making contact with the parked car. This time Darden lost control of the wheel momentarily and they raked the length of the other car with a screeching sound of slashing metal.

No one had been hit, but all three men were clutched by a paroxysm of terror. The sniper was a crack shot. The third explosion rammed into the back side of the car like a huge steel boot. The entire car seemed to be lifted. John was thrown forward against the dashboard and a rictus of pain shot through his right side. Darden was practically climbing over the steering wheel. One minute Harry Downs was sprawling in the floor space behind the back seat, the next he was pulling himself up on the seat again in blind terror. His head bobbing around in the back seat was a challenging target for some one or more snipers in the darkness behind them.

Darden had the car under control again, finally, and was pushing down on the accelerator. The car surged forward, hooked up in some way with the car it had sideswiped, clashing and tearing amid the sound of scraping metal and breaking glass, until at last it tore free and skidded out toward the center of the road. The men were screaming, yelling, cursing senselessly, their control shattered by their terror.

John's heart pounded as he thought, the whole thing was preposterous. Who was out there shooting at them?

What the hell am I doing out here anyway? What's the point in it? Sal was right, he should have stayed home where he belonged. Suppose something should happen to him, what about his wife and kids? Suppose he got himself killed. Would it be worth it? Would anything be accomplished?

As the car careened into an intersection, they heard the crack of another rifle shot. The lack of impact was almost as terrifying as the shattering jolt of the previous three shots.

Darden worked the wheel furiously. The rear tires spun and shrieked on the pavement, and the car somehow finally started forward again with a renewed burst of speed.

Out of the line of fire, Darden slowed the car and just sort of hunched over the wheel, trembling with the ordeal of normality. John was leaning over the back seat in an effort to determine whether or not Harry Downs was injured. He could see shattered shards of glass all over the back of the man's head and shirt collar, and there was a great swath of blood across the back seat.

"Harry, are you hit? For Christ's sake, Harry—"

"No," came a weak voice from the floorboards. He raised up slowly, tightly clutching his left wrist with his right hand. It was covered with blood.

"What the hell—"

"That gash of steel," said Downs, nodding toward the door just behind Darden's seat.

It was a pretty nasty cut. John couldn't tell for sure in the darkness whether a vein had been cut, but was afraid to take any chances. He pulled off his belt and wrapped it around Harry's arm above the elbow, fashioning a rude tourniquet. "Let's get the hell out of here," he said in a thick anxious voice. "The hospital's less than a mile away."

As they entered the receiving station at the hospital, heading for one of the examining bays, John was momentarily stunned to find himself face to face with Chester Biggs.

The sheriff, standing there like a khaki-covered mountain, his hands on his hips and a surly, sarcastic expression on his face, said, "You fellas been out for a nice summer ride?"

# Chapter Seventy-three

"My God," Sal said. "You're falling on your face. Let me help you."

She began stripping off his grimy clothes and led him into the bathroom to settle him into the tub of hot water. She poured an extra measure of bath salts under the flowing spigot and it bubbled up above his legs and belly as he slid down lower in the water.

"Feels like embalming fluid," he said, his head to one side, eyes half closed.

"Honey, I've been so worried." Sal lowered the top on the commode and sat down across from him. She had pulled on a soft blue nightgown when she heard his car approaching on the gravel. She was barefooted, her hair loose about her shoulders. She had not been to sleep. "Are you...?"

"I'm okay, now."

"Do you want a drink?"

"It'll probably knock me off my ass, but I'd love one."

When she came back with the drinks she thought for a moment that he was asleep. But he heard the ice cubes rattling in the glass and reached his hand up out of the sudsy water. She noticed the bruises on his ribs for the first time.

"What in the world—"

"Nothing serious. Got tossed up against the dashboard. Just bruises, according to the nurse in the emergency room."

Sal knelt down beside the tub and put her hand on his arm. "I'm so glad you're safe," she said. "I've been worried, of course. But mostly I... I've been so upset because of the way I've been acting."

"Hell no," he said wearily. "You were right all along."

"I kept telling myself that if anything should happen to you—"

"I had no business out there. I had no responsibility for any of that, my responsibility is to you and the kids."

He paused. "I love you, Sal. And I love the children too, and the life that we have together. But I don't think I've been playing fair with you. I've got you into something without telling you the whole story. And now there's no other way out except for me to come clean.

"Sal, something happened today, and I have to tell you about it. I'm not a hundred per cent sure that it would all come out, so I might get away with it. But that just isn't the thing to do. I know that now. I think I made my decision in a split second out there tonight when I was trapped inside that car with live rounds of ammunition ricocheting around my head."

Sal shuddered, and put her hand up to her mouth.

"It's all right. It could have happened but it didn't. That's over. I won't be out there again. But now we've got other dangers to face. Sal, I had a run-in this afternoon with Chester Biggs."

"What's new about that?" she laughed dryly.

"I punched him, Sal."

"You *what?*"

"I punched the big tub of guts and left him gasping on the floor like a fish out of water."

"What in the world are you talking about?"

He took a deep breath, a swallow of his drink, and then looked up at her with resignation. He had to get it over with. "Chester is trying to blackmail me."

Her mouth moved incredulously but she made no sound. She just looked at him in astonishment.

"He wants me to get off this Eddie James case," said John. "He knows about the diary. You know about the diary, but you don't know what's in it. Chester doesn't really know what is in it either, but he thinks he does. Furthermore, he's afraid that he might be right." John knew he was beginning to babble but he couldn't stop himself. "That diary is absolute dynamite, Sal. Chester tested me this afternoon just to see how I would handle. It didn't work exactly the way he was hoping. But I know good and well he doesn't intend to stop there. He learned something from the experience, and he won't make the same mistake twice. He certainly isn't going to just let me off the hook."

"I still don't know what you're talking about."

He took another deep breath. "All right," he said. "Here it is. To hell with legal ethics. Enough people in the criminal justice system will have to know about it, I don't see any reason under these circumstances why a man's wife can't also know what he's involved in. The truth is, I just can't subject you to any more of this without letting you know what's in store for you."

John finished his drink, set the glass on the floor, raised himself a little higher out of the water and went on.

"Sissie Cubbage's diary is like a blueprint for crime. It diagrams an incredible amount of criminal activity in Taliawiga County, and Sissie was right in the middle of most of it. For example, that boy Elton Pittman, the one who was killed with her on the night of the Eddie James rampage. Sissie had been involved with Elton for a long time. He's been in and out of trouble all his life, here and everywhere else he's lived. You know he's the son of that prostitute out on the old mill road, the one that's in cahoots with Chester Biggs..." He paused and his thoughts gathered momentum.

"I don't know exactly what Sissie's connection had been with Elton in years past, but after he got out of prison last year up in Illinois, he gravitated on up to Chicago at the same time that Sissie was there. Sissie had run away from home some months before and had settled, temporarily, in Chicago. She lived a communal sort of life with a rotating band of young drifters, kids given to drug taking and all forms of sexual promiscuity. Eddie James, it seems, was one of the group. For months, L.G. had been on the road looking for his daughter. When he finally tracked her down and stumbled into that mixed pad of drugs and perversity, he found Sissie paired off with Eddie James, and to make matters worse, she was some four months pregnant. L.G. tried to talk her into leaving with him. but she refused. He tried to take her away with him one night but the others, including Elton, bodily threw him out of the house. A few days later L.G. caught up with Sissie alone on the street when she was on her way to a neighborhood Laundromat. In effect he just plain kidnaped his daughter. He took her with him, forced her into an abortion by some hack who put her up on a kitchen table, and then he brought her back home to Adelphi."

"The poor kid," Sal said. "No wonder she was so hard to handle."

"Well now, don't go feeling too sorry for Sissie on that account. It's pretty obvious from her diary entries that she hadn't much cared about the whole thing one way or another. She hints in a couple of places in the diary that she had no intention of keeping the baby. After it was born, she would have either abandoned it with those in the commune or she would have given it to some sort of health agency. But she made one big mistake. She figured without the feelings of Eddie James. Eddie was not only in love with her, he wanted their child. So, there was the motive for what Eddie James did at the Cubbage house that night. L.G. had not only kidnaped his girlfriend, in Eddie's eyes he'd also procured the murder of Eddie's baby."

"That's the most incredible thing I've ever heard."

"No, it isn't," said John. "It gets more incredible by the page, so to speak. In order to establish this motive, don't you see, I would have to put the diary into evidence. It's in a sort of code, but we've cracked it now and more or less have a key to the whole thing. No matter how hard we try, once we reveal the importance of the diary, there would be no way to keep the contents secret. It would literally tear Taliawiga County apart at the seams."

"Why? I don't understand—"

John dipped a washcloth into the hot sudsy water and squeezed it over his head. "Sissie Cubbage was a very enterprising young lady."

"What do you mean? Tell me, John. This is worse than a TV soap opera."

He laughed hollowly. "Believe me, Peyton Place was tame by comparison."

"Well, *tell* me!"

"For one thing, at some time or another—I haven't established exactly when—Sissie entered into some sort of working relationship with Chester Biggs."

"Surely she wasn't—"

John paused for a moment, gathering his thoughts. "As you know, Chester has his hand in just about every illegal activity that occurs in Taliawiga County. Nothing happens here that he doesn't control. If he allows gambling, prostitution, illegal liquor, dope—whatever—it's either because he is taking a rake-off or there is some sort of political advantage in it for him. You know something about his relationship with Lucy Pittman...But he also had this deal going with Sissie. Chester was not a dope runner, mind you. On the other hand, he had a couple of 'clients' here who had a need for such a service. And Chester had reason for wanting to keep these people under his thumb. There was no better way to control them than through their illegal habits. One was Gordon Joyner—"

"The congressman's son?"

"That's right. Biggs figured this was the best way for him to control the old man. Then when old man Joyner stepped down—which, by the way, he decided to do as soon as he discovered his son's propensity for marijuana and very young girls—when Joyner decided to step down, Chester figured that sure enough Gordon would take his place. Chester would then be in the catbird seat with the congressman from our district right in his hip pocket. He could get just about anything he wanted."

"So Sissie supplied Gordon with pot and kept Chester Biggs informed every time the hapless jerk lit up," said Sal.

"That's about the size of it," John said, and continued, "You know sweet little ol' Miz Aimee MacAtee? Well, she was on Chester's list too," he said, squeezing the washcloth over his stomach. "Cocaine. Sissie got it from a contact in Atlanta and turned it over to Chester. Chester gave it to the old lady, free of charge. Just a good public-spirited servant of the people. No wonder old Chester has never wanted for financial support in any of his campaigns. And Miz Aimee is just one of many. He also has a strangle lock on Orin Pettigrew."

"Kitty-Kat's daddy?"

"That's right," he said, ignoring her remark. "They have a real sweet deal going, and have had for many years. It seems that Chester keeps Orin supplied with cheap labor for his lumberyards and wood-cutting teams. He picks up blacks on trumped-up charges and instead of bringing them before the court, he simply assigns them to work out their sentence with Orin. Of course they don't get paid for it, but they're glad enough just to stay out of jail. Nobody complains. And if they wanted to they'd have to complain to Chester. They would be afraid to go to Judge Harbuck—even if they were smart enough to figure out what had happened to them—for fear the judge would slap some sort of fine or prison sentence on them."

"It sounds like something out of a grade-B movie."

"It goes on and on. This is just the top of the list. The girl had something on almost everybody. At least on enough people—"

"What did she have on you, Professor?"

He gave her a sour look and said, "You've missed the mark a little bit with that shot. But you're not entirely off base."

"What do you mean?" Sal sat up, her face tight with apprehension.

"I told you that today was a very eventful day." He sighed deeply. "The Orin Pettigrew story. Oddly enough, it was one of the incidents that wasn't detailed in Sissie's diary, wasn't even mentioned. But Biggs couldn't be sure of that, you see. So he decided to test the water. He had Rachel pressure me into coming out to Oak Grove."

Her dark eyes chilled. "Rachel? You went to see her?"

"I went out to Oak Grove, in response to a hysterical phone call in which Rachel said she knew what I was trying to do, and if I didn't come out to see her she would blow my whole scheme out of the water. I obviously had to go—"

"Obviously," said Sal coldly.

"Knock it off, Sal. This is hard enough as it is."

"And how was the reunion? Filled with bittersweet tears and kisses?"

He looked at her and his own voice went flat. "Do you want to hear this, or do you want me to stop, here and now?"

"Go on," she said softly, and took a sip of her drink.

"Well, I got the story out of Rachel. She was waiting for me when I got there, demanding to know what I intended to do about her father. Of course I didn't know what she was talking about. I didn't intend to do anything to him, but she didn't know that. Anyway, I finally pried the story concerning the arrangement with Biggs out of her. But when I tried to explain to her, to convince her that I really had no intention of indicting her father, she simply wouldn't believe me. She became hysterical. And she'd been drinking. She's something of an alcoholic, you know. She's had a pretty hard life."

"Poor thing."

John looked at her sourly. "Anyway, the whole thing was a setup. The next thing I knew she was all over me. Arms and legs. We were stumbling around the room. She fell down on the floor and pulled me down beside her. Then she ripped at her clothes, pulled her blouse open, bounced her bare titties all over me. At that same moment flashbulbs started going off all around the room."

Sal sat up straight, the color draining out of her face. "Flashbulbs?"

"That's right. Photographs. And standing in the doorway with a big shit-eating grin on his face was none other than—"

"Chester Biggs."

"Exactly. The whole thing had been a setup."

"And that's when you belted him?"

"A few minutes later."

"Good for you," she said enthusiastically. "If I had been there I would have kicked him in the balls."

John laughed. "The next time you see him, why don't you just do that."

Sal grew serious again, disturbed. "What does it mean? What is he going to do?"

"He's going to try to blackmail me," John said. "That's what Sissie was planning to do to everybody. Including Chester."

"That's why she was keeping the diary."

"That's right. Planning to use blackmail to get herself a stack of traveling money and then split from this place once and for all."

Sal shook her head in wonder. "Home sweet home."

"Ain't it though. Well, that's the whole sordid story, Sal." He paused. "Most of it."

"There's more?" she said incredulously.

"Well, as I say, Chester was just testing me. He knows now that it isn't going to work. Of course he could raise a hellofa stink with those photographs, but it really wouldn't serve his purpose much. So I don't think he'll pass them around, knowing that it isn't going to shut me up anyway."

"What do you think he'll do?"

For a long moment John was silent. He dipped the washcloth into the sudsy water and began scrubbing it across his chest. Then he looked up at Sal again. Finally he said, "I think he knows something that even I don't know, Sal. And I think he's prepared to use it."

She felt a chill at the back of her neck. "About you?"

"No. I don't think there's anything that he can use against

me directly. I think he knows I wouldn't knuckle under to that sort of thing." Again he hesitated. "But there *is* one thing that I haven't told you...about myself."

"Oh God," she said. "You and another old girlfriend. You were just walking down the street, minding your own business—"

"It ain't funny, Sal," he said morosely.

"Well, tell me."

"It really isn't such a momentous revelation, I suppose. I don't know why I've always made it seem so important in my own mind. I guess it has a lot to do with the way Ida Belle has reacted all these years." He laughed dryly. "No telling what she would do if she knew I was aware of the big lie."

*"What* big lie?"

He looked at her. "About my father. The fast-talking salesman. The war hero." He laughed and paused. "War hero, my ass. One time, while I was in the Justice Department in Washington, I was running a check on the administrative capabilities of the Records Department. On a lark I decided to run down the name of my father. After all, I didn't know very much about him. He had supposedly succumbed to his war injuries while I was still quite young."

"Go on," Sal urged gently.

"He was never in the military," he said flatly. "But then, they say there's not much difference between the military and prison life."

"Prison? Your father?"

"No big deal. Nothing spectacular. He was no Al Capone— just a petty little thief. Times were rough for them, there's no doubt about that. He probably wasn't making any money. If the truth be told, he probably wasn't a very good salesman anyway. At least he didn't seem to be very good at anything else," he said wryly. "He got caught, the last time burglarizing a goddamn candy store." John laughed brusquely and threw the washcloth down at the foot of the tub. "Can you believe it? A goddamn candy store."

"Oh, John," she whispered. "I'm so sorry."

"Sorry? Don't be sorry for me. It doesn't matter much one way or the other. Anyhow, that's not the end of it. Dead war hero he was not, but he was dead enough all right. That part of the story was true."

He looked over at her and she cocked her head quizzically.

"The inept sonofabitch went and got himself killed in an attempted prison escape."

292

They just looked at each other for a long moment. Neither spoke. Sal put her glass on the window ledge, pulled her nightgown over her head and got down on her knees beside the tub. She fished the washcloth out of the water and began scrubbing his chest and shoulders and neck. He leaned his head against the back of the tub and closed his eyes, relaxing under the soothing balm of her gentle hands.

Later, in bed, she remembered to ask him what it was that he thought Chester was planning to use against him, if it wasn't the knowledge about the way his father had died. In the darkness he put his hands behind his head and thought about it for a long moment. Then he said, "I can't be sure, but I think it probably has something to do with Homer."

"And Bigg thinks that because of your friendship with Homer you'd be willing to suspend your investigation rather than have the truth divulged?"

"I think that's about it," he said with a deep sigh. "And I guess he's right. Before I'd do anything to injure Homer, I'd take that diary and throw it in the Taliawiga River."

# Chapter Seventy-four

**The next morning John, still shaken and sore, met** with Robert Tribble in Judge Harbuck's chambers to hear the medical report concerning Eddie James.

The call from Harbuck's office had come over just after nine o'clock. The judge's secretary had said that Harbuck had decided to receive the report in his chambers rather than in open court due to the tension already existing in Adelphi. Doc Whipple was standing before the judge, surly and impatient to get away and back to his duties at the hospital.

Judge Harbuck looked up from the medical report, then handed a copy to John and one to Tribble.

"Any questions?"

It was not unexpected. Although the report did not pronounce Eddie James incompetent or unqualified to assist in his defense, it did recommend that he be transferred to the state mental hospital for a thorough examination before any such determination should be made.

"No questions," said Tribble, and it was all he could do to contain his elation. It didn't really matter what the psychiatrists said, ultimately. He had gained the time he needed to make this case a national *cause célèbre*.

John had no legal grounds for contesting the medical recommendation, nor had he any ethical quarrel with this particular course of action. He did not particularly want the delay, but he did want a determination of Eddie James's mental status. It was as important to John as it was to Tribble. "No questions, Your Honor."

"All right," said Judge Harbuck. "I will enter an order in due course transferring the patient to the state hospital in Milledgeville." Then he looked over at John. "It won't be long for word of this to get out on the street. I'm sure I don't have to suggest to you that whatever precautionary measures you plan to take ought to be put into effect without delay. If you really want that fellow to receive all those psychological tests over at the state funny farm, you've got to get him there first."

John went directly back to his office and put in a call for Charlie Tate. He wanted a double guard placed on Eddie James's hospital room. And no one other than the medical staff was to have access to him without John's personal permission. Next, he scanned through the stack of telephone messages that had piled up over the course of the morning and the previous afternoon. There were at least six calls from Homer Stokes. There had even been a call from Rachel Pettigrew. And there was a call from Dean Witcomb and from one of the university trustees. But John had no time for any of that nonsense.

Ellie Fletcher's death was common knowledge in the county now. Josie had identified the shoe and the scraps of clothing found in the cave, and Doc Peavyhouse had compared the girl's medical records with the deformed footbone to his satisfaction. Plans were already being made for her funeral, and it was likely to be the focus of another black-white confrontation. Since it would be held outside the city limits, it would come under the jurisdiction of the Sheriff's Department. John wondered what Chester Biggs planned to do about it.

A sudden chill swept over him at the thought of Sheriff Biggs. He had been too busy in the last hours to give the events out at Rachel's house more than a passing thought. But now the image came swarming back before his conscious mind and all of a sudden there lay Chester Biggs on the floor at his feet.

What would happen next? Chester certainly wasn't the type to forgive and forget. What would he do with the photographs of John and Rachel? Were they being prepared even now for circulation?

Why had Rachel called this morning? Did she really think they had anything else to say to each other? But he didn't have time to speculate about such matters now. The most important thing he had to do was coordinate the transfer of Eddie James from the local hospital to the institution at Milledgeville. He would just have to trust Charlie Tate, simply because he didn't know who else to turn to. Tate had a reputation for being a straight arrow. John couldn't put him down simply because they differed philosophically.

When the phone rang it was Tate. He was coming in. In the meantime he thought John ought to know that a new project coordinator for the SCLC had arrived in town with the mission of organizing the funeral of Ellie Fletcher. Also, rumor had it that Bo Washburn, the imperial wizard of one of several Klan factions in the South, was on his way to Adelphi. A Klan rally for that evening was being planned just across the Taliawiga County line.

Downstairs in the Sheriff's Department Chester Biggs was sitting behind his desk in conversation with two of his own trusted aides.

"Well, that's all there is to it," Biggs said. "That's the end of it. Alvin Boyle is bad enough. We just ain't gonna tolerate Bo Washburn stirrin' up things enny worse than they already are. Boyle's already gone, but it don't take no investigative genius to know that he was behind the bombin' of that church yesterday. And there ain't no tellin' what else he's already arranged with some of his Cracker contacts here in the county. But we ain't puttin' up with Washburn. They ain't holdin' that rally inside our county and that's for damned sure. And what I want you boys to do now is put out the word that the minute that sonofabitch steps foot over in our county he's to be picked up. You unnerstan'? Scoop 'im up, bring him here and lock his ass up in the jail."

"But, Sheriff, ain't that a violation of his civil rights—" began one of the deputies, and Biggs abruptly cut him off.

"Fuck that man's civil rights. His civil rights are what I say they are. And I say that in *our* county he ain't got none." Biggs sat forward and leaned both beefy arms on the table. "Now you two listen to me and you listen good. I want the lid put back on this here thing. We got a problem, there ain't no doubt about it. But we're gonna handle it ourselves. We don't want no outside niggers, no outside Crackers, no outside investigators... we damn sure don't wanna give the dadburn FBI no more reason to come snoopin' around here. You know damn good an' well they done got five or six agents right here in town nosin' into all 'a this. Now we gotta get a handle on this here thing an' get rid of 'em."

"But I don't see—"

"You don't haveta see. All you gotta do is what I tell ya. Now get the hell outa here and start doin' it."

When the two men had left Chester swiveled around in the creaking chair and stared at the door for a long moment. He realized he was facing the most dangerous challenge in all the years he had been sheriff of Taliawiga County. Everything he had worked for, all he had built up, was on the verge of coming unraveled. But he had finally thought it all out. At the center of his problems was the case of Eddie James. Because it was this case that had brought into play the Cubbage cunt's diary along with the appointment of John Winter as special prosecutor. Handle that part of the problem and all the rest of the turmoil would gradually subside. Eddie James, he thought, the diary and John Winter.

His hands went involuntarily to the ache in his stomach muscles. He couldn't remember the last time a man had dared to take a poke at him. But it was his own fault. He had played Winter wrong. He had figured him right a few days before, when he had decided the best way to get at him was through his buddy Stokes. Then he had gone and got sidetracked on the Pettigrew idea instead of driving home with his power play. Winter wouldn't go out on a limb for Rachel Pettigrew or her daddy. Hell, if John had cared anything about the cunt he would have married her years ago and taken the old man for all he was worth. Course the pictures might come in handy

296

someday, you never could tell. Chester felt a sudden chill at the base of his scrotum as he thought of Rachel's big pink-ended titties. The pictures would come in real handy all right. He wondered if...naw, he would take 'em home with him and look at 'em in private. He might even stop by Lucy Pittman's with 'em.

He wondered if maybe—just maybe—he might be able to use the pictures for a little leverage against Rachel herself. Maybe he could get Rachel and Lucy together some night—he began to dig excitedly at his crotch. He felt the bulge in his trousers and stood up abruptly.

He had to stop. He went over to the sink in the corner of the room and washed his face in cold water. He would think about Rachel Pettigrew later. It was through Homer Stokes—not Rachel—that he would get to John Winter. He had already put the bug in Homer's ear. Scared the pluperfect shit right out of that mincing poof. Biggs wondered if Homer had made contact with Winter yet. Biggs had no doubt that he would do so. Homer had no other alternative.

No, he could count on Homer doing what he had to do. Right now Biggs had to concern himself with the other part of the problem. Eddie James.

He went back to the desk, picked up the phone and dialed for an outside line.

# Chapter Seventy-five

After John hung up the phone he sat behind his desk for a moment as though pressed down by a great weight. Sal, in her most exasperated voice, had just called to tell him that his mother refused to move down to the house in spite of the fact that she was worried out of her mind. Now, busy as he was, John would have to take the time to run out there and see what he could do about getting the old girl settled in. What he didn't need, in view of everything else, was trouble with Ida Belle.

Shortly after the call from Sal, John drove to his mother's house. He banged on the door and then waited impatiently for her to get all the locks undone so that he could be let in.

"Momma, you're closed in here so tight a molecule couldn't get through your defenses."

"I'll thank you not to come here with all of your smart-aleck remarks at a time like this. Especially since just about all that's goin' on out there is your fault."

"My fault!" he exclaimed. "What the hell are you talkin' about?"

"Don't you *dare* curse at me."

"Momma, I didn't curse at you and you know it."

"Usin' that kind of language to your own mother. I just don't know what's got into you. You were never like this before. But ever since you went off to Europe...ever since you...got messed up with..."

"That *woman*," John said sarcastically. "Jesus, Momma—"

"There you go again—cursin' our Precious Lord now."

Less than five minutes with her and as usual he was on the verge of exasperation. "What do you mean, *my* fault, Momma? Is that what all your friends are saying?"

"Nobody else's," she snapped. "If only you'd left all this nigra mess alone—"

"Now, Momma—"

"Or if you did feel you had to go and get involved in it, if you had only done the right thing by your own kind instead of takin' the cause of those—"

"Listen, Momma. I didn't come out here to argue race relations with you again. But you're right about one thing. We've got trouble out there. At the moment I don't really care whose fault it is. I want you to pack up some things and come down to the house—"

"No. I'm not goin' down there. I'm stayin' here."

"You *can't* stay here, Momma. It's dangerous. There's no tellin' what might happen. Now I'll send Steve Hines up here—he's the state trooper who's stayin' with us—and he'll load up your overnight bag and anything else you think you might need. If you forget something he can come on back up and get 'em later."

He started backing toward the door. She followed but the interval between them stayed the same. "Son," she said, her eyes bright and feverish, "do you know what you're doin'? To your family, to your people? Do you know you're gettin' set to turn loose the nigras—the black Mohammedans—in a race war that'll see most of us murdered in our beds before the week is out?"

John couldn't help laughing. "Momma, that is not what's going on in Taliawiga County. When did you see it, last night on the late show?"

"You make fun of your poor old mother all you want. But I'm tellin' you what I know. This town is headin' for trouble and you're just as much the instigator of it as anybody else. You and that rabble-rousing, nigra-loving Bobcat Tribble. Why, if old man Tribble had any idea what his boy was doing, the grave wouldn't be deep enough to hold him down."

John stepped out on the porch and said, "I gotta go now, Momma. Steven Hines will be up to get you in a little while. Now you be ready."

He turned and ran out to the car as his mother began setting locks and throwing bolts.

John drove out to the edge of the highway. He hesitated before heading back to town. Should he go on down home and try to square things with Sal first? Things were beginning to get to her now, as he had feared they would. On the other hand, he had so damn much to do at the office. He drew a deep breath and decided he had better get on back to town.

While he was making up his mind, John noticed the old pickup truck coming down the county road. He waited as it slowed and then turned in front of him onto the dirt road that bounded his property.

Lamar Stick passed on by without looking in his direction, and John pulled out onto the county highway to drive toward Adelphi. On the highway he met another battered old pickup that didn't look much different than the one Stick was driving. He looked up in the rearview mirror. That truck turned onto the dirt road too, and followed the red cloud of dust that Stick had raised moments before.

There was more than one man in the second truck. There were at least two, perhaps three. John didn't know any of them, but they made little impression on him. He had other worries.

# Chapter Seventy-six

Sal froze when the telephone rang. A chill swept down her spine and she stared at the instrument on the wall as if the phone itself were an obscenity.

Steve Hines answered the ring, in case it was another crank call. But it was John. He had been to see Ida Belle and she would be ready shortly. Steve was to go up and get her.

Before Steve left, Sal telephoned Ida Belle just to confirm the plans. The old woman was cold and distant but apparently reconciled to doing what her son had instructed. At the last minute Ida Belle asked if Davey would come along. Steve said it was all right with him and wild horses couldn't have kept Davey from riding in the patrol car.

Steve carried the bassinet out to the barn for Sal. She settled Cathy in the bed with a rattle and one of her favorite cloth dolls. Then Sal went to work.

She had not painted in days. She needed to do something to focus her thoughts. Although from the looks of the absurd blotches on the canvas in front of her, she was having little success. John had left a note thumbtacked to the edge of the easel. *It's wonderful. What the hell is it?* She smiled absently, concentrating on the writhing shapes on the canvas. What had she been trying to get at? And why was her inspiration darkening again? *That's* what John didn't like. He wanted the sunshine and brightness of Italy again.

Sal wondered suddenly where Clyde and J. Edgar were? She needed their customary support. The dogs usually hung about the studio whenever she worked, her most astute critics.

She backed off a few paces and stood absolutely still, staring at the canvas. The dominant colors were yellow and pale blue. There was a splotch of blue paint on her blouse just above her left breast, a dab of blue the size of her fingertip resembling a beauty mole on her right cheekbone. Her hair was piled up on top of her head and tied in place with a yellow ribbon.

Picking up a jar of paint, Sal swirled it thoughtfully for a moment, staring intently at the canvas in front of her. In the crib Cathy gurgled and played with the rag doll. Suddenly, Sal flicked her wrist forward and dashed the liquid paint all over the canvas. It struck the painting in the upper left-hand quarter, splattered outwardly in all directions and then began to drip downward.

She was breathing harder now, her eyes shining. Something about the shapeless mess on the canvas began to present creative possibilities in her mind's eye.

If John could make some sort of sense out of the chaos surrounding his life, surely she could do the same. When he had come home the night before, exhausted and shaken by his experience on the streets, her own complaints had seemed so petty by comparison.

After all, a good deal of what she was stewing about was of her own making. She had encouraged John to accept the job. Her liberal, pacific, humanitarian beliefs had left her no alternative.

And now, here they were, living with killing all around them, in spite of John's role in the affair.

Coming out of her reverie, Sal stepped over to the crib. Cathy had fallen asleep with the rag doll on her chest. Going back to the worktable beside the easel, Sal picked up one of her palette knives and started to turn toward the canvas when she heard a scraping noise behind her. She jerked her head around and gasped.

Two men wearing ski masks were standing in the open barn door.

# Chapter Seventy-seven

"What do you want?" Sal whispered, terror clawing at her chest and throat. Even behind the masks she could see that they were laughing at the question.

One man was tall, thin, and although the ski mask covered the top of his head and his face, she could tell that he was a redhead from the hair on his arms. The other man was short, fat and swarthy. Both wore jeans and short-sleeve cotton work shirts. The tall man wore tennis shoes, the other work boots.

The tall man took a few steps toward her. Sal moved as far away from the crib as she could. Cathy slept quietly on. The man pursued her slowly in a circular fashion as she moved, apparently in no hurry to close the distance between them. When she had moved across the barn as far as she could go, the man stopped about ten feet away from her. He stood, hands by his side, fingers curved, thumbs rigid.

The other man, the short fat one, had come into the barn only a few steps. Sal looked at him now, her eyes wide and feverish, her heart pounding wildly.

"What do you want?" she asked again, her voice a hoarse croak.

The tall man said in a husky voice, "Take that shirt off, Pocahontas, and show us them there purty titties."

She stared at the man unbelievingly. It had to be a bad dream. It couldn't be happening. Not to her.

The man said, "I done asked you once, I ain't gonna ask again. We want you to show us yore titties."

Her heart sank and her knees went limp. It was no dream.

It was real. She still had the palette knife in her hand. Slowly, almost as if in a trance, she began to raise the terry-cloth blouse up over her body. What else could she do? Even if she were able to get away she couldn't leave Cathy with them. When she got the blouse in front of her face, revealing her naked breasts to their gaze, she heard the man closest to her suck in on his breath.

"Gawd," he said wondrously. "Look at that."

She stood staring at them, holding the blouse in her hand, wrapped around the palette knife.

The first man stepped up a little closer to her and moved around to her side. Sal's legs were so weak her knees began to buckle.

"What do you want?" she whispered.

The man spoke over his shoulder to his companion. "The lady wants to know what it is we want." They began to laugh. Cathy slept on, undisturbed in the crib.

Sal's conscious level of thought began to drop lower and lower even as the men continued to talk. What could she do? Did she have any choices? She had to *think!* But her mind was stunned by fear and the suddenness of it all. She couldn't run away and abandon Cathy. Could she fight? *Should* she fight?

The first man said, "You ain't much of a tit man, are you, buddy? You reckon Pocahontas here got ennything else might get a rise outa you?"

"I wanna see them short hairs," said the second man. "I wanna see me some cunt."

"You heard it, princess," the tall man said. "My buddy here wants to get a look-see at that there pussy of yours. Now you get them pants off and do it in a hurry."

*That's* it, she thought wildly. *Delay.* They want me to do things in a hurry. I've got to stall. Talk to them, anything—just keep them talking until Steve gets back. They can't know about him, or they wouldn't be here. They wouldn't risk doing this if they didn't think I was alone. Stall them, Sal. Use your head. Use your body too, if it will help hold them off.

She hadn't moved a muscle, and the second man came across the barn floor, brandishing his massive fist under her nose. "If you don't get 'em off, dolly, I'll make you wish to hell you had."

Like a robot Sal raised her hands to the elastic band of her shorts, paused, took a deep breath, hooked her thumbs over the top and began to peel them down her hips.

"Ooee," said the first man.

Her head was spinning as she stepped out of the shorts and dropped them on the floor beside her feet. She was barefooted and stark naked. She was still holding her blouse wrapped around the palette knife in her right hand, and the blood had gone ice-cold in her veins.

"Spread 'em, little lady," said the first man, and when she failed to respond, he said, "Do it or I'll do it for ya."

She felt the rush of hot air against her genitals.

"On your knees," he said. "Right now, squaw—down on yore knees."

Sal sank to her knees as if in a dream, watching with detached amazement as the first man unzipped his fly. She was surprised at how calm she was; she felt dazed, drugged all of a sudden. She was completely at their mercy...Steve would not get back in time...Ida Belle was probably acting up.

The men had come closer to her and were still talking...to her...about her...but the only thing that clearly registered on her conscious mind when the tall thin man began to dig his genitals out of his pants was the fact that he had a thick mass of bright red hair growing around his shaft.

"She won't like that, man. That's not her kind. This here ol' squaw is the wife of that there nigger-lovin' special prosecutor. Why, she must be a nigger lover, too. That's it, ain't it, Miz Winter, Pocahontas, honey? It's nigger dick you loves."

Sal had involuntarily begun to cry. She was not making any noise, but the tears were running down her cheeks. She could taste the salt on her lips. She looked past the first man's big red extended shaft to the cradle across the room. There was no motion from inside, no noise. Cathy was sleeping peacefully.

Suddenly, it was so hot, the air so thick and close, that Sal could scarcely breathe. Her head was spinning and she could not maintain her balance. *Am I going to faint?*

The first man moved in front of her, clutched the pile of hair on top of her head and jerked her face around to his penis. With his other hand he began to rub the end of his shaft over her face. First her eyes, then down the sides of her nose, then over and across her top lip. He moved it down under her chin and then came up the side of her cheek and back over toward her mouth again. He paused with it there, rubbing it back and forth across the line of her mouth. He seemed on the verge of prying open her lips, but for the moment he was only taunting her.

He backed off and the other man said, "Looka here, nigger lover. Look what I got for ya."

The man had slipped a plastic dildo over the end of his penis. It was enormous, provoking the most obscene images her terrified mind could imagine. And it was crudely painted black for the occasion.

Her mind began to shriek with fear as the man came slowly toward her, holding the long glistening dildo in his hand, brandishing it obscenely in her face. She shut her eyes, trying to ward off an inclination to faint. The man said, "I reckon this here is more to your liking, hey, Miz Winter?" She began to gasp, her body in the icy grip of a freezing anger that literally made her shake all over. The pitiful helplessness of her posture—and the degradation of it all—enraged her.

The man repeated the process that the first had followed. She could feel the cold slippery plastic rubbing against her skin and lips. All she could think of was a huge black snake wrapping around her face. Chills swept the length of her body and she broke into a cold sweat. But her brain was clearing, her mind was talking to her. Her entire being was engulfed by her rage.

The man stepped suddenly back and she almost fell on her face.

"Tha's it," he said in a rasping voice. "Get on yore hands and knees."

She hung there for a moment without comprehending his meaning. Then he cuffed her roughly with the palm of his hand on the back of her neck, knocking her forward to the ground. She threw out her hands just in time to keep from falling on her face.

"Further! Stick it up here in the air. Tha's it."

Sal closed her eyes and clenched her teeth as the man moved around behind her and got down on his knees. The other man standing in front of her came down on one knee and grabbed her again by the knot of hair.

Her head came up sharply, and so did her hand, which still held the palette knife.

"Jesus!"

He ducked sideways just in time to avoid the blade as she slashed with all her might at his grimy freckled face.

The edge of the palatte knife opened a superficial cut along his jawbone and nicked into the fleshy part of his shoulder. Had he not ducked in time, he would have been wearing six inches of steel in his neck.

"Bitch!" he screeched, slamming her on the side of the head with the back of his hand, as the other man buried ten inches of plastic between Sal's thighs.

Lamar Stick was standing on his tiptoes outside the barn watching his cronies at work on both ends of Sal's contorted body. He was masturbating with such wild abandon that it would be hours before he realized he was rubbing splinters into the head of his penis against the barn wall. When he ejaculated he had to hang onto the windowsill to keep from falling in a swoon of ecstasy.

Both his friends were halfway into the woods before the crunching sound of tires on the gravel driveway registered in his feverish brain.

Sal lay face down on the floor of the barn, scarcely cognizant of the shouts and sound of running feet outside. The acrid odor of semen on her face first roused her, but then as she moved to brush at her bruised lips she felt the lingering intrusion in her body.

She almost screamed at the thought. And even worse was the idea that someone might come in and find her like that. Steve Hines...Ida Belle...Davey?

"Oh God!" she gasped aloud and reached quickly to her buttocks and clutched the dildo. Her teeth began to chatter and her body shuddered as she drew the filthy thing out of her body and flung it across the room.

Then, as she heard the muffled sound of gunshots in the woods, she dissolved in a hysterical fit of tears, while in the crib nearby, Cathy pushed the ragdoll in the corner, gurgled and slept on peacefully.

# Chapter Seventy-eight

Instead of driving home after his hasty visit to his mother, John had returned to the office. He had restrained an impulse to drop by and see Sal, even if it was only for a cup of post-luncheon coffee. He had wanted to talk with her...He was having second thoughts now...perhaps he shouldn't have told her about Sissie's diary...about his suspicions concerning Homer and Chester Biggs. He had had to tell her about Rachel, in case a packet of those photographs had suddenly arrived in the mail one day. But should he have told her about his father? Had he been disloyal to his mother...?

Hell no, he thought. His mother had never yet seen fit to confide in him.

He hoped Ida Belle would do as he had instructed her without any further resistance. It would be tense having her in the house with them, but he didn't want her staying home alone at a time like this. There was no telling what might happen. There were a lot of nuts running around out there. He thought of the rash of hate calls, the notes in the mail, and even the public slurs chalked on the sidewalks.

On an impulse, he picked up the phone and dialed his mother's number. He let it ring but there was no answer. He felt better about it as he hung up.

Then he considered phoning Sal. Just to see how things were going. Poor Sal, he thought, having to bear this all alone. Ida Belle would be more than a handful. He looked at his watch. He had sent for Charlie Tate...he would be here any moment. John picked up the phone as the intercom buzzed.

It was his secretary telling him he had a call.

"John—? It's Harry Downs. Come home, man. Right now. There's been an—accident."

Doc Whipple, his face contorted with rage, was coming out of the house with a worried Harry Downs when John arrived. John dashed across the concrete apron of the parking pad before his car had completely stopped.

"John...easy now, easy," said Harry.

"It's Sal, John," the old doctor said thickly. "Now she's all right...I mean, she's resting comfortably..."

"What happened? *Tell* me!" John could feel his heart sinking, his stomach beginning to crawl.

"I...I don't know exactly," the doctor said miserably. "I've given her a sedative, she's going to be—all right."

John turned to the governor's aide. "Goddammit, Harry!"

Harry Downs gripped John by the forearm. "Now get hold of yourself, John. This is gonna be rough. When Steve went up to get your mother—Davey went with him, thank God—Sal went out to the studio to paint. She had the baby with her, in the crib."

Already John could feel the bile rising in his throat.

"It was just a goddamn fluke," said Downs. "A terrible coincidence that Steve was away from the house momentarily. Even Moses was gone. You know he went over to Shad Row this morning to see if that sister of his was all right. So Sal was alone—for just a few minutes. That's when they...there were three of them, John..."

"Oh God," he groaned, and put both hands back to lean on the car.

"Sal insists there were only two. But Steve says he chased three men—"

"Oh my God," said John.

"He chased three men into the woods. Two were wearing ski masks...Steve fired at them, thinks he might have nicked one in the ass."

"Ski masks?" John muttered numbly.

"And Sal says she stabbed one of the men in the face, with a painting knife of some sort."

"Palette knife," John mumbled. "It's called a palette knife. She uses it to mix her paints, and to scum large background areas." He was talking to hear himself talk. Anything to avoid conscious thought. He would give the men a lecture on the technique of scumbling in oils.

There were tears in his eyes, an agony of pain in his throat.

"Why didn't he kill them?" he demanded. "Why didn't Steve kill the slimy bastards?"

"John—come inside and have a drink?" said Doc Whipple.

"I want to see her," he said, starting abruptly for the house. "Where is she?"

"John—she's resting, son."

"Where *is* she?" he demanded.

"In the bedroom," said the doctor, following him inside the house. "But only for a few minutes now, you hear...?"

John got halfway down the long hallway, then turned around and came back.

"Did they...?"

The doctor avoided the agony in the man's eyes.

"Oh God," said John again.

At the door to their bedroom he paused, took a deep breath and went inside.

# Chapter Seventy-nine

"Sonofabitch," he growled. "He'll pay, it's just a question of how." Chester Biggs was on the highway that crossed John's property. Merely the thought of John Winter caused Chester to wince, and he experienced a sharp pain in his belly.

"He'll pay."

For the last five or six miles traffic on both sides of the road had begun to thicken. The county line was only about ten more miles. Chester wondered how many would show up—a dozen, a hundred, a thousand?

The demonstration that afternoon hadn't amounted to much, maybe this shindig tonight would fall just as flat. Maybe. About a hundred blacks had marched on the courthouse protesting police brutality. But the whites didn't throw up much of a counterdemonstration. No more than a dozen hotheads, and the few Klansmen that showed up were barely noticeable without their robes and pointed hoods.

Some people breathed a sigh of relief and considered it a good sign. But Chester wasn't fooled. They hadn't backed down; they were simply biding their time. The word was out. A big "Klanvocation" was scheduled for that evening just over the county line out of reach of the local authorities. The Crackerheads were just storing it all up. Let a few niggers march around town with a bunch of signs above their heads; come nightfall the soldiers of the Lord would pick up the tune.

Chester began to laugh. He didn't see how those dumb Cracker bastards continued to survive. With all the crosses they were burning lately it was plumb miraculous they didn't set themselves on fire. Oh, they were horse's asses, all right, but he wasn't going to make the mistake of taking them for granted. A lot of people had done that and not lived to regret it. They was dumb, all right, but mean as snakes in the bargain, he thought. And dangerous as all get-out.

Would Bo Washburn dip down into Taliawiga County on his way to the rally? Chester didn't really expect him to. The sheriff had already put out the word to the right people. Washburn knew by now that he wasn't welcome in Biggs's territory.

As Chester took the ramp onto the Interstate, he had to restrain his speed in the congested traffic. "Don't these goddamned Crackers know there's a gas shortage?" he said.

He wished he could attend the rally himself. But he knew Washburn would have a crew of his security guards down for the occasion and it wouldn't take them more than a minute to spot an old adversary like himself waddling around the cow pasture. Still, he planned to have his eyes and ears all over the place come sundown.

His brow wrinkled as he reached for a cigar. He had been trying all afternoon to reach Lamar Stick. He knew damn good and well he wouldn't have to force the Cracker sonofabitch to attend the meeting, but he did want to give him a couple of special assignments. Biggs lit up, threw the spent match on the floorboard and wondered why the scrawny maggot hadn't called in.

"Hot damn! Ain't this gonna be something!" exclaimed Lamar Stick, jumping out of the truck almost before it had come to a halt. The two men riding with him got out at a more leisurely pace and came around to meet him in front of the truck.

"I'm so hongry I could eat the rear end off a skunk," said the short stocky fellow.

"From the way you was lookin' at that there pussy," said the skinny fellow with the flaming red hair and the long bloody scratch on his jaw, "I expected you to be down on yore hands an' knees rootin' in the mush afore I could so much as git me a stiff pecker."

"You sonofabitch," said the first man. "You worked her over good, I gotta give you that."

"Tell you what though, I almost shit my pants when she come up with that fuckin' butcher knife."

*"Butcher* knife!" said Stick.

"Looked like a goddamn butcher knife to me. Looked like a goddamn machete!"

They were laughing and the fat man said, "Wadden nothin' funny about that there bastard a-blastin' away at us in the woods though."

"Jesus, I'll say," the redhead agreed.

"Who the hell was it—her old man, you reckon?" the fat man asked as they started toward the hot dog stand.

"Naw," said Stick. "I don't think it was Winter."

The fat man chuckled. "How would you know, fast as you was runnin'?"

"I didn't notice you standin' still."

"Ooowee," he said. "Hadn't been for that liddle ol' pine tree I'da took some lead right in the ass."

"Bet that there Winter gal could take it in the ass," said the redhead and they began to howl again.

"God, I can't wait to see the look on old Chester's face when I tell 'im what we done," said Stick. "I tell ya, fellas, by this here little day's work we done fixed ourselves in so solid with the sheriff that even one of Alvin Boyle's firebombs couldn't knock us loose."

311

"You reckon," said the fat man, "he really gonna let us become deputies one 'a these days?"

"Jethro, I tell ya here an' now—you can count on it. That man owes us now. And ol' Chester he sure ain't one to welch on his debts!"

Hearing the door handle click, Sal thought, *They've come back*. She couldn't survive another attack. If only she had had time to tell John she loved him. The thoughts were plodding about in her mind now like footsteps in quicksand.

The room was dark, all the shades were drawn; but a shaft of light entered from the hall as the door opened. And she could see feet now. *I'll scream!*

She was so tired. Her brain seemed incapable of rational thought. This man is kind and gentle.

"Don't hurt me," she whimpered.

"Oh, Sal. God, I'm so sorry."

She took a deep breath, her heart against his face. "John...?"

"I'm so sorry, honey..."

"John, they were just awful men." Her voice was a soft slurred whisper. "They did terrible things...unspeak—unspeakable things." She sounded drunk.

"Hush now. Shhh, it's all right now."

"But John—I have to tell you...in case they come back—"

"They'll never come back," he said harshly.

"I have to tell you I love you."

"Oh, Sal..." His voice cracked. He couldn't hold it any longer. With great shuddering gasps, he dropped his head against her breast and began to cry.

"And I love you, Sal. I'll always love you," he said fiercely.

# Chapter Eighty

**Chester sat in his car on the side of the road,** looking down at the activity in the field below. The old Stovall farm lay just across the county line, a thousand acres of overgrown woods and unused pasturelands. Hundreds of rusted-out vehicles had already rattled their way across the bumpy pasture to the area that had been designated for parking. All along both sides of the highway hand-lettered cardboard signs—mostly misspelled—announced the meeting and pointed the way. Men, women, children. Some of the boys wore Klan T-shirts, a number of men had already donned their robes and peaked hoods. Security guards stood all around the field dressed in paramilitary gear, carrying foot-long stanchions. Some tourists had stopped, mostly out of curiosity, to watch the fun and goings-on. Chester wondered how many in the crowd were undercover FBI agents.

Beyond the cluster of cars a few of the more commercially minded Klansmen were busily erecting their portable stands for the dispensation—for an appropriate price—of a wide variety of Klan paraphernalia. Farther on down the pasture a jerry-built wooden platform had been hastily constructed, and Chester could see three or four men scurrying around under the platform in an effort to hook up the public address system.

"Be nice iffen they'd just go on an' electrocute theirselves," Chester said aloud.

At the far end of the field a cluster of men were busy wrapping oil-soaked sheets and blankets around the center pole of a giant wooden cross. It would make a hell of a sight, Chester had to admit.

He looked up in the rearview mirror as one of his radio cruisers pulled up behind him.

"They sent me out with a message for you, suh. One they didn't want to put on the radio."

"What is it, boy—an' make it quick."

"All they tol' me was to tell you to come on back to the station lickety-split. Got somethin' to do with that there special prosecutor."

Biggs cranked the engine and started to slip the car into gear. It would soon be dark. He wanted to get back in time for the speeches and the bonfire. The crowd was thickening. There was a festive mood; every other car seemed to have a cooler full of beer in the trunk and bags of sandwiches and snacks—like a church picnic on a warm summer evening.

Chester eased the car onto the road and let it roll downhill slowly. They were really piling out of the cars now; men, women, children and a slew of babes in arms. He started to pick up speed and then suddenly hit the brake, saying, "What the hell—?" as he saw Lamar Stick ambling off into the woods behind the platform with a pair of his cronies.

"Goddammit," he said. "That Cracker sonofabitch is more trouble to me than he's worth."

# Chapter Eighty-one

L. G. Cubbage was speaking. Two or three others had already preceded him, and the crowd was pretty well pumped up by the time he got the microphone. He was not the featured speaker; that honor would fall to Bo Washburn. On the other hand, L. G. had a real opportunity to make a name for himself and to do some good in the coming election. As he stepped up on the platform, Lamar Stick had slapped him on the back and said, "Go get 'em, Mr. Mayor."

L. G. wanted to concentrate on his speech, but even while he raved on, his mind kept wandering back to what Stick had just told him concerning the incident out at John Winter's house. The goddamn fool must have been crazy. And he thinks Chester Biggs is going to reward him for it! L.G. realized now that he was going to have to be a lot more careful about who he picked to work with in the future. A mistake like the one Stick had made today could be fatal. He would disassociate himself from the fool as of this night on.

The sudden roar of the crowd jarred his conscious mind.

"And I know," Cubbage continued, "that all you good Christian people agree with me when I say that never did I think I would live to see the day that such as this would be happenin' right here in our own home community. The Northern liberal, nigger-Jewish-communist conspiracy forced us to integrate more than two decades ago. And just look at what it has finally led to. Niggers accostin' white folk right here in our home-town streets. It's unsafe for our womenfolk to go to town or to church...it's unsafe for our children to go to school...it's unsafe for us to go to work or even to drive our cars out on the streets after dark.

"But I for one—and I know there are a great many out there like me—have no intention of laying down like a sniverlin' dawg...no intention of invitin' the communist masters in Moscow to come walkin' into my living room parlor. The last commie-nigger who come walkin' into my house come in with a gun!" Tears involuntarily began to trickle down his cheeks, his voice trembled with the amplified sobs that wracked his stunted body. "And when he was done, when this murdering devil was gone, I was left alone in this here world...my entire family gone, dead, murdered. And this creature is *alive*," he continued in a rasping voice. "Why, he's being tended to right this very minute, tended to by the sovereign state of Georgia itself. Clean sheets, three meals a day, all the medicine he needs. Doctors, nurses and policemen standin' guard in order to protect him, to make sure he's comfortable, an' safe, an' all his constitutional rights and privileges are honored. *This* is what our country has come to!" he bellowed, his whole body quivering with indignation.

"Instead of the black murderin' sonofabitch danglin' right

now from the tops of one 'a them trees over there, he's a-layin' up in that clean sweet-smellin' bed while *my* fambly," he said, dropping his voice an octave lower and moving his mouth closer to the mike with an instinctive showmanship that even L.G. himself had no idea he possessed, "while my fambly even now lies a-rottin' in their cold lonely graves."

For a full ten seconds there was absolute silence in the crowd. Then a sudden collective roar of anguish came up out of those people, as if the group itself had somehow been grievously injured. And then, gradually, their roar of woe began to change in tone and quality. Finally the new sound began to take shape and L.G. was able to discern the nature of their message.

"Cubbage! Cubbage! Cubbage!"

Though it wasn't planned that way, Bo Washburn, experienced manipulator of hysterical crowds that he was, realized the high point of the night had just been reached. Though two other speeches, including his own, were yet to come, he made the instant decision not to allow the spontaneity of the moment to slip away unexploited.

He signaled quickly to one of his faithful followers. The man scooped up the skirt of his satin robe and raced across the lumpy pasture as fast as his booted feet would carry him.

While the crowd was still shouting, "Cubbage Cubbage Cubbage," the base of the gasoline-soaked cross ignited in a spectacular explosion of orange flame and a deafening WHOOMPH! that almost blew the unsuspecting spectators to the ground.

The crowd turned in awe, like a dumbstruck animal standing in the field, staring at the burning cross silhouetted against the darkening sky. They stared with fascination and reverence as the breeze whipped the brilliant flames around the wooden beams. They stood there in their jeans and seersucker suits, in their cotton blouses and silk dresses, in their satin robes and pointed hoods—men with potbellies and rotten teeth, women with neat permanents and plastic jewelry, children with gaping expressions of wonder and awe—watching with religious fervor as the burning cross of Jesus once again lighted their way.

# Chapter Eighty-two

**Some while after midnight, Chester Biggs finally made** it over to Lucy Pittman's house. He parked his sedan directly in front of her house and waddled slowly up to the porch. He didn't want any interference tonight, so he left his car in plain view.

Lucy took her time to get to the door. But he was too tired to just kick the damn thing down. He took off his hat and wiped his forehead with a large dirty handkerchief. He had about a dozen other things he ought to be doing at the moment but was so damn tired he couldn't hit a lick at a snake if it was wrapped around his boot. And he was emotionally drained.

As if all the goddamn nigger mess goin' on in the county wadden bad enough, he had to worry about asshole Lamar Stick and his latest piece of Cracker nonsense. Merely thinking the man's name made Chester blind with rage. He could feel his fists, stomach and sphincter knotting in unison. He had nearly wet his pants when they told him. If Winter thought Chester had ordered such a thing done to his wife, the goddamn man would hound him to his grave.

"Lucy! Goddammit, open this door!"

What he had to do was wait and see how bad the woman was hurt and what John Winter was gonna do about it. Somehow he had to get word out to Winter that he had had nothing to do with what happened. A stabbing pain began to throb in his temples. Winter won't believe it. He must know that Stick is my man. Chester began to grind his teeth as he thought of the creep. He didn't have any problems about what to do with Stick. He would put the word out first thing the next morning; have the ignorant bastard's bones broke in a dozen places. Then he would run Stick and his trashy family out of the county forever.

"Open the door, Lucy, or I'll tear your goddamn house down!" He drew up his big booted foot just as she opened the door.

"I'm sorry, Chester. I was just getting out of the shower when I heard you knock. I...I wasn't dressed..."

"Like I ain't never seen you nekkid before, hey, Lucy?"

He brushed past her uninvited and went into the living room, where he flopped wearily down on the sofa. She followed him with her robe pulled tightly around her body, digging in her pocket for a cigarette.

"What the hell's the matter with you?" he asked, watching her light the cigarette with a shaky hand.

"Nothing," she said quickly, then shrugged. "Oh, it's all this violence and carryin' on, I reckon."

"Bad for business, too, I s'pose."

"My mind is hardly on business at the moment."

"Well now, you know what I'm in the market for tonight, Miz Lucy? To see you do one of them there special gypsy dances I like so much. Put on one 'a them records and dance me a crazy Hungarian fandango. An' then you can get me out them pictures the Cubbage cunt left behind."

Lucy moved roughly in time to the music, dropped her robe to the floor and turned her back to him. Shuffling over to a nearby table, she opened the drawer and took out a large manila envelope. She swayed a little with the music, came toward the sofa and offered him a full frontal view. He was sweating now. She handed him the photographs, backed off a few steps and slowly began her bumps and grinds.

Chester opened the envelope and took out the photographs. There were only five or six, but those were Chester's favorites. He began now to look through them with hot red eyes. Lucy continued to dance sluggishly, her pinched face a study of fear and anxiety. But Chester was too far gone to notice. He was wheezing like an asthmatic hog. He unzipped his fly, sitting with his meaty thighs spread, and beckoned to Lucy to get on with it.

Like a sleepwalker, she knelt before him and dug into his pants.

Chester put his head back on the seat and closed his eyes.

He gasped at the touch of her lips. He had never known her to be so rough, so unprofessional.

He raised his head to censure her. As he opened his eyes, he saw them in the mirror on the wall across the room. His eyes filled with horror. They were standing behind the sofa like ebony bookends. Tall, broad as doors and black as the ace of spades.

Chester gasped, thrust his pelvis forward and ejaculated in Lucy's throat, as the two black men systematically began to crush his skull with their leaded socks.

# Chapter Eighty-three

**John was up early, having scarcely slept all night. His** grief, even on a subconscious level, was too severe to allow for sleep. The last thing his mind and body could accept was rest. He looked in on Sal; she was sleeping heavily, lying on her side, her body drawn into a knot with her knees practically beneath her chin. An attitude of self-protection? Ida Belle was sleeping too, and so were the children.

Was it safe to leave the house? He went back to the guest room, where Downs and Steve Hines were asleep. The door was cracked, their room full of shadows and heavy snoring. He decided to wait a while longer. They might not hear Cathy if she cried. He didn't want Sal disturbed under any circumstances.

He took another cup of coffee and went back to the den.

It had been a hell of a night. He didn't like to recall the sort of thoughts he had wrestled with during the endless nighttime hours. He was tired of the sofa now, so he sat down in the swivel chair behind the desk. Every bone in his body ached. His heart muscle felt as if it had been run through a meat grinder. He felt—suddenly—old and defeated.

It had rained during the night, and he had spent the hours lying on the sofa listening to the heavy drops splatting against the window. How could he face Sal in the cold light of day? What could he say? That he was *sorry?* That everything would be all right, that he would make it up to her?

His stomach knotted up and his eyes burned against the images that attempted to intrude upon his thoughts. All through the night he had kept imagining the events of the afternoon. Details were scarce and his imagination ran wild. All that he knew for certain—according to Doc Whipple— was that Sal had been raped, brutally, was when the effects of the sedatives wore off she would experience considerable pain.

What had they done? His mind was awash with obscene images. The rage in his chest, the desire for revenge that burned in his veins, was all but suffocating. Who were they? Why had they chosen Sal? He would destroy them with his bare hands. Had he ever doubted his capacity to kill?

A sudden thought shook him like a cold fever. *Chester Biggs!* The incident with Rachel had not been enough to shake John; something closer to home was needed. Sal first, then perhaps Davey or Cathy.

John stood up, fists clenched at his sides, knees shaking. *I'll kill him,* he thought savagely. I'll spill his big fat tub of guts all over Taliawiga County. John's face was grim, tight-set, bloodless.

He went to a closet in the corner of the den. The shelf across the top was enclosed, the paneled doors locked. He took a ring of keys out of his pocket and opened the doors. Across the back of the shelf lay a pump-action shotgun and a box of shells. He took the shotgun down and examined its working parts. Methodically, he inserted eight rounds into the magazine and then racked a shell into the firing chamber.

Taking it outside, he put the gun in the trunk of his car and locked it. As the sun rose through the trees, his old friend the whippoorwill could be heard welcoming the day down by the creek.

A light went on in the guest room; either Harry or Steve Hines was up. Suddenly, John turned on his heels and began to run. He ran like a madman, his arms and legs flailing the air.

He raced down across the yard and bounded onto the footbridge across the creek—as he had been doing for so many mornings the last few years. But it was not the same without the dogs nipping at his heels. Both were dead; they had been poisoned. No wonder they hadn't come to Sal's aid, or at least sounded an alarm. But it wasn't only the dogs...nothing about this day was the same. Nothing would ever be the same again.

As his running feet hit the path the thoughts jarred about loosely in his head. Poor Sal. She had been through so much. First her entire family...and now this. Why? What had she ever done to deserve something like this...except marry him?

His lungs were burning. He pushed himself relentlessly. His calves were taut, his insteps beginning to knot. As the path twisted and steepened abruptly his legs began to wobble. Occasionally he stumbled and lost his footing, but still he pushed on.

Somewhere along the way he had begun to cry. There were more tears after all.

If only he knew who they were...if only...

*Chester would pay.* Sweat was running into his eyes now, his lips were coated with grime. He would make Chester pay in full.

He increased his pace as he hurtled up the leafy hillside, punishing his legs and lungs beyond the point of endurance. Up, up he ran...ten, fifteen, twenty minutes...until his aching legs would support him no farther.

He slowed, stumbled, fell to the ground on his hands and knees, gasping, sucking the hot dry air into his tortured lungs, eyes clenched, fighting off the spasm of nausea that gripped him.

"Oh God," he groaned. "If only...if only she could have fought them off!"

As the russet balm of morning burst fully upon the silent woods, John vomited his shame and disgust onto the footpath between his hands.

# Chapter Eighty-four

**John wanted to shower and clean up before Sal woke.** Doc Whipple said he would look in on her around eight o'clock. After he was satisfied that she was okay, John planned to leave the house for a while. He would tell Chester Biggs he wanted to talk. He would tell him he had had enough. He would arrange a place to meet. A private place.

As he started into the house, John heard the tires on the gravel. It was probably Doc Whipple. He waited as the car came up the drive and stopped behind the parking pad. It was not the doctor. It was Jim Darden.

"Have you heard?" the patrolman asked, getting out of the car. With Ida Belle in the house there wasn't enough room for Jim; he'd spent the night at a motel in town.

"Heard what?"

"About Chester Biggs."

When the news about Sheriff Biggs got around town and county, a general mood of stunned disbelief seemed to grip everyone, black and white alike, so that rational thinking was almost as difficult to come by as reasoned activity.

The Sheriff's Department was in turmoil, and the P.D. was not noticeably any more efficient. An APB was out for any suspicious-looking persons in the county. And that was a laugh. The county was populated with suspicious-looking persons. Anyone having information concerning the attack upon Sheriff Biggs was urged to contact law-enforcement officials at once.

Investigators had no idea where to begin. When the sheriff

went off duty the night before it could only be assumed that he went home. He had no wife or family, no close friends or neighbors. The only person who might have helped was nowhere to be found. Lucy Pittman's house was as clean as a whistle. All her clothes and personal belongings...her car...gone. And Lucy herself had vanished.

By midmorning the shock still had not worn off. People could talk of nothing else. The sheriff's body had been found out in the country, his head beaten to a pulp and his severed pecker stuffed up his asshole.

"Didden have a stitch of clothes on 'im," said the coroner. "The damnedest-looking spectacle I ever seen."

"Where'd it happen?" asked Captain Tate. "Not out there where he was found?"

"Naw," said Doc Peavyhouse. "No idee."

Tate shook his head and started into his office. "What the hell's gonna happen next around this place? You'd think it was New York City."

It was almost more than John could absorb. Too much had happened too fast. And Chester was gone. Someone had avenged John's honor for him. Something else to live with, he thought.

He made sure the diary and Sharon White's report were securely locked away in his reinforced desk drawer. Then he checked his watch. Ten-thirty. He ought to hit the road if he wanted to be in the governor's office by noon as planned. Governor Barrow had tried to dissuade him but finally bowed to the inevitable.

Ida Belle had Cathy on the porch and was playing with her. Steve Hines was showing Davey how to whittle in the barn. Harry Downs had already left for Atlanta. And Doc Whipple had come and gone, leaving Sal under sedation again with the promise to return in the early afternoon. The doctor thought that one more night's medicated sleep would see her through the worst of it and she would be up and on her feet again.

At that moment Bobcat Tribble was in his office above the pharmacy, proofreading a new stack of dilatory motions that he was planning to file in the James case. And the staff at the county hospital was making preparations for the transfer of Eddie James to the mental institution in Milledgeville for the tests ordered by Judge Harbuck.

# Chapter Eighty-five

**Hours had fused into days, days into weeks. He had no** idea how long he had been held prisoner, no idea where he was, nor what they wanted of him. He couldn't quite remember how they had got him and had no idea what had become of his buddies. He still had the shooting pains in back of his eyeballs and in his temples, and the wound in his shoulder throbbed dully. It must have been a bayonet, but he didn't remember the precise moment of confrontation. He couldn't remember when he'd bought it with an exchange of small-arms fire either, but he knew what had opened the gaping wounds in his side and shredded his left arm. The long blazing scar on his arm was what really puzzled him. It was an old scar, healed over and painless. Why haven't the other wounds healed? How long have I been here?

He could hear movement outside his door in the corridor, and muted voices. What were they saying? He couldn't understand the language. He wished the one with the beard would come again. He didn't understand him either but there was something in his eyes, in his tone of voice. He doesn't hate me like the others do. But then why shouldn't they? They know what I've done. I can tell from their questions. They want me to confess, probably record it all on tape and film and use it against America as dirty lying propaganda.

Except it *isn't* dirty lying propaganda.

Someone touched the door, but didn't come inside. His hair bristled on the back of his neck. What can I do when they come for me? They *know*. They know all about me and what I have done. I'll give 'em my name, rank and serial number.

I'll confess to nothing. I'm not guilty. I'm a soldier. I'm fighting for my country. I only did what I was ordered to do. I only—

Oh my God.

The door opened. Just a crack, but it opened and he saw—

Oh my God. It was all there: the hot sun, the pale green ocean shimmering beyond the white sand beach, the shoreline edged with tall coconut palms, the village cluster of tin and wood and metal...the scarlet flame trees licking the blue sky like tongues of fire...the chatter of small-arms fire, the shouts and screams and—

Oh my God. *That little baby girl—*

The door slammed shut.

I'm a soldier, thought Eddie James. I do what I'm ordered to do. He was drenched in sweat now, his pillow sodden beneath his head. They call it an atrocity now, but to us it was nothing more than a hit-and-run military operation. We thought there were enemy agents in that village. We didn't know it was only old men, women and—children.

Eddie began to cry. She couldn't have been more than five. He didn't know she was there. He had kicked down the door, heard a noise across the room, turned and fired. "It's not my fault," he said aloud and the sound of his own voice astonished him. It was the first time he had spoken in weeks. What if one of the guards hears me, he thought. They'll come for me. They'll make me talk...

He had to think. He had to remain calm and decide what to do. He was a soldier. He knew the code. He had to escape. At least he had to try.

It was quiet in the corridor now. No sounds, no voices. What did it mean? His mind was so hazy with drugs and fatigue that he couldn't think clearly. Was it possible that they had removed the guard? Why?

The silence was menacing. Perplexed at suddenly finding his room unguarded, he felt unnerved—alone and lost in an alien land, unfamiliar with the language, unprepared for the terrain. Nevertheless, his duty as a soldier was to escape. He had to do what was expected of him by his country. He had withstood the enemy's interrogation for weeks; he had admitted no atrocities. But his final duty was to escape.

He struggled to keep his eyes open and to move his arms and legs. His body ached. The pain in his temples screamed and his vision went spinning wildly as he sat up on the side of the bed. Slowly, painfully, he made his way over to the door.

The door was unlocked, the sentry's chair unoccupied. There was no one on guard! He froze instinctively. Something was wrong. His mind was trying to warn him of something but the message was blocked. It was as if all the main circuits in his brain were closed down. Barefooted and wearing only the green hospital gown, Eddie stepped cautiously into the deserted corridor.

He stopped suddenly, his heart in his throat. At the far end of the corridor a pair of large glass doors opened onto a covered courtyard of sorts. In the courtyard he could see the back end of a parked ambulance, its rear doors thrown open, the driver leaning against a fender smoking a cigarette.

*They're taking me away,* he thought wildly. Instinctively he knew the ambulance was for him. He was being moved, farther back into the jungle, perhaps even to Ho Chi Minh City itself. There he would be subjected to far more devious methods of interrogation—perhaps even tortured. He couldn't hold out much longer. It was now or never.

He turned in the other direction and moved down the corridor toward a door marked EXIT. Unable to read Vietnamese script, he was unaware of the sign's message. Facing a choice of terrors, he had no alternative but to take a chance.

But before he could extend his hand, his hair bristled and his skin began to crawl. Though the exit door remained tightly shut, the door in his mind opened a crack.

"Oh Jesus," he said.

It was night, hot and sultry. There was a flavor of jasmine on the breeze. A swing was creaking in the darkness. He had found her. He would make her and the others pay. Especially her father. He was the guilty one, not Sissie. She would not have murdered his child had it not been for her meddling father. She knew how much it meant to him to have their baby. She knew it was his only means of redemption for the unpardonable sin he had committed in that Asian village. She knew—

Oh my God.

They all had to pay. Her father was the worst, but they had all conspired to kill—

Oh Jesus Lord. *Not again.*

The door was swinging shut.

Wait!

That sudden metallic sound in the adjoining hallway. The

plastic duck rocking back and forth on the cold linoleum floor. The little girl's wet soapy body—

The door slammed irrevocably shut on the agonized shriek of momentary comprehension.

And the exit door swung open with a metallic creak.

He started down the steps and set his course across an open field. All a soldier could do was try. No country should ask more than that.

# Chapter Eighty-six

**By the time John reached the courthouse square,** Sharon White was on the steps watching for him. When she saw the red Toyota coming, she ran down the steps and out to the curb, waving.

"They've got him!" she said anxiously, jumping into the car. "He was too weak to get far. A patrol car picked him up three or four blocks away from the hospital. They're on the way to the police station with him now."

"Police station!" John swung the car around in the middle of the street, shot out through a caution light and headed for City Hall.

As they rushed up the City Hall steps, they met Charlie Tate on his way out.

"Have they got him? Is he okay?"

"The sonofabitch!" Charlie said furiously.

"What's wrong?"

"He shot another cop, that's what the hell's wrong."

They turned and started running after Tate.

Tate's car was parked at the curb. He got in and John ran around to the other side, while Sharon jumped into the back seat. The car was moving before John could get the door closed. It took less than five minutes to get to their destination.

There were a half-dozen police vehicles nosing around the bloody scene like a pack of hungry sharks. They jumped out of the car and made their way roughly through the gawking crowd of spectators and uniformed policemen.

Tate grabbed the nearest cop by the arm and swung him around furiously. "Who got shot? One of our boys is down. Who is it?"

"Naw, Cap'n, sir. Ain't none of our boys been hit."

John pushed past them and went over to the ditch that paralleled the side of the road. He shoved his way through a cluster of gloating officers.

Eddie James was sprawled face down in the mud; the back of his head resembled a smashed melon.

As Sharon White came up behind John, she gasped at the grisly sight. John looked up and locked eyes with Robert Randolph. The D.A. was standing stoically on the other side of the ditch. Neither man spoke. At least, thought John, the bastard wasn't laughing, like so many others back in the crowd. He wondered how long it would take for L. G. Cubbage to get to the scene. And maybe Alvin Boyle, or Bo Washburn. And what about the two sub-cretins who attacked Sal? He looked around the crowd. Surely they wouldn't miss a good free show like this. This kind of thing ought to be right down their line.

Captain Tate stepped into the breach and began snapping orders. "Okay, you guys—we got a crime scene to protect. Sergeant, get on the horn and get the boys from my office over here pronto. Meanwhile, some of you boys begin clearing all of these vultures out of here. And keep the fuckin' newspaper termites outa my sight till I tell you it's okay!"

John and Sharon backed away from the scene and started back toward Charlie's sedan. They met Bobcat Tribble coming through the mob. The two men stopped and stared at each other.

"Well, Cat—there goes your national showcase," John said dryly.

"Look, son. I...I know how you must feel."

"No you don't."

"John..." He shook his big shaggy head. "It isn't that simple, man."

"It's pretty simple for Eddie James, isn't it? Now."

328

Tribble looked at his client lying in the mud with his head half blown off. "It isn't *my* fault," he said. "I was trying to get him out of here. Before something like this..."

He saw the agony in Winter's eyes and stopped.

"John...about Sal..."

"It's not your fault, Cat. Nor mine. It's nobody's fault. None of us is responsible for any of this." He paused, looking at Eddie James. "Right?"

# Chapter Eighty-seven

**Homer Stokes finally caught up with John in the court-**house as he was leaving the special prosecutor's office. It was almost two o'clock. After the shooting of Eddie James, John had canceled his appointment in Atlanta with Governor Barrow.

"Where are you going, John?"

"Home. I haven't even stopped for lunch. And I want to check on Sal."

Homer ran along beside him as John hurried out of the building. "How is she, John? I mean, is she..."

"She's as well as can be expected—under the circumstances."

At the car, John opened the door and turned to Homer. "Is it—all over town?"

Homer stared at him, tight-lipped.

John took a deep breath. "Yeah, well...it's all over now." He paused. "I was gonna kill Biggs, you know. I think I would have too. I can't say for sure, but I think I would have."

Homer was visibly moved. "Biggs?"

John nodded, then got in the car.

"John, please..."

He closed the door and looked up at him. "What do you want, Homer?"

"I have to talk to you."

John shook his head. "Not now you don't. Not anymore."

"I..."

"Homer, I'm through...finished. I don't want anything further to do with any of this."

"I've *got* to talk to you." Homer looked extremely agitated.

"Get in," said John, starting the engine.

They rode out to the house in silence, a part of the common mood in Taliawiga County. Activity in the county had all but come to a standstill. With the death of Eddie James, coming so close on the heels of the equally violent demise of Chester Biggs, most people were simply stunned into immobility. It might not last, but for the moment activists on all sides were motionless. At least things had slowed down long enough for the authorities to regain a measure of control.

Even so, a new ingredient had recently been introduced into the uncertain equation: the FBI had moved into Taliawiga County in force to investigate a host of civil rights complaints. The death of Eddie James would go to the top of their list of priorities.

How had the boy ever managed to get out of his bed and his room, let alone the hospital itself? Had it been a setup? On whose orders? The answers to those and a lot of other questions may have perished with Chester Biggs.

I'll help them all I can. Up to a point, John thought.

As soon as he checked on Sal, he would call the governor and make another appointment.

At the house he chatted for a few moments with Steve Hines, sent Homer into the den with a platter of sandwiches and a pitcher of beer and then went to look in on Sal.

Steve had said she was awake and much improved. John found her that and more.

"Honey, you look wonderful!"

"I feel so much better."

He kissed her forehead and lips, and then sat on the bed beside her.

"Are you all right?" she asked.

"Don't worry about *me*."

She smiled weakly and glanced at the unused side of the bed. "And where have you been sleeping?"

"I'll trade with you. Tonight you can have the sofa in the den."

"Poor baby," she patted his hand.

"Sal—" His voice broke over the lump that suddenly blocked his throat.

"No, no, not now," she whispered. "I'm fine, really I am, but I'm not up to talking about it. I...I don't even want to think about it."

"That's right," he said firmly. "Don't talk or think about it. Let's just forget it ever happened."

He buried his face in her shoulder and held her to him.

She put her hand behind his head and squeezed weakly. "Wouldn't that be nice," she said drowsily.

In the den, John sighed as he sank down into the sofa with a tall beaded glass of beer. But he couldn't yet focus upon whatever Homer's problem was.

"What's going to happen now? Is it over, do you suppose?"

"Over?" John grunted. "It may have just begun. Oh, some of the stars are gone, but there'll be plenty of tyros to rise up and take their places. And the others—they've just paused to regroup, to figure out what the hell to do next."

He paused, then added, "No, it's not over. This sort of thing won't just go away."

Homer said, "At least the capital punishment issue may have been defused."

"They'll find another fish to fry."

"Eddie James is dead," said Homer. "Does it really matter *how* he died?"

John looked at him sharply. "It matters and you know it does. When Eddie James killed, he was probably not a rational person. The state is *supposed* to behave responsibly."

"Tell me, John, what do you think personally? Is capital punishment a deterrent to crime?"

John shifted in his seat and looked hard at Homer Stokes. "It will always deter *some* people from committing crime. Others—" He paused, his eyes hardened to match his voice. "—there are some crimes that nothing in God's green earth can prevent. I would have gut-shot Chester Biggs this morning just as sure as I'm sitting in this room. If I ever catch those other creeps I'll take them apart with my bare hands."

"John, you don't mean that."

"Don't tell me what I mean," he said glumly.

"Heavens, man, it contradicts everything you've ever professed to believe in. You're tired, and sick. You need rest. You're not bloody Superman, you know."

John got up abruptly and went over to the corner bar. He poured a shot of scotch and downed it neat.

"Homer," he said with a grimace as the whisky exploded in his throat, "I don't want to seem inhospitable, ol' buddy. But I really am awfully busy."

Homer stood up. "Are you going to resign?"

"I think so. Yes, of course I am."

"Have you told the governor?"

"I was going to this morning. Then the Eddie James thing... I'll go up to see him tomorrow."

Homer sat down again, as if his legs had collapsed. "Before you resign... before you talk to him..."

"Homer, what the hell *is* this?"

"Please, John. Could you give me a good stiff drink?"


Sal wondered who was in the den with John. So many people coming and going. But John was here; he was spending as much time at home as possible. She knew how many things he must have to attend to. He had so many worries. What to do about that boy, Eddie James. And the racial animosities—he seemed so *surprised* by it all. Didn't he know this was the way it was? These are his people. Doesn't he *know* them? Poor dear. And now all this mess with Rachel and her father and Chester Biggs.

Oh that *awful* man, she thought. What would he do with the photographs? Sal smiled as she thought about the look on John's face when he had told her about the incident out at Oak Grove. Did he really think she would suspect him of carrying on with Rachel Pettigrew? Silly boy. She knew her man better than that.

But he was worried. About so many things. And now—*this*.

If only... what? If only it hadn't happened? That's wishful thinking. Wouldn't it be nice if nothing bad ever had to happen. What kind of life would that be. Still, maybe if... stop it! There was nothing you could have done. But maybe... no!

And John had been so sweet, so gentle and understanding. He would realize there was nothing she could have done to prevent what happened. Wouldn't he? Of course he would. She had had to consider Cathy. Even if she had been able to somehow get away from them, such an option had been denied her because of the baby. She couldn't have run away and left the baby with *them*.

She couldn't have survived at the expense of her own baby, the way she had survived despite the outrage against her parents and baby brother. No one could carry that much guilt.

She was so drowsy. She wished Doc Whipple would stop giving her those shots. He was such a nice little man. Kind, gentle hands. Not at all like those others.

A chill rippled along her spine.

Don't! Please don't. She shut her eyes and leaned against the images pushing into her mind. They didn't come so often anymore. She was growing stronger against them. She didn't want them, but she was no longer terrified by them. It was very curious...but somehow she was able to handle them now.

Each time the images came to her—as in a dream—they were all mixed in with those earlier dreams, the ones she had suffered for years after the murders of her family, and they always came clothed in dark heavy shadows, amid terrible earsplitting noises that tore at her nerve endings like broken shards of glass. But now...somehow...all that was changing. The faces of her parents were fading...her little brother was smiling happily...her family, she suddenly realized, was at peace. *Peace*. And the dark shadows were lifting. The noise—it was *music*, of all things—strident at first, a blaring cacophony of sound...but now it was softening.

And those men—they were not real at all! No faces...empty ski masks...no substance at all. Wait! The darkness—fading—sunshine and light everywhere. And faces—yes!—John and Davey and Cathy...and she slid into a deep, easy sleep, the whispering rain against the windows...and she was running down a long dark tunnel with the terrible shrieks and cries of pain and fear and—guilt—wailing in the darkness behind. And then...there was a door at the end of the tunnel ...it was open and there was light everywhere, a field of light and color and music and...

The terror was gone!

On the gigantic canvas of light were the smiling portraits of John and Davey and Cathy...

Sal turned her face into the pillow, smiling. For the first time in years she slept with a heart and mind at peace.

# Chapter Eighty-eight

"Let me say it all at once, John...without interruption...before I lose my nerve."

John sighed, nodded, took a drink over to the sofa and sat down. Homer had another shot to settle his nerves and turned around.

"I know you've been curious about my behavior recently. No need to deny it. It has been odd, to say the least. Ever since the disappearance of poor Ellie..."

Homer paused and came a few steps nearer the sofa.

"Until then, I was your most fervent supporter. I even helped get you into all this."

"Didn't you though."

"I'm sorry, John, truly sorry. If I'd had any idea—"

"Go on, Homer. You were about to tell me that you abducted Ellie Fletcher."

Homer smiled ruefully. "Not exactly, old man. But I am involved and it does concern Ellie and her mother."

John shook his head in exasperation. "That old gossip means nothing to me, Homer. Hell, I don't care one way or the other—"

"It's more than gossip, John. And what I have to say will be of considerable interest to the special prosecutor."

"Which I won't be after tomorrow."

"So I have to tell you this today." His eyes misted over with tears.

"Homer—"

"Please, John. I *said* no interruptions." John settled back in his chair and Homer took a deep breath. "There have been so many times I wanted to tell you this. I just couldn't do it." He sat down heavily, his face in his hands. "I was just so bloody *ashamed!*"

John leaned forward and touched his friend on the knee. "Homer, there's nothing you can say that will ever change the way I feel toward you."

Homer looked up, his eyes scorched with pain and remorse.

"D'you remember that summer when we went away to college? Josie was working for us at the time, cooking and cleaning. And her husband Jesse did all sorts of odd jobs for Daddy. And then—suddenly—just before we went away to school, Jesse disappeared."

"Sure, I remember. And Josie was pregnant with Ellie." John shrugged. "It's unfortunate, but those things have been happening for a hundred years down here."

"Of course Josie couldn't stay on with us. Daddy fixed her up with the family of one of his friends and she's never wanted for work since. And Ellie's been taken care of too. It's so bloody ironic," he said hollowly. "She died out there in the woods a mighty rich young woman."

"How so?" John leaned forward, his curiosity aroused.

"From the day she was born she received a check every month, first from Daddy, then after he died, from me. It's all been handled through a blind trust, anonymously, by Judge Bradshaw over in Macon. The money was to see to her education and then the rest was to be divided equally between Ellie, Otha, Mandy and Josie. Now—now of course it will all go to Josie and Mandy."

"What about Otha?"

"I had him removed as a beneficiary some years ago. When Josie disowned him, so did I."

"He never knew?"

"None of them did. Not even Josie."

John leaned back against the sofa and said, "Well, you've done the best you could. Certainly your intentions were good. None of what happened to Ellie was your fault. Given the circumstances, you couldn't acknowledge her as your daughter. You did the next best thing."

Homer shook his head sadly. John had never seen him look so long-faced.

"You still don't understand, John. No one does." His voice cracked, his hands began to shake, his lips quivered. "Ellie isn't my daughter. I never had an affair with Josie."

"Then what—?"

"It was Jesse I loved."

John's mouth fell open, but he was speechless. A chill began to spread over his scalp.

"Daddy caught us. In my room at the top of the stairs. You know the one, you've slept there often enough. And Daddy actually *caught* us."

"Good God Almighty," John whispered, his face as white as a sun-dried bone.

"I...somehow forgot to lock the door. He opened it, flicked on the light and there we were. On the bed . . . naked . . . Jesse black and glistening in the garish light . . ." He spoke in a dull monotone, his gaze vague and fixed on a past image that must have ruled his adult life.

Homer dropped his face into his hands again and began to weep. He cried in a way that John had never known. No woman had ever cried quite like that in his presence. John didn't know what to do. Just sit there; speak to him; touch him? How could you comfort such heartache?

"Homer, listen to me," John said finally. "It's over and done. It was a long time ago. You're not the only kid who ever had a homosexual experience."

"It's more than that," Homer sobbed between his fingers. "You don't understand. It wasn't sordid, not a bit. I loved him. At that time in my life I actually *loved* him. I'm no queer," he said vehemently. "I had two or three relationships after that in Paris. I had to find out, you see. But they wouldn't do. It was all over, it couldn't be recaptured. It was only with Jesse. And I've never had those—urges—since."

"Well, all right, there it is then. Don't you see—"

"There's more, John."

"Oh Jesus, Homer. There can't be. C'mon now—"

"Didn't you ever wonder what happened to Jesse?"

John looked at him quizzically. "I always thought—like everyone else..."

"Now you see it had nothing to do with me and Josie."

"Oh Lord, Homer. Don't tell me—"

"You remember what Daddy was like."

"God yes."

"He killed him," Homer said softly, and his words had the impact of exploding hand grenades. "Right in front of me...right there in the room...in my bed. It all happened so fast. He came across that room like a wild animal. You remember his hands—they were like steel traps. He throttled poor Jesse right there in front of me. Blood gushed from his nose, his eyes popped out of his head in terror and pain. I just sat there, in the bed, watching in stunned horror, pissing all over myself."

Homer stopped, unable to continue. Tears streaked his cheeks and his eyes burned in his head. He wept in silence and his grief seemed boundless.

John moved to the arm of the chair and sat beside him, his hand gently on Homer's shoulder. It was all he could do at the moment. It would be a long while before Homer Stokes would know comfort.

# Chapter Eighty-nine

**John left early the next morning for Atlanta. Once** again the governor had tried to delay the inevitable but had finally bowed to John's insistence.

Certainly Homer's story had in no way persuaded John that any other course of action was indicated. Incredible tale that it was. Especially the part about Chester Biggs. Just when John had thought it was all over, lo and behold, Homer had pulled himself together and related the most shocking part of the entire tale.

The old colonel had had damned few options under the circumstances, but he could have selected a little more wisely than Chester Biggs. *Chester Biggs!* thought John, as he cruised along the Interstate toward Atlanta slightly in excess of the speed limit.

Chester had performed a few minor services for the colonel in the past. The old man knew of the young deputy's ambition. The current sheriff was in the colonel's hip pocket then, and could be expected to do as he was told. Chester rendered that particular favor to the old man and the sheriff was told to groom Chester as his successor. Within the hour the young deputy had arrived at the Stokes mansion, sized up the situation and gone into action without asking question one.

Of course there was one little fact about the incident that even Chester didn't know. By the time he had arrived at the bedroom at the top of the stairs, the corpse of Jesse Fletcher had been dressed and dumped on the floor away from the bed. Chester, too, had always believed the killing to have been inspired by a jealous husband's lack of control upon catching his wife in the boss man's bed.

In any case, Jesse Fletcher's body had gone into a bottomless sump hole, never to be seen again, and the Stokes family had gone rather nicely into the hip pocket of Chester Biggs.

"And that's what the bastard had up his sleeve," thought John, "as his ace in the hole."

The staged incident with Rachel Pettigrew hadn't worked, so Biggs was going to blackmail John into inaction with the threat of exposing Homer's longtime secret. He knew John wouldn't permit the destruction of his friend's reputation and career. And John certainly couldn't allow Homer to be prosecuted as an accessory to a murder that had occurred almost twenty years before.

John took his eyes off the road momentarily and looked at the package on the seat beside him. Then he gripped the wheel with both hands and concentrated on the road.

Sal felt it was wonderful to be up and about again. It seemed as if she had been in a state of suspended animation for years. And perhaps she had been.

Heading outside, she paused on the back steps, her face turned up to the blistering sun. It felt marvelous. She took a deep breath, rising on her toes and stretching both arms high above her head. Her lungs filled with air and oxygen raced to her head with exhilarating swiftness.

She went into the yard and started purposefully for the barn. At the door she stopped. *I can't do it.*

She knew she had to, but she couldn't. It was like getting on a horse again after a bad fall, or taking an airplane after a crash. You had to go right back again or else you would be crippled for life.

*I have to,* she told herself. She took a deep breath and stepped inside.

Instinctively she shied away from the area in which the

attack had occurred. She went instead to her easel and stared for a while at the canvas. Dark, she thought. Too dark and somber by any standard of measurement. She removed the canvas and put up another that was fresh and untouched. She smiled at the notion of a new beginning.

It was a relief to know that she could stand there without succumbing to a flood of overpowering associations. But life went on. Survivors had to live.

Her reaction to all of it was astonishing. She had not experienced a psychic collapse this time, as she had when faced with the earlier tragedy involving her parents. This time she accepted what had happened to her, and there was absolutely no reason to invest herself with a shroud of self-guilt. What was done, was done. Her task was to live now and in the future.

She spun around and hugged herself with both arms. Never in her life had she felt so free. Somehow, her own private ordeal had unlocked the psychic vise of guilt that had shackled her mind since the deaths of her family. This time she was *happy* to have survived!

"Free," she said aloud.

She went over to where it happened. She stood on the very spot. Nearby lay the palette knife with which she had raked the man's face. She shuddered now at the recognition of the capacity for violence that lay so close beneath the surface. Perhaps she would never again be quite so smug in her beliefs and assertions concerning the conduct of others.

Slowly, she turned and walked toward the far end of the barn. She went in behind one of the old stalls in which John's grandfather had spent so much of his passion, if not love. She hesitated a moment, breathed deeply, then moved aside an old unpainted woodbox.

The dildo was in the same spot where it had landed the day she flung it from her body. No one had seen it. No one ever would. Quickly, without really looking at it, she wrapped the dreadful thing in an old rag and took it outside to the garbage dump. Touching it made her flesh crawl and she felt queasy in the pit of her stomach.

Kneeling beside his four-poster bed, hands clasped in white-knuckled intensity on the satin spread, Homer stared at the wall. His face was streaked with tears and twisted in pain.

"Oh why, why?" He begged in a groan. "Why couldn't I tell him the truth? The whole truth?

"I love *you*, John," Homer sobbed. "I always have. I always will."

# Chapter Ninety

John had stopped the car in a roadside park a few miles outside Atlanta. He couldn't put it off any longer. It was the long-delayed day of decision. The moment of decision. Subconsciously, he had been wrestling with this moment for weeks.

He turned off the ignition and sat for a few moments staring into the woods beyond the red brick barbecue pit. He had gone into his own woods earlier that morning, sat for a time on the crumbled windowpane of his grandfather's old dugout. From his perch on the mountaintop he could see the house on the slope across the branch. His grandfather's house, his great-grandfather's land. It was now his and soon would be his children's. He could feel the pincers of generations working against him from both sides.

In my place, what would Papa have done?

John snapped out of his reverie and looked down at the package on the seat beside him.

It *looked* harmless enough, he thought grimly. Yet the contents were menacing, as any combination of truth and past events menaces the future. How few are the people, the towns, the counties that can survive publication of the naked truth?

Can I turn my back on my family, my people—my county? I have the power—here on the seat beside me. Do I have the right? Loose ends, I could call them. The final process of tidying up...a facing up to responsibility unsought and reluctantly borne.

And what then, for me? Do I hand this information to the governor and then accede to his wishes and stay on as special prosecutor? Of course not. Do I return to the university—as president or professor? He laughed ruefully. If I do this responsible thing, they wouldn't have me back on the maintenance team.

Cut and run, there's always that. Governor Barrow would find a spot for me in Atlanta. And there's always Washington, D.C. And Europe again. What the hell do I owe these people—family, countians, any of them?

What would Sal say? Burn our bridges and just *go?*

Poor Sal. It had been so hard on her. There was so much yet to come.

He took a book of matches out of the glove compartment, the package off the seat, and went over to the barbecue pit. He threw the package into the fire pit. In some ways, it was like having done with part of his own life.

He struck a match and set a loose end of the package afire. He fanned the blaze, then touched flame to the other end of the package. He stood back and watched as the flames ate at the wrapping and then began to lick and taste of the foul pages of Sissie's diary.

John began to smile. There would be no editorials in the *Oracle* about this deed, favorable or not. It was not exactly the kind of public service he could brag about. But Taliawiga County would be in his debt forever. Biggs blood, Cubbage blood...Fletcher blood...Stokes blood and Winter blood. It was all the same. Tainted.

It didn't matter that no one would ever know of the debt. He would know. That's all that counted.

He went back to the car, his mind at rest at last.

# Chapter Ninety-one

At his press conference Governor Barrow had been gracious in accepting John Winter's resignation as special prosecutor and lavish in his praise of John's service, his ability and, above all, his integrity. Reporters had attempted to expand upon John's simple statement as to his reasons for submitting his resignation at this time.

"My job as special prosecutor is completed," he said again. "I originally accepted the appointment for the limited purpose of prosecuting the case of Eddie James in the Cubbage murders in Adelphi. With the recent death of Eddie James, my position has become superfluous. I have therefore tendered my resignation to Governor Barrow and he has graciously accepted it."

But they would not leave it at that. The cluster of reporters moved forward, a battery of microphones were shoved into his face. Television cameras angled in such a way as to catch his handsome profile.

"Mr. Winter, what is your personal opinion concerning the eruption of violence in Taliawiga County after your appointment as special prosecutor?"

John looked at the reporter and smiled thinly. "Are you suggesting that *I* caused it?"

Another reporter quickly said, "Is Taliawiga County the most racist county in the state of Georgia?"

"A fellow named Bobcat Tribble made that statement, not me," John said affably.

"Is it true that you're going to run for district attorney in Taliawiga County in the autumn election?"

"No," said John.

"Are you going to run for Congress against Robert Randolph, as was suggested by this morning's editorial in the Adelphi *Oracle?*"

John's eyebrows raised. "I hadn't read that one," he smiled. "I have no intention of running for Congress. As my gran'daddy used to say, he brought me up with more ambition than that."

Amid a spate of laughter a female voice asked, "Are you going to run for U.S. Senator against your recent benefactor?"

John was surprised by the question. Governor Barrow was surprised by the question. They looked at each other over the forest of microphones, and then John laughed.

"I have agreed to help Governor Barrow in his bid for the Senate," John said. "If he thinks I can best serve his candidacy by running against him..."

He let his voice trail off and there was a ripple of laughter again in the press group. John thought that he detected a sigh of relief in the governor's reaction.

"Are you going to work in the governor's campaign?" came the same woman's voice.

"I am going to help him in every way I can. I will do whatever he asks me to do."

"Will you campaign for him on an anti–capital punishment platform?"

"Yes. I will support him on that platform," John said firmly.

The governor's aides were on the verge of breaking up the conference. One more question was taken.

"Mr. Winter, since you are not running for public office in the fall, have you decided to return to your teaching duties at Adelphi University?"

John looked at the reporter with a mischievous expression. "I didn't say that I was not going to be a candidate for public office in the fall."

For a moment there was a long silence. Finally someone said, "Are you going to run for President?"

John laughed and so did the others, including the governor and his aides.

"No," said John. "I'm not going to run for President. But as soon as I return to Adelphi it is my intention to file the necessary papers at the Taliawiga County Courthouse for the newly created office of County Public Defender."

\* \* \*

JOHN WINTER FOR PUBLIC DEFENDER.

Once again he was in the headlines, on the front page and the subject matter of editorial comment. And for the most part it was all supportive. The reservoir of good feeling that existed in Taliawiga County for himself, and for his late grandfather, was brought into focus by his recent announcement. No political figure other than Judge Harbuck could do as well at the polls countywide as John Winter. After all, John *was* Flood Hightower's grandson. There were some four months yet to go before the fall balloting but the die, if not the vote, was already cast.

The decision had brought a certain measure of peace to the Winter family. And so had confrontation.

"You've got to do it, John," Sal had said. "It's long overdue."

"But it's hard to say exactly how she will react."

"It doesn't matter how your mother reacts. Having it out in the open is the thing that counts. Reaction—any kind of reaction—is better than the limbo she has lived in for so many years."

"I wonder..."

But he knew Sal was right. Finally he screwed up the courage and plunged in.

"Hello, Mom. How you feeling today?"

"About as good as I feel any day. As good as I can ever expect to feel."

Ida Belle was sitting beside the picture window in her customary Gone-with-the-Wind chair beside the Gone-with-the-Wind table which held her precious Gone-with-the-Wind lamp; all of which must have cost her about three hundred dollars some thirty years before. She would not exchange them for love or any amount of money.

"You had anything for lunch?" he asked.

"I'm not hungry."

"You've got to eat, Mom."

"I had a bowl of cereal about ten o'clock. Maybe I'll have a doughnut in a little while."

"That kind of food won't keep a bird alive," said John, taking a seat in his favorite old rocking chair beside the fireplace.

"Well, even birds have to die," she said.

"Now, Momma—don't go talking about dying again."

"Lord knows enough people around here have been dyin'

right and left lately. I s'pose we ought to be thankful for every day that's given to us.".

"That's right, Momma. We should."

"Don't go lecturing me, young man!"

"I'm not lecturing you. I'm just trying to say—"

"And how's my boy this morning? What is Davey doing and when is he coming up to see me?"

"When I left him he was digging for worms down by the creekbed with Moses—"

"You better keep that baby away from that old creekbed if you don't want one of them moccasins takin' off his hand."

"He's with Moses. He's perfectly all right."

"Moses," she scoffed.

"Besides, Momma, the boy's got to learn to stand on his own two feet. We couldn't keep him a baby for the rest of his life even if we wanted to."

Her tired old eyes snapped defensively. "You gonna start tellin' me again what a terrible job of raisin' you I did?"

John sighed. "Momma, I didn't say any such thing."

"Well, you might be right. Maybe I did do a terrible job. Lord knows I did my best. But the way things have turned out—"

"Maybe what you needed was some help, Momma." He paused and took a deep breath. "Maybe you needed a man to help you. Maybe I needed a father."

She averted her eyes, her hands came together in her lap and her skin began to twitch beside her nose. "That's probably true," she said cautiously, not at all certain where this line of conversation was going. "If only your daddy hadn't had to go off to that terrible old war—"

"Momma," John interrupted. "Don't you think it's time we stopped this silly game?"

"What? Whatever are you talking about?"

"You know what I'm talking about."

"Why, Buddy, sometimes I swear I just don't know what has got into you."

That was where it had always become so hopeless in the past. John had gotten that far on a number of other occasions; but she always turned and ran away from it though, and he had always thrown up his hands and beat a collusive retreat. Not this time.

"Stop it, Momma. I can't do it anymore, that's all there is to it. It's not just you and me any longer. This is not a decision I've come to hastily. I've given it hours and months and years of thought. I just don't think it's the right thing to do. It's not right for you or me or Sal. It's not right for the children. Once and for all, let's get it out in the open."

His mother issued a tiny little gasp and attempted to raise herself from the chair. A stab of arthritic pain shot up her arms and she fell back into the chair. She still wouldn't look at him. Her chin was down on her chest. The gray hair was shockingly thin. Her mouth was trembling as she looked at her hands clasped tightly in her lap. Her hands were thin, veiny, and the skin was spotted on top like the underbelly of a fish.

"I *know*, Momma."

She looked at him in horror.

"I've known the truth about my father for years," he said gently.

Her eyes puddled up and her mouth began to work soundlessly.

After that, everything was a jumble of words and sounds. She didn't say a thing. He tried to talk to her about all the good things he could remember, the things for which they both had reason to be happy. And then he tried to talk to her about the other things, the things that had kept them apart, even during the years in which they seemed to be so close. He said he understood about her marriage and the way things happened and that he certainly didn't blame her or anyone. He didn't really want to know all the details. Details didn't matter. At the time, she had done what she thought she had to do. He understood that. Things happen sometimes that are no one's fault. Certainly they had both been wrong in perpetuating the lie. Did she really think it would be better for a child to grow to manhood believing that his absent father was a golden war hero, when in reality he was nothing but a petty thief who went and got himself killed in a prison riot while doing time for a candy store robbery? How could she have been so confident as to suppose that John would never learn the truth?

Ida Belle didn't say a word. She sat twisting her hands this way and that, her head shaking, her eyes turned downward, her thoughts her own.

John was sweating as if he had been jogging through the woods for hours. In fact, he had been running from this scene for his entire mature life.

"You wasted most of your life up until now—surely you realize that. I'm not blaming you. I'm not saying it's your fault, but once the years are gone, they're gone. There is so much you might have done, if only you'd acknowledged your early youthful mistake and then set about putting your life together again from that point on. Instead, you ran. Instead, you hid. Instead, you let life ride you instead of you riding it. It's been a secondhand life, Momma, a counterfeit life. But it isn't over. You're lucky after all. You've got more time. I'm even luckier. I found out sooner than you how destructive it is to live a lie. I couldn't do it any longer, even if it hurts you now to have to face this. I *had* to bring it out in the open. We can't let what has happened to you and to me repeat itself in the lives of Davey and Cathy. We just can't do that. Life is for living. It's too precious to waste. We don't have enough of it as it is."

He stood up, his chest was aching. Perspiration was running out of his armpits and his knees were shaking. His mother kept turning her hands without looking up.

He went to the door and stopped.

"I know we can't talk about this now. Not in any great detail," he said. "It's too soon. The wounds are open now and raw. Later, perhaps, we can close the wounds."

He opened the door but her voice stopped him before he could leave. Her words were barely above a whisper. He had to ask her to repeat herself.

"Do you ever pray anymore, John?"

That came as something of a shock. "I talk aloud," he said. "Or maybe I'm still praying to a God I'm no longer sure I believe in."

"You ought to *try* praying, John."

He smiled wryly. "I'll make a bargain with you, Momma. I'll try praying again if you'll try living."

He closed the door and went down the wooden steps. He began to trot out toward the old dirt road. He turned at the road and began to sprint for home as fast as his legs would carry him.

# Chapter Ninety-two

**The rainy season was upon them. One of the rainy seasons.** John sat in the red Toyota, waiting for Sal outside the new Red and White supermarket. He was growing more impatient by the moment. She had said she only wanted to make a few last-minute purchases; she had already been inside for a good fifteen minutes. He could see the rainstorm coming up, moving toward the city. Even without seeing it, he had felt its approach for the last twenty or thirty minutes in that little quivering change in the air that he had learned to detect in the woods as a boy.

But the rain was nearby. He could not only see it over the treetops, he could smell it. In another ten minutes they would be inundated.

He got out of the car and went inside the market. Maybe if he hurried Sal along they could make it out to the house before the deluge.

As he entered the door she was just leaving the checkout counter. But she stopped suddenly as if some unseen hand had flipped the switch on her motive power. John stopped, too, and then caught her line of sight.

She was staring at a man near the magazine rack, looking at him the way she would have gaped at a hydra-headed monster. He was tall, skinny as a rail, wore bib overalls without a shirt and heavy scuffed work boots. There was a long jagged scar along his jawbone. The hair on his head, chest and arms was red and fuzzy.

The man shook like a bag of bones when he looked up and

caught Sal staring at him. He put down his magazine and started for the exit.

John turned and went back out the door he had entered. Sal saw John through the plate glass window and she started for the exit as fast as she could move with the grocery bags in her arms.

By the time she caught up with him, John already had his hands on the man's throat from behind. The man was trying to open the door of his rusty old pickup truck and John was pulling him backward with his hands on his throat, his knee in the small of the man's back. Sal could hear the man's gasps deep down in his throat.

"John!" she screamed. "Stop it! *Stop* it!"

But John wasn't about to stop. He was blind with rage. He had seen the look on Sal's face, the knowing expression on the man's face when he realized Sal had recognized him. Nothing in the world was going to stop him now. He pushed with his knee and squeezed on the man's throat as tightly as he could.

"John! You've got to stop before you kill him!" Sal dropped her packages and began pulling at John's hands and arms.

He tried to fight her away and retain his grasp on the man's throat at the same time. He could feel the man's legs beginning to go limp. In another few seconds... but he didn't have another few seconds. Sal had grabbed his right forearm and pulled it down, away from the man's throat, with all her strength. The man rolled instinctively toward the side of reduced pressure and his neck snapped out of John's hand. The man fell forward against the body of the truck and rolled to the side as John made a dive again with both hands for his throat.

The man kicked with all his might. His knee caught John in the genitals as his body was hurtling forward. John had never known such blinding pain, not even in his football days. He went to the ground in a blackened daze and tasted the vomit rising into his mouth. He felt Sal's arms clutching at his head, twisting his body away from the tires of the truck.

He was doubled up in agony as the truck careened down the exit lane from the parking lot, heading for the open road. But pain or no pain, there was no way John Winter was going to let this encounter end there on the concrete parking lot.

He struggled to his feet just as the big flat raindrops began to explode on the parked cars and the surface of the parking lot. He was on his feet, stumbling toward his car with Sal's aid, oblivious to the crowd that had gathered to watch from inside the store.

It didn't take long to catch sight of the rusty old pickup. It was moving out the south road as fast as it could go, which unfortunately for the driver was not nearly fast enough. John's Toyota sliced through the windless sheets of rain like a red fish. The staccato noise on the rooftop was so loud he could scarcely hear Sal's pleas for him to stop.

But he wasn't going to stop. He had already begun to catch up. The truck, though, was only a blue haze in the middle of the road ahead, what with the heavy rain and the dazzling pain that John was still experiencing in his groin.

Finally the Toyota roared up behind the outclassed pickup truck. John banged once into the rear end and Sal screamed as she flew up over the dashboard. She had thrown both hands up just in time to prevent smashing her head against the windshield. When she fell back into the seat, she began hooking up her seat belt, screaming at John to stop before he killed them all.

He stamped on the gas pedal and swung out around the side of the truck. He wasn't going to stop until that Cracker sonofabitch was in his grave!

Before John could pull beyond the truck's front fender and cut him off, the man frantically accelerated and inched the old truck ahead just enough to keep abreast of John's front end.

The quality of Sal's next scream finally made an impression on John. He was never sure whether he actually saw the car heading toward them or merely sensed it. He braked as hard as he could, swung the wheel to the right, and fell in behind the truck with only seconds to spare. The other car zoomed past in the other direction and John immediately began to pull up behind the pickup truck again.

He rammed the back end a couple of times then pulled out into the passing lane and started to overtake it again. But this time the man wasn't about to let him get that far without taking defensive action. He cut his wheel to the left and bumped John's right front fender with his battered flank. John had to move away for fear of getting hooked up. He could no longer feel the ache in his groin. His throat was constricted, his blood sang in his ears a song as old as man itself, and he knew the lyrics that fit the music. Kill! Kill! Kill!

He was roaring ahead on the left again, the tires and engine of the Toyota shrieking with such unwarranted punishment. This is it, thought John. This time he would finish it. Not for a moment did he consider that he might finish things for himself and Sal as well. He was beyond that kind of rational thought. He was beyond all thought at all, going on instinct, blind, atavistic, animal instinct.

"John!" Sal screamed, her voice splitting through the noise of the crashing rain and the roar of the vehicles.

They had approached the Taliawiga River, and the bridge on that part of the road was barely wide enough for two lanes of traffic. He had him now, thought John. There was no way for the sonofabitch to maneuver. It was either off the road and into the roaring river, or smash head-on into the concrete abutment of the narrow bridge. John was biting down so hard on his teeth that he worked a filling loose. He spit the grit out of his mouth, hunched over the wheel as close to the windshield as he could and kept the pressure on the accelerator steady.

There was no way out now. He could see the driver of the truck fighting the wheel frantically, twisting his head this way and that. But all his options had been denied him.

John saw the hands first, then the tousled hair standing on end, long before he saw the eyes rising like twin moons of disaster above the back windowpane of the truck.

The little boy had finally managed to pull himself up off the seat and was looking out the truck's back window. His face was a gray mask of innocent fear.

John jammed on the brakes and wrestled the wheel with all his strength. Their vehicles bumped once and there was the sound of metal tearing, and then the truck bounced off to the right shoulder of the road, skipping, swerving wildly out of control. It was all John could do to hang onto the wheel and keep the Toyota from flipping over as the front end of the car receded behind the rear of the truck. Somehow, the man cut his wheel and pulled the truck back onto the road, just in time to swerve onto the bridge at the very last instant.

John also made it onto the bridge and across to the other side of the river before bringing the car to a halt. By the time his eyes began to focus on the scene, the pickup truck was completely out of sight. They sat there for a long moment, emotionally and physically exhausted. John was trembling in every inch of his body. His face was white as death. Sal looked at him through her tears as John struggled to catch his breath.

"My God," he said in a throaty whisper. "I might have killed us all."

Absolutely stunned by the enormity of the moment, they turned to each other and embraced. Rain pounded on the rooftop and sharp eddies of wind shook the little car like a leaf. Below them, the river boiled and roared downstream like a runaway freight train.

The killing season was over.